A PERFECT DISGUISE

As security chief of the supernaturals' ruling council, Michaela Chui has seen more than her fair share of disaster. For centuries, she's survived through caution and strategy. But when the only human councilor is viciously murdered, Michaela knows the coincidences that keep blocking her investigation are a sure sign of bad things to come. She needs answers fast. And her only ally is Cormac Redoak: wild, unpredictable, unreliable—and worse, distractingly attractive.

A HIDDEN TRUTH

An exile from the court of the Fairy Queen, Cormac has all the experience with careful strategy and veiled intentions he can stand. But he also has the fey talent for getting his way, and he's sure his way lies with Michaela's. No matter that she can change her lovely face at will; there's a clarity to her being that he'd know anywhere. Working with her will be temptation and frustration bound together. Somehow, though, he must convince her to trust him—without revealing the secrets he dares never share . . .

Visit us at www.kensingtonbooks.com

Books by Alana Delacroix

Masked Arcana
Masked Possession
Masked Desire

Published by Kensington Publishing Corporation

Masked Desire

A Masked Arcana Novel

Alana Delacroix

LYRICAL PRESS
Kensington Publishing Corp.
www.kensingtonbooks.com

Lyrical Press books are published by
Kensington Publishing Corp. 119 West 40th Street New York, NY 10018

All Kensington titles, imprints, and distributed lines are available at special quantity discounts for bulk purchases for sales promotion, premiums, fundraising, and educational or institutional use.

To the extent that the image or images on the cover of this book depict a person or persons, such person or persons are merely models, and are not intended to portray any character or characters featured in the book.

Special book excerpts or customized printings can also be created to fit specific needs. For details, write or phone the office of the Kensington Special Sales Manager:
Kensington Publishing Corp.
119 West 40th Street
New York, NY 10018
Attn. Special Sales Department. Phone: 1-800-221-2647.

Kensington and the K logo Reg. U.S. Pat. & TM Off.
LYRICAL PRESS Reg. U.S. Pat. & TM Off.
Lyrical Press and the L logo are trademarks of Kensington Publishing Corp.

First Electronic Edition: April 2018
eISBN-13: 978-1-5161-0362-1
eISBN-10: 1-5161-0362-9

First Print Edition: April 2018
ISBN-13: 978-1-5161-0365-2
ISBN-10: 1-5161-0365-3

Printed in the United States of America

For E

Chapter 1

Michaela Chui lifted the lid of her white-and-blue glazed teapot and poured in the water with deliberate care. Morning tea was a ritual she'd observed for as long as she could remember and it never failed to fill her with a sense of calm.

Sometimes, though, the calm was illusory and she knew it. For the last six months, Michaela had lived with an ever-increasing sense of dread. No surprise, she thought, as she watched the pale gray leaves swirl under the tendrils of steam. The masquerada were in the final stages of mopping up what had been a nasty insurrection of chauvinists and bigots led by Franz Iverson. It was a big job and Eric Kelton had asked her to oversee it.

The death threats had been irritating but expected.

She glanced at her watch. Soon she'd need to leave for a meeting with her mentor, the vampire Madden. More secrets. While she wasn't alone as a shape-shifting masquerada in a human world, her role on the Pharos Council couldn't even be shared with Eric, her Hierarch. Charged with keeping the arcane world hidden from that of the humans, the Pharos walked unknown among their compatriots and ensured all followed the Law.

The tea was perfect now and she stood at the window to enjoy it, relishing the familiar, almost ritual action. Her friend Caro nagged her about her painful lack of spontaneity, but Caro was young. The thought wasn't catty or malicious; Michaela admired Caro and her strength. However, she knew living in the moment wasn't a trait she herself had. Centuries of watching the world's many casual cruelties had created a need to make life as predictable as possible.

It was how she survived.

Time to go. She sighed and focused inward for a long moment. She'd worked since childhood to master the perfect natural poise that still betrayed nothing of her inner self. Although not a physical masque, Michaela was a tougher version of the Miaoling she had been in her youth. Stronger, less vulnerable. A colder face she had created to survive the demands of life away from her family and one she now found invaluable for the arcane society in which she lived. She hadn't allowed herself to truly embrace being Miaoling for centuries. As Michaela—suspicious where Miaoling was natural, cold where the other was warm, and deliberate rather than impulsive—she was more suited for success in this world, and she meant to succeed.

Her drive took her south through Toronto's downtown core, a cold valley of bank headquarters and overpriced restaurants, to a small heritage building that had been partially incorporated into a skyscraper. Even in temporary headquarters, Pharos members demanded elegant and old-fashioned surroundings with every modern convenience.

Michaela locked the car door and was checking the handle when a soft, low growl came from behind her.

"Councilor. You're here early."

Not now. It was too early in the morning. She steeled herself to face Cormac Redoak, exiled fey, special ambassador to the Pharos Council, and world-class pain. "Ambassador," she said briskly, heaving her bag over her shoulder.

"May I take that for you?" Even after centuries away from the fey homeland, he still had a bit of an accent, almost but not quite Irish.

"No." She walked towards the door. Although they had known each other for decades, she'd had few conversations with him, and in fact tended to avoid him. Not because of the wild rumors that surrounded his exile from the fey court or because she'd been on the receiving end of more than one of his inquisitions when she'd objected to his schemes. He was too erratic for her. Wild. Unstable. Even his eyes refused to stay a single color. Right now they were a light jade but could easily change to gray or brown depending on his mood.

This criticism was grossly hypocritical coming from a masquerada and she knew it. Her eyes, like the rest of her, could be transformed in a breath to become part of any masque she chose. That was the point, though. While Cormac was at the mercy of his emotions, she needed to keep perfect control at all times. Failure—if her masque slipped and humans witnessed a shift—would result in a breach of the Law. Worse, she could lose her natural self in a sea of other personalities: the dreaded convergence.

Cormac said what he wanted, did what he wanted, and damned the consequences. The ambassador was not a man who accepted limits to his desires and it made her wary.

"I want to speak about our discussion the other day," he said.

She didn't bother to look at him. "By discussion you mean when you attempted, and failed, to humiliate me in front of half the Council?"

He made an airy *details, details* gesture.

"I asked for a simple clarification."

"About a subject you had no business with and at a meeting to which you were not invited." She reached out to pull the door open but he moved in front of her with the fluid grace typical of the fey. For a moment she breathed in his unique pine scent—the one thing she enjoyed about him.

Then she silently brushed by with a nod of thanks, mind already on the day's agenda. She had about ten minutes before she was due to meet Madden, enough time for a few emails and to re-check her calendar.

"I assumed my invitation was lost. Luckily Hiro told me about it."

She kept walking. "Which he also had no business doing. We have meeting procedures for a reason."

"Procedures are for the masses." He paused when they reached her office door. "Look, Michaela, my point remains valid."

Michaela opened the door. "As I said before—" Her voice trailed off as she flicked on the light. "Good God."

Cormac peered in, then tried to block the door. "You don't want to see this."

Did the man not remember she was the Pharos security chief? She shoved him aside. "That's Hiro. In my office."

Cormac stood beside her, his cool skin brushing her hand. "It *was* Hiro," he corrected. "It's not anymore."

* * * *

Cormac knew Michaela was not the type to scream and faint at the sight of blood, but this was a truly monumental amount. The copper smell that rolled out of the open doorway was thick and rank, enough to give most people nausea and probably send vampires into a frenzy.

Michaela, however, was not most people. Her sharp gaze darted around the room, taking in details and assessing the situation.

"Don't go in," she said in her usual crisp voice, her arm flashing out to prevent him from going farther when he took a step.

"I want to check that he's dead." The response was automatic.

She shot him a glance with those gorgeous obsidian eyes. "Seriously?"

He assessed the gore of the murder scene. "Right." Hiro was human, not arcana. There was no way he could have survived such an assault.

She pulled out her cell phone and called Anjali, her witch deputy, providing a summary with military conciseness. It gave him time to absorb what he was seeing, and more importantly, what it meant for him.

Hiro Murakami was dead.

That a human was dead was no surprise. In Cormac's eyes, humans died with astonishing frequency and he often watched with wonder as so many of them squandered their short years on silly pastimes and trivial vengeances. But a Pharos councilor who had been essentially gutted in a colleague's office? That was unusual, and for Cormac personally, extremely inconvenient.

Michaela pulled her laptop out and balanced it open on one arm to take notes.

"Aren't you going in?" he asked. Was she afraid of getting bloody? She didn't seem to be the squeamish sort.

She shook her head and kept typing. "Don't want to contaminate anything."

Of course she would have a logical answer. He wasn't even sure she had feelings—she certainly wasn't displaying any now. Time to ask the second most obvious question. "Why was Hiro in here?"

Now her fingers paused. "I'd like to know as well."

Well, Hiro at least had the good sense to be killed in Michaela's office. If anyone on the Council could find an answer, it would be her. She'd been the Pharos security chief for as long as he could remember and was one of the most formidably effective women he knew.

He watched as she continued to type. As usual, it was impossible to tell her true thoughts. Was she horrified by the body? Saddened? Curious? Titillated? Probably not the last, although reading a masquerada's body language could be fiendishly difficult.

He'd never seen Michaela in any masque but the current one and he assumed, though he would never know, that it was her natural self. Like many arcana, it made him uneasy to know that Michaela could easily become Michael or anyone else she chose. Other arcana could change their appearance temporarily, but none with a masquerada's expertise or proficiency. He'd heard they could take on the same masque for years if they wished, or rotate through an endless parade of personas. It struck him as unnatural. Sinister. Completely shady.

That being said, he had zero complaints about how Michaela chose to present herself. The security chief had a fragile, austere loveliness that roused the same admiration he felt for exquisite sculpture. Michaela was art, in a way, a practiced and deliberate performer. She had the usual aggravating masquerada haughtiness in spades, and her every glance, word, and movement was as choreographed as a dance. She would have done well in the Lilac Court, he mused, a court where everything was judged and assessed.

He had not.

"You can go." Michaela put down her laptop and pulled out a thin black notebook. "Anjali will come by your office to ask questions."

"No, thank you," he said pleasantly. "I'm going to stay."

"It wasn't a question."

"I know." He smiled, knowing that she wouldn't lower herself to debate with him.

Nor did she, but instead returned to work on what looked like a sketch of blood splatter. He spared it a quick glance—Michaela's sure fingers had created an almost photographically accurate representation of the horror in the room—and turned his attention back to the body, diminished by death.

Damn Hiro. How dare he get himself killed, right when Cormac needed him? The *only* time Cormac had ever needed him? Time, usually not even on his radar, had become his enemy. Under his shirt was a pendant containing a leaf fragment given to him by his tree, a great red oak that rose high above Yetting Forest.

The leaf had been green when he'd been forced to leave the fey Queendom. Six months ago, he'd seen traces of brown outlining its edges. Every fey forest needed a steward to survive and his had been without for three hundred years. The deal with Hiro would have given Queen Tismelda matchless forest in northern Japan, forest that would have laid the foundation for Cormac's campaign to thaw the queen enough to reverse his exile, even if only to re-establish himself as steward. Yetting Hill had to survive. Without it, there would be no Redoaks. Fey and forest lived and died together.

He'd been so *close*. Who had known of his plans? Had someone killed Hiro to thwart him, to prevent him from returning to his forest?

He had to know. He turned from the room's carnage to regard Michaela, who ignored him as her fingers flew over the page. He *would* know, even if it meant working with a masquerada with ice in her veins. Or around her.

Anything he had to do.

Chapter 2

Focusing on the sickening scene in front of her took Michaela's mind off Cormac's irritating hover, but his question continued to echo through her thoughts. How had Hiro come to be sitting at her desk, in her locked office, when he was killed?

Anjali appeared around the corner, followed by other members of Michaela's security team. "Ma'am, we're—" As Michaela's had, Anjali's voice stuttered to a stop when she saw the extent of the carnage. "Goddess."

Michaela didn't hesitate. "Anjali, you're with me. The rest of you, escort Ambassador Cormac to his quarters and one of you stay with him until I call. He is not to communicate with others." She ignored Cormac's rumble of protest. Until proven otherwise, he was a suspect and she wouldn't allow him to eavesdrop on her investigation.

Anjali finished gawking and rummaged through her bags for disposable latex gloves. "It's fresh," she said as she tucked her curly black hair under a shower cap. "Smell's still strong and the blood's only tacky around the edges. Why was Hiro in your office?"

"Good question." Michaela pulled on her own gear and stepped into the room, laid out with elegant dark woods and marble floors. Getting to Hiro while avoiding the blood was slow work and when she finally managed it, she gazed down at his wide, still eyes. His arms were flung open from the ferocity of the attack, but she knew he'd been typing at her computer. Even with the slaughter in front of her, that minor violation—his fingers on her keyboard—was disturbing. An office key sat on the edge of the desk, marked with blood.

Anjali joined her. "There's a stab wound near the neck, much deeper than the others."

"He's been skinned." Michaela pointed at his forearms, which showed large, gory patches reaching almost to the bone.

Anjali blanched. "Did he have tattoos? They might have pointed to the killer."

"Not that I recall."

"Torture?"

"Anything is possible."

Dev, her forensics expert, arrived back on the scene. "I left Nadia with the ambassador," he reported. "He wasn't too happy."

Michaela felt a petty surge of unprofessional satisfaction that she instantly repressed. "Come see."

Weres might be stereotyped as thoughtless and impulsive, but Dev's process was slow and thorough. He never hurried. The two women left and shut the door, each sighing with relief at the fresh air. "We need to tell Madden and the other councilors," said Michaela.

"Yes, ma'am." Anjali's gaze slid to the door hiding the carnage. "Are you going to tell them everything?"

Michaela stifled a sigh, knowing the multiple layers of drama and paranoia that would ensue if—when—the Pharos councilors discovered the gruesome details of Hiro's death. "Only Madden. He can decide what to tell the others."

"Some help?" called Dev. Anjali wrinkled her nose and steadied herself before heading back into the room.

Michaela stayed out. At least Madden was in the building for their meeting, so she wouldn't have to wait. He answered the phone on the first ring.

"You're late." He was testier than usual but she ignored it.

"There's a reason." She told him about Hiro.

"In your office?"

"Yes."

"I'll be there immediately."

No wasted words. She approved. Michaela stood at the threshold and peeked in through the crack in the door at Anjali and Dev as they muttered to each other. Hiro. Of all the people on Pharos to have been killed, he was both the most and least likely. He was a strong advocate for his fellow humans, and Michaela suspected he harbored an active dislike of his supernatural colleagues. Hiro made a habit of phrasing his points in a way that made the arrogant blood of his arcana fellows boil.

The phone buzzed again and filled her with distaste for this fast-paced modern life. When she was a child, it took weeks for news to travel. Months, even. There was time for people to absorb information and make a sensible decision before they reacted. Not now.

It was a text from Nadia. *C made call before I could stop him. Didn't see him.*

Michaela breathed deeply. Cormac had no respect for appropriate process at the best of times. She shouldn't have assumed the gravity of the situation would cause him to behave any differently. Then, as a fey, he could glamour himself when desired. Nadia, young and cocky even by vampire standards, had probably not known he could, or that Cormac was a rule unto himself, not to be halted by irrelevant things such as rules, or protocol, or minding his own damn business.

"We've got incoming," she called in to Anjali and Dev. "You keep working."

She shut the door and stood planted in front of it like a sentinel as a babble of voices rose from around the corner. The six or seven councilors were led by Oksana, the other human representative on the Pharos Council. Uneven red blotches stained her leathery, weathered face and her mouth worked as though she chewed a rubbery bite of steak.

"Michaela." Oksana's voice rang out over the others. "What are you hiding from us? Is it true? Hiro is dead?"

"Yes." Michaela kept her voice cool and face smooth but cursed inwardly. It would have been proper for Madden to give the news, but there was no point lying.

Another reason Cormac should have kept his mouth shut.

Oksana stiffened. "I demand to be let in." Michaela looked over the woman's shoulder to the huddle of councilors, including Baptiste, her own masquerada counterpart. A slight relief pulsed through her. Although she had no problem standing against the group, it was always good to know that Baptiste was there to have her back.

"You can't go in, Oksana. We're conducting an investigation." Michaela didn't try to soften the rejection with a gentle touch or tender smile. In her decades as security chief, she'd found the only way to manage the imperious and demanding councilors was to avoid any gesture that might be construed as weakness or reluctance.

"I *insist* on seeing Hiro with my own eyes."

"No." Michaela had often dealt with honest grief but didn't see much anguish when she examined Oksana's very dry eyes.

"Michaela is right." The crowd of councilors parted as Madden approached the door, as imperturbable as always. "There will be a briefing in one hour," he said. "Michaela will tell you what her team has found then."

Madden's intimidating presence, made more effective by a low-level vampiric compulsion, was enough to disperse the group, albeit with some resentment. Baptiste raised his eyebrows and made an almost imperceptible slashing motion at his throat. Michaela nodded in answer to his silent question: Hiro's death had been murder. He closed his eyes and his lips moved in a silent prayer as he left.

When she and Madden were alone, Michaela opened the door. The vampire's nostrils flared at the reeking scent of blood but aside from a slight flush displayed no other indication that it affected him. "What do you know?" he asked the team working around the body.

Dev straightened up. "Sir. Councilor Hiro was murdered earlier this morning. We think that he was killed with a single stab wound to the neck and then mutilated further after death."

"Why?" Madden gazed around at the mess with his pale eyes. "This speaks of a great anger. Hiro was disliked but I wouldn't say he was hated."

"We don't know," Michaela said. The unknowns at the beginning of an investigation both frustrated her and filled her with anticipation. "Nor do we know why he was in my office."

Madden rubbed his long fingers along his chin. "This is not good for Pharos."

Michaela knew he wasn't referring to the murder per se, which was of course bad enough. The Council had experienced low levels of infighting over the last year. Hiro and Oksana had rounded together some of the weaker factions and occasionally the vampires to vote against the masquerada and their allies. It had brought the simmering tensions that lived between the groups close to the surface and suspicion had run particularly high after the others had learned about Franz Iverson's rebellion and the popularity of his belief in masquerada superiority. For many, it confirmed what they had always suspected: the masquerada viewed the rest of them as lesser beings. Michaela and Baptiste had been unable to convince them otherwise.

Pharos had been created centuries ago for a single purpose—to uphold the Law that kept the supernatural arcane races hidden from the huge mass of humanity. Should the council rip apart, the Law would be upheld only in pockets by arcane rulers strong enough, and willing, to keep their people hidden. Unpoliced, it was inevitable that some arcana, somewhere, would reveal themselves to the humans. Michaela shuddered at the violent effect this would have. She was under no illusions about how humans dealt with what frightened them.

It would be a bloodbath.

"We'll check the security tapes and councilors' alibis," she said. Tedious but necessary footwork.

"Do you think it was one of us?"

Michaela shrugged. "I don't want to bias the investigation with an assumption." The words were rote; both knew the chances were good. Her security had been designed to keep those not affiliated with the Pharos Council out of any of their headquarters.

Madden chuckled drily. "I'd expect nothing less. Have something to present in an hour."

"I will."

He turned at the door. "Michaela?"

"Yes?"

"Be ready for questions."

With that, he was gone. Michaela frowned after him. Why a warning? Then she shrugged. She had fifty-five minutes left and no time to worry about mysteries apart from the one right in front of her.

Chapter 3

Cormac swept into the council boardroom, bidding farewell to his bitter little security shadow at the threshold with a big, eat-shit smile and wave that nearly made her head explode. He would have felt pity for the vampire had she not treated him like a prisoner. She wanted to play? Then she'd learn to lose.

Speaking of losing, he wondered if Michaela had enjoyed her visit from Oksana. Judging from the expression of utter disdain she leveled at him across the table, he thought not.

Excellent. They were even.

Michaela opened her laptop and began to tap away, busy organizing some bloody list or another. In the time they'd been councilors together, he'd never seen her without one. Lists, plans, strategies, all laid out and ready to be plugged in and presented, with appropriately colored graphs, at a moment's notice. He wouldn't be surprised if underneath her flesh were Excel spreadsheets.

How dreary, to spend one's life mapping out the entire journey to prevent any surprises or wrong turns. So safe. So boring.

The other Pharos masquerada, Baptiste, slid into the tufted velvet green chair beside Michaela and the two chatted in low voices. Unable to eavesdrop, Cormac glanced around the room. The Toronto headquarters were not as chic as some of the other locations—the Cairene building in particular came to mind—but it was the most comfortable. Cormac liked it, and he enjoyed the city. Toronto had enough green space that he could soak in the energy all fey needed without going out of his way. Too much concrete destroyed his ability to focus—as well as being hideous.

He winced. Truly, humans had an innate ability to kill every enchanting thing in their realm. They were parasites.

Of course, the arcana seated around the table would probably have done the same thing. Pharos had representatives from all the major arcane groups, two each from the fey, masquerada, witch, warlock, vampire, and were. The *lithu* seats were vacant, as their people had not attended a meeting since the Pharos was established seven hundred years ago. Other, smaller groups, such as ghouls, were called in when necessary to canvas their opinion.

Then there was him, the special one. Cormac had managed to wrangle his position from the previous council head after coming into possession of some fascinating information about the warlock's personal life, but it meant nothing. He had no vote, and no say. The only thing it did was keep him busy enough to avoid insanity, allow for a little intrigue, and ensure he knew at least some of what was going on in the arcane world. It was amusing, and provided an anchor in an otherwise untethered existence. In the endless years of his banishment, Pharos had ended up being the only place where he could return and see familiar, if not necessarily friendly, faces after each of his haphazard journeys.

Rendell and Drina, the two fey councilors, came into the room talking animatedly. Since they refused to speak to Cormac, a dishonored exile, he didn't bother to greet them.

"I heard he wanted to be mated but she refused," Rendell said. Cormac listened shamelessly. Information was always valuable.

Also, he wanted to know who they were gossiping about. The fey took mating so seriously that he knew very few who had taken the step. Not even his parents had been mated. Like most, they preferred the much less intense legal partnership.

Drina's lilting voice carried from down the table. "That's why she left, then. I'd refuse too. Who in their right mind would risk mating?"

Cormac mentally shuddered at the thought of the mating bond. Bond was the right word—mating resulted in an unbreakable union as appealing as being roped to a dying tree. The two fey councilors changed subjects before revealing who the poor lovelorn bastard was. Cormac caught Michaela's gaze and for a moment had the singular sensation they were the only ones in the room. His hands instinctively sought the wooden hand rests of his chair before pulling back to lay on his thighs. It had been centuries since he'd allowed himself to link with any aspect of the *dolma*, the natural world. That connection would have exposed him as one of the outlawed *caintir*, a risk too great to take and a secret he'd buried deep in his heart.

Michaela broke their glance and a pang of disappointment surprised him. She was too rule-bound for his tastes, attractive though she was. Paradoxically, she was also one of the reasons he continued to return to the Council from his journeys. She was always…Michaela. Whether he'd been gone for a week or a year, she was always the first Pharos member he'd seek out, knowing that when he saw her she would be dressed in the same neat black outfit with her hair tied back in a smooth bun. In her hands would be her laptop or a notebook. She was a small slice of security in this world and he'd come to crave that unchanging support.

Ironic that it was a masquerada who had provided him with that sense of ageless permanence.

That she didn't like him was moot. Few did. Despite her many flaws, he liked her.

Well, admired.

Fine. Lusted after. After all, she *was* stunning, even if she had the emotional capacity of a marigold.

"Let's get started."

Madden's deep voice drew Cormac's attention. Michaela glanced back at Cormac and shook her head slightly as though forcing herself out of a dream. She laid her hands on the varnished oak table and sat still with her head tilted down.

They were back in the council room, tainted by murder.

Cormac leaned back to enjoy what he anticipated would be a very interesting meeting. The air almost vibrated with the ghoulish curiosity of the councilors. Madden sat down at the head of the table and nodded to Oksana. "We will find the one who killed your counterpart," he said. "We stand with you in your grief."

A murmur went around the table and Cormac hid a smile. Few, if any, of the arcana muttering their condolences cared if Hiro was dead. Hypocrisy and politics were eager bedmates. Down the table, Baptiste rolled his eyes.

"I will grieve for Hiro when his killer is found." Oksana kept her voice steady.

Madden nodded with approval. "This seems like a good time to hear from Michaela."

The security chief's findings were meager. Beyond knowing Hiro had been killed and how, there was little to tell. There were no fingerprints or a murder weapon. Her office, like all of them, was spelled to ensure privacy, which meant that neither witches nor warlocks could be called in to raise Hiro's spirit and question it.

"We're investigating and will be speaking to each of you today," Michaela finished. "I know you'll be happy to cooperate." Her dark eyes lingered in turn on each individual but deliberately passed over Cormac. He grinned at the stab, subtler than he thought Michaela capable of.

However, she was still no match for one raised in the Lilac Court. Time to get this show going. "Michaela. Let's discuss the political angle of Hiro's death."

Madden answered before Michaela could. "What do you mean, *Special* Ambassador Cormac Redoak?"

Cormac ignored the deliberate use of his formal title—Madden's attempt to remind him he had no real role on the Council—and continued to address Michaela. "There are many suspects."

"Are you making an accusation?" Michaela glanced up at him with deliberate unconcern. "Because now would be an ideal time to share whatever information you have."

"Accusation is a harsh word. Hiro was a man with a strong mind and many ideas. His killer could be anyone." He looked pointedly around the table and for fun paused at Pilar, one of the two vampires. "Any one of us."

The table erupted into predictable outrage. Pilar and her compatriot Abdul both leapt to their feet, fangs bared. Cormac leaned back with his hands behind the back of his neck in a pose that reeked of unconcern and smiled at them. This was going better than he'd expected. The vampires were such a beautifully touchy bunch.

"Ambassador." Madden's voice cut through the din. "Explain yourself."

"Michaela is an excellent security chief but I am concerned at the potential for bias in the investigation."

Michaela changed the grip on her pen. "Bias? Mine?"

As tempting as it was, he decided against leaving a pregnant pause that would doubtless send the council right over the edge. He didn't want this to devolve into a yelling match before he achieved his goal. "Naturally not. However, you are an active council member. Hiro was in your office. Killed in your office, I may add. Your locked office."

Baptiste, the other masquerada councilor, rose to his feet with a vicious scowl and Michaela waved him back down to his seat with a casual gesture. "These are all accurate. However, Hiro had a key to my office that we found next to the body. How he obtained it is one of the questions we need to answer."

Cormac let the heavy silence say what he didn't need to. That the councilors thought Michaela was the most likely killer was clear.

Pilar, the vampire, knocked the table for attention. "The masquerada are the only ones who are openly anti-human," she said pointedly.

"That may be so, but I personally am not." Michaela's gaze was unblinking.

"Redoak, is there a point to all of this?" Madden spoke to Cormac, but watched Michaela.

Cormac paused to make sure all ears were on him. "I offer myself as Watcher."

A dumbfounded silence filled the room, broken finally by Michaela.

"A Watcher is not required." Her words were untroubled. Her icy glance said, *You bloody bastard.*

"Aye, it is," Cormac said casually. "As I made very obvious. Shall I go over it again? Hiro is dead. In your office. Only months after the masquerada tried to destroy the Law and enslave humanity." He smiled inwardly, pleased to have gained a point over her for sending him to his office like a child.

A slight quiver shook Michaela. Had he finally managed to get under her skin? Years of delicate needling and all it took was a public accusation of murder. Perhaps she would lose control and unconsciously take on a new masque right there in the boardroom, a lapse of etiquette that would demonstrate a stunning lack of discipline. Baptiste laid a hand on Michaela's arm and both masquerada gave Cormac an identical glower.

Across the table, Abdul cleared his throat. "As much as it pains me to agree with anything Redoak says, he may have a point. In all our years, we've never had a councilor murdered in our own headquarters. It may be best, given the circumstances." He nodded to Michaela. "A Watcher is meant to protect the investigators."

She swept the table with a cool smile. "Our protection is sufficient." Cormac gave her a long, slow wink that she ignored. Abdul was correct in his interpretation of how the role was intended but Cormac gave zero fucks about intention. He needed to be close to the investigation to see if Hiro's death was related to the sale of his forest.

"I agree with Abdul." Madden tapped the table harder. "This is a special case but it will be noted that the assignment of Ambassador Redoak as Watcher is in no way a comment on Michaela's competence or culpability."

"Agreed." The word rose as a chorus, even from his fey compatriots. Cormac accidentally caught Rendell's eye but as always, his rival deliberately looked right through him. The cut direct had been perfected by fey at the Lilac Court, where the protocol of manners had reached a ridiculous degree, and Rendell was acclaimed as one of its most skilled practitioners. Cormac expected nothing more from him. Nor did he want anything but for Rendell to suffer a slow, painful, and preferably hideously disfiguring fatal illness. They had been on opposite sides of the war that had resulted in the deaths of his parents and mentor, and Cormac's subsequent banishment. While Rendell had not been the one to deliver the blows, his unwavering support of Tismelda had made them permanent enemies.

After a few more instructions, the councilors filtered out, leaving only Madden, Cormac, and Michaela. Michaela leaned over to Madden, murmuring in a voice low enough that Cormac couldn't hear more than her inflections. Madden listened, frowned and gave a sharp shake of his head before he replied, then took his leave. Michaela stared after him until Cormac sat on the table beside her. "Interesting conversation?"

She stood with a deliberate, slow movement and stood away from the chair. "You son of a bitch."

Considering what he'd done to her, Cormac considered this mild.

He crossed his arms. "It's necessary and you know it. One wrong step and this council will be in chaos. Madden should have suggested it right away."

"You didn't do this out of altruism." Her eyes narrowed. "What's in it for you?"

He ignored that. "Hiro was killed in your office. What does that tell you?"

"I search for evidence before conjecture."

He brushed away this typically pompous masquerada response. "Then you're a fool. Hiro was either waiting for you or trying to break into your files. Either way, it's bad for you, isn't it? Do you even have an alibi?"

"We'll examine the scene to find the answer." He noted that she ignored his last question. No alibi. "We need more information. That's my job. Not yours. You can watch all you want, but stay out of my team's way. Stay out of *my* way. Am I understood?"

The security chief stared up at him with glowing black eyes. With her cheeks flushed and lips red from where she'd pressed them, she looked like she'd been tumbled in bed.

She resembled a woman and not a statue.

Well, he'd been in trouble with beautiful women before. Best to let her get her temper out quickly so they could move on.

He gave her a mocking salute. "Yes, ma'am."

"This is not necessary."

He smiled broadly. Getting a response out of Michaela, minor as it was, was more pleasurable than he anticipated. "You mean you don't like it. And it doesn't matter."

Cormac remained a step behind as he followed Michaela back to her office crime scene. When she opened the door, her deputy and investigation team looked up at her, then him.

"The council has appointed Ambassador Redoak as Watcher," she announced. "It's only because of the political sensitivity of this case. Pharos has full confidence in your work and integrity. The ambassador will in no way interfere with you or the investigation." Her tone said that she would gut him if he even tried.

None of them answered, but their expressions were easy enough to read. Cormac gave a jaunty bow. One thing the Lilac Court had taught him was the value of appearing indifferent to hostility. Not that he was offended by their animosity, but it was good to show he had a tough hide.

Michaela ignored him as she wound through the close quarters of the office speaking to her people. Cormac regarded the empty chair where Hiro's body had been as the team went back to work. Death was bad enough, but to be stabbed in the back was such an ignominious way to go. It was also a cowardly way to kill.

Who owned that forest in Japan now that Hiro was dead? Tismelda would soften the moment he could present her with that beautiful land, and then it was only a matter of time until she reversed his exile. He touched his pendant, knowing that each day he remained in this realm, away from Yetting Hill, was another day his forest had to die.

When the forest died, so would he and his sister.

The fading leaf told him it was time to put aside pride. He'd tell the queen he'd learned his lesson. Once home, he could connect with his land and become a proper steward again. He could protect Isindle from the queen's many small biting cruelties. *I can stand up for myself, brother.* The memory of his sister's exasperation made him smile. She was correct. On her own since his exile, and now a full-fledged mage, Isindle was strong enough to deal with the Lilac Court. Yet he was eldest and she would always be his responsibility. Isindle might be a mage, but the girl-fey he remembered was soft-hearted and kind, no match for Queen Tismelda.

Michaela sighed and rose to her feet. "Keep working," she ordered her team. "I'm going to start talking to the councilors."

"Good luck," someone mumbled.

"Thanks." She swung open the door and left as though Cormac didn't exist. He shook his head as he followed. It would take more than common rudeness to turn him off his job.

She had no idea what was at stake for him. None at all.

Chapter 4

Michaela eyed Cormac with veiled resentment. It had been a long and tiresome day and having Cormac shadow her every move had not helped. True to his promise, he had stayed out of the way, but his obtrusively unobtrusive lurking had been more distracting than if he had taken part in the interrogations. Every time she'd looked up, she'd been confronted by his bright green, then brown, then dark green eyes watching her every move with a disconcerting intensity, as though he was stripping her to her very soul. She'd done her best to ignore it.

Michaela ran her hand quickly over her hair, tucking in loose strands as she glanced down her list and fixed the neatness of one of the lines. The councilor interviews had been frustrating. To her mind, having to waste time discussing their relationships with Hiro was also useless since she was almost certain she was the intended victim. She'd said as much to Madden after the council meeting.

"He was found in my office," she'd said. "You know what the Dawning has threatened to do to me."

"You promised me that our security here was tight."

"It is, but it doesn't prevent someone on Pharos from acting on their behalf."

"Yet you are alive and Hiro is dead," he'd said. "I need to you to focus on the man who's dead. It may not be about you."

As if she was such a narcissist. The stress of running Pharos was getting to Madden. His temper had been short for the last few months and although she'd not commented on his new attitude towards her, it had hurt. For years, Madden had been one of the few people she'd regarded as a compass—wise with experience and generous with advice.

She sighed, suspecting she'd outgrown him as a mentor. Perhaps he knew it too.

She thumbed through her notes as Cormac guzzled down water. Every councilor they had spoken to had an alibi, or an alibi of sorts. Cormac had been seen at breakfast. The witches had been at a Zumba class. One of the werewomen had been with her alpha, while the other had a dentist's appointment.

"This room is grim," observed Cormac from his seat near the wall as he put down the empty glass. Michaela had commandeered an empty office space for her interviews. "Like tedium came to life with a career in interior decoration."

"It's a meeting room. Cover it with one of your fey glamours if it bothers you so much."

His arched eyebrows rose high. "We usually only glamour ourselves."

"Like you did to hide from Nadia?" The young vampire had been furious Cormac had hoodwinked her and had blamed everyone and everything except her own inattentiveness.

He leaned back and crossed his arms. Michaela kept her gaze up and away from the very unprofessional observation of noticing how good his biceps looked. For a lean man, Cormac was impressively muscular. "Is that what she told you? Sorry. She was simply unobservant. It would be a crime to glamour myself. How would people admire me?"

"Arrogance." Not that it wasn't well-deserved. Cormac was a very striking male, though his appalling personality negated any attraction his tall body and chiseled features might have had. Or his broad shoulders and muscled thighs. She'd noticed, but that was to be expected. As a masquerada, she always closely observed people's physical appearance; it meant nothing.

"Truth." He sat down and settled down in the chair, fiddling with a pen. "We aren't all thieves, you know." He sounded amused.

She hid her surprise. "I didn't say you were."

Cormac snorted. "Right. You looked at my hands and tapped your jacket pocket. Your keys are safe."

"How do you know I have keys there?"

"They leave a bulge and jangle. Like a dungeon keeper." He made a gesture of twisting a key. "You know, we still haven't discussed your alibi."

No, they hadn't. She ignored him and checked her watch. "Rendell is on his way."

"Rendell is always late. Where were you this morning before you arrived here?"

She was the one in charge, thought Michaela furiously. "None of your business. You may have someone to vouch for you, but I still want to know about your dealings with Hiro."

He leaned forward. "First you. I repeat: Where were you when Hiro died?"

Michaela smiled and looked him in the eye. "This is not your investigation."

"Nor is it completely yours. No one will be so crude as to say it aloud, but the reason you have a Watcher is because deep inside their nasty little souls, your colleagues all think you did it."

"At least they have souls," she snapped. Not the best comeback, especially since the fey absence of soul was still a matter of debate. *You're getting too involved. Step back.* It had been a long time since someone had managed to get under her skin the way Cormac could without even trying.

"Where were you?" His eyes didn't leave hers and despite herself, Michaela was impressed. Cormac had a commanding presence that made him an intimidating interviewer. She straightened her back. She had faced worse than an exiled fey.

The heavy silence filled the room and Michaela settled herself to wait him out.

"You could be the killer," he said. "In fact, you are the most likely killer."

She yawned and paged through her notes. "Tell me about your deals with Hiro," she said.

"Of course, whatever alibi you could give would be close to meaningless," he said thoughtfully. "It could be anyone in your masque."

"You and Hiro?"

"I'll tell you about Hiro if you give me your alibi."

Michaela smiled. "So tell me."

"I had a meeting with him at ten this morning," Cormac said promptly. "Or would have."

"What about?" She had to ask even though she doubted his honesty. Cormac could protest against the fey reputation for thievery all he wanted, but no one in their right mind would believe a word out of one's mouth. They were golden-tongued, renowned liars and storytellers.

"A forest. I was negotiating for the rights to one of his forests in northern Japan."

"Why?" The fey had plenty of forest. "What made this one so special?"

He shrugged. "It's a lovely place, worthy of the queen. I thought she would enjoy it."

Michaela regarded him. Gratuitous generosity was not a fey trait. "You mean give it to Tismelda so she'll reverse your exile."

"That's one part of it, certainly," he said smoothly. "Humans are encroaching on the area. All that beauty will be gone in a human generation without protection."

She had to admit this was reasonable. The fey were fanatical about keeping woodland, even though their primary abodes were in their own realm. If that was true, then it would have been in Cormac's best interest to keep Hiro alive. *If* it was true.

"Are you done, Inquisitor?" His gaze was mocking but she noticed that his eyes lingered on her lips. "Ready to keep your end of the bargain?"

"I made no bargain," she said. "Now be silent. I hear Rendell."

He sputtered as he realized that she hadn't committed to the deal he'd offered but took a seat with ill-grace as Rendell thrust the door open and entered with a slow and languid elegance that made her feel lumpy and bumbling. The fey often had this effect on other arcana. As he passed Cormac, she compared the two. There were similarities, to be certain. All fey had a particular puckishness to their features. In Rendell, it came out in a strangely gleeful expression as if laughing at a cruel joke. Cormac had a bit of the same but without the underlying nastiness. On him, it showed in the occasional wicked and knowing smile that swept across his face like a cool wind.

Rendell brushed an imaginary speck of dust off his spotless silver-gray suit. "I keep thinking of Hiro. Poor man. Such pain."

The words were right, but Rendell's voice was thick with a horrible excitement. He kept talking. "You saw him. Were the cuts deep? Were the blood drops like rubies on his skin?"

Michaela barely avoided rolling her eyes at his blatant attempt to shock her but Cormac growled. "Why don't you tell us?" he asked.

"Cormac." Her voice carried a warning.

Rendell's eyes flickered over him, deliberately dismissive, before turning back to Michaela. "Should we be frightened? Can you protect us all?" He licked his lips.

It only took her seconds to decide how to deal with him. "You've nothing to be afraid of," she said in her chirpiest voice, patterned after the most irritatingly cheerful barista she knew. "We think the attacker is only targeting important Pharos members."

Rendell laughed. "Charming, Michaela. You know, of course, that unlike you, I have no reason to kill Hiro. Or any human for that matter, although Oksana is so irritating she should be exterminated on principle."

She caught Cormac leaning forward as if to say something and shot him such a look that he held up his hands in mock surrender.

"You were seen speaking to him in the library several days ago," she said to Rendell.

"Perhaps. I speak to many of my colleagues."

Investigations would go so much better if she only had to deal with things and not people. "What did you discuss?"

"I don't remember."

"Let me help jog your memory. You were overheard talking about money. Quite a vast sum."

Rendell yawned and cast his eyes up to the ceiling in an exaggeratedly theatrical attempt at recollection. "Now it comes back to me. He offered me some land, a forest. I have plenty and declined, but he was extremely pushy. I told him I'd think about it."

"What land?" asked Michaela. Across the room, Cormac's eyes were trained on Rendell but he remained silent.

"A Japanese mountain, or some such thing."

Japan. Michaela kept her focus on Rendell. "Northern Japan?"

"Now that you mention it, yes." He smirked. "Did he offer it to you, too?"

"I don't need a forest."

"Oksana says Hiro's death is a violation of the Law, you know." Rendell cocked his head to the side, then crossed his legs. "Is she right?"

"Human councilors are outside the Law," she said. "Obviously, since they need to know of arcane existence."

"The Law and the peace it brought hangs by a thread." Rendell's comment made Michaela wonder how much of his attitude was simply show. The Law that governed all arcana and hid them from human view had worked for the last seven hundred years and, on the surface, still seemed to be working. Rendell was one of the first Michaela had heard openly admit to the potentially devastating cracks that were forming underneath.

"Why do you say that?"

"Hiro is one of only two humans on the council. If I were Oksana, I would be very worried indeed."

"An interesting theory." She had an inkling of where this was going but would let him say it.

"Didn't the masquerada have a little problem with humans recently? Franz Iverson?"

She didn't bite. "All the arcane groups have a love-hate relationship with humans, not only the masquerada."

Rendell gave her a nasty smile. "Last time I checked, the fey weren't the ones trying to, oh, dominate the world and subjugate humanity."

Deep breath. "That was one twisted man's thinking." Franz Iverson had not made them many friends by declaring humans were at the bottom of a pyramid of worth that placed the masquerada alone at the top. While most arcana would agree with humans at the base, they disagreed vehemently about having masquerada at the apex.

"One?" Rendell examined Michaela with his pale blue eyes. "We all know how hard it's been for you to take control of your insubordinate groups. I doubt he was the only believer."

He winked at her and swept out of the room, a king ending an audience with a supplicant.

Once he was gone, Cormac scowled, his jaw tense. "Does that worm bother you?"

"I'm not interested in your petty rivalry."

"Petty? No. Rendell is one of the queen's pets and he has even less morality than most fey. Stay clear of him."

"It's my investi—"

He smiled at her, the corners of his eyes crinkling in a way that made her heart beat faster. Attracted to Cormac? Impossible. "Michaela. I know you can take care of yourself. I give you only a warning about an individual of whom I have more experience than you."

She listened now. It was difficult to find accurate information about the fey. "What do you mean?"

"Rendell is the queen's master torturer. He enjoys his work."

She blanched. "That's barbaric." The masquerada had abandoned torture decades ago. Arcane groups didn't interfere in each other's internal discipline, but such practices still came in for a good amount of superior tut-tutting.

"That is how the fey court works." Cormac yawned as if this was normal. "He did bring up a good point, however."

"I don't recall asking your opinion."

"I know. That's why I'm giving it unsolicited."

"What exactly are you blaming on us?" Her day with Cormac had caused a headache that had settled directly behind her eyes.

He gave a languid shrug. "Not Hiro's death, necessarily. The tension between arcane groups, yes."

"This is not our fault." Why was it her job to defend her race against the stupidity of a single bigoted man who the Hierarch had killed in combat? Hadn't she spent the last half year fighting death threats to make sure masquerada with such heinous beliefs were taken into custody?

It must have been chilly in the room, because she shivered as he moved by her to flick open the window curtain and check outside. "No need to get high and mighty. Perhaps if you treated the rest of the arcane world with the respect you demand, it would be easier to work with you."

True enough for some of her compatriots, but no need to get into it. The other groups were no better. She refused to get defensive.

Cormac pushed on. "Iverson might be dead, but can you tell me that what he believed died with him? Obviously not, with the amount of work you've been doing to crush his supporters."

It wasn't surprising others knew of her role in clearing Iverson's poison out of the masquerada. Franz Iverson had been vile and Eric had killed him and then systematically destroyed his networks. Most of his lackeys were either dead or imprisoned—thanks in a large part to her.

"Rumor has it that you let Iverson's deputy escape," he said. "You can't even find her."

Time to end this conversation. "Frieda is of no concern to me." Michaela glanced down at her notebook. Right now she had a murder to solve.

Chapter 5

Cormac paid little attention to the other councilors who came in to provide their alibis. His gut already told him what he needed to know.

Rendell was the killer. Looking for more money, Hiro had offered the forest to the other feyman, who had immediately seen an opportunity to thwart Cormac. A foolish and greedy thing to do, but that was the kind of man Hiro was. As if reading his thoughts, Oksana admitted to Michaela that she, no surprise, hadn't liked her compatriot. "Trying to keep a united front with Hiro was impossible," she said bitterly. "He would turn on you in a moment. His principles were as fluid as water."

Turn on you in a moment, like he had with Cormac's forest. Since Rendell was not one with a huge respect for human life, it was reasonable he would consider Hiro's death an appropriate price to keep Cormac from returning to the Queendom. It ended the risk of Cormac ingratiating himself with Queen Tismelda before it even began. Cormac never would, of course, but Rendell was a courtier to the bone. Court politics would be his default—and probably only—consideration.

After Oksana took her leave, Michaela turned off her digital recorder and flipped through her notes, written in a compelling Chinese running script. Cormac considered her. She was as fresh as when they'd started, except her normally pale lips were even paler. Red lips might be the usual standard of beauty, but there was something about the way hers blended in with the skin that he found almost stunningly erotic. He wanted to see that lower lip crimson and full with desire.

"Curious."

Cormac tore his attention away from her mouth. "What?"

Michaela capped her pen. "Oksana wasn't frightened."

He replayed the interview in his mind. Michaela was correct. "She thinks Hiro was specifically targeted as an individual, not a human." Instead of congratulating his perception, Michaela bent and added a few more notes as he stared at the precise part in her black hair, straight as a sapling.

"I have enough here to get the teams started," she said.

"They all hated him. You didn't get anywhere."

"What were you expecting? One of them to jump up and admit their guilt?"

"Don't be ridiculous. Not to mention that you're still no closer to knowing why he was in your office."

"An investigation takes time."

She stood while Cormac watched her unabashedly. Michaela was slender and straight as a reed but when she stretched, her body curved to emphasize a waist almost narrow enough for his hands to span. That blue-black hair remained tightly coiled, and he wondered how long it would be when she took it out.

Get it together, Redoak. Michaela was a beautiful woman, but he'd always found her coldness a turnoff.

Didn't he? Or was it a challenge he'd never thought to accept?

"I'm going to check in with the team and then go home." She packed up her bag and double-checked the desk to see if she had all of her papers.

He followed her to the security office. She paused with her hand on the door and he heard the voices inside.

"It's her. I'm telling you." Nadia's voice, an annoying mix of whiny and strident. Cormac winced.

"For the tenth time, that is Hiro. They look completely different." Dev sounded exasperated.

Nadia snorted. "How can you tell? All Chinese look the same. Even their hair is the same."

Beside him, Michaela stiffened.

There was a long silence and when Dev spoke again his voice was cold. "Hiro is Japanese. If you're going to be ignorant, keep it to yourself."

"Chinese, Japanese, whatever. Look at that security shot and tell me it couldn't be either of them."

Michaela must have thought this was a good time to interrupt, because she pushed the door open. Cormac came in behind her to see Dev's poorly disguised fury and Nadia's surly expression. Michaela didn't mention what they'd overheard but went straight into updating her colleagues.

On the screen was a security shot of a figure in black coming in the main door, head down and with dark hair smoothly tied back in a bun. He was about to examine it closer when Michaela gestured him out the door.

"What a bitch," he said conversationally.

"She is that," Michaela agreed, to his surprise.

"You didn't say anything." He would have thought that Michaela would have taken the opportunity to lay down some home truths to the vampire. She was not a woman who shied from necessary confrontation.

"Dev handled it well enough that I didn't need to." She picked up her bag and touched the pocket where her keys were. "I'll see you tomorrow."

Tomorrow? "No need for good-byes."

Her thin black brows knit together. "What are you talking about?"

"I'm your Watcher."

"I know. You've watched. All day."

He cocked his head curiously at her. Could she not have known? "I don't leave your side, Michaela. Not until this is done."

Her face said she hadn't. He nearly rubbed his hands in delight.

She didn't even bother to answer. Instead, she took her phone, made a call, and spoke without any greeting. "When were you going to tell me about Redoak living with me?"

She must have called Madden. There was a long silence. Cormac could hear Madden's warm soothing tones, his vampire's compulsion at work, and also knew by Michaela's expression that she was not convinced.

Then she turned her back to him. "I don't want him at my place," she hissed.

Pause. "I'm *not* going to a hotel with him."

Pause. "That's not the point, Madden."

Long pause. "Yes."

Very long pause. "Right."

Michaela hung up and Cormac leaned over into her view. "Your place or mine?" he asked innocently.

She took a deep breath and Cormac took a prudent step out of her strike range. "You'll come to my apartment," she said, having regained her calm. "Do you need anything from your house?"

"I keep an overnight bag in my office."

She raised her eyebrows. "Prepared for anything?"

He nodded, deciding to take it as a serious question. "Yes."

Cormac grabbed his bag as they passed his office and they walked in silence to the garage. He remained a few steps behind and watched Michaela's straight back. Being her Watcher was turning out much better than he had imagined. He'd confirmed Rendell had the motive to kill Hiro—he would do anything to keep Cormac away from court—and he'd managed to get a rise out of Michaela.

She pointed her key fob towards her car and it unlocked the doors with a series of cheerful beeps. Then she made a careful tour of the exterior. Was she worried about her safety, or was this another manifestation of her excessively cautious self?

Cormac slid in as she checked the mirrors. "No need to be angry at me."

"You don't know what I was thinking." She shoved the key into the ignition so hard that he winced as it jammed into the palm of her hand.

"Of course I do. You're furious I offered to be Watcher. You think the council doesn't trust you." He considered this. "They don't, but they don't trust anyone."

She drove onto King Street at a speed more suited to the autobahn than the busy downtown core. It didn't matter; traffic ground them to a stop before she'd even gone twenty feet. Damn. They were enmeshed in the tail end of rush hour. More time trapped in the car, cooped up in a metal cage in this concrete valley.

"Might be faster to walk," Cormac offered finally. "How long have you had this car?"

"Five years." She paused. "Why?"

"No reason." It was spotless and even had that chokingly chemical new car smell. He pulled the seat back and stretched out to relax as she chauffeured him around. It would be better if he had his eyes closed.

She stared straight ahead. "What was that about?"

"An observation about the speed of traffic." Let her work for it.

"I don't mean that and you know it. There hasn't been a Watcher appointed for over a hundred years."

"As I told the council, this is sensitive. You know it, Michaela. In fact, in different circumstances, I'm sure your fine mind would have been one of the first to suggest it."

She inched the car forward and swore as the light turned red. "You decided you would be the best choice? An exiled fey?"

He put a hand on his heart. "Wounding but technically accurate. Who else would be acceptable? None of the others trust each other. I am the only one with no master. Or mistress."

He said the last in an arch tone that made Michaela's lips thin. She must know he was right. Every member of the Pharos had a dual role. The first was to make sure the Law was obeyed by every arcana and to punish transgressors. The second, and unspoken, role was politics. Pharos was the unofficial overarching council for all arcana. So secret that not even their rulers knew they were members, the councilors worked outside the official avenues to solve disputes that threatened to destroy the delicate balance of power between arcane groups. Secret though they were, there was a clear loyalty to one's ruler and one's race above all.

Cormac, as an exile, was beyond at least this level of local politics. The other fey didn't even acknowledge him.

"I meant what I said about staying out of my way."

"And I have." He yawned and nestled back into the seat. "At least in public."

Chapter 6

Damn him. Damn. Michaela wanted to scream with the intense frustration of being stuck in traffic with the world's most irritating feyman. Of course she didn't. As a masquerada she could maintain precise control over every nuance of expression she wished to reveal.

Cormac, though, had the disturbing ability to peel back her defenses until she felt as open and unsophisticated as a child.

She glanced over at him when she stopped at the next light. Cormac lay with his eyes closed and his arms tucked behind his head. He was tall for a fey. His hair was golden but by his ear she noticed streaks of what looked like silver, as if the metal had been coated with pearl. His face was perfect, of course, although slightly more rugged than the other fey she'd met. The body was…nice. Exceptionally nice.

Over generations, humans had imagined fairies into tiny winged creatures that tended to flowers and giggled behind trees. The fey were nothing like those translucently dressed beings. Like the rest of his kin, Cormac exuded an aura of wild power.

His eyes opened and she was taken aback by the motley mix of grass-green and dark sable, illuminated by the fading sunlight. It shadowed his face and highlighted his bone structure, almost too lovely for a man but still enticingly masculine.

"What do your eyes mean?" she asked abruptly.

He looked confused. "That I can see?"

"No. The colors."

"There's no guide." He gave her a whimsical smile. "Like to a box of chocolates. Are you looking for the caramel or the candied cherry?"

She ignored that. "They must reflect something about how you're feeling or what you're thinking."

"If you want to know that, why don't you ask me?"

"You lie." The words came out before she could check them and a quiver ran over him, gone so fast that she wondered if she'd even seen it.

"Aye. I suppose I do." He glanced up, eyes now a cool gray. "You know I love your admiration for my good looks, but the light changed."

Michaela hit the accelerator.

"Nadia might be an idiot, but I saw the screen," said Cormac. "The figure was clearly Hiro, but it did resemble you."

"Generic Asian?"

"Generic business casual. He wore all black, like you, and he had his hair pulled back, like you. If you ask me, he was impersonating you." And if he was, then Hiro wasn't the target.

Rendell might not be the killer.

"First, I didn't ask. Second, we're in Toronto. Everyone wears black." Michaela kept her voice cool, but inside pieces were clicking together. Hiro was in her office, dressed like her. It was so obvious whoever killed him thought it was her, especially since there was no reason for Hiro to be there at all. She now needed to find enough incontrovertible proof to convince Madden.

Too bad her own mentor didn't trust her.

They drove a few blocks in thick silence until her phone rang.

"Auntie! *Ni hao le ma?*" Ivy's cheerful voice filled the car and Michaela's entire body relaxed.

"*Hao le, xiao xiao.*" She ignored Cormac as his entire, rather distracting, body swiveled towards her. Best to keep the conversation in Chinese so her Watcher couldn't spy on this part of her life.

"You sound stressed, Auntie." Ivy was excellent at reading people and Michaela hadn't been surprised last year when she decided to go to medical school. "Are you driving?"

"Stuck in traffic."

"I won't be long. I wanted to remind you about dim sum this weekend. My parents are coming to visit."

"Wouldn't miss it."

Ivy chattered on a little more about her schoolwork and roommates and job. "Late shift tonight," she said.

"Your parents won't like that." Her parents thought Ivy's efforts should only be academic but Michaela had supported her. A woman had to know how to earn money of her own.

Ivy's happy laugh came down the line. "That's why they don't know. I keep safe."

"I love you."

"Love you too, Auntie. See you this weekend."

Michaela hung up and stared at the bumper sticker of the car in front of her. *Hanging with my gnomies* was inaccurately pictured with a line of small, colorful goblins. Yao would have been proud of Ivy, thought Michaela, reeling with a momentary grief for her old friend, dead these many years. Not that he ever would have had a chance to meet his great-great-granddaughter. A human's life was so very brief and his had been cut even shorter.

"A friend calling?" asked Cormac neutrally.

"Yes."

"She sounds young." He said it in perfect Chinese.

"Your accent is very good." He wasn't going to shock her.

"I'm an exile. I have plenty of time to practice."

"Where did you learn?"

"Here and there."

She almost grinned, knowing he was remaining vague to irritate her.

"I have a sister," he said.

She glanced over in surprise. "You do?"

He laughed and regarded her with eyes that were now deep gray. "Is that any stranger than a human niece for a masquerada? Isindle stays in the Queendom."

"Do you see her often?" Michaela could have bit her tongue off the moment she saw Cormac's face go blank. She hadn't meant to be deliberately cruel and had forgotten his exile.

"No. Tell me about Ivy and why she thinks you're her aunt."

"She doesn't. It's a term of endearment. She knows me as a family friend." Although she watched over all Yao's descendants, she rarely made herself known. It was too difficult to explain her lack of aging. From the first, though, Ivy had spoken to her heart.

"Are you?"

"I knew one of her ancestors." Michaela skirted around the issue, not wanting to discuss Yao.

Incredibly, Cormac seemed to respect her reticence. "She seems happy," he said. "You must watch out for her."

Michaela laughed. "Ivy wouldn't like that." Which is why she didn't know.

He shut his eyes. "When has that stopped you from doing anything?"

* * * *

Cormac kept his eyes closed.

He didn't like going to Michaela's box in the sky any more than she wanted him in it. Like a proper fey, he made his home in a tree. Not the great oak of his forest—he prevented himself from instinctively touching the pendant at his throat—but a perfectly serviceable chestnut tree he'd found in the hidden depths of High Park. Keeping himself isolated (not that other fey would risk being seen with him) was necessary to hide his physical need to be close to the *dolma*.

That he was a *caintir*, a forest talker, was a secret he could never allow out. Queen Tismelda would have him clapped in irons in the bottom of her dungeon. The *caintir*'s deep connection to the *dolma*—the world and its living things—far outstripped that of all other fey, making them both powerful and dangerous. Tismelda would have considered his mere existence a challenge to her throne. Not even Isindle knew, though he was sure his sister suspected.

He was the last existing *caintir* in or out of the Queendom and had survived because he'd buried his ability so deep he often wondered if he'd lost it forever. The only other he'd known was the bitch queen's own sister, Kiana, an extraordinary feywoman who could effortlessly impress her will on the *dolma*. Animals had done her bidding and trees would flower at her word. Kiana had secretly trained Cormac to do the same, all the while covering for both of them so Tismelda would never know of their existence as *caintir*. With a fierce sense of loss he remembered the communion he felt when he opened himself to the world, and sent his mind to fly with the birds and hunt with the wolves.

That had ended when the bitch queen had holed Kiana up in a room devoid of any natural element and watched without mercy as Kiana's very skin and bones had faded and turned to dust.

Kiana had forced him to swear on his tree that he would remain hidden after her death and he had done his best to avoid the slightest lure of his power. It had been so difficult during the first years he thought it would send him mad. He stared at his hands and flexed his fingers. Only fear for Isindle helped him persevere. He monitored every action to ensure he didn't give himself away, fighting the enticement of wood whenever possible, knowing he could lose himself in a single touch. A physical ache filled him when he thought of how complete he had felt in discuss Yao.

Correction: Michaela skirted around the issue

those days with Kiana.

He opened his eyes to watch Michaela weave expertly in and out of traffic. Like everything else she did, she drove well. How old was she? Younger than he was, that was certain, but there was a wariness around her eyes he'd seen in other arcane beings. She'd seen many things, and few of them had left happy memories.

She loved that Ivy girl, though. He considered Michaela under this new light. To be able to love like that after so many years was unusual, and many arcana avoided love, especially love for a human. Experiencing the death of a loved one hurt as much the tenth time as it did the first, even after centuries. After a while, the heart couldn't take it anymore. The scars surrounding it tightened until it was so tough nothing could penetrate it.

Yet impassive Michaela risked her heart to a young human. Seeing Michaela's unguarded joy as she spoke with Ivy had stirred a primal and almost foreign emotion in him, and he didn't like it at all.

Tenderness had no place in the fey world.

Not only that, it was laughable. Tenderness for Michaela Chui, the most hardheaded woman he'd known outside of his own queen? She'd see it as weakness.

But she'd laughed so freely when she was talking and her entire face had lit up like a diamond hit by the sun. Seeing her with her guard down had unleashed his instincts to keep her from harm. The fey were almost ferociously protective once they formed a connection. He could take her out of the damn car and dance her over to the big chestnut, where he would wrap her in his arms and…

And what? His priority was getting the proof to show that Rendell had killed Hiro out of spite to prevent him from getting that forest. Seduction had no place in his plans. He tried to hide his sudden iron erection. Knowing Michaela's hard exterior hid such a caring gentleness was extraordinarily alluring.

This was bad. *She's a masquerada,* he thought desperately. *Who even knows her true face? Her true self?*

"We're here." Michaela pointed up to a very modern building, all shiny chrome and bluish sheet windows.

"You live here?" He'd expected something with stained glass and old dark wood. Red and green accents. When she led him in, even the elevator was lined with gleaming black granite.

They stepped out and he almost walked right into her when she stopped halfway down the hall. Before he could open his mouth, she held up her hand in an imperious gesture and motioned for him to stay still.

"I should have mentioned this in the car, but I've done my own security," she said, pressing a button on her keys. A series of soft trills came from the dark apartment and she listened before moving ahead. "All good. Come in."

The next few minutes were a lesson in paranoia. Cormac watched in increasing wonder as she stood in the foyer and methodically checked through a catalog of security measures she'd installed in every location.

"How do you know if the door has been tampered with?"

Michaela waved her phone. "I monitor the hall during the day. There's also a motion sensor."

"This seems excessive." Was the woman expecting an army? Multiple assassins?

She slid off her shoes and lined them up neatly near the door, which he now saw had been sealed around the perimeter to form a barrier against any gases or powders being forced in. "It's been a rough few months," she said.

Cormac followed her in. "Your civil war."

"It's not a war."

"Excuse me. The minor disagreement that split the masquerada into warring factions and forced the Hierarch into mortal combat to keep his throne."

She didn't crack a smile. "True, though dramatically phrased."

A blue light glinted from the balcony door. A motion sensor? "How many death threats have you received?"

"Enough." Michaela sat on the couch and closed her eyes.

"Any attempts?" That someone even considered laying a hand on her was enough to start a dull red climbing up behind his eyes. At least now he was with her to add a measure of protection. Relief flowed through him but he told himself it was only because of his pride. It would be deflating if she was injured while he was Watcher.

"Not often," she said, eyes still closed.

"You do get them, then."

Now she met his gaze. Her eyes were almost black and fringed by thick lashes that tipped very slightly downward. He wanted to trace his finger along them. "If I did, it would be neither new nor unusual."

"Despite that, you still think Hiro was the intended target?"

"Since he is the one who is dead, yes."

She was lying.

Michaela stood. "Tea?" She shut down the conversation and he let her go, watching her straight back as she left the room. She didn't think Hiro was the target. Why was she pretending that he was? Michaela never did anything without a reason. Perhaps she was covering for Rendell. A feeling of discontent rolled over him that she might be in league with his enemy.

"Sit down, Cormac." Her voice floated out from the kitchen. "I can hear you thinking from here."

He did, and finally let himself take stock of her apartment. Then he blinked, a bit stunned. Michaela's place was a collector's wet dream. An exquisite jade melon sat in the center of a beautiful carved lacquer table. To the left was what appeared to be an entire herd of Tang dynasty ceramic horses, their distinctive glazing perfectly lit by a small light. He stood and wandered in awe, categorizing her treasures before ending up in front of an achingly lovely brush painting of a crane about to take flight. The Chinese characters on the side evoked a similar sense of movement. Kiana would have loved it. He took his time examining it, then wandered slowly through the rest of the room before returning to the painting. It had a poignancy that attracted him powerfully.

"Here's your tea." Michaela gave him a handless cup of flowered tea. "Imperial jasmine."

He inhaled the steam. "This painting is extraordinary."

"Thank you." She stood beside him and tilted her head to the side. Even here, safe in her domain, she stood straight and her hair was still tied tight. "It took me some time to decide how to place the bird."

"You did this?"

"Yes." She said no more. "I'm going to bathe. It's been a long day."

With that, she left him in a cloud of jasmine-scented steam. He forgot the crane and instead thought about how she would look with her skin pinked from the bath.

Never mind.

Chapter 7

Michaela checked the time and rose from her bed. The evening had been quiet and the two had bid each other an early good night. Was Cormac planning something? He didn't even try to annoy her once.

The whole experience had been far less aggravating than she'd expected, but still uncomfortable. Having him in her space was far beyond dealing with him as a partner in an investigation. This was personal. Her home was where she could be herself, where she could lower her guard and relax.

Still, it was preferable to risking her life at a hotel, where she could be easily tracked by one of Iverson's followers.

She dressed in the chilly room. Her silk pajamas slid to the ground with a whisper and she pulled on black pants and a black jacket, tucking her long braid down the back. Cormac had joked about watching out for Ivy, but he didn't know the half of it. She'd played invisible guardian angel to Yao's descendants for over a hundred years and would until the end of her long life.

Of course, she thought wryly, Ivy had many times the freedom and independence of her mother and grandmother. Not that Michaela was complaining—she wanted Ivy to lead a life unfettered by expectations— but it did make being a guardian a little more difficult, especially now that she had to worry about idiots prancing around who thought killing Michaela might in some way advance their cause of domination over the humans. She could never lead her opponents to Yao's family. Not that it would happen. She was a masquerada, after all, and confident she could fool her enemies.

Cormac's door was closed; he'd never even know she was gone. Michaela slid out of the apartment on light feet and ran down to her car. Sneaking by Cormac had given her a silly sense of naughtiness that she hadn't had in years, like a kid who snuck a cookie out of the jar. *You're over five hundred years old. You should be more mature than to enjoy sneaking around at night.*

Should be, but then she hadn't had much of a childhood. Her first marriage had been at age fourteen and the old man had kept a close eye on her. Even the beautiful garden had been off-limits. Instead she'd been dressed like a doll and forced to sit and sing endless songs to old Zhang as he coughed and wheezed.

Never mind. That marriage, and all the others, were long past.

It was almost one in the morning and drunk people stumbled out of the bars as she parked a few blocks away from the pub where Ivy worked. All Michaela had to do was check that Ivy caught a cab. The alley to the left was dark and Michaela slipped in. When she came back out a block down, she was in what she thought of as her invisible masque. It had taken her multiple tries to discover that no one in the city seemed to notice an older, heavyset black woman dressed in dark clothes.

Today was as true as any other. She walked down the street and saw the eyes of the mostly young crowd skate right over her as if she didn't exist. How different than when she took on other masques. When she was a man, most people gave her space as she walked, moving out of her way unless they wanted to make some sort of point. As a young woman, it seemed that every eye on the street was on her. She'd spent years experimenting with clothes, hair, skin, and attitude in cities around the world, gauging reactions to her various masques. The only ones she couldn't use were the very young and very old. Her power, unlike Eric's, wasn't strong enough for that drastic a change.

Ivy's pub was across the street. Michaela bought an orange juice from a hot dog vendor—Toronto's street food of choice was hot dogs, of all things—and sipped it slowly as she waited on a bench. Ivy usually came out at exactly fourteen minutes past one. Michaela could watch Ivy hail the cab, then get back to her own apartment by half past one. There was no remorse at leaving Cormac ignorant. This had nothing to do with the investigation, so there was no need to involve him.

There was Ivy, right on time. Michaela stood, her body moving slowly against the twinges of age and hard work that came with taking on the masque's persona. On the sidewalk, Ivy yawned, pulled her hair into a high ponytail, glanced at the sky, and smiled.

She walked east.

Michaela groaned. It was a lovely night and not surprising Ivy wanted to stroll home in the fresh air. Well, it wasn't a long walk. She limped down the street and crossed to keep Ivy in sight. The walk was pleasant until Ivy decided to take a shortcut through an alley to the right, forcing Michaela to hurry her step. The alley appeared empty, but there could be people hidden in garage niches or in the shadows. Night was a time for arcana as well as humans. Not all of them were sweethearts.

"Check out that one."

The call came from the other end of the alley as Michaela came up behind a rank, rusted dumpster. A group of young men had appeared at the end of the street. Even at this distance she could tell they would reek of alcohol.

"Out all alone, huh?" The tall one with the ball cap moved forward with a nauseating smile. Ivy had half-turned and eyed him cautiously. A short blond in the back snorted nervously.

"Hey, guys, she's—" he started, but shut up when the leader elbowed him hard enough to cause a cry of pain. Michaela focused on the tall one. He had something to prove. The others would break if she took him down. Would she wait until he touched Ivy, or do it now? Ivy's eyes were huge and Michaela could almost hear her heart thumping. She seemed too frightened to run.

There were six of them. Michaela had seen how cruel humans could be when they hunted in packs and found a victim weaker than they were.

Ivy stepped back and tried to scream but it came out as a whimper that acted as a signal. It took only a moment for them to surround her. The tall one licked his lips, and even in the dim light of the alley from her location behind the dumpster, Michaela could see how huge his dilated pupils were.

"Look at you, standing with the garbage, where you belong. Should have stayed in your own country." A high, wild giggle escaped him and he wiped his mouth with the back of his hand. "Too bad. Now it's time to have some fun."

Then he reached out and grabbed Ivy's arm.

* * * *

Cormac stood in the shadows, watching the young woman, Ivy, as she stood against the group of men who now circled her. Men. Humans were brutish, with the same dominance displays as animals, and some were only happiest when they were inflicting pain on others—and even better, had it witnessed by their cronies. Michaela was nearby, masqued and hiding behind the dumpster. She must be too panicked to act. Not what he expected from her, but even the strongest warriors could freeze.

One made contact with Ivy and her strangled moan made his rage spike. On the rooftops above sat a flock of pigeons, the only animals in sight. He could bring them down, send them to Ivy's aid. Even as the thought occurred to him, a surge of power blasted up from the ground as the intense desire to connect with the *dolma* overwhelmed him.

He could bring it all under his control again—the trees, the drooping dandelion growing from a crack in the asphalt. It had been 312 years, 5 months, and 13 days since he'd had this.

No.

It took all his willpower but he managed to pull back, dampening his thoughts and forcing them away from the *dolma*. He had to. Too much would send an upwelling in the natural world that even Tismelda would sense.

He would not break his vow to keep his *caintir* power hidden, and his sister and forest safe.

However, his brief weakness had been enough to turn fifty pairs of beady eyes towards him before fluttering down. A thick, gray-brown cloud surrounded Ivy and her attackers, whose swagger crumpled as they tried to beat the birds off with weak slaps and shrill squeals.

Even as the flock of pigeons descended, the figure near the dumpster abruptly grew two feet taller. Cormac gaped. The being with the cadaverous face and wicked fangs worthy of a saber-toothed tiger had to be Michaela, but masquerada only took on human forms. He didn't even think they *could* take on the masques of other arcana.

The nightmarish vampire-Michaela loped over and took hold of the leader's hand, giving his arm a vicious twist. Cormac winced as he heard the bones crack and grind. The human's agonized scream was enough to send the others running. Michaela hissed into Blondie's face and Cormac saw him whimper and clutch his ruined arm to his chest. He doubled over as she gave him a vicious kick to the groin.

"Leave this place." The voice was every horror movie come to life. It brought shivers to Cormac's spine and he wasn't surprised when the damaged man desperately tried to pull himself away, the birds pecking at his face. He groaned and stopped, lying in an oily puddle.

Ivy had already gone running, screaming at the top of her lungs.

Cormac strode over to Michaela. She made a superb vampire but, as he watched, became herself again.

They regarded each other.

"I didn't know you could take on arcane masques," he said evenly, though the vampire had been more of a human perception of a vampire than any vampire he'd come across in real life.

"I didn't know you could summon a bird army."

Detente. He glanced down at her hands, which didn't tremble in the least. Apparently he had been wrong about her fear. "Are you injured?"

"No. How did you call the pigeons? Why pigeons?"

"Why don't we discuss this later?" He nodded to the twitching human.

Michaela ignored the human, now vomiting in pain. "Ivy. I need to check on her."

She dashed out and down to the street, making sure not to take the same route as Ivy. Cormac kept close as Michaela peeked around the corner. A group of people were soothing a young woman who cried as she pointed back at the alley.

"She's safe," Michaela said with relief.

"You're not going to see her?"

Michaela had already turned to walk away. "Why? To tell her what happened? That I transformed into a giant vampire to save her life?"

A siren shrieked in the distance as Cormac followed. "Good point."

She stumbled as they ducked into a side street and he instinctively laid a hand over hers. Her skin was warm and he was astonished when a shiver ran through her.

Then even more surprised when he felt a strange twist in his gut, a warmth that replaced the cold anger that had filled him.

Impossible. They didn't even like each other.

Yet he hadn't imagined that shiver. Or his matching reaction.

"How did you find me?" she asked.

"Heard you leave and flagged a cab."

"No, I mean my masque."

He could tell this bothered her, and at least this gave him the upper hand. "Instead of that, why don't you tell me about sneaking out past your Watcher? Your council-mandated Watcher?"

She grimaced. "Look, sneaking sounds so—"

"Correct? Dammit, you could have been killed."

Michaela glanced around and when she turned back, a thick man with glaring eyes and heavy, pale brows stared back at him. He had no neck, just a solid trunk of muscle from his ears to his shoulders.

He reeled back. "Good God. *What* is *that*?" Was it more disturbing to see her as this hulking man or as the ghoulish vampire? He shivered. Both were wrong.

Yeah, like talking to birds is totally normal.

"I am Yuri."

Her clothes had stretched to the ripping point around the masque's husky barrel of a chest. She must have considered her point made because she shifted back into her natural self.

"Who the hell is Yuri?"

"I am a masquerada," she said with heavy patience. She stepped close to him, so close he could smell the tuberose that wafted from her skin. "Not a human woman. Frankly, even if I was a woman, I wouldn't need—or want—you to take care of me."

"I was right to intervene."

"I'm the judge of that."

"You could have been injured," he said evenly.

They arrived at the car. She glared at him. "I needed to check on Ivy and I had it under control. They were only humans."

"What if they hadn't been?"

"Get in the car, Cormac. Now."

"Not until we discuss this."

"Here? You want to discuss this on the street."

"Yes. Better start talking."

She opened the door with a savage yank. "Fuck you I will. Walk if you don't want to drive with me."

"I need to drive with you, remember? I'm the Watcher. Mandated to be with you every minute. Watching your every. Goddamn. Move."

"Let's get this sorted, right now. I don't like being with you. I don't like you around me. I don't like having you hanging over me, breathing down my neck as I try to work." She blew her breath out and controlled her voice. "Yet I bowed to the will of the council."

"With such grace."

"That wasn't part of the deal."

"No, but you know what part of the deal was? You don't go out alone. You did. I can report this to the council and have you removed from this case."

She got in the car and powered down the passenger window. "This had nothing to do with Hiro, and I don't like threats."

Didn't she get it? It didn't matter what she thought. They were stuck together. "Then stop acting like a petulant child and giving me something to threaten you with."

* * * *

Michaela laid her hands carefully on the steering wheel, the right at two o'clock and the left at ten, before she leaned over to address Cormac through the open window. She wanted her hands fixed on something to prevent her from getting out and throttling him.

"I fail to understand how continuing my commitment to Ivy makes me more petulant than the man yelling at a car in the middle of the street."

She could almost hear Cormac grind his teeth as he got in the car and slammed the door.

When he huffily crossed his arms over his chest, she laughed out loud.

He glanced over, a small reluctant smile quirking his lips. "Not funny. You broke the rules." His eyes widened as if he just realized what he'd said. "*You* broke the rules."

"Not that big a deal."

Now he faced her with a huge grin. "Wait until I tell the Council this. They probably won't even believe me. Michaela Chui, stickler extraordinaire, sneaking out of her room in the middle of the night like she's trying to beat curfew."

"Look, I really—"

He didn't even pause. "Do you even feel guilty? I didn't know you had it in you."

Michaela focused on driving until he finally stopped. "I don't know that the Council needs to hear about this," she said.

"Oh, I think they do." Now Cormac sounded serious, and when Michaela checked his expression out of the corner of her eye, she saw that he was frowning slightly. "The Council assigned you a Watcher for a reason. Your protection. I can't protect you if you're sneaking around. I'd be derelict in my duty."

Did he think she was so stupid? "Please. Don't make my car a den of lies. We both know that your offer had nothing to do with me. You want something."

"Maybe I want you to be safe."

"Maybe I've managed to do that myself for a half-millennia and have a pretty good handle on it." Now she was getting a little pissed. Her own protection had been the same excuse her parents had used when they brokered her first marriage to a doddering old man. By the time they'd married her the third time, she'd realized she'd had enough of people protecting her. Whenever someone decided to protect her for her own good, they usually had a stake in the result, one of more benefit to them than her. She'd learned the lesson early and learned it hard.

"My reason doesn't matter," Cormac said with delight. "What matters now is that we have a situation where you have a secret you don't want me to tell."

"Blackmail?"

"Think of it more like a negotiation for mutual benefit."

"What do you want?"

"An apology," he said softly. "I want you to say you were wrong and I was right."

"The hell with that."

"Fine." He spoke with an air of extreme unconcern. "We'll chat with Madden in the morning."

"Fine."

"Fine."

They said nothing to each other for the rest of the ride but by the time she pulled into her parking spot, the car was filled with words left unsaid, mostly hers. She wanted to point out—God, that she didn't need a Watcher and that he was an asshole and how dare he treat her like some stupid underling and she didn't owe him an apology and he should screw right off.

The problem was, as her temper cooled, she knew she couldn't.

She didn't like his motives but Cormac had acted correctly and was well within his rights to report her. She had broken the rules and left him behind. She was going to have to apologize. Not to avert the threat, but because she was in the wrong and owed it to him.

Goddamn it.

Michaela did not enjoy apologizing. Best to get this over with.

Cormac had already cracked open the door when she held up a hand.

"I apologize," she said.

"For what?"

"That you felt I shouldn't have left without you. Even for Ivy."

Now he turned back and Michaela dropped her eyes. "Look at me."

The power in his voice forced her eyes up. "What?"

"That's a shite apology and you know it. I want you to say I was right."

"I…you." It was difficult to concentrate. Cormac leaned towards her, his tall body twisting until she was almost suffocated by his closeness and even then wanted him closer.

What? No, she didn't.

"Say you won't leave again."

She shook her head. She'd experienced vampire compulsions before and this was similar, though far more intense. With a quick motion, she opened the car door and let the cool night air flow in, restoring her equilibrium.

He might be her Watcher, but he wasn't her controller.

He got out of the car and came around to her side while she sat thinking, then opened the door and held out his hand.

Slowly, she pulled the keys out of the ignition with trembling fingers and brushed him away as she got out of the car.

A mocking voice came from behind her as she walked to the elevator door. "Apology accepted."

Chapter 8

Cormac watched Michaela shut the bedroom door behind her. He was fairly certain she wouldn't leave without him again…but not completely sure.

Now he sighed and regarded the couch. Since it was a little too short for him to sleep comfortably, there was only one thing to do. He pulled the pillows and thick duvet from his bedroom and settled down in front of her door. There was no way Michaela would get around him again.

He had only himself to blame. He should have kept a better eye on her. She resented his role as Watcher, but he'd thought her slavish adherence to orders meant she would play by the rules. That she hadn't done so intrigued him. There was more to Michaela than he'd thought.

The apartment was peaceful despite the annoying little blue security light beaming on the balcony. She didn't need the rest of the beeps and bells. He was here to protect her now.

He paused. That's not what he was here for. This was a problem. Like all fey, he possessed a protective streak and as a *caintir*, it was almost impossible to combat. Kiana herself had warned him about it during one of their first training sessions. "The *dolma* wants all," she'd said, her amber eyes wise. "Look at a fallen tree overgrown with vines."

He'd laughed. "I'm a vine?"

She'd remained serious. "Yes. Your connection to the *dolma* means you will always have to fight a poisonous possessiveness. Otherwise, you too will choke the life out of what you love."

Since he only loved Yetting Forest and his sister, and was now in exile, that hadn't been a problem for him. Michaela had roused those latent, primal emotions and made it clear that she expected him to mind his own business.

Not an easy ask.

Michaela was also more powerful than he had anticipated. He dredged his memory for what he knew about the masquerada. They had status levels, he knew, that were dependent on how many masques an individual could shift into. They were notorious for their blind worship of power. He frowned. Eric, the Hierarch, could shift into any form he pleased, and wasn't constrained by race, gender, or age. In her life outside of Pharos, Michaela was the highest ranking member of Eric's advisory council. Eric had made a Herculean effort to get his people to accept each other's worth regardless of how many masques they could take on, but it was a slow process. To be on that council, Michaela needed to be strong.

Seeing her as a vampire had been a shock. While there was no treaty against it, there was an unspoken agreement that masquerada only appeared in human masques. They were already the most numerous of all the arcane groups, and their ability to take on other personas made them feared. Who could know how many infiltrators one had when they wore the faces of your friends?

Physically, she was also capable of almost ripping out a human's arm without even blinking. That part, he had no problem with. It was kind of sexy, in a way.

Michaela's wooden floor hummed softly beneath him and he adjusted the blankets to prevent his flesh pressing against it. What had occurred in the alley with the pigeons couldn't happen again; he'd been weak. Cormac wouldn't be surprised if his old enemy Rendell made a habit of spying on him in the hopes of finding something to further discredit him to the queen, as if he could drop any lower in her eyes. Finding out Cormac was a *caintir* would be a choice morsel for him to bring back to the queen.

The pendant, with the leaf from his tree, lay heavy on his chest, a countdown clock reminding him of his first and only real responsibility. His forest needed him and nothing would distract him from his goal. He'd taken on the Watcher role to find out who had killed the man he needed, not as Michaela's guard or protector.

Nor could he get drawn into the easy, perfect joy of being a true *caintir* again. That power was what got Princess Kiana slaughtered. No. He corrected himself. The power didn't kill her. Kiana's ability to speak with wolves didn't kill her. Her influence over the forests and its creatures weren't what tortured her to death.

Tismelda and her insecurity had done all that.

To speak with the wolves again…He tucked his arms behind his head and stared at the smooth curves of a vase in the living room.

A creak came from Michaela's room and he listened closely before dismissing it. She was still there and not climbing out a window. He adjusted his pillows and propped his head on his hands. The day had been a series of unanticipated events, especially those involving her. Michaela was aggravating beyond belief. Devious. Robotically rational. Strong-willed. Make that iron-willed. Gorgeous. A vicious vampire. A huge, rough Russian man.

Right. That he'd never seen her shift had blinded him to the point that not only could she shift, but it was the central part of her being. She was a masquerada and he could no more separate that from her than any other trait. *What does it feel like for her to be Yuri, or any other masque?* he wondered. He would ask one day.

Though not tomorrow, which looked like it would be more irritating hours of by-the-books investigations. His gut still said Rendell had murdered Hiro in a power play to prevent Cormac's return to the Queendom, but another possibility had come clear the moment he'd seen the security footage of Hiro and had solidified when he saw Michaela's security precautions. Her work neutralizing the rest of Eric Kelton's enemies meant she was a high-profile target, and she knew it. Hiro's death could reasonably have been the result of mistaken identity. If Michaela was the target instead of Hiro, then he would need to find a way to bow out of his Watcher role to pursue other avenues of satiating the queen.

He'd think about it tomorrow. It would give him a puzzle to ponder as he listened to toothless interrogations.

His mind drifted to how to deal with Queen Tismelda. He'd make some discreet checks about the ownership of the forest, but it could take months to settle it. It was almost laughable that he, a creature who had lived for centuries, was now desperately measuring months. Hiro's forest was the only leverage he'd had to end his exile and it was slipping out of his grasp.

Well, it's not like he was going to come up with a grand plan in the middle of the night lying here on Michaela's floor. He shut his eyes, put one hand on his fading leaf pendant, and willed himself to sleep.

* * * *

Cormac woke when a door slammed into his ribs. He groaned, his dream state dropping him for one harrowing minute back into the battlefield of his youth, when he'd been woken by a spear in the side.

No, he was too warm and comfortable for the battlefield. He opened his eyes to Michaela's triangular face poking through the small gap that led to her bedroom.

She tilted her head. "Were you lying in front of my room all night?"

He rolled slowly to his feet. "Clearly."

She edged out. Her hair had come out of the braid she had twisted it in for the night and lay in a jetty fall around her face. He blinked. The morning sun streaming into the room lit her eyes and he saw they were a delicious chocolate brown, not the black he assumed. A small spray of freckles dotted her nose and cheeks, and one dark freckle lay near the cupid's bow of her delicately etched mouth, the lips the palest pink he could imagine.

His gaze travelled down to the white silk she wore, which clung to her every curve.

Michaela cut the reverie short. "Was that necessary?"

He moved out of the way. "After our adventures last night, yes. I think it was."

She muttered a vile insult in Chinese and stomped her way to the bathroom, hair swishing behind her as she gave her head an indignant toss.

Cormac yawned. Yesterday, Michaela had shown him a small, plain room to use as an exercise space. He folded his blankets and made his way down the hall. Bamboo palms lined the room, narrow leaves shining in the sun. Their simple energy called to him, and he yearned to hover his hand over them to connect to the *dolma*, but he wouldn't. Not after last night's incident. He couldn't risk it.

He stretched his arms up and out, feeling the aches and stiffness disappear. After moving to the center of the room, he began the meditation exercises Kiana had taught him when he was a child. Combined with physical poses that resembled the yoga practices of the humans, the practice had saved his sanity through the endless years of his exile. During these almost sacred minutes he was able to mesh his fractured self together and believe himself back in his forest, his oak rising high above him.

Michaela entered the room and waited quietly in the corner as he released the final pose.

"There are some mats in the closet," she said. "Straps and blocks as well."

Cormac blew stray hair out of his face. "I hope you don't mind me using your room."

"Not at all."

"You use it often?"

"For tai chi, mostly. Very good for mental clarity. Your practice was unfamiliar." She hesitated, unusual for her. "Will you show me?"

He smiled at the peculiar delight that coursed through him. "If you'll teach me tai chi."

She laughed. "I'll do my best. What's your practice called?"

"*Dolmatan*. It promotes inner silence."

"I like that." She moved into the room, closer to him and bringing the smell of tuberose in her wake. "I often think those of us born into earlier ages had more silence, more room for thought. I don't think I've managed to outgrow that."

"Nor I. Although I remember London being loud, with the calls of the sellers and the eternal clacking of horses' hooves."

"Wharves were always chaotic." Michaela's face was lost in memory. "I was a merchant and the docks were always deafening. Combined with the smell of the fish and the garbage people threw into the water, it made me nauseous."

"Really?"

"Until I got used to it. Then it smelled like coming home, no matter where I was."

The kettle whistled from the kitchen and Michaela's expression instantly reverted into her usual smooth mask. "Can you make the tea?" she asked. "I'll be there in about twenty minutes."

As a dismissal, it was clear enough, but he lingered in the door. Michaela stood with her hands on her hips, watching him in the long mirror that lined the wall. "The tea?" she repeated.

Was she giving him orders like a servant? He settled against the wall, ready to contradict her when a flash from her eyes warned him to back off. For many long-lived arcana, meditation was a necessity to mentally process the demands of their many years. He shut the door behind him, feeling momentarily ashamed to have prevented her peace.

He went to make the tea.

Precisely twenty minutes later, Michaela came out with tidy hair and calm eyes. She took the cup he gave her with a nod of thanks and sipped. She sipped again, her eyebrows raised. "This is good."

Despite himself, he felt a rush of pleasure that she enjoyed it.

Ridiculous. What did he care if she liked the tea?

It was nice that she did, though.

* * * *

Although their discussion in her apartment had been polite enough, as Michaela started the car, she felt a barrier slam down between them. It had been difficult for her to get to sleep again last night. The memory of how he had leaned in towards her before they left the car had kept her tossing and turning all night. She'd wanted more.

It was bizarre. She didn't even like the man. Not only that, she'd seen his face when she'd shifted into Yuri. Under his initial shock was an expression she was used to seeing from other arcana—suspicion mixed with horror. The masquerada were too different from the rest of the arcana. She sniffed. Somehow vampires drinking blood was considered more normal.

She passed a human in a BMW whose rude gesture stopped dead when he saw the glare Cormac gave him.

Now. Just say the words.

"You were right." Unlike last night, this time she meant it. "I should have woken you. I'm not used to answering to another person about my whereabouts."

"Thank you." He touched her hand and that simple gesture nearly skyrocketed her heartbeat. She pulled away, not comfortable with her reaction. "So. You were a vampire last night."

She didn't take her eyes off the road. "You had pigeons. I didn't know fey could summon animals like that."

"Fine. Let's make a deal."

"Shall I buy a vowel?" She glanced over.

His lip quirked. "Wrong show. Here's what I suggest. We say nothing about last night, at all. That's it. What happened will stay our secret."

"Agreed." Her answer was so prompt that he laughed.

"I'm not done yet. You tell me about taking on arcane masques. That's not supposed to happen."

"There's no rule against it."

"Then you won't mind if I mention it to the other councilors."

She definitely would. "Then you need to tell me about the animals." She stopped at a red light and faced him, waiting until he started to speak.

"What do you know about the fey?"

She turned back to the road, frowning slightly. "You draw energy from nature, I know that, and protect the forests you're bonded to. Queen Tismelda's court is said to be quite an experience, though she doesn't welcome strangers."

"True enough. We can sense nature, but most are limited to the plants and animals that are individually located in their ancestral forests."

Michaela nodded. "I thought it was mostly trees."

"It is, for most. I've lived in the city for so long that the animals are used to me. They reacted to my anger but it was unconscious." He shrugged. "There's no more to it than that."

When she parked the car and made to get out, Cormac stopped her. "No, you don't. You don't get to leave when it's time for my questions."

"I wasn't done with my questions but I want out of the car." Away from being close to him.

"Fine. In my office."

"In the security room." Since her own office was a crime scene.

"No, Michaela. You have a team who will want to talk to you and interrupt us. Mine."

It made sense. It was a logical decision, Michaela told herself. Still, she didn't like him ordering her around. "The boardroom."

Now he laughed. "You never give up, do you?"

She smiled. "We're agreed? The boardroom?"

He shook his head, still smiling. "Agreed."

A small victory, but after last night, good enough.

Chapter 9

He wondered if she knew he'd lied about the pigeons. The garage was open on one side and the reflected morning sun from glass-fronted buildings was a mere ghost of the bright light that cut through the trees of his forest. He hated it. Much more scenic was Michaela walking in front of him. Her tight black pants hugged the curve of her ass and she'd wrapped a thick gray leather belt twice around her waist before knotting it. Seeing it made him think of untying it before slowly stripping her to her gorgeous skin.

Cormac's breath almost whooshed out. The thought of having Michaela Chui nude in front of him, those pale lips growing redder, combined with her rich perfume, almost leached the will out of him.

If he wasn't careful, that woman would have a power over him that would be unacceptable. He'd been alone for so long that his isolation had gone from a punishment to a necessity. To let another being into his heart was unthinkable. Good thing this wasn't love. He only wanted to touch her. That was physical and it was completely acceptable.

Apart from the extra security Michaela had posted at all the entrances, they met no one on the way to the boardroom. It gave him time to think about how he would handle the rest of her questions. He might want her, but he hadn't decided on how much he trusted her. She might be angry with him, but Madden still had a heavy call on her loyalty. Better to keep it simple.

The boardroom was empty and Michaela took the head seat. He hid a grin as she nodded him to the seat on her right, and instead sat on the table in front of her.

"Ask away," he said.

A momentary look of dismay crossed her face as she realized that Cormac loomed over her. He deliberately leaned into her personal space and watched her struggle to not move back.

He saw the slight quiver that presaged a shift. He moved back, fast. It was too early in the morning for him to have to face that hulk of a man. Yuri was someone best experienced after a few good pints at the pub.

Michaela narrowed her eyes, then cleared her throat. "Pigeons?"

"Still nature. Birds are animals." He gave up the game and sat down in the chair. "Those men had probably been drinking. If they report they were attacked by a flock of birds in a back alley?"

"Not the most reliable witnesses. The same as if they say they were attacked by a seven-foot-tall vampire."

He restrained the desire to shudder at that grotesque image. "Now you."

Her smile lit up her whole face. How had he ever thought her a statue? Michaela was a vibrant, elegant, incredibly desirable woman—when she was not Yuri or a vampire or god-knows-what. Then he considered her. It was more accurate to say *this* masque was a stunning woman. It might not have any resemblance to Michaela's natural self.

Damn it. Masquerada were confusing. No wonder no one liked them.

"We're not supposed to take on arcane masques and I didn't. The masque I took on wasn't an actual vampire. It was a human idea of a vampire."

"Semantics." He moved an inch closer and her breath hitched. That little sound made his knees weak.

She kept her composure. "Important differences. I needed to protect Ivy and I don't want police sniffing around. Ivy had her eyes shut, so she'll say she didn't know who helped her and tell herself she was seeing things. What are the chances anyone is going to believe a group of drunk, high assholes who claim they lost a fight to a vampire?"

Cormac laughed, picturing it. "Not many."

"It might stop them from attacking another lone woman." Her mouth was a thin line. "One who might not have me around."

Cormac's mood darkened. "I should have let the pigeons peck out the eyes of the lead one."

She shrugged. "He'll probably lose the arm."

He grinned at her. "Aye. We understand each other."

"So it seems. About this."

"About other things." He leaned over, forcing her to look up at him. Those tilted lashes would be his downfall. One more inch and they would be touching.

Michaela pushed her chair back and away, no expression on her face but with a quick intake of breath she couldn't quite cover.

Cormac straightened up and mirrored her. "Michaela—"

She didn't look at him. "Time to work."

He cleared his throat. "Right. I was going to say that."

Exactly that.

* * * *

It took most of the morning to go over the evidence with the team. At the end, they all sat back glumly and gazed at the list of findings Michaela had jotted onto the whiteboard.

"We have nothing," said Michaela.

"On the surface." Anjali spoke grudgingly. "We need to dig more. You can't slaughter a human in these offices and walk out. Whoever did this would have been covered in blood at the very least."

Michaela squinted at the ceiling, trying to avoid Cormac's gaze. True to his word, he'd left the team alone to work, but she was sure she'd heard the gears grinding in his brain during the session. "We have no suspects. Everyone has an alibi. No security footage."

"The camera was down in the hallway near your office and the guard on duty was on cold medication. She fell asleep and didn't notice a thing." Anjali sounded wrathful. "I didn't even think vampires caught colds."

"Nadia?"

"That's the one."

Michaela sighed. "No weapon. No evidence on the body."

Dev cleared his throat. "There may be one thing." He seemed taken aback when every eye at the table twisted in his direction.

"What?" Michaela prayed it would be along the lines of, *Oh, I saw so-and-so coming out of your office covered in blood and forgot to mention it.*

"I thought I saw Hiro at a bar I go to the other night. He was with some arcana, which I thought was weird, since he didn't really like us."

Anjali tilted her head. "You didn't think this was important to mention, why?"

"I didn't think it was a big deal." Dev wiggled his shoulders uncomfortably. "It was awkward."

"We understand," said Michaela. Dev rarely spoke about his private life but she knew he had been outed involuntarily—it wasn't something he would easily do to another. "Did he see you?"

"I don't know. I wasn't even sure it was him. I thought I saw Madden with him, but that would have been weird since it's not a vamp place. The night's all a bit fuzzy." He shrugged. "Beermosas."

"It's probably nothing," said Michaela, "but, Dev, I want you to investigate whether there were any more meetings between Madden and Hiro."

"Yessir."

Michaela rubbed her eyes. "The rest of you, keep working on it. I refuse to believe there was nothing. Ambassador Redoak and I need to go see Eric Kelton."

Cormac's brows rose and he spoke for the first time. "The masquerada Hierarch? The one who mated a half-blood?"

"Who is a wonderful woman and a friend." Michaela spoke firmly. Many arcana disapproved of mixed relationships. It was best to make it clear where her loyalties lay right away to prevent insults or prejudice from the beginning.

He smiled. "You know, myths of racial purity lead to stagnation. I couldn't give two flying fucks about who's in bed with whom."

"Good."

Cormac didn't seem to be lying about meeting Eric's mate, thought Michaela as they drove to a district of refurbished warehouse space near the lake. That was a relief. Eric and Caro were two of her closest friends, not that she had many.

"I've met Eric a few times," Cormac said.

"What did you think?"

"I've got the utmost respect for what he's trying. You're a very conservative race, the masquerada."

"Some of us." In her kinder moments, she might consider calling Iverson's stalwart followers conservative and uncreative instead of selfish, narrow-minded bigots. Luckily, she rarely felt so generous.

"Pulling them kicking and screaming into the modern world has to be hard. We don't have it so bad."

"The queen keeps the fey in line?"

He laughed humorlessly. "There is that, but we can also go back to our forests in the Queendom and escape the human world. You can't."

"We share the world and have a responsibility to live in it."

"Thanks, Madame Morals. How's that working out for you?" He didn't wait to see the face she pulled. "Eric must have unlimited patience combined with balls the size of a building."

She'd heard her Hierarch described many ways, but not like that. "You can talk to him about that yourself. We're here."

Michaela led them into the warehouse building and turned at his sigh of relief. "Are you feeling okay?"

"It's always good to have trees nearby," he said simply. He waved his hand at the old timber interior.

What? "It's wood, not trees. Dead trees, ones that have been cut down in their prime. Shouldn't this feel like a tomb?"

Cormac hovered his hand over a glossy pine bannister without touching it. "It should—but it doesn't. They still contain an element of their life force."

"They aren't angry about being cut?"

He laughed. "Trees aren't people. They don't think of it like that. Yes, they prefer to be in the forest, but they are existing here."

"I don't understand. Either you're alive or dead."

"Not for a tree."

Before they could continue this, a man's voice called Michaela's name from the top of the stairs. Her body relaxed. "Stephan!"

He came down and they bowed to each other. Over the past few months, their friendship and respect had deepened, but Michaela was still not the huggy type. She turned to Cormac. "Ambassador Cormac Redoak, meet Stephan Daker, the Hierarch's Chief of Staff."

Stephan nodded. "Ambassador. Friends of Michaela are welcome here."

"We're not friends." Michaela felt her smile fade. "Cormac and I are working together on a security issue."

"Does it have to deal with the masquerada?" Stephan demanded.

"Possibly."

Stephan's next look at Cormac was several degrees cooler. "I see. Pharos business."

"I'm not sure what you mean. It's Council business," she corrected. Stephan always tried to catch her out.

The tall masquerada gave a heavy sigh. "Worth a try. Well, come on."

Chapter 10

Cormac wasn't surprised when Michaela sidestepped the truth and that Stephan didn't press her. It was *Pharos* Council business, but since Michaela was also a member of Eric's own masquerada council, her phrasing kept it ambiguous. To keep them from being unduly pressured, Pharos members were meant to be totally secret, even from their own rulers.

That didn't mean that the brighter rulers didn't have their suspicions. However, suspicions were not confirmation, and Pharos members took care to keep their work concealed.

Michaela didn't bother to answer Stephan. "Is Caro coming?"

"She'll be a few minutes late, but Eric's almost ready. Tom wants to talk to you, though. Says you texted."

Michaela turned to Cormac. "Tom Minor is the Hierarch's security chief and an expert in information security. I consult him when our High Council has questions."

High Council. That meant the masquerada, not Pharos.

Stephan's phone beeped and he checked the screen. "Follow me."

Eric's office was exactly what Cormac would expect from the human CEO of a successful tech company, which was how Eric portrayed himself to the rest of the world. How the man found time enough—or even the inclination—to take on so much work was beyond Cormac.

Then again, he thought, catching sight of Eric behind his desk, the Hierarch was a different beast than the fey, who were a more passive group in general. Others, such as the witches or the masquerada, even the weres, had to deliberately activate their power. They had to choose to cast a spell, or choose to take on a masque or were form. Fey energy came from the *dolma*, and was best achieved by simply being one with the environment. That's not to say that the fey were not a conniving bunch of schemers. They were, to a fault, yet their energy was more specifically focused. The masquerada ability to take on different masques, to become others, struck him as a huge waste of time. Why not focus on exploring the unlimited potential of oneself? Or, for many of his compatriots, the benefits to oneself?

His inner philosophical debate halted when Eric waved them to seats in front of the desk. When away from humans, arcana rarely shared touches such as handshakes that brought one close to a potential enemy. The chairs were comfortable and spoke to the depth of Eric's calm confidence. This was not a man who needed to resort to childish dominance tricks. Quite a change from Queen Tismelda's court, where her seat was on a high dais. Even walking around, the queen wore stupidly tall platforms decorated with bells that allowed her to tower among her people.

Eric took off his glasses. "Good to see you again, Ambassador. You're well, I hope?"

"Thank you, yes. May I congratulate you on the elevation of your mate?" Caro Yeats had recently been declared consort, news that had ricocheted around the arcane gossip circuit. Half human and half masquerada, Caro was a lost daughter of the European ruling house, a masquerada said to be as powerful as the Hierarch himself.

Eric's face broke in a broad smile. "Caro should be here soon. She's curious to meet you."

Cormac's eyebrows rose. "She harbors no ill-will towards us?" A fey had been involved in Caro's kidnapping by one of Eric's rivals. Queen Tismelda had been quick to disown Julien D'Aurant, but masquerada could be unreasonable when it came to their mates' safety. He respected that.

"None at all, Ambassador." A small woman wearing jeans and low brown boots strolled into the room. Her dark hair was held up in a messy topknot. "I don't judge all fey by Julien, since the man was a complete and pathetic ass. I greatly respect the environmental conservation work many of your people do."

She gave Michaela a quick hello wink and went to stand beside Eric, who pulled her hand down to kiss the palm. For a second their shared gaze made Cormac uncomfortable, as though he was witnessing an intimacy that was meant to be private. Then Caro gave him a beaming smile. She was pretty, but more than that, Cormac could almost see the vitality of her life force. It illuminated her from within.

No wonder Eric could barely keep his eyes off her. Caro was magnetic.

Still, she was no Michaela. The thought came unbidden and, surprised, he turned his gaze towards her. Michaela's perfect features were set in the same aloof expression that he realized was as much a masque as Yuri. She was the most intriguing woman he'd ever met. She caught his gaze and although she didn't go as far as to smile at him, he thought he detected a slight softening of her lips.

Good enough.

Caro sat down and crossed her legs. "Not a social call, then, is it?"

Michaela shook her head. "A human named Hiro Murakami was killed and there may be arcane involvement. That means it comes under masquerada jurisdiction."

Cormac had forgotten that little bit of arcana legislation. Any wrongdoing that involved a human and arcana was investigated by the closest geographic ruler. It helped delineate responsibility among rulers with multiple overlapping territories. If it had been further to the south, it would have been the vampires' problem, since the vampire queen Wavena was currently living in Florida. Toronto meant Eric, and the masquerada.

"Hiro." Eric tented his fingers on the desk. "We saw him at a human technology event recently but had only the usual superficial social conversation."

"How did he seem to you?" Michaela had her notepad out, writing without taking her gaze from Eric.

Eric didn't hesitate. "Calm on the outside, but I sensed he was tense." He gave his mate a teasing look. "Humans are very difficult to understand sometimes."

She rolled her eyes. "Luckily, masquerada are as transparent as water."

"Sorry I'm late." A slender man, composed of wiry muscle and weapons, stood in the door. "Michaela." He spoke with military precision but it was clear that he liked her.

"Tom, this is Cormac Redoak. Cormac, Tom." Cormac saw that like Stephan, Tom was a man to be reckoned with. His sharp eyes took in Cormac with a glance and slid back to Michaela, who had turned serious as she glanced down at the desk. "Good God, Eric, what are those?"

What had been hidden from Cormac's seated perspective was visible when he stood. It took him a moment to understand, but then he saw it.

Images of human remains, rotted and horrifying.

"Good question," Eric said, moving aside a paper so they could see clearly. "We've found bodies in some of Iverson's hidden cell locations. They all have strange punctures, some in the back of the neck near the head and sometimes on the arms."

"Torture?" Michaela picked up one of the photos and squinted at it.

"No evidence," Tom said. "Nothing on tox scans either. We're still investigating."

She put her hands on her hips and stared Eric down. "I haven't heard of this. You know you're supposed to report this kind of thing to your council, sire."

"A lot of things seem to miss getting reported," he said smoothly. "For instance, Hiro."

"I told you about Hiro."

"When did he die?"

Michaela thinned her lips. "You know that we triage what you need to know."

"Is that the 'we' of my council? If I asked them, would they be familiar with Hiro's death?"

"It's a security issue." She cocked her head to the side. "So of course not everyone will know."

"Then it will be no surprise to you that I make sure my advisory council doesn't get overwhelmed." Eric grinned and a smile twitched the corners of Michaela's lips. An old game between old friends.

Eric glanced at Cormac. "Ambassador, would you mind stepping out for a moment? I assure you it's only masquerada business."

"Sorry, no." Cormac kept his tone pleasant.

Tom stepped forward, his body relaxed but alert.

"He's right." Michaela rubbed her temples. "There may be fey involvement as well, and we have an agreement that we stay together to keep it all transparent."

Eric's and Caro's eyebrows both shot up, giving them matching looks of astonishment. "Can he be trusted?" demanded Tom.

Michaela turned to Cormac with a thin smile. "Can you?"

"I swear on my tree," he said promptly.

Her chin jerked up, her eyes wide. "On your tree?"

Out of the corner of his eye, he saw Eric whisper to Caro, no doubt explaining that this was the fey equivalent of a blood vow. "For you. On my tree."

There was a charged moment between them. She dropped her eyes. "He can be trusted," she said.

"I can't tell the council, Michaela, and neither can you." Eric stood, then paced around the room. "Only you and Baptiste will know."

"Know what?" she asked.

"These remains were found in Iverson's combat cells. We've been finding similar atrocities since the *defie* with Iverson."

The reason dawned on Cormac. "You have divisions in your council. You don't know who to trust."

The Hierarch laughed without humor. "The rumors are that bad?"

"Not at all, but it's a reasonable assumption."

Eric paused at a bookshelf and picked up a carving, a little songbird in wood. "Reasonable and accurate."

"I know who to trust," Michaela said. "The problem is I don't trust who they trust."

"Which is why I want to investigate from here. I don't like it. We don't know what they were doing to these humans, but it can't be good."

"Evil," put in Caro quietly. "I went to one of the sites. It was wrong in a way I can't understand."

Michaela caught Cormac's eye and glanced down at one of the photos. The woman in the photo was well-preserved, perhaps dead only a day or two. On her arms were two large punctures, in precisely the same spots as where Hiro had been skinned.

A connection.

Michaela shuffled through the rest of the photos and Cormac saw that the stomach-turning level of decomposition had erased any similar clues on the other bodies.

"Tell me if you need help." She put the photos back down.

"It gets worse." Eric paused and faced Cormac. "On your tree?"

Cormac spoke the formal vow in his native tongue, then translated: "I swear my truth to you. Let the breaking of my word be as the breaking of my tree in a storm."

"We heard an Ancient is back."

Michaela and Cormac shared an incredulous look. Cormac found his voice first. "Sorry. What did you say?"

"An Ancient is back. One of the original masquerada."

Michaela sucked in her breath. "Yangzei?"

Eric put the bird back down. "We think so. You can see, if that's true..." He turned around. "Well. We have a problem."

"Especially because one of ours would have had to find him. He wouldn't have come for any other than a masquerada."

"He's bad?" Cormac asked. He'd never heard of Yangzei.

They all laughed and Stephan was the one who took pity on him. "Yeah, fey. He's bad. Real bad."

"He's also supposed to be dead," Michaela said.

Eric snorted. "Do you think a small thing like death would stop Yangzei if he wanted to cause trouble?"

"No." She sighed. "Shit."

The silence in the room seems to say she's summed it up well, thought Cormac.

Great.

Chapter 11

Michaela didn't even wait until they reached the car to speak. They finally had a clue. "The arms of the woman in the photo."

"Same location as on Hiro, but it doesn't help until we know why those humans were killed."

"Or why they were there in the first place." She opened the car and slid in. "What was Hiro up to? He didn't even like masquerada."

"At least we know whoever killed Hiro is also involved in what Eric showed us."

She shook her head morosely. "Unless Hiro was already dead when they came in." Michaela pulled out into traffic. Although it didn't answer why Hiro was in her office, the marks on his arms provided a connection as to why he might have been killed. It was a selfish relief to know she might have been wrong about being the target. "We need to know more about Hiro."

"Agreed."

Michaela looked at him out of the corner of her eye. This was a side of Cormac she hadn't seen before, serious and resolute. She'd heard that he'd been a military leader back in the Queendom, but assumed it was rumor. Perhaps it wasn't. This was a man she could picture in command.

It was attractive. Extremely attractive.

Since she didn't want to linger on this and also had zero desire to talk about Yangzei and to air masquerada dirty laundry, she asked, "What did you think of Caro?"

"I liked her." He said it casually. "Do they know you're Pharos?"

Michaela grinned, thinking of the little traps Eric had laid for her over the years. It was a game they both enjoyed and he had never won. "He suspects, and likes to try to catch me out."

"What about the security man and the deputy? Tom. Stephan."

Was there a pause before Stephan's name? Surely he couldn't dislike Stephan. Tom, she could see—Eric's chief of security wasn't the friendliest man in the world and his default mode was distrust. People liked Stephan.

"Incredible men. Eric's lucky to have them. Stephan in particular is smart, charming, and extraordinarily effective."

"Have you known him long?"

"Perhaps a century or so," she said, thinking back. "He and Eric were already a team to be reckoned with when I came to Canada in the 1800s."

"You came from China?"

With a shock, she realized how rare it was to speak about her past. The people she knew were either human, and to them she was a data analyst from San Diego, or had known her background for decades. "Guangdong before I moved to Malaysia. Melaka."

Cormac nodded. "I've been there. Gorgeous city."

"When?" she demanded. "Why?"

"To see a tree."

He has to be kidding, she thought suspiciously. "A tree? Is that what fey do in their time off?"

"This one does." He twisted to face her. "It was a very special tree. I was curious about it."

"A *tree*?"

"Why do you sound so surprised? A fey would go to the end of the earth to see a special tree."

"Why? What can a tree tell you?" Cormac had a golden ring in his ear, she noticed, high up and tucked so tight to the skin that it was hard to see until the sun hit it. She restrained an urge to touch it.

"For a fey, a tree is more real than many of the people they met. Trees have personality, hopes and desires." His voice deepened. "Anger and rage."

"I never thought of it like that." To her, trees were, well, trees. She looked at the line of maples along the road, wondering what they were thinking.

"Imagine a living being who never moved from a single spot, for hundreds of years. A tree can tell me about the changes in the earth from its roots, and in the air from its leaves. It bears witness to the world."

She nodded and considered this. Arcana also lived for centuries, but to see the changes from only one spot would be an intriguing perspective. "This tree was special?"

"Yes." Then he turned away. "Tell me about Yangzei."

Damn. Well, she knew he would ask. "I don't even know where to start," she admitted.

"He's a negative force?"

"Very negative." Yangzei was the dark monster behind all their fears—what they could become. There were myths about the Ancients, primeval beings who were part of the ancestral rootstock of all arcana. They hadn't been heard of in so long that many arcana had decided they were simply stories. Not all Ancients were out-and-out evil. They were simply vampires, masquerada, and the rest in all their complexity, and much, much more powerful. The stories said current arcana were a faded shadow of what earlier ones were capable of.

Before they went insane and started to kill each other.

"I haven't heard of him before."

"We don't trumpet it to other groups."

"Like a black sheep?"

"Like a very strong, mean, and selfish black sheep who is happy to kill."

Cormac pulled out his phone and looked up a moment later. "His name means *Eye Thief.*"

She pulled into the garage and stopped the car. "That's a literal translation. He doesn't steal eyes."

"Good news."

"Not really. He apparently stole souls. Or personalities. He's masquerada, after all." She got out of the car.

Cormac slid out and caught up to her. "Wait, what? You don't steal souls."

"According to one of the stories, masquerada used to steal a little of a person's life force whenever they took on their masque. It's not true, obviously." There was enough fear and trepidation about the masquerada that when you added soul-stealing to the mix, it made for a potentially explosive situation.

He caught her arm before they reached the door. "You said that a little too fast, Councilor Chui."

"We don't steal souls."

"Don't steal souls, or don't steal souls *now*?" His hand slid up her arm.

"We take on masques, Ambassador Redoak." No need to go into the debates she'd had with Stephan about whether or not it was true. Cormac didn't need to know that. He was an outsider, after all, and she owed him no answers.

"Still not an answer." He pulled her a little closer and she shrugged him off. She was starting to like it when he touched her. That was something she didn't like at all.

"This is not the time and has nothing to do with Hiro."

He smiled, a wicked glint in his eyes as he bent over her. "Then later. At your place."

There was no answer to give, so she gave none. Instead she held her wrist up and looked at her watch. "Time for lunch."

"At an intimate little bistro?"

"If by intimate bistro you mean at work. My team won't have eaten."

"With wine?" he asked hopefully.

"Tea. Lots of tea."

He groaned but followed her outside.

* * * *

Once out on the street, they automatically moved to topics that were safe for humans to overhear. Movies, the weather. Of necessity, it mimicked the boring small chat of acquaintances.

Cormac didn't care. Here in the sunlight, Michaela's skin was a creamy pearl tinted a perfect faint rose and extraordinary against the blue-black of her hair. The gazes of human men and women lingered on her as they passed.

Michaela seemed utterly oblivious to the attention, but Cormac made a point of looking each of the humans in the eye.

His threat was no less serious for being silent. *Don't even think of it.*

They got it.

They turned into a bento place and cleared out most of the trays. Michaela muttered under her breath as she matched her team with likes and dislikes. "Anjali likes the sashimi. No rice. Dev will want glass noodles. Get him a diet Coke. Says the real stuff is too sweet."

In seconds, Cormac's arms were piled high. She grabbed him a seaweed salad and a few avocado rolls without even asking. Fey were vegetarian, and he was impressed she remembered.

Back at Pharos headquarters, Michaela laid out the food and called in her team. "Working lunch," she declared. "What do you have?"

Anjali cracked her wooden chopsticks open enthusiastically. "Not much, ma'am. We confirmed there were no strangers in the building."

"Hiro was killed by one of us." Michaela said the unspoken thought. "We suspected so."

A glum silence hung over the team. Cormac sat back and sampled his seaweed, curious to see how Michaela handled it. Motivating a depressed team was the mark of a good commander.

He'd once been good at it himself.

"I want to focus on Hiro and who he's been speaking to lately," Michaela said as she passed the napkins. "I also want to find out the story behind those patches on his arms."

From the way they threw out ideas, the team was clearly cheered to be given set tasks. By the end of the lunch, they had a new plan and Michaela had invigorated her team. They left chattering in low voices.

"That was well done," he said.

Michaela blinked, then narrowed her eyes. "What do you mean?"

He sighed. Normally he approved of suspicion when it came to fey compliments but this one had been real. "Good God, woman. I'm offering you a compliment. Don't let it go to that swollen masquerada ego of yours."

"Oh. Umm. Thank you." She glanced down and up in a shy way that hooked his heart.

"Michaela." Madden's deep voice came from the doorway.

"Madden." Michaela's smile disappeared. Cormac knew she had a close relationship with the vampire, but it looked like it was fraying. Not surprising. It was unusual for mentorships between different arcane races to happen in the first place, victims of inter-group mistrust and posturing.

"How is the investigation coming along?" Madden asked.

Michaela gave him a quick update and he frowned. "The fury of the attack concerns me, and those patches of skin missing are more than unusual. No arcana takes trophies like that. Do you have any leads there?"

Madden's voice was calm and soothing. A vampire's ability to charm was one of their greatest assets and even those on their guard could be lulled into complacency under a vampire's compulsions.

Interesting that Madden had honed in on that one topic for his compulsion. Cormac cut in before Michaela could reply. Fey were less swayed by vampires than other arcana.

"Not yet," he said.

"It's painful to discuss as I know it will hurt you, but I also know that it's pertinent to what you're doing." Madden gazed at the door. "I should have mentioned it before. Hiro had no love for the arcane world."

Cormac waited. This was no shock. Hiro had been open about his belief that the Law was not enough to keep humanity safe from what he once called cold killers. He had not been pleased when Cormac had pulled out a list of environmental degradations, massacres, and various villainies perpetrated by humans on their compatriots. In fact, Hiro had blamed all of those instances on arcana interference. Rather hysterically, Cormac thought.

A ghostly smile crossed Madden's face. "I see you know that."

"He made no secret of it," Michaela pointed out.

"No, I suppose he didn't. He spoke of his concerns with me a few times. He was particularly against masquerada."

Michaela shrugged. "Not surprising. Many distrust us, find us more unnatural than the others."

Cormac wondered if she was directing this at him.

"You in particular, Michaela. Personally."

This seemed to sincerely surprise her. "Me? What about Baptiste?"

"Only you," Madden said. "You are in a powerful role that he wanted."

"He wanted to be in charge of security?" Michaela leaned forward. "When did he say this? I didn't know."

"Didn't you ever wonder why he was so opinionated where you were concerned? Why he always challenged you? Questioned your decisions?"

"He was being contrary. He did it to everyone."

"No. Not all of us." Madden smoothed his cuff. "You. He was found in your office."

"I knew nothing of this," she said. "I didn't kill him."

"No one would accuse you of such a thing," Madden said with a slight scoffing tone. "I merely thought to provide you with some insight."

Michaela's face maintained its usual blank slate. "Of course," she said. "Thank you."

Madden stood. "Now, if you'll excuse me…" He left, and Cormac leaned over to shut the door behind him.

"What an asshole," he said.

"He's my mentor," Michaela said automatically. Some of that old loyalty still remained, then. "It's his job to tell me about"—she paused—"things."

He rolled his eyes. "He accused you of killing Hiro. With me in the room."

"Because he wanted me to know that I was vulnerable there."

"I think that was clear enough when he appointed me Watcher. Maybe he could have done it in private?"

She glared at him. "You follow me everywhere. When would he have the chance?"

She shut the conversation down by sitting at the computer and typing at a furious rate. Cormac let her stew for exactly three minutes by the clock and cleared his throat.

"I don't think you killed him."

The typing stopped. "Thank you?"

"No need to thank me," he said expansively. This made her lip quiver and she finally smiled.

"The rest do."

"Certainly. However, if you killed Hiro, you would have had the sense to not do it in your office." He paused. "Unless you were enraged by him using your keyboard. I think that's grounds for murder."

Now she laughed out loud. "Me too." She pushed away her laptop. "If you don't think I did it, why did you bother being Watcher?"

Time for the truth. "I wanted that forest from Hiro and needed to make sure he wasn't killed to stop me from getting it."

"You could have asked for updates."

As if she would have provided him anything but obfuscating claptrap. There was no point in even dignifying that with a reply. "Here are the three options as I see them. You were the target. Hiro was the target. Someone who is not you killed Hiro, either to set you up or out of convenience, because that's where they found him."

"A set-up would answer why he was in my office," she said.

"Can you think of any enemies you have?"

She looked at him with wide eyes, and they both burst out laughing.

Chapter 12

Her enemies. Where to even start? She shook her head. "This is like a locked room mystery."

"A what?" A shock of shimmering hair fell over his eyes and she stared. "Your hair shines," she blurted out. It did, too, almost rippling with pale morning sunlight.

"I use a great shampoo. Tell me about that mystery."

"People in a room and one is killed, except there's no way any of them could get in or out." She paused. "Sort of like that book about the train."

He moved closer. "In these mysteries, who is the killer?"

She was a bit breathless. "The one you think has a cast-iron alibi."

"Which is not you." Cormac stood beside Michaela. She'd forgotten what it was like to work with an equal, rather than to lead a team. Surprisingly, she realized she'd been enjoying their discussion.

He bent down to her and Michaela's gut clenched at his mouth being so close to hers. A kiss.

She pulled herself away. No. Too intimate. She'd never shared a kiss with a lover, only had them taken.

Her phone rang, interrupting the moment. "It's Brad from IT."

Brad was as laconic as ever. "Found something. Come see."

Finally, a lead. She led Cormac into the hall.

"I was looking for you." Baptiste came around the corner in his favorite masque, based on an old Creole undertaker he'd once known. "Got anything?"

Baptiste was the only person on the council who could come out and ask her without causing her to bristle. He was renowned for his honesty and Eric often consulted him for advice.

"Not yet." It hurt to admit it. She'd never failed to solve a situation before.

"Man was an asshole, *mei mei*. You know that. He probably rubbed someone the wrong way. Definitely one of us, though."

Cormac glanced over. "How do you know?"

"Go talk to your trees, plant man." Baptiste's eyes were wide and knowing. "See what the *dolma* tells you."

"What the hell does that mean?" Michaela scrutinized them both but neither man's face revealed a thing. What could trees tell them about Hiro's killer?

"What about the trees?" repeated Michaela impatiently.

Baptiste laughed. "Not my story, *mei mei*. Heard you visited the big man today."

"Eric tell you?"

"Stephan." That made sense. The two men were old friends. "You see him?" Michaela knew what he was asking. "He's looking better."

"Needs to get over that vampire woman is what the fucker needs."

Cormac's eyebrows shot up and Michaela took pity on him. "Stephan was seeing a vampire for a while but it didn't work out." That was an understatement, but Stephan wouldn't thank her for sharing his emotional baggage. He'd tried to hide it but he had fallen for Estelle hard and fast. Michaela pitied him. She let only Ivy that close to her heart, and that was mostly because of her promise to Yao's memory. It was safest that way.

Baptiste shook his head. "Can't live your lives for you, sadly. Look at you."

She gave him the same look she used to quell overenthusiastic salespeople. "We've been through this." Baptiste was a vigorous proponent of using emotional ties to ward off *le vide*, the fatal ennui that could affect arcana. He constantly pointed to his relationship with his mate Keenan as a model for Michaela, who he claimed was withering without passion.

"I still don't like it. Keenan is the heart of my soul. He keeps me sane and grounded." Baptiste stared at Cormac as he spoke and Cormac gave him a big grin, then winked at Michaela.

"I have Ivy," she said firmly.

"A human," sniffed Baptiste. "She will die and then where will you be?" He caught sight of Michaela's expression and grimaced. "I apologize, *mei mei*. That was unforgivably rude."

Michaela glared at him. "Stop living my life, Baptiste. I don't live yours."

Baptiste shot his eyes over to Cormac but said nothing.

"Stephan tell you about the dead humans?" Michaela changed the subject.

The masquerada nodded. "Heard. Going over later to see for myself. Get Eric to spot me a meal, Caro to tell me a story. Fine storyteller, that woman." He waved and left.

"He calls you *mei mei*," Cormac said. Little sister.

"Baptiste is about a decade older than I am, we think. He likes to remind me of it."

"Michaela." He stopped. "That's not Chinese. What's your real name?"

"Miaoling." She frowned. "Why, what's yours?"

An incomprehensible stream of silken sound came from Cormac's lips. She tilted her head. "That doesn't sound like Cormac."

"I know. That's the point. Names have power, Michaela." He looked over as he said her name, intimate as a caress.

"What power did I give you?" The teasing question came out before she could monitor herself.

He didn't answer but gave a long, raking look that made her belly heavy.

In the middle of the hallway.

During a murder investigation.

She clenched her fists and forced herself to focus. "We should, ah, get going." *Nice. Very articulate.* She couldn't help it. It had been a long time since a man had looked at her with such desire.

She didn't even like Cormac.

Did she?

Cormac looked over. "Over to IT?"

Work. Right. They'd been on their way before Baptiste had come. He fell into step beside her and his hand brushed hers. A shock, so sudden it felt electric, shot into her very bones and forced her to skitter away. Cormac seemed not to notice and she was grateful. What was going on with her? Working with the fey ambassador was definitely better than she expected, but her bar for success had been admittedly low.

Very powerful fey had the same compulsion powers as vampires. Was he deliberately clouding her judgment?

That had to be it. There was no way she could be attracted to Cormac.

* * * *

The moment she jumped back Cormac knew two things.

First, he wanted Michaela Chui so badly he could almost taste her.

Second, Michaela wanted him.

The thought made him harden instantly. The remote Michaela Chui wanted him. She might not even know it herself, but one of the earliest lessons of the fey court was how to read hidden desires. She was good at hiding her feelings, but he could see the need in her body as clearly as if she had announced it on a megaphone. Her eyes had closed, so briefly, and her breath had quickened. He had wanted to feel her desire since that moment in the car.

The question was, would she ever admit it? Would she act on it?

Christ, he hoped so.

He thought not.

He hoped not.

Yeah, right. Who was he kidding? He'd spent more of this investigation thinking about her than he had Hiro but he had no guilt. Michaela was a flame under that marble exterior and he wanted to see it burn hard—turn it into an inferno.

Those were thoughts for another time. She wouldn't thank him if he interfered with her work. There was time to do it properly and that time was not in front of her security team, who were waiting outside of the IT office to usher them in.

Michaela didn't pause. "Tell me."

Brad pulled out a phone. "We took another look at Hiro's phone with advice from General Minor. He was right. There was an app we missed."

"How?"

"It's usually used by human teenagers to save illicit images and files. It's hidden behind an innocent app, such as a calculator."

"Remarkable." Cormac stared at it. Human adolescents showed much ingenuity when it came to sex. "How did you find it?"

"The storage used didn't match what we were seeing, so we went looking. Found screenshots of messages but we don't have all the details. It looks like they go back about a year. Maybe less."

Cormac scrolled through the messages. "I'd like to take this home to study it," he said.

Brad glanced at Michaela. "It would be good to get some help," he said apologetically.

Michaela nodded. "If you don't have a problem, Brad, fine."

Cormac shut his mouth. He'd been ready to argue with her, sure she was going to—rightfully—point out that as Watcher, he had no right to take part in the investigation. He examined her out of the corner of his eye. Was she permitting him to help because she believed in his ability and wanted to get Brad some much needed assistance? Or was it for a more personal reason? Perhaps Madden's accusation had rattled her more than she let on.

If her own mentor had turned on her, she would need all the allies she could get to prove her innocence. Even him.

Chapter 13

When Cormac leaned over her to take the phone, his lush pine scent immediately derailed her thinking process. It took a moment for her to regain her control. She casually stepped away as though simply looking for a good place to take some notes. She'd been attracted to men before but this was unexpected and very bad timing. Not to mention ill-advised. She had no problem taking pleasure on offer, but she made sure of her partners beforehand. No strings. No lingering attachments.

Brad's eyes were already fixed longingly at his computer again, so Michaela took her leave. Dev caught them in the hall and brought them into a nearby room.

"I checked into Hiro's relationship with Madden, as you asked," he said. A single dark curly lock had escaped from his usual slicked-back hair and he pushed it away impatiently.

"Doesn't sound good." Michaela braced herself.

"They've been seen at the bar before," he said. "It could be for a personal or a business relationship, but my gut says business."

"They left at different times?" she asked.

"Arrived separately as well, and never touched."

That didn't sound like a couple. "Anything else?"

"Haven't tracked them anywhere else, but sometimes they had other men with them. Don't know who but we assume they weren't arcana. They arrived and left with Hiro."

"Thanks, Dev."

"Hey, any time I can expense my bar tab is good for me."

Cormac put his hand on her arm when they were out in the hall and a wave of comfort overtook her. How ironic it would be if Cormac ended up being the one she could trust. She nearly laughed.

"You're tired," Cormac said.

"It's been a busy day."

"Time to go home?"

She ignored the suggestive way he phrased the question. There was nothing more she could do here. It might be best to go back to disconnect from the case for an evening and sleep on it.

She took out her keys.

"I'll drive." Cormac held out his hand.

Now she did laugh. "I thought you didn't know how."

"Really." He arched his brow. "Give me the keys."

Bemused, she handed them over and followed him to the car. Without asking, he held her back as he checked before opening the doors.

"Thanks," she said.

"Self-preservation," he said as he put the car in reverse. "If they blow up you, they blow up me."

Michaela observed him as he turned out. Cormac was a good driver. Why this should surprise her, she had no idea. "You drive well."

"I do."

"Where did you learn?"

He merged out of a construction lane. "Here and there."

"What else can you do? Scuba?" She said it as a joke but wasn't surprised when he nodded.

"Yes."

"Rock-climb."

He glanced over out of the corner of his eye, his mouth lifted in a slight smile. "Don't forget ice-climb, sail, Morris dance, and God knows what else."

"How many languages do you speak?"

"I've lost count." He spoke in Chinese.

She stared at that rugged profile. "Why? Why do you do all this?"

"I've been in exile a long time. It's either that or die." He spoke matter-of-factly.

She was silent the rest of the drive, thinking about Cormac—the man, a person—for the first time in the many years she'd known him. To be exiled from your home and people would be horrific. She'd had a taste of that when her father had sent her to her uncle's house, but that was nothing compared to what he'd experienced. Michaela had always been surrounded by her own people, even when her family had been less than satisfactory. She had found Caro, and Eric and Stephan, and even humans like Yao and Ivy.

Cormac had no one.

They arrived home. She turned the key and led the way into her apartment, grateful the alarms were still set. She couldn't afford to relax her guard.

Cormac steered her to the couch with a gentle hand on her lower back. Even that slight touch was enough to send a soft burn shivering over her skin, so she shook him off. Cormac nodded at the cushions. "Sit down. I'm getting you a drink and we're going to talk." He smiled. "Have a conversation, like regular people."

It was a relief to not have to think for a moment and it had been a long time since she had been able to react, rather than give the orders. With a heavy sigh, she leaned her head back, only to find her knot of hair in the way. With a quick movement, she untwisted it and let it flow over the back of the couch.

Even her apartment's pleasant order failed to cheer her. Having to deal with Madden's hostility and accusations had been more shocking than she'd let on. She'd hidden the pain, but she'd trusted him. Suddenly her mentor was becoming a man she didn't know, and liked even less.

Contrary to what she let people believe, Michaela didn't enjoy confrontation. She rubbed her jaw, trying to relax the deep muscle tension from keeping herself under control. It was a skill she had practiced for centuries, but she'd never had to invest so much to govern her emotions as she had recently. Part of her wanted to take on her biggest, meanest masque and go pick some fights. Or become a long, lean runner and race for miles.

She wouldn't, though, because that wasn't who she was. She was Michaela and she faced her problems head on. At least she did now. It had taken multiple marriages for her to take control of her own life, and she would never relinquish it again.

The ring of glass against a granite counter came from the kitchen, and she hoped it was the sound of a drink being made that was not tea. When she was in her Yuri masque, Michaela drank like a fish. As part of the persona she'd developed for him, Yuri was a man of the earth, a heavy drinker and big eater with tremendous physical strength. He swore and fought, held grudges but was a loyal friend. As Yuri, she had been able to face tragedies that would have crumpled her had she been in her natural masque. She rolled her head to her chest, then around in a circle, wincing as her vertebrae popped alarmingly despite the daily exercise. Masquerada depended on supple muscles for easy transitions to other masques.

How long had it been since she created a new persona? Years, maybe. Frightening the humans in the alley as a vampire had been the first time she had shifted in a while. It hadn't even given her the joy she was used to. Dread knotted in her stomach. Was *le vide* creeping up on her? It was insidious, that empty tedium that eventually sucked all of the color out of life. She had fought it once in the 1800s. Fear of *le vide* was what had forced her to leave her comfortable merchant's life in Melaka to face the terrors of the New World.

What would her life had been like had she stayed? She closed her eyes, bringing back the sights and smells of China. The first part of the Ming dynasty had been decadent if a family had wealth and Michaela's didn't. Or at least, her parents had decided that they needed more and had honed in on the humans as easy marks. And they were, once Michaela had been established as a young, fertile woman who would provide many sons to the aging merchants. She shuddered. They had married her six times, each as a different masque, before she'd refused to go again, unwilling to feel those cold hands parting her flesh and the whip when she'd been without child month after month, until the old men died. Her old *amah* had given her the herbs she needed to prevent pregnancy and she'd taken them religiously, even when bedridden from a beating.

After her unfilial refusal, her parents had sent her to her uncle's in Malaysia as punishment. He was going to find another husband for her when she'd finally run, knowing that leaving her family would be the only way to escape that horrible cycle. Captain Lu had taken her in as a cabin boy.

Cormac came out with a tray. He'd created a veritable feast, complete with wine. On a tray were olives and nuts, cheese and crackers. "How did you know what I liked?" she asked in amazement.

He passed her a glass of white, perfectly chilled. "It wasn't hard to tell. Your kitchen had an entire cabinet of bar snacks."

She took a handful of salted almonds. "I usually eat at work."

"I'm not complaining." He cut himself a large hunk of brie and popped it in his mouth. "The fey usually live on nectar and sap, so I'm not much of a cook myself."

They ate in companionable silence for a few moments. Michaela thought about what he'd said. "Do they?"

"Do who what?" Cormac poured himself more wine. Under the light, his hair shone almost opalescent.

"The fey eat sap."

He passed her a cracker. "I'm exaggerating a bit. Most fey make a show of only eating that kind of fare, flowers and nectar, when they are in public. It's too corporeal. Too crude."

"In private?"

"They wolf down whatever they like."

"No meat though."

He shuddered. "Only the most debauched would even consider such a thing. One day Isindle was…" He broke off. "Sorry. More wine?"

"Isindle. Your sister."

He held his glass up to the light and gazed at the pale liquid. "That's right." He put down the glass, looking resigned. "Before you can ask, here's what you need to know. She is younger than I am, and as bright as a star. Yes, I miss her greatly. Yes, she lives in the Queendom and as I pointed out before, our meetings are rare as I am an exile."

Michaela flushed. "I wasn't going to interrogate you."

"You weren't?" His peaked brows rose. "I thought you were interested in me."

She opened her mouth and shut it, realizing how he had caught her. To say she wasn't interested would be unnecessarily rude. To say she was would be—well, what would it be? He did interest her.

The silence grew as Cormac drank his wine and regarded her. She should speak. She didn't want to. The heavy quiet in the room was charged with an energy she wasn't sure she wanted to break up or tap into.

What she did know was she was exhausted. Mentally and physically.

Cormac broke into her thoughts. "You're tired."

His voice was firm and brooked no subterfuge. She didn't give it. "I am."

"Tell me."

Michaela took an olive and let the salt fill her mouth. How to answer this? What she was truly tired of was the ever-present solitude, the split life of being a Pharos member. Covering so many secrets from those she wanted as friends. No matter to whom she turned, there was an invisible barrier that she couldn't pass, knowledge she needed to hug close.

Cormac spread his arms over the back of the couch and spoke when she didn't reply. "You're a member of Eric's High Council. The head of it, if I recall correctly."

She nodded. This was public information, as was the fact that she had been the one appointed to oversee the *defie* challenge six months ago that nearly cost both Eric and Caro their lives. She had seen blood before, lots of it, and on the bodies of those she loved, but the *defie* had been shattering.

"I was involved in cleaning house after Iverson lost the *defie* against Eric." She shrugged. "You saw how some reacted to it. I didn't make friends."

"A lot of work, I'm told."

She rubbed her eyes. "That's an understatement. It's still going on, half a year later."

"Eric handles insurrection much differently than I've seen it done."

Michaela knew exactly what he meant. "Eric is unusual both as a masquerada and a leader. He isn't vengeful and made a point of allowing those who honestly regretted their decision to have another chance."

"He was turned, not born, if the rumors are true."

"For once, they are." Eric had been a *coureur de bois* in the 1600s. He was still a noted expert in determining fur quality, not that it came up much in his role as Hierarch.

"Exceptionally strong, then. Those who are turned are notoriously powerful."

She laughed. "You know?"

"I make it my business to know." He poured them both more wine and Michaela drank it down without thinking.

"What else can you tell?"

Instead of answering her directly, Cormac stood up and walked to where she sat on the couch. She poured herself another glass of wine, welcoming the slight dizziness. The room was getting hot, and she stripped off her cardigan. Cormac's eyes flickered slightly as she also unwrapped the long, heavy silver chain she'd wrapped around her throat that morning and tossed it with a clank on the table. For a moment, she felt like her true self, Miaoling, but she pushed it down deep. Miaoling had been forced to deal with enough of life and once she stepped foot on Captain Lu's ship, she'd sworn that she would never let Miaoling, her real, true, secret self, be hurt again.

She must have sat there drinking her wine and thinking idly to herself for some time because Cormac reached out and laid a hand on her knee. "Tell me about Ivy."

Michaela nestled back into the chair, letting the warmth of his touch spread over her skin. "She's a descendant of an old friend of mine." A branch of Yao's family that had remained in China.

"Who?"

Yao. Being his friend had been Michaela's privilege. She ran her hand along her left arm, feeling the slight ridge of the scar on the back from the overseer's whip.

Cormac caught her hand and ran his finger along the scar. "This is part of your story. Tell me."

She hesitated and he brought his hand to her chin, tilting her face to look him in the eyes. It was hypnotic, Michaela thought, staring into his clear jade gaze. There was an old compassion in his expression that she recognized. It was a rare arcana who had not known loss and pain over their long lives.

She wanted to tell him.

"His name was Yao," she said.

Chapter 14

Cormac released his hold on Michaela once she started speaking. He'd felt the shudder that had run along her slender body at his touch, and his response.

He wanted her badly. He'd never felt this way about a woman before, but Michaela was no simple woman. Inside that tiny body were lifetimes of experience, and he wanted to know every part of her.

She stared at her glass, swirling the wine inside. "I came to Canada in the late 1800s. I was facing *le vide* and I thought that things would be better over the sea." She sighed. "There were stories about gold lying on the ground. The usual tales immigrants tell themselves to help make the decision. It seemed exciting."

"Was it bad?" Cormac paid little attention to human history, but even a fey knew that humans cycled from cruelty to enlightenment to cruelty.

She laughed shortly. "It was slavery. Yao became my friend after I was whipped by the overseer. I was working on the railroad and I hadn't broken the rock fast enough. Yao came to me that night with some salve he'd smuggled in, an herbal remedy from home I hadn't seen in years."

That definitely didn't match his recollection of history. "There were women on the railroad?"

Michaela snorted. "No. I was a man back then, of course."

"What?" The casual gender-swapping of the masquerada still threw him.

"We were considered subhuman. There were few safe places for Chinese and hardly any Chinese women here because they didn't want us to breed and start families, put down any roots." She turned her hand over and pointed at a pale round scar on her palm. "Got this from the Swedish foreman when he scorched me with a poker. I was sleeping when he thought I should be awake."

"Why don't you heal the scars up?" Like the fey, masquerada could heal quickly.

Her gaze burned him. "There are some things that you never recover from. Some experiences that should be remembered. This"—she jabbed her finger—"it's not a scar. It's a memorial to Ming and Yao and Bian. Men who had the misfortune to be poor and Chinese while here in the Americas."

Cormac refilled their wine. "You're a masquerada, a strong one. You could have changed your appearance to look like that Swede, could have walked away."

"I won't lie." She put the glass on the table with a soft clink. "I thought about it. Even tried. I wasn't able to. It would be a betrayal of myself."

"How so?"

"When we take on a masque, we take on more than the appearance. I would have been tainted with the attitudes of those who looked like that overseer. I feared as John, or Sven, I would have seen Yao and the others only as tools to be used and discarded, not as men with value and individuality and worth. Those smugly superior thoughts would have been mine." She paused, dark eyes further shadowed with memory. "I didn't know if I was strong enough and I couldn't take the risk of losing myself like that. We Chinese were hated, degraded in every way. An obnoxious pestilence to be used grudgingly for the hardest work and then discarded. To take on a masque that would harbor such despicable thoughts was unacceptable."

Cormac leaned back, fascinated by this window into her mind. "Yao helped you?"

"He was a good, kind man. Even among our own, there were bad men, the kind who would run to the overseers and report on any indiscretion. We despised them. They were the same men who would tattle to the magistrates back home. The reason didn't matter—whether it was for extra food, or to make others suffer, or to experience a little bit of power themselves. Yao and I found friends. It was a hard life, but we could laugh. I couldn't leave him there while I walked away in a different masque."

She smiled, her gaze distant. "We played jokes on each other. It's odd now, to think of what we found humorous. Then Yao died."

Cormac had expected this, but the desolation in her voice caught his heart. "How?"

"I had been told to blast a tunnel with dynamite. He knew how much I hated the job—we all did—but he hated it slightly less and took my place without me knowing."

A tear fell down her cheek. "They didn't bother to bury him. Left him in that tunnel, parts of him sprayed over the walls so nice people who wouldn't even look at us could have an easier train ride."

"I'm sorry."

She shivered. "We worked hard, Bian and Ming and I, and we paid the head tax and brought his family over. Said they were mine. All the Chinese looked alike to the customs men so I didn't have a problem. I've watched over them since."

"Ivy is related to him?"

She smiled. "His great-great-granddaughter and more like him than any member of the family."

"Tell me more about him."

Michaela opened her mouth to speak but bent her head as a storm of weeping shook her body. Cormac, though he was fey and soulless, felt something tear at him. He leaned over and wrapped his arms around her, letting her cry as he whispered into her ear.

* * * *

It had been many years since Michaela let herself think of Yao. She remembered his death each year as was proper, but she wouldn't let herself dwell on him. In Cormac's embrace, she recalled Yao's mischievous smile. "He was a good thief," she said.

"Then he would have been respected by the fey."

"You said you weren't thieves."

"Perhaps I exaggerated our virtue. In any case, we all admire expert technique. What would he steal?" Cormac's voice was soft and he brushed her hair behind her ear.

"Food, mostly. Clothing. Only from the company men. He'd never steal from another Chinese. None of us would."

Cormac nodded. "During the war, we did the same. The idea of stealing from a warrior on your own side was anathema."

"The fey war?" Michaela leaned back and wiped her eyes, which seemed to have lightened to bronze from her tears. "I don't know much about what happened."

No surprise. It had been a sordid civil war because Tismelda wanted the Tansy Throne. "We don't celebrate it much. Even our songs are more about the nobility of sacrifice than Tismelda's grubby greediness."

"You were in it." Michaela sat facing him.

"We all were." Cormac drew his fingers through Michaela's hair. It felt like heavy silk and slid out of his grasp. Her eyes didn't leave his, but her lips opened slightly.

A faint pulse beat in the hollow of her throat.

"Cormac." Her voice was unsteady.

He wrapped her hair around his hand and pulled them closer. "I've been dying for this."

He should have known it wouldn't be that easy. She twisted away so that his lips landed on her throat. Before he could react and claim her mouth, her hands moved up the outside of his chest and along his shoulders. If Cormac had been hard before, feeling Michaela against him turned his cock into a length of steel. She ground into him and he actually saw lights flash behind his eyes.

She brought her mouth to his shoulder, licking the skin by his collar and making him shake. Without breaking their embrace, he urged her to her feet. He lifted her so that she instinctively wrapped her strong legs around his waist. His knees almost buckled. She felt incredible. No, more than incredible. Perfect.

His hands kneaded the rounded curves of her ass and he moved towards the bedroom. She made a small noise against his neck but the tilt of her hips let him know it wasn't in protest. Her skin tasted like brandy and his lips burned with the liquor.

In the bedroom, he let her down gently on the bed, curving over her. She avoided his kiss again, skillfully sliding her fingers on his lips. "No kissing," she murmured. "No sex."

He pulled back to look at her. Michaela's hair was spread over the white sheets, so shiny that it reflected the dim lights from the lamps. "Anything you want." Though he was dying to taste her mouth, already temptingly full with desire, he wouldn't push her.

Cormac leaned down and trailed his tongue lightly along her throat, finding a spot so sensitive that she instinctively clutched him tighter. Fire scorched through him as he felt her move beneath him. His attention narrowed until it was filled by her. The softness of her skin. The heavy black silk of her hair. She arched up and slid a hand across his back, scratching him delicately with her nails. He moved his hand down her stomach, then, without warning, slid his fingers deep into her.

That was all it took. Michaela's body spasmed around his hand as she arched and cried out. Her hands gripped his and her eyes shut. Cormac watched, more aroused than he'd ever been in his life, as his fingers moved deep inside, seeking the spot that would bring her to the edge again.

"No," she gasped. "Not again."

"Yes." He groaned it against her hair. "Come again, Michaela."

There. He curled his finger gently and Michaela screamed out loud, bucking against him again. She was soaked now and he could barely restrain himself from stripping her and fucking her until she begged him for mercy and he exploded deep inside of her.

That would be next time. For now, he would focus on her. He bent his head as he moved his fingers quickly in and out. His mouth closed around her nipple, sucking it hard through the thin silk of her blouse.

"I can't..." Michaela's voice shook.

"You can."

How many times did he make her come? He couldn't even tell. By the end Michaela was limp, her legs spread and her mouth almost burgundy. Cormac had refused to let himself come, out of some insane decision he'd made to not come until he was inside her.

He deeply regretted that decision because Michaela sated was almost sexier than Michaela aroused.

He gave her a last gentle kiss on her temple. "Sleep now."

She did and he watched over her, his eyes trained on a small blue light that flashed in the corner of her window and his thoughts on her.

Chapter 15

A beam of sunlight woke Michaela and she shot up in bed, images of last night tumbling through her mind. Cormac. His hands on her skin. His fingers. How many times had she come? They hadn't even had sex and that was still the most incredible experience she'd had. She glanced down.

She was wearing clothes. If a tiny pair of panties counted as clothes.

"Good morning."

She twisted around. The sheets only covered up to his hips and she gazed down with a mix of desire and dismay. In the morning light, Cormac's hair was luminous, reflecting the light so it danced on the walls. His eyes were dark green and he tucked his arms under his head, leaving his sculpted torso bare and uncovered. Michaela's hands itched to touch him, yank off that damn sheet, and ride him until she collapsed.

"We can, you know. The only one stopping us is you." Cormac lifted one of his hands and traced a teasing line over her thigh as he gazed at her breasts. She resisted the temptation to cross her arms over her chest. She wasn't a protected young virgin, taught to be ashamed of her body.

It would be nice, though, if her reaction to him wasn't so obvious. Her nipples hardened as his touch on her leg grew firmer.

"Come here."

It probably wasn't a good idea. Now in the bright morning light, she could count a hundred reasons, a thousand reasons, why she should instead get up and have a cold shower. The investigation, first. The fact that she wasn't entirely sure how she felt about Cormac. It would be a mistake to add in a physical relationship while they were still colleagues. Then the light caught the tiny ring in his ear and reflected a small dart of gold at the wall. She lay down next to him, loving his cool skin against hers. He avoided her mouth and she relaxed deep inside, grateful she wouldn't feel that terrible desire-killing tension of having to be on alert all the time.

Instead, he pushed her down deeper into the bed as his body covered hers and his face tilted to the side.

"Only this," she panted as his fingers slid down her hip and plucked at the lace on her hip. "No more."

He pulled her closer, his mouth trailing down the line of her jaw and to her ear. "This," he promised. "I'll wait for you to ask me to fuck you. Until then..."

The dark heat in his promise made her open her thighs, enough for him to bring his hand over and cover her mound. His long fingers pulled aside her panties and stroked her with a gentleness that made her entire body clench. She bit her lip and reached down for his cock, but he moved so she was trapped. "No. You don't get to make all the rules." His fingers moved deeper into her body and she knew that he was going to make her come shamefully fast again. Then his thumb moved over her and that was it.

She exploded, crying out as her body arched and her hands clenched handfuls of sheets.

Cormac's rumble of desire echoed in her ear. "God, I love listening to you come."

Michaela didn't answer. Her eyes were closed as her body rocked with the waves of her orgasm and she cursed her traitorous self. She had wanted and not wanted this. Well, that was a lie. She had totally wanted it, but her sense of duty had come down heavy.

It was wrong to have sex with a colleague. That's all it was. Even when that colleague wasn't a true colleague. Madden would not be pleased to know that she was intimate with Cormac, and the rest of the council would take it as a sign of weakness. She had to be careful.

She wanted him, though. After all, this wasn't *sex* sex.

Cormac had been respectful of her limits every step of the way. It was her decision to make.

Her eyes fluttered open as Cormac straddled her and took her hands in his. "Soon, Michaela. You'll ask me soon."

She struggled against his grasp, conscious of a surge of longing when she realized how strong he was. She always chose human males as partners in the knowledge that they could never physically overpower her.

Cormac could.

She couldn't want that. She was the one in control. Then he took both her hands effortlessly in one of his and reached back down to her soaking slit. Every attempt to buck him off sent his fingers deeper inside until she came again, fiercely.

This time Cormac released her. "Ask me soon, Michaela."

She couldn't reply.

She could barely breathe.

* * * *

Cormac sat in the kitchen staring at Hiro's phone. He was supposed to be looking at the messages Hiro had sent to try and make sense of what the man had been up to. He had opened it up when the shower started.

That was enough to shoot his concentration to shit.

Michaela. Miaoling. Whoever she was, in his arms, under his body, she'd been all that he'd ever wanted. He hadn't realized how deep and hard her shell was, but hearing some of her story made him understand the safety that she found in it. All arcana lived through horrors, as likely to be perpetrated by their compatriots as well as humans. To be arcana inevitably meant a natural resilience to loss. The emotionally fragile generally didn't live long.

He stared at the golden tea he'd chosen at random from her shelf. There was far more to Michaela than he expected. He'd thought she would be demanding in bed, a nocturnal version of the steel-edged woman visible during the day. That was enough for him. Hell, he would have been happy with whatever she decided to grant him.

That she moved away from his kiss disturbed him, but he would let her take her time. Her smile when she was about to come was the hottest damn thing he'd seen in his life, and he'd lived a very long time.

"What did you find?" Michaela came into the kitchen, her skin still damp from the shower and opened the cabinet for another cup. "Is that tea still good?"

It took Cormac a moment to gather enough of his wits to answer. The morning sun slanted down on her blue-black hair, making it gleam like a dark-hearted sapphire. "Do you wear jewelry?" he asked abruptly.

She poured out her tea and gave him a confused look. "A strange answer."

"You need emeralds in your hair. Rubies. Gold."

Michaela sipped her tea. "I have all that," she said indifferently. "I don't bother to wear it often."

"You'll wear it soon. I want to fuck you with your hair covered in gems, wrapped with gold chains."

"It will have to wait until I find Hiro's killer."

He grinned at her response, exactly as he would have expected from her, and caught the slight breathlessness in her voice. He wanted her unbalanced when it came to thinking about their relationship—whatever it was. From the way her nipples hardened under the thin top she wore, he knew that being unsure was unexplored territory for her. In this one area, he could teach her. It had nearly killed him to stop her from making him come, but he'd decided that he'd wait until he could come in her.

Waiting would make it even better. If he survived it.

"Did you find anything on the phone?" Her hands shook slightly when she brought the cup to her lips, but her voice was now steady.

"I started but it doesn't look good."

Her shoulders sagged. "Tell me."

Time for business. Cormac motioned her down to sit beside him. "I still don't know to whom he was speaking, but he was taking orders." He pointed at the lines of text he'd noticed the previous day.

"To do what?" Michaela's usual tuberose rolled over him and he struggled to concentrate. He'd noticed last night she applied it between her breasts and along her belly and now all he could think about was her standing nude in her bedroom, letting the fine fragrant mist land on her satin skin.

Back to reality. "I don't know."

She gave him a stellar smile. "Then figure it out."

"Yes, ma'am."

After all, Michaela was the boss.

He rather liked it.

Chapter 16

Michaela sat alone in the office answering emails. She and Cormac had come to an agreement about how to function while Michaela worked and Cormac fulfilled his role as Watcher. The compromise was to have Cormac work in her antechamber, with the door open.

It worked well, because Michaela found having Cormac out of sight did wonders for preventing her need to walk over, push him against the back of that padded chair he was sitting on, and straddle him. She clicked *Send* and put her head in her hand. This was not the type of woman she thought she was. In all of her masquerada masques, she was always in control. She was meant to lead. She was the one who set the terms.

She never had trouble focusing on work. Anjali came by with some tea and food from the kitchens. "Nothing new," she reported glumly. She pointed at the pastries. "Someone brought in cheese straws. They're good."

"Thanks." Michaela nibbled at one as they chatted about Nadia, who was still sulking.

She was newly absorbed in mapping out Hiro's relationships when she heard a step.

"She's not in." Cormac's lazy voice drifted in.

"You weren't asked."

Rendell? What did he want? Michaela came out of her office to see the two fey standing almost nose to nose. Rendell smiled at her and tried to step forward. Cormac shadowed his every move.

"I came to speak with you, Michaela, but your dog doesn't seem to approve."

"You have nothing to speak with her about." Cormac's tone tightened and Rendell took a discreet step back. Both had the radiant good looks and tall, lean bodies of the fey, but Cormac now exuded a dangerous aura of protection that filled the room. Michaela had no doubt the moment she indicated Rendell was a threat, Cormac would kill him.

She was horrified to find this aroused a primitive gratification deep inside of her that went against everything she treasured about her hard-won independence. She didn't need protection. Her pride fed her anger as she nodded at Rendell. "Come with me."

Cormac didn't move, forcing Rendell to shoulder by him, which he did with his mouth turned down in a moue of distaste. Michaela ignored this ridiculous male posturing and gestured Rendell to a chair. As he settled in and steepled his hands under his chin, Rendell watched her with eyes that couldn't ever be called anything so boring as blue. Azure, perhaps. Were there ugly fey? She'd certainly never seen one. They were beautiful by arcane and human standards and many worked as models in the human world, their slender otherworldly height a highly demanded commodity.

He didn't say a word, so she prodded him along. "Well, Rendell?"

The fey leaned back and crossed his legs. "You look different, Michaela. More...vulnerable. Accommodating. Open." He almost whispered the last and a low growl came from the front room. Rendell smiled and his gaze moved to the door.

"What do you want?" She was in no mood to let her sex life be used as a way to irritate Cormac. The two fey were notorious enemies.

If he noticed any difference in her tone, Rendell didn't mention it. "You know what."

Interesting. "You're taking unusual interest in Hiro's death," she said. "I didn't know you were friends."

"Friends." He tucked a long thin braid of dark hair behind his ear. "That we were not. My queen is curious."

Michaela gave him a huge smile. "About the death of a human on a council she is not to know you are part of?"

Rendell smoothed his hand along his thigh, deliberately calling attention to the lengthy bulge in his pants. Michaela clamped her lips to avoid giggling. "Never underestimate Queen Tismelda."

"Well, you can tell her we're doing our best," she said with as much firmness as she could muster without sounding defensive. "The team is working hard."

"Oksana is demanding answers."

"Oksana will get the answers when we have them. Was there anything else you wanted?"

"Madden was once your lover, was he not?"

The sound of a pen snapping came from the front room and Rendell looked wickedly gleeful.

That was enough. Michaela pointed at the door. "Good-bye, Rendell."

Instead he leaned forward, his eyes suddenly serious. When he spoke his voice was low. "Do you know about your guard dog? Know what he's like? He was one of the most respected commanders in the war, though he was on the wrong side."

"Is this ancient history lesson necessary?" She kept her tone bored as she lifted her tea to her lips.

"That's not why he was exiled, though. The queen is generous and many of her opponents were allowed to remain. What he did was so unforgivable that she had no choice."

"Hard decisions are made in a war."

"Indeed, but not all of us betrayed our families and our soldiers. He had a choice—to save his forest and himself or those he was sworn to protect." He stood and swept her a bow. "You're a smart woman. I don't need to tell you what happened."

Rendell left, tension rolling out of the room as he went through it. She wondered how much of the story was true. The fey were exquisitely skilled liars and Rendell was a shit-disturber of the highest degree. In any case, it was irrelevant. She wasn't in a relationship with Cormac, and although their physical attraction was undeniable, she was hardly about to let that lull her into a sense of complacency around him. Cormac offered to be her Watcher because he wanted something for himself. She knew it and would act accordingly.

Two seconds later, Cormac appeared in the door, coldly furious.

That was good, because so was she. He had no right to dictate with whom she spoke. "What the hell do you think you're doing?" she demanded.

Those green eyes went almost black. "Was Madden your lover?"

No, but what business was it of his? "Not even discussing this."

There was a tense standoff and then Cormac gave a slight nod as though admitting her point. "He wanted to make trouble."

"That's your problem how?"

"I protect you."

Michaela looked at him and spoke slowly. "I take care of myself, Cormac. Understand that now. Right now. I don't need your help. I don't want it. In fact, I reject it. I have survived without you."

There was a long and tense silence. Then he threw back his head and laughed.

"What's so funny?"

Cormac rubbed his forehead. "This. Michaela, I know this. You're the most capable woman on the Pharos Council and you always hold your own."

She blinked. "Thank you."

"The issue is that I am fey. We are possessive about those who are important to us."

He said it simply, his eyes trained on her. Michaela's breath caught. Important to him? Since when? How? There was chemistry—if a desire that intense could be called that—but that was physical only.

It still didn't give him rights over her.

Cormac didn't give her time to reply. "That being said, Rendell was more of a pompous dick than usual." He looked thoughtful.

She was grateful to get off the topic of feelings. "He was."

Cormac sat down where Rendell had been minutes before. "He wanted to get something from you."

"Perhaps." She didn't want to go into it. "What was on Hiro's phone?"

Cormac shook his head. "Still working on it."

Her phone rang. "One second. This is Eric." She answered to find Eric sounding more pissed off than usual.

"We have a problem," he said. "There's a meeting in one hour at my house. All advisory council members in the city are expected to attend."

"What is it?"

"You'll know soon enough."

"Eric, I am the head of that council. I deserve a bit of advance warning."

"I know. That's why I called you first. See you soon."

She was left with a silent phone. Cormac took her shoulder. "Everything okay?"

She shook the phone as if it could magically impart more information. "I don't think so. We're going to find out."

Chapter 17

Stephan stopped them at the door. After greeting Michaela with a touch on the arm while Cormac tried to control his desire to knock the guy out, Stephan raised his perfectly groomed eyebrows. *"In camera* meeting, Michaela. Ambassador Cormac can stay out here."

"The hell I will," Cormac said politely. "Michaela does not leave my sight."

The tall masquerada sighed and ran a hand over his shaved head. "Dude, don't make this worse. You can't go in. This is our business."

"Then she doesn't go."

As Michaela opened her mouth, Stephan jerked back as if Cormac had hit him. "Who do you think you are? She doesn't need a keeper. Especially you."

Michaela stepped between the two, her tiny body dwarfed by the angry men. "Time out. Stephan, I need to request special permission for Cormac to come in. We have precedent in Caro's attendance."

Her voice wavered slightly and Cormac glanced down in concern. She looked tired, but he couldn't tell if it was deliberate to play to Stephan's soft side. Damn the masquerada. They could be tricky.

Stephan started shaking his head before she even finished the sentence. "No can do. This is big, Mike. Too big to let outsiders in."

"Michaela's life is under threat," Cormac said. "I'm her bodyguard." This was close enough.

If he thought this appeal to Michaela's safety would work, he was wrong. Stephan's face went tight as he turned to Michaela. "Is this true?" he demanded. "Why didn't you tell me or Tom? You went to an outsider?"

The hurt in his voice was clear to both of them. Michaela shot Cormac an agonized glance and in that millisecond he knew whatever came out of her mouth was going to be insane.

"We're mated," she blurted out. A heavy flush started up her neck. "I've taken Cormac Redoak as my mate."

The pendant hanging around Cormac's throat burned with a sudden heat and he tried not to keel over at the intensity of the pain that ricocheted through him. Michaela gasped and her hand flew to her chest as she stared at Cormac in shock. She was breathing harder but so was he.

Luckily, Stephan was too stunned to notice their reactions. His mouth fell open as his eyes bounced between the two of them. "Holy Jesus Christ, what the fuck did you say?"

Cormac mentally seconded that. Did she have any idea of what she'd done? He was desperate to see what sigil the pendant had branded on his flesh.

After all, it would be a match to the one that appeared on Michaela.

"You heard me." Michaela tried to smile but it came as a grimace. "We've known each other a long time and been working closely lately and, well…" she trailed off. "You know how things happen," she finished lamely.

A complicated mix of emotions streamed over Stephan's face before the masquerada moved forward and embraced Michaela. Cormac's hearing was good enough to hear what he said into her ear. "All these years, I hoped you would find someone who was worthy of you. It's what I wanted most for you."

He turned to Cormac and gave him a bone-cracker of a hug. He understood the implicit threat. Treat Michaela wrong and he would be crushed. This didn't bode well for when he told them that he had no desire to be mated, even to Michaela. "Welcome," Stephan said simply. "Now is not the time to announce such a joyful union, as you'll see in a minute. We'll say you're here as a consultant."

Michaela nodded weakly, her face sallow and clashing with the flush that lingered at her throat. She cast a beseeching glance over her shoulder at Cormac, who managed to mouth "What the fuck?" at her before she turned back.

Cormac was still too shocked to give full range to his fury and he forced himself to try to stay calm enough to get her side of the story. She had no idea what she'd done. Cormac's mind boggled at the trouble those simple words would cause him. *I've taken Cormac Redoak as my mate.* To Michaela, she'd blurted out a lie under duress. It was stupid, and ill-considered, and frankly not in character for her at all but he could see, if not understand, why she'd done it. As a member of the North American masquerada's ruling council, Michaela was expected to attend meetings, even emergency ones. Since she was also not supposed to reveal her work with Pharos, it now put her, shite, both of them in the awkward position of trying to explain why Cormac needed to shadow her.

To her, the lie was a quick fix that could be eventually solved. Stupid but somewhat reasonable. He supposed.

The problem was, the moment the words came out of her mouth, they'd stopped being a lie.

Michaela would have seen only the many superficial amours and dalliances the fey played at. What she didn't know was how seriously they took mating. A fey's mate was as important as their family forests and the mating bond so strong the death of one mate meant the death of the other within days. It was more common for fey to enter a partnership with a compatible other, easily dissolvable and often political. To mate was to open oneself up to ecstasies and torments deeper and more intense than most fey wanted to risk.

Why mate? went the old joke. *My tree will never die on me.*

Not even his parents had mated.

Cormac stared at Michaela. Was it possible that she knew what she was doing? It was…but he dismissed it as improbable. An exiled fey was hardly a catch, and he couldn't think of a single reason why she would pick him over, well, anyone.

As a *caintir*, any mate of Cormac's would have to deal with the greater intensity of his attachment to the natural world. Fear of what that would mean for a mate had even kept him from pursuing deep relationships. It would absolutely, definitely prevent him from saying the words that changed everything for a fey, the public announcement that sealed the deal.

When Michaela declared him as her mate, he had become her mate. His pendant had confirmed it for them. They were bonded for life. To make it even worse, Queen Tismelda insisted on approving any matings. She also disapproved of mixing blood between groups.

Those words had doomed him. He was never going to get his forest back. A dull pain formed in his gut. Yetting Hill would be gone forever from the Redoaks. Isindle with no home. His tree…dead.

If his tree died, he died. As his mate, so would Michaela.

Six, seven words and one minute to create this absolute fucking mess.

Stephan's phone beeped and he excused himself to meet the next councilor. "You know the way, Michaela."

Cormac waited, almost on his toes, until Stephan's steps faded away. "Are you out of your fucking mind?"

She still looked stunned. "I must have been. I can fix it."

No, she couldn't. "What were you thinking? What were you *thinking*?" Perhaps if he kept saying the same thing he'd get...what? Magically transported to his non-mated state? She looked so wretched that he almost didn't have the heart to blame her.

But not quite. Cormac turned away, doing his best to keep his self-possession. Letting loose his rage on his new mate in front of the masquerada would be a death sentence.

Like the one Michaela just put on you. You and Isindle.

Did it make it worse that she didn't know the consequences of what she had done? In a way, perhaps. To lose his forest and be force-mated as a result of deliberate malice would have been understandable and probably would have happened in retaliation for one of his own insults or actions. He would have deserved it.

Instead he'd lost everything so Michaela could get in a fucking *meeting*.

"Cormac, I..." Michaela stood beside him but she stopped talking when he turned to face her. He relented slightly. It might have been her fault, but they were now stuck in this nightmare together. Still, they needed to discuss this reasonably before he hit her with the mates-for-life whammy. She was still rubbing her chest but hadn't checked to see what had caused the pain. He didn't want to reveal it right now. Beads of sweat appeared on her forehead.

"Are you well?" he asked.

She was still rambling. "I...I don't know. I froze. There was nothing else I could think of. Caro comes to meetings. I didn't have another plan that didn't involve telling Eric's entire advisory council that we need to be together because the super-secret group we're both members of has said so."

Footsteps approached. "We need to talk about this later."

"I know. I'm sorry." She looked wretched.

Then Stephan was there with another masquerada councilor and motioned for them to enter the room.

Good God. He had a bloody mate. No forest, but a gorgeous, sexy, intelligent mate. For a brief moment, Cormac wondered crazily if being mated would be all that bad.

Perhaps it wouldn't. Until his forest died and they died with it.

* * * *

"What's the meaning of this, Michaela?"

Every masquerada had stopped what they were doing to stare at Cormac. Michaela took a deep breath, feeling it hitch in her throat. Her idiotic mating comment had affected her more than she had thought. Even her heart was racing. She put it aside. She was the head of the High Council and the others were right to expect an explanation.

"Councilors, may I present Cormac Redoak, our fey consultant."

Josiah rose from his seat near the end of the table. "I don't recall approving a fey to join us." *Fey* was uttered with almost visible distaste.

"If the Hierarch said it's fine, then welcome aboard," said Phoebe. Michaela smiled and stopped herself from shading her eyes with her hand. The lights were too bright in the room. It was too hot as well. Or too cold.

Josiah slammed his meaty hand on the table. "This is a closed meeting, Michaela. Who the hell do you think you are, to bring in this outsider? This is a huge disrespect to the council and Eric."

"On the contrary. I'm honored we have such a guest." Eric came into the room followed by Caro. Josiah clenched his fists and sat down with a bump.

Another wave of dizziness came over her. From the look Eric and Caro gave her, then shot to Cormac, it was clear Stephan had wasted no time in telling the Hierarch what Michaela had said. She tried to keep her face impassive, but noticed Cormac giving a ghost of a nod, handling it with a level of grace she knew she had no right to expect. She wouldn't have been surprised had he stormed out after she'd made such a stupid, presumptuous comment. She rubbed again at her chest, wondering if she'd been stung by some bug. There was a slight burning itch on the skin over her left breast. She would have checked was it not generally frowned on to look down one's shirt during important business meetings.

Eric tapped the table and the room quieted instantly. "First, thank you for coming. As you see, we have a visitor, Ambassador Cormac Redoak, who is here at my request. I'm sure you made him welcome."

He paused, but no one said a word. They were all capable of reading their Hierarch and it was clear that he was immersed in an icy fury. Even those who were antagonistic to him were smart enough to keep their mouths shut.

Michaela did her best to concentrate, but her thoughts refused to stop spiralling. How could she have told such a lie to Stephan? There was no hole on Earth deep enough for her to hide. The only thing to do was to get him after the meeting and explain that…even here she broke down. It was a mistake? How can you make an error about being mated? That she misspoke? *Oh, sorry, I meant we were dated. Rated. Bated.* She shook her head to interrupt the rhyme of words. It was too bright in the room, so hard to concentrate. When had Eric changed the lights?

Then there was Cormac. She owed him a huge apology for such a transgression. He must be furious. She would have been.

She laid her hands on the chair arms and willed herself to find some amount of peace for this meeting. Abject apologies to Stephan and Cormac would have to wait. Eric had not called an urgent meeting in months, not since he told the council the details of what had happened with Iverson and announced his plans to clean house.

She swayed in her seat, then sat snapped-up straight, wondering if she was falling ill. It was rare for a masquerada to be sick, but when it took them, it took them hard. That would at least explain why she was making such stupid decisions.

Like saying she was mated to Cormac.

Mated. To Cormac.

Cormac met her eyes across the table. His were filled with the anger she expected—she would be furious—but for a moment she thought she saw pity. Odd.

Eric leaned forward and rested his palms on the table. "I called you here to tell you that I have confirmation Frieda Hanver has resurfaced."

Michaela pressed her hands down harder on the chair arms to steady herself. Eric would be counting on her to assess the reactions of the others in the room. Caro's cool gaze flitted from one face to the other, doing the same thing. There was nothing but disbelief and consternation, even among Eric's enemies. What Frieda had done when she impersonated Caro and tried to kill Eric was so beyond the pale that no masquerada with minimal moral sense could countenance it. If they lacked even that small core of goodness, then self-preservation would have kept them still and mum.

"My informants say she is in North Africa building a small army of disenfranchised arcana. I am telling you this before I tell the other rulers." He paused. "Frieda is no longer a masquerada problem. She and her followers have taken Iverson's ideas and expanded them drastically."

"No," gasped Phoebe, who was one of Eric's strongest supporters. "They want another war with the humans? That will break the Law. The humans will massacre us."

"She's gathered vampires, weres, and a mishmash of others. There are masquerada. Many of them." He nodded at Cormac. "Even some fey. They call themselves the Dawning."

A loud mutter burst from around the table. Cormac's brows lowered thunderously but he stayed silent.

Michaela heard this as if from a distance. Sweat dripped through her tightly bound hair and down her face as her dizziness grew.

Eric's voice boomed in her ears. "They want to end the Law. For Frieda's army, the only success is the total annihilation of humanity as an independent race."

A babble burst out as the councilors all spoke at once. There were calls for Frieda's arrest, to know who her collaborators were. Eric's plans. The trustworthiness of his informants.

She tried to rise but wavered as she stood.

"Michaela!" It was Cormac, already vaulting across the table.

That was all she heard before she toppled into his arms.

Chapter 18

Eric insisted Michaela stay at his house where she could be treated properly. Cormac agreed instantly once he found out the reason for her collapse.

Michaela had been poisoned.

"We don't get sick like this," the lead medic had said as she ordered a full toxicology screen. "There's another factor at play."

The other factor, they soon found out, was a deadly combination of liquid minera and other nerve agents. Tom Minor, Eric's security chief, was visibly torn between admiration for the recipe and disgust for its creator when he reported to the others.

Cormac, on the other hand, felt nothing but rage. His anger towards Michaela's damaging lie had been shoved to the side in light of this more recent danger. Cormac might not want to be mated but he was, regardless of the circumstance. That still had meaning.

The killer had tried to harm his mate, under his nose, and that was an action he could not let go without retribution.

"How the hell could this have happened in your house?" He tried to keep his voice level as waves of anger continued to spill through him.

Stephan held up a hand. "Our medics say it could have been administered any time in the last six hours and most likely in food or drink. Apparently it's designed to only affect masquerada."

Cormac narrowed on this. "Most likely or definitely?" The tea. The food Anjali had brought. Rendell's visit.

"It's possible she touched it and consumed it that way," Stephan said. "I think less likely, though."

The killer was getting bolder. Cormac's thoughts were in such a rush that he didn't notice the others in the room staring at him expectantly.

"What?" he snarled.

Caro pushed back her wavy dark hair and sighed. "Ambassador, we want to help."

He knew where this was going and made up his mind before she even laid it out for him. The branded sigil under his pendant throbbed. His link with Michaela was still strong; she was recovering. Michaela trusted her compatriots. The only question now was how much he would tell them.

He examined each of the masquerada around the table. The three men reflected his own wrath back at him. They loved Michaela, he realized as he registered the deep concern in Caro's voice. Respected and loved her.

Fuck the Pharos.

"We didn't lie when we came to you about Hiro's death," he began. "We may have neglected a few details."

A ghost of a grin flickered across Eric's face. "We know. You're a good liar, fey, but we're masquerada. We're born to read others."

Cormac would have laughed at the Hierarch's firm confidence, so like Michaela's, but he was too tense. He gave them a précis of the facts, including his role as Watcher.

Stephan groaned out loud at this. "I can't believe Michaela agreed to that."

"She had no choice," Cormac said. "She's the security chief for the Pharos Council."

That was it. The secret was out. He waited for a response, but the four masquerada simply nodded as if he was confirming old information.

"You knew."

Eric gave a *well, yeah* shrug. "We suspected. An individual of Michaela's caliber was an obvious choice. Also, she would disappear for weeks with some flimsy excuse. Pharos needs better cover stories."

"What about the mating?" asked Stephan, his gaze boring into Cormac.

Time for the other bombshell. "We weren't mated then. That was Michaela's excuse to get me into this council meeting."

Eric's gray eyes narrowed. "You said then."

"I did."

Eric dropped his face into his hands. "Fuck. Tell me she didn't say it. Please."

"Said what?" demanded Caro. She looked at Stephan and Tom, who gave her confused shrugs. "Said what, Eric?"

Eric pointed at Cormac. "Better ask Michaela's new mate."

"She said we were mated." Cormac pulled down the collar of his shirt to show the edge of the sigil. "We are now mated."

Caro's huge brown eyes grew round. "Are you fucking kidding me?"

"No."

"She says you're mated and that's it." Caro shook her head. "You're lying."

"The fey don't approach mating lightly. To us, the words have meaning."

"Oh my God." Caro blanched. "Does she know?"

"Do you think she would have said it had she known?" Known that those words would doom both of them?

There was silence around the table as they all absorbed this. From the expressions on the faces of the people who knew her best, Cormac gathered his new mate had not been in the market for a life-partner.

"The poison must have messed with her mind for her to even say such a thing, especially given her history," Stephan said firmly.

"Her history?" Was she already mated? Cormac wasn't even sure what would happen then. Would their link be done? Ignored? A surge of hope shot through him.

Stephan glanced at Caro, who said, "Michaela has been married before—"

"Married?" Could this entire issue be put to rest on a technicality? It was impossible for a mated fey to mate again. Perhaps, because Michaela was a masquerada, this had gone unnoticed.

"—though she isn't now." Caro finished. "You need to give her an out."

Shite. They were still stuck. "I agree, and I would never force her in an unwanted mating if I had a choice." *Like she had with him.* No. It wasn't her fault. She didn't do it deliberately. Remember that before he started hating her. "But there's no going back. My forest has blessed the union. We're mated."

A moment of silence as they all considered how Michaela would react to this news. Eric shook his head. "Incredibly, you stealing away one of the most powerful women in my nation and the shitshow that will occur when you tell her is the least of my worries. Who poisoned her?"

Cormac's heart thumped when he remembered Michaela's white, still face. "It could be any of the Pharos, if your analysis of the poison is right. How easy is it to obtain?"

"Since we just discovered its existence, I'd say difficult," Tom said.

"We need to get to the bottom of this," Eric said. "Will you accept our help? I know it's a Pharos issue but by attacking Michaela we now have a stake in this."

"Yes." Cormac didn't even hesitate. She was his mate, for all the trouble that it was, and worthy of his respect. "Fuck Pharos anyway. I'm taking her away to recover, away from any danger."

Eric didn't bother to ask where. "Keep in touch." Then he smiled. "Good luck with your mate."

His mate. A hot spike of pleasure pulsed out from the brand, quickly followed by a rush of fury. His mate. His killer.

Cormac nodded and left.

Chapter 19

This was a hell of a hangover. Michaela groaned and coughed, cursing inwardly as the slight movement made her head pound. She was going to have to control her drinking as Yuri. This was agony. She opened her eyes then squinted them shut again. Even the dim light in the room was like a searchlight pointed directly through her pupils and into her brain.

A cool hand lay briefly on her forehead, then stroked her hair back. "You need to drink this."

Her eyes flew open. "Cormac?" Her throat was dry and raspy.

"Drink first and then I'll tell you what you want to know."

A cool glass touched her dry lips and she drank reluctantly, then gulped it down. The liquid was sweet but not cloying. "What…"

"You were poisoned. Liquid minera. Eric's medics stabilized you and I brought you to my tree to recover."

Poisoned. Tree. Michaela wondered if she was hallucinating. Cormac pressed another glass into her hand and she drank greedily, propping herself up on one shoulder. When she put the empty glass down with a sigh, she let herself relax against the pillow again. "Thank you."

"You're welcome." He sounded stiff, but it was hard for her to think analytically. No doubt he was uncomfortable she was in his space, the same way she felt when he was in her apartment.

"Tell me all that again. I think I misheard you say, 'It's a hangover.' " Obviously she wasn't in a tree. The room was huge.

He spoke so slowly she would have thought it was an insult had she not had trouble following it. It was too surreal. "You collapsed during the masquerada council meeting. Eric's medics identified it as liquid minera mixed with some other elements to create a poison they haven't seen before. I took you to my tree to heal."

His tree. She couldn't believe so much weirdness was going on that being in bed inside a tree felt normal. There would be time later to go into what rules of physics and perception had been altered to let that happen. "Why? Why didn't you leave me with Eric?"

His eyes burned green and there was a strange tug near her heart, like a healing scar. She glanced down but Cormac grabbed her hand. "I wouldn't."

She tossed his hand away. He hadn't told her everything. "Tell me."

"I told Eric you were Pharos."

She squinted at him. Cormac wasn't looking directly at her. She pulled herself together, shifted into Yuri, and leaned her hulking form forward.

"Feyman." Her voice was deep, rough and impatient. "Do not fuck with me."

"We're mated."

Michaela felt Yuri disappear as she laughed, then groaned as her head pounded. "No, I only *said* we were mated. I remember that. I apologized." An awkward situation, but at least being near death had taken some of the sting away. She cheered slightly knowing that she had a ready-made excuse in being near collapse when she'd said such a senseless thing.

Mates. With Cormac. Preposterous. She'd been married enough to last lifetimes. Certainly he was gorgeous, but mating required more than physical craving, no matter how intense it was. After so many years with those walls over her heart she didn't know if it was possible to break them down even if she wanted to. Not that she would. Love caused too much pain, and all she was willing to risk she had given to Ivy.

He didn't flinch but she could feel his repressed anger. "Now is probably the time to look at that itchy spot over your heart."

How did he know it was over her heart? The question died on her lips the moment she pulled her shirt open and saw a strange black blotch on her skin.

"Oh. My. God. What is that?" Was this an aftereffect of the poison? She looked up to see Cormac pull his shirt over his head. While part of her ogled the perfection of his musculature, the more with-it section of her head zeroed in on a matching design on his chest.

"We're mated." His expression said nothing, but she sensed his disquiet and that made her even more tense.

"You didn't answer the question. I didn't ask if we were mated. I asked what the hell it is." Michaela prevented herself from shifting into Yuri again, even though her take-no-prisoners masque would be better able to deal with this than her natural self. Yuri would have the guts to take a knife and cut that damn thing out of his flesh.

Cormac traced his design with gentle fingers, and she noticed that it was intricately constructed. It drew her in as if he was touching her own skin. "It's our mating brand. Our sigil."

Her jaw dropped. "You branded me? Like cattle?"

For a moment, his temper flashed. "In case you haven't noticed, you're not the only one walking around with a surprise tattoo stamped onto their skin and a brand-new partner for life."

Michaela gaped in horror. She'd been so caught up in herself she hadn't thought about what Cormac had gone through. A mating bond went two ways. They were shackled together. "What have I done?" she whispered.

He burst out laughing. "Don't look so tragic," he said flippantly as he yanked his shirt back on. That stupid, non-thinking part of her brain sighed in disappointment to see that splendid flesh disappear.

Unable to have this conversation lying down, she struggled up until she sat cross-legged on the bed. "I said we were mates, but there was no ceremony. You didn't say a thing. You didn't even say yes."

The crooked smile he gave her took away some of her fear. No, concern. Uneasiness. Never fear. She was Chui Miaoling, no, she was *Michaela*, and she was not a woman who allowed herself to be frightened, at least not for non-life-threatening situations. "I didn't have to. The fey mating ritual is simple. One of you says you're mates. That's it."

"Wait a minute." The sheer injustice of such a system cut through her incredulity. "That's it? One of you declares it? What if you don't want to be mated?"

"Penalties for forcing a mate are severe. Death for you and your family, and your forest is confiscated by the queen."

The rational part of her was slightly soothed by this, but... "I still did it though, and you can't take any revenge on me. I have no family and no forest." *Wait a minute.* "I'm not even fey."

"The union also has to be blessed by my forest. If my forest thought you would be a poor match for it, it would not have allowed the mating."

"You trust your forest."

"Yes." It was a simple declaration. "If Yetting Hill says you are a worthy mate, you are."

"For you. What about you for me?"

He shrugged. "I guess it figures you'd be sure I was a good match before you announced we were mates. It's a forest, not an omnipotent god. Look, I know it's a lot to absorb, but you need your rest."

Rest? Like she was a bloody invalid? When there was a killer on the loose at Pharos and Frieda Hanver was back? When someone tried to kill her? She wasn't sure if it was a relief to know Hiro had probably been killed because of her, and it still didn't answer why the hell he was in her office. It was all a blur. She threw the crisp covers aside and moaned as she saw stars. Cormac pushed her back on the pillow. "No."

"Yes." Even as she said it, she knew it was a lost cause. She could barely move. That poisoner had done a real number on her, and she probably hadn't helped things by taking on a masque.

"Eric and I agree that your priority is to convalesce. He's going to work on it from the other side."

"I am so glad you two men decided what I should do."

"It was Caro's idea. She was worried about you overextending yourself."

Damn Caro. Michaela had another wave of dizziness. Cormac laid a cool hand on her cheek, and she was oddly soothed.

Then her heart spiked. Mates? What did that mean?

"We'll talk later." His voice was a promise and almost against her will, Michaela found her eyes closing.

Mates.

Chapter 20

Cormac watched Michaela rest. All in all, the conversation had gone better than he had anticipated, and he congratulated himself on getting the shock of it over while she was still woozy from being poisoned.

Not the noblest of sentiments, but times were hard. He paced around his tree. Avoiding touching his new mating sigil, he pulled up his pendant and assessed the leaf. Had the brown expanded? The edges looked darker.

Maybe it was paranoia.

At least he had remained calm. He'd also not mentioned that she'd sentenced them to inevitable death once Tismelda found out what had happened, if Tismelda didn't have his tree cut down or order their executions simply out of spite. His only hope was that she wouldn't find out. No one had witnessed it happening, after all, and he wasn't about to send any announcements. This was cheering. He had a good chance of keeping it secret and avoiding the queen's rage.

Don't be an idiot. She would know. The queen's spy web—centered on Rendell—was thorough.

There was no point dwelling on this. There was nothing he could do. He couldn't repudiate his mate. In fact, even as he mulled over the problems, he felt a pull towards Michaela, one that rendered him almost incapable of anything but protection.

He sat in a chair beside his sleeping mate and pulled out the messages from Hiro's mobile phone. Although he had faith in Eric's team, it was killing him to simply wait for them to find answers about Michaela's poisoner. He'd sent a message to Madden under Michaela's name—he'd have to deal with that when she woke up, damn it—telling him that she had been taken ill. The flurry of subsequent demanding texts had gone unanswered.

The poisoning had also forced him to re-evaluate Hiro's death. If he had any doubts that Michaela had been the original target, they were now gone.

Michaela sniffed and curled up on her side. She was small under the white covers and so pallid she almost blended with the sheets. He leaned over and tucked her in, then smoothed her hair back.

His mate. What did that even mean? He stared down at her, the lashes a long dark slash across her high cheekbones. He was mated to a masquerada. She'd turned into that hulk of man only minutes before. Then he sighed. Dealing with Yuri was still a thousand times better than the idea of having to explain what happened to the queen and beg for his forest back. He shuddered.

Begging.

Him.

He'd never begged for a thing in his life.

It was time to focus on tangible problems, like the messages on Hiro's phone. Returning to his work, he let himself be absorbed by the messages. Hiro's skin had been removed in the same place as the marks on the dead humans in the insubordinate masquerada dens. Eric had mentioned the Dawning in the meeting, and it was logical to assume Frieda Hanver was directing whatever was happening to those humans. The Dawning might want to make slaves of humanity, but Hiro wouldn't be the first collaborator to sell out his people for the right price.

By the time he shook out his hand, sore from writing notes, he had a good idea of what Hiro had been up to. It was as he feared. Hiro had shared information from Pharos with the Dawning. Several messages referenced an individual referred to as Three, who seemed to be at a higher level to Hiro and directing him. Cormac would have rolled his eyes at the pathetic cloak-and-dagger aspect of this had he not lived through his own war. The anticipation of battle seemed to bring out the most juvenile aspects of arcane groups as well as humans.

He propped his feet up on a low table and considered this. While they were waiting for the medics to stabilize Michaela, Eric had elaborated on Frieda Hanver.

"She's smart and cunning," Eric had said. "More than that, she's tapped into a vein of hatred that we've known existed but perhaps had underestimated."

"Against humanity."

"Even when we lived openly with humans, there were factions in all arcane groups who felt humans were not worthy equals."

Cormac had nodded. "That they were unevolved."

"Throwbacks, yeah." Eric had pinched the bridge of his nose, the universal sign for fending off a bitch of a headache. "We need more intel on what she's planning, and I'm going to get it."

The mysterious Three could be Frieda, but she had been also referred to by name in the texts. He ruffled through them again. Another collaborator? A spy? Yangzei? Might as well get a wild card Ancient prancing through this mess to make it fun.

Brother.

After a quick look at Michaela, who slept with a slight frown on her face, as though she was even in her sleep thinking of ways to void their mating, Cormac went out to the clearing in front of his tree. The misty outline of a tall woman turned to him, panic in every line of her body.

"Isindle?"

"Cormac, what have you done?" His sister was nearly in tears. "The entire forest shook. Your tree is in white flower it's so happy. The queen is furious."

Shite. "I have a mate." He said this as proudly as he could. It might have been a mistake, and he might be personally furious, but he would not let others think he felt anything but confidence in the match.

"I know you do. We all do, even the queen. Rendell said it's a masquerada. Is that true?" Isindle sounded horrified.

"*It* is not. She is, and her name is Michaela."

His sister sagged against a tree. "Tismelda will have your head for this. A mixed mating while you're exiled? She's already furious that you aren't doing more to get her forgiveness."

"I was—but my plan was delayed." *Damn Hiro's killer.* "Has she threatened you?"

A small smile flickered across his sister's ghostly face. "Of course. She can't do much though, since I was elevated to mage status."

Cormac breathed a sigh of relief. At least Isindle had the backing of the powerful Fern House, mages who held secrets that even the queen treated carefully. Still, the thought of the queen having power over Isindle made him furious. He should be there to protect her.

Idiot, if it hadn't been for you she wouldn't be in this predicament in the first place. You were the one who was exiled.

"It's not what you think happened. It was an accident."

"The queen will not accept that as an excuse. Matings don't happen by accident."

It does when one is mated to Michaela. "You need to trust me. Find out if there is a way to annul it." That would solve their problems but he had a feeling it would be impossible.

Life did not like making things easy for him.

"I will try." She sounded doubtful. "That's the best I can do."

Isindle faded and she put her hand over her heart as a farewell before she disappeared. It took great energy to project like that—Cormac couldn't even attempt it now that he was keeping himself sequestered from the *dolma*. Seconds later, she was gone and he was left staring morosely at an empty clearing. Rendell's spy ring was good—he must have found out about the mating soon after it happened. He couldn't even blame the fey for spilling his cowardly guts. Tismelda would have been in a right rage when she found out about his tree in flower, and Rendell would have been the first to be summoned. Knowing the little weasel had received the first rush of the queen's anger cheered him slightly.

There had to be something else he could gift the queen. As a *caintir*, he could find out from her tree what her greatest desire was, yet the moment he accessed the power, she would send hunters after him. Could he do it fast, without her knowing? A quick dip?

He eyed the rough bark of his tree. In High Park, with his glamour on it, the tree looked like any other chestnut. He hadn't been able to bring himself to live in an oak, but this was a nice tree, with a leafy squirrel drey wedged high between two branches. Slowly, he brought his hand up to the trunk. All he had to do was reach out. That was it. Put his hand out and touch the damn wood.

Then he'd hear the forest sing again. He'd be one with the *dolma*. He could placate the queen. It would only take a second.

"Cormac?" Michaela's voice drifted out from inside the tree, and he put Tismelda's rage out of his mind as he drew his hand slowly back.

Chapter 21

Cormac was up before dawn. Michaela lay beside him, curled up on her side with her hair tumbling across her face. Incredible how her hair always stayed tied up neatly during the day but fell out of whatever braid or bun she tried to contain it in at night. He pushed a tress off her cheek and she murmured and rubbed her nose without waking. Resignation rolled through him.

She'd been poisoned.

She'd been in no way to blame for their mating.

It was just a shitty, fucking accident.

Since he couldn't reasonably take any anger out on Michaela, he'd have to redirect it to a better target—the one who had tried to kill her and caused this whole extravagant mess.

The bed was warm, and he decided he could think cocooned there as well as he could walking around the clearing. Not that there was much to think about. He knew what had to be done.

Michaela had to recover. That was the most important step. Rest and the medicine from Eric's medic were already taking care of that. When Michaela was well, they needed to return so she could track down and beat Frieda's ass and send that army running. Here he frowned and tucked his arms under his head. She would be working closely with Stephan. Michaela said they were only friends, but what she thought and what Stephan might have as a deeply hidden hope were two different things.

He'd keep a close eye on that.

Then, of course, he needed to get his hands on her poisoner and wrap them like a pretzel around the nearest tree. That would be most satisfying.

After that, he'd have to find out who had ownership of Hiro's Japanese land, convince them to sell, and get it to the queen to save his forest. Hopefully it would still be enough to placate her despite his mating. He pondered this as he stared at the dappled shadows on the ceiling.

Better make that two forests, just in case.

Right, and Hiro. While Cormac didn't care personally about Hiro, finding who killed him remained a priority so he could mete an appropriate punishment on whoever had dared think of harming Michaela. The poisoning had made it clear that she was the intended target.

Finally, get this mating annulled. He had no desire to be mated, nor, apparently, did she. He was a *caintir* and couldn't risk his mate to the same dangers he faced, especially if she could sense the *dolma*. Michaela was brilliant, strong, and gorgeous but she was also a rigidly inveterate rule-follower. He shuddered at a life filled with endless routine. They were not a good match outside of bed.

But in bed…He shook his head to clear it of the image of Michaela, mouth relaxed and her whole body satisfied.

Pale light filtered through the windows and he stretched, feeling somewhat gratified now that he had the priorities straight in his head. It had been a long time since he'd had meaningful work to do, and he'd almost forgotten how much he enjoyed being busy. He thought back. Yes. Fighting in the war had been the last time.

He controlled a shudder. The war had been made more terrible by how much he'd anticipated it. Like a fool, he'd thought battle was exciting and combat the true test of a man. Kiana had warned him but he'd ignored her. "You're a *caintir*, Cormac. You will feel the pain of every tree felled and every animal killed." He hadn't believed her and he'd been wrong. By the end, even the trampling of a single blade of grass had been agony.

All that pain for so many, and in the end, what had it been for? Simply a new face on the throne.

He didn't want to think about the horrors that brought the bitch queen to power, so he slid out of the covers and pulled them over Michaela's shoulders. She was improving, he noted gratefully. A small flame lit in his chest but he fought it back.

He was mated. His forest had confirmed it.

It didn't mean he had to accept it.

* * * *

Michaela opened her eyes, yawned, and knew she was healed. For two days, she couldn't even stand up without wanting to simultaneously throw up and fall down. Cormac had been a superb doctor, dosing her with what she assumed were medic-mandated cures.

Cormac sat with his feet up on a table, golden hair smoothed back and a sheaf of papers on his lap. He twisted to look at her.

"Good morning," he said gravely.

"Morning." After he'd dropped the mating bomb on her, she'd been reluctant to talk. Luckily, her illness meant she'd spent most of the time sleeping. Now there was no excuse.

He assessed her with a critical eye. "You look better. Much better."

"I am."

Cormac nodded with approval, the gesture of a man who had done a task well. "You'll want to wash and eat. There's a stream outside and food will be waiting."

Questions about the mating, what was happening with Pharos, and where the hell his tree was exactly could wait for ten minutes. The lure of being clean, combined with the idea she would be more formidable with her teeth brushed and hair untangled, was too great.

Also, she had a bad feeling that the rank, goaty smell was coming from her.

"Through the door to the left," he added. Under the thin white cotton of his T-shirt she could make out the dark emblem on his broad chest. Her sigil pulsed in response, sending a hot, lazy sensation through her body.

Nope. Nope. Think of it later. In fact, don't think of it at all. Cormac might think that the mating was irrevocable, but there was always a solution. Michaela tipped her chin down as she pulled out her shirt to look at the light green tracing on her skin. How did one reason with a forest? She frowned. That was Cormac's job and once this was all over, she would see that he did it.

She walked out the door—it looked like regular door, but rounder—and into a bright clearing unlike anything she'd seen. The grass was green and cool on her bare feet though the air was a balmy kiss. Birds chirped. Straight out of a Disney movie, she wouldn't be surprised if a singing line of cuddly animals came marching out of the woods.

Behind a strand of trees was a perfect babbling brook, so clear she could see the small pebbles lining the sandy bottom. She wrinkled her nose, wishing it was a steaming tub that she could wallow in instead of a cold stream. Never mind. She'd once washed in water collected in a ditch and should be grateful this was at least private and clean.

A row of stone steps led down the bank and a small bar of soap and a thick white towel lay with a cotton robe near the stream. It *did* look enticingly fresh. She shrugged off the loose pyjamas and poked in a tentative toe.

Within seconds of plunging in, Michaela never wanted to leave. The water bubbled around her and was deep enough to have a real swim, her hair streaming out behind her. Under the dappled light, she flipped on her back and let herself float with only her face out of the water. It was so calming she could close her eyes and drift off. If there was any poison left in her system, it must be draining out of her.

Poison. All sense of well-being deserted her and she sputtered into the water with an inelegant splash. She couldn't play in a stream. There was a job to do. No, more than that. Crises to avert. The killer might have claimed another victim while she lay unconscious, although she was now certain, despite Madden's accusations of ego, that she was the intended target. Yangzei was wandering around. Eric's warning about Frieda. She'd need to get back to the masquerada council and talk to Tom Minor about their security. That bitch might be in North Africa now, but Eric, and by extension Caro, would be Frieda's primary target. Eric was strong, had chased her out of masquerada society, and was mated to a woman Frieda hated with a passion that was roundly reciprocated.

The pleasure gone from her bath, Michaela reached for the soap for a quick sudsing. Her soapy hands ran over her new tattoo. It had gone from a light jade to a dark forest green that reminded her of Cormac's eyes. She sighed. Incredible that being mated had become simply another item on a long list of things she had to deal with.

She'd sworn that she'd never marry again. Six rounds of unwilling marriages had been enough for even a masquerada lifetime. Now she was mated—even the word seemed so much more serious than mere marriage—and it was her own fault. That stupid, stupid lie, now turned truth.

That she was mated, to Cormac of all people, was…bad. He was exasperating, but she was beginning to enjoy his company. She definitely and very much enjoyed his touch and those strong hands with the long fingers that stroked her so confidently. She shivered with a mix of desire and something close to trepidation. None of her past partners had matched her in strength. They respected her. Sex had been pleasurable with a parallel level of give and take, but she had been safe in the knowledge that she'd always had the upper hand if necessary.

Cormac was not like that.

A burning flash rolled over her, emanating from her tattoo and turning her insides to liquid. Cormac. All her other worries dropped away as she soaped her breasts, thinking about how he touched them. She wanted him. She could almost feel his mouth sucking on her flesh.

Her hands smoothed down her belly. She spread her legs and rubbed, wishing the fingers sliding through her wet folds were Cormac's.

* * * *

Cormac dropped his feet from the table and groaned. Pinpricks of pleasure rippled over him as his cock thickened. The sigil on his chest almost burned.

Michaela was touching herself and thinking about him.

That was almost enough to make him come, but he managed to control himself long enough to unzip his jeans and spring himself free. Fisting himself, he let her sensations flow over him as he tried not to come before she did.

No one had told him this was what being mated would be like. He muffled a groan in his shoulder as he forced himself to slow down. If it was this incredible now, he might actually pass out when he was able to sink deep into her. He closed his eyes and imagined how he would pleasure her. On her knees, holding her hips high? Then he could reach under her. Against a tree outside?

He could almost see her, right now. She lay back on the steps, her knees too weak to hold her and her legs spread wide. One hand rubbed frantically as she pounded the fingers of her other in deep. She was panting, her chest heaving and so gorgeous he wanted to eat her.

Please let her come. He'd die if she took this precise moment to show her usual self-restraint. His hand moved faster, matching her rhythm.

Then, she called out with a deep shuddering cry. Cormac exploded, stars in front of his eyes as he sagged deep into his chair and felt his cock pulse.

It took him a minute to recover. Then he leapt to his feet in a desperate attempt to tidy up before she came back. The last thing he wanted was to have totally misjudged the situation. It would be awkward if he was standing there with his pants down as she innocently strolled in from her bath and he realized the whole thing had come out of his imagination.

Not that he had. The one thing in this whole crazy mess he was sure of was that Michaela had made herself come in the stream while thinking about him.

Jesus. He was hard again.

Think of rain. Ice. Cold things. He straightened everything out and put the water on for tea with a shaking hand before sinking into a chair. He'd rarely had a more intense experience. The mating bond had both deepened and tightened his connection to her.

The kettle started to boil when Michaela walked in, her hair tied up in a turban. A long lock she'd missed hung down her back in a slight wave.

"Hello," she muttered.

He turned off the stove and poured the water into the teapot, letting the fragrant steam fill the room. "Did you have a refreshing bath?"

Any doubts about the reality of what had happened were put to rest when Michaela's face pinked. She avoided looking him in the face as she tightened the robe. "Very refreshing, thank you."

He wanted her. That's all there was. He sighed. "Sit. We need to discuss our situation."

Instead, she turned in a slow circle, inspecting the room. "This was a tree on the outside."

"I told you it was."

"No, but look." She waved her arm. "This is definitely not a tree."

Cormac tried to see the space as she did. This had been one of his living trees for a long time and he hadn't looked at it in a while, at least not with a stranger's eye. "It's a fey tree."

"That doesn't answer how it made a tree trunk large enough to live in, but only from the inside." She sat down and pulled off her turban, letting the ebony vine of hair unwind down her back. His hand twitched as he thought about wrapping it around his hand to reveal the soft skin at her throat. He could almost see the delicate pulse quicken as he gazed at her. Was his arousal affecting her the same way hers did him? "Cormac?" Her voice went husky, then she coughed. "Excuse me."

She was out of the room and through the curtain before he could speak. Cormac shut his eyes and tried to breathe normally. The mating bond was far more intense than he had anticipated. He ran a shaky hand over his head as he heard Michaela rustling around behind the curtain. To be honest, he had never anticipated it because he never thought he would be mated. It could be that she was a masquerada mated to a fey, or that he was a *caintir*.

Or perhaps because he was Cormac and she was Michaela.

Michaela strode back into the room with a grim expression that said she was ready to tackle multiple unpleasant conversations. "Where am I?" she demanded. "Where exactly is this tree?"

He pulled out some fruit and poured a tall glass of tree sap. "Eat."

"Talk." She crunched into a deep red apple.

"We're in High Park, still in Toronto. Deep in the forest, so not many come by except some coyotes and raccoons."

"That's not High Park out there."

Cormac pointed to another door that lay behind a curtain. "Out that way it is." He ran his hand along the wall. "This is a fey living tree. To others it looks like a regular tree—this one is a chestnut—but it's a portal to the Queendom. We're in both the tree and not-tree."

She chewed for a while, her eyes distant, before she nodded. "Okay."

Cormac waited, but that was all she said. "Okay?"

She laughed, a light and pretty sound that he hadn't heard before. "We're arcana. This is fairly normal when you think about it. Is the portal open?"

He shook his head. "I'm an exile, so mine goes only to a predetermined space outside the Queendom proper." There was a tug on his sigil.

Michaela winced and put a hand to her chest. "I'm sorry." She glanced down, her eyes wide. "I felt you."

"We're mated," he said simply. He caught her gaze with his own. "We're one. It might not have been deliberate, but we need to deal with it. Perhaps in time it will seem normal."

Michaela tugged on her earlobe. "I can't apologize any more for what I did."

Cormac sat down across from her and sliced a golden ripe pear for himself. The juice dripped down his hand. "I'm not trying to make you feel guilty. Mating was never on my list of things to do, but that's moot. Our goal now is to understand how to deal with it."

"You can annul it," she said stubbornly. "You haven't even tried."

There was no point going into the details of what trouble this mating had caused for him, since it would only deepen her guilt. Yet she didn't seem to grasp that there was no way to break a fey mating. "In fact, I have. I spoke to Isindle and she will see if there is a way," he said, handing her a slice of pear. "Though I don't believe there is."

"Oh. Thank you."

"I propose that we focus on the world-ending issues first and then how to break the mating. Or is being mated to me so abhorrent to you that we need to prioritize it?"

She went bright red. "I can wait. Lives are at stake."

Cormac lowered his voice. "Is it that bad being mated, Michaela? To me?"

Michaela dropped her eyes and said nothing.

"Answer me."

"It's not you." Her reply was only a whisper. "It's the situation. Being mated, to anyone."

He nodded. "I know."

Chapter 22

Michaela looked up to see Cormac staring at the wall. This whole thing was her fault and yet she'd only given Cormac a fleeting thought. He hadn't wanted to be mated either.

"You too?" she asked.

"Me too, but I seem to dealing with it better than you." He leaned across the table. "Since we'll be stuck together for quite some time, we should probably discuss it."

Michaela didn't want to talk about why she didn't want to be mated. Wasn't it enough that she didn't? When he spoke to her in that tone, the one that made her think of his hands sliding over her, she felt almost compelled to do his bidding. She didn't like that. It had to be a fey compulsion.

Which, then, she didn't like.

God damn him.

At least it was only desire. There was no more to it. He had no claim on her heart and never would. Even if this entire mating catastrophe hadn't happened, she desired him and would still be in this same position of wanting to yell at him while begging him to hold her down and take her.

Ugh. What was the matter with her? This was intolerable. She couldn't allow emotion to get in the way of her work. Of course being mated was bad—but in the grand scheme of things, it wasn't as bad as world war. She needed to keep perspective.

If her entire being wasn't rebelling under these forced partnerships, having him first as her Watcher and then as her mate, she might be able to view it with the distance that perspective needed.

Mated. She remembered the triumphant smile and cold hands of her first husband and shuddered.

"Why don't you want to be mated?" she evaded.

He shrugged. "I told you. There is no more serious choice for a fey. To be plunged into it like this is…intolerable."

"Is that it?" she probed. There was another reason, she knew it. "Did I take you from a lover?"

He laughed. "No. You? Do you have one?" A muscle in his jaw jumped.

"No."

"Good."

She took the last bite of her apple and put the core down. "We're going to set out some ground rules."

"I'm listening." He sounded serious enough for her to take it at face value. "We need to be able to work together," he added.

Michaela watched him lick the pear juice off his wrist as she tried to summon her thoughts and finally had to force her eyes to the ceiling to not stare.

"You've gone well and beyond the role of Watcher," she said. "You have much to offer. I recommend you continue your active involvement in this investigation in the way we've been approaching it."

"We don't tell Madden?" He cut right to the chase.

Madden. He had nothing left to offer her. "No."

"Works for me."

"We won't talk about the mating until we've come through this crisis. We pretend it didn't happen."

"That will be hard." He pulled his shirt down and wordlessly pointed to his tattoo.

That body. His skin was flawless except for scars that she instinctively knew came from combat. "I want to not talk about it. I want to not refer to it. I want us to act as we did right before I said those words."

"I will try."

"Why try?" This was exasperating. "Can't you do it?"

He shook his head. "Mating is the most significant action a fey can take. I simply can't pretend it means nothing, when to us it means everything."

"I know, but—"

"Michaela. Close your eyes."

"Why?" She eyed him suspiciously.

"It's an experiment."

Reluctantly, she did as he asked.

"Now, clear your mind."

"Meditation?"

"Of a sort. Focus on your present. The now."

It was impossible. Alien thoughts intruded, intense feelings about the wind and cool earth and…Her eyes flew open.

Cormac held up a hand. "Close your eyes."

She did and this time, she felt the same way she did in the pool. A languorous heaviness filled her body and her skin tingled.

She lifted her eyelids a crack to see Cormac watching her intently. His hands hovered over the table in front of him.

"What's going on?" Her voice cracked.

"It's difficult enough for me to try to cope with a mistaken mate, let alone pretend that it's not real. It is. These feelings—you can experience what I do. We're connected and we can't ignore it."

This was her fault. She caused this. The least she could do was try to be understanding. "I truly am sorry."

He grinned at her. "I know. Look, at the minimum, you need to accept it happened. You can't pretend it didn't. It did. Face up to it. We are mated. *Mated.* M-a-t—"

"I can spell," she said sourly.

"—e-d," he finished.

"For now."

"This is not facing up to it."

"I want—" She paused. Cormac was right. She did want to pretend it didn't happen.

"Michaela, what is the problem here? Let this develop and see what happens. There is nothing we can do about it at the moment."

She shuddered at the idea of letting something happen. That's not how she worked. Proper planning made things occur as they should, without leaving things to chance. "We aren't truly mates. It was a mistake."

"True." He shrugged. "Compromise. We continue on, period. I'm still your Watcher, so little is going to change."

This was probably the best she would get out of him and he was right. They couldn't separate even if they wanted to until she solved Hiro's murder.

She nodded. "The last one is no sex."

"Nay," said Cormac amiably. "I refuse."

"We are not going to consummate this false mating."

"So, one, that's not how a fey mating works. The assumption is there was plenty of consummation before the mating to ensure compatibility. The mating is final when you say the words."

"Oh."

"Second, if I have the opportunity to spread your thighs, sink deep inside of you, and fuck you until you cry, I will. In a bloody instant."

Michaela gaped at him and tried to ignore the flood of desire that overwhelmed her. Cormac's eyes were now a dark green and her sigil burned against her. In that moment, she knew that she was well and truly screwed. Cormac was right. No matter what she said, or wanted, they were connected.

She couldn't think about it now. Best to ignore what he said. She cleared her throat. "Umm, the last is." What the hell was last? She couldn't remember. Cormac's steady gaze on her mouth was not helping. Work? Was it about work?

"We, uh, get to work."

Cormac nodded. "I am in full agreement with this last point, particularly where it does not interfere with your second point."

He'd rendered her speechless again. Never in her life had she come across a man who so unashamedly asserted what he wanted.

While she was still thinking about this, and how she desperately wanted to hear more, Cormac pulled out Hiro's phone.

"While you were recovering, I went through Hiro's communication." His professional tone brought her back to her senses.

Priorities, Michaela. End of the world. War.

Sex with Cormac.

Michaela reached for some almonds. "Tell me."

"This is bigger than Hiro. He's with Frieda. Or was. I still can't tell who he was talking to because the texts are only his. Frieda is setting up bases here in North America. Eric was right about their membership. It's grown. Vampires, weres, all of them."

Michaela let out a controlled breath. "All reporting to Frieda?"

"She's somehow convinced them that once the humans are dominated, all the arcane races will be left to their own devices."

"She's lying. Iverson was all about domination. Masquerada at the top."

Cormac sent the phone spinning lazily across the counter. It came to rest by her hand and she pulled away. That battered black rectangle had transformed into a beacon of hate. "I have some suspicions."

"About Frieda."

"You were in charge of shutting down Iverson's supporters."

Michaela nodded. Iverson was an internal masquerada issue but as Cormac had pointed out, this was no time for hiding information. "It's still going on. His support was stronger and more deeply rooted than we thought." She paused. "That's why Hiro was in my office. He was looking for information to send them."

"It seems likely."

"Then how did he get my key? The only copies are in security."

Cormac sighed. "Let's go for a walk."

"I don't want to walk." She spoke to his back. He was already headed out the door. With a curse, she stood and followed after him. "Did you not hear me?" she demanded.

"I heard you."

Even more galling than Cormac's high-handed behavior was that Michaela's spirits started to rise the moment she dug her toes into the grass. A deep breath brought fresh air rushing through her bloodstream. Even her step was bouncier. She looked closely at the trees as they walked. "It feels like spring, not autumn." Toronto in November was damp and chilly.

He looked down at her and her breath sucked in. The golden light lit him up like a halo, shadowing the sharp lines of his face. "We're actually near the borders of the fey homeland." He waved lazily to the left and she saw a pale pink glow in the distance. "I can't go in, but this remains open to me."

If this was the borderland, his real home must be magnificent. A pang went through her at his isolation. How terrible to see the home you love and never be able to return. Cormac took the lead through the forest and into a clearing. A small pagoda sat in the center, crowned by sunlight. Vines with big yellow trumpet-like flowers hung down from the sides.

"Come." Cormac motioned her to enter. Michaela sat down on one of the softly padded chairs and let the breeze sweep over her skin. Cormac's smile was crooked. "I come here to think sometimes," he said. "This is designated for exiles, so it's usually quite quiet."

Michaela sat up straight. "How many exiles are there?"

"One. Now. Let's talk."

The brisk corporate voice was jarring in this tranquil retreat, and it didn't help when he moved over to sit beside her. Cormac pulled out a notebook and opened it to a page of what, to Michaela, looked like beautifully rendered runic symbols. "Sorry." He flipped it to English and handed it to her.

His closeness distracted Michaela enough that she had to lean forward to get her eyes to focus on the page. Hiro's messages. Cormac's graceful writing laid out the mind of a traitor exploring his options. She skimmed across the vitriol that seemed to overtake Hiro any time he referred to her, unwilling to read those words of ceaseless revulsion. To be detested this much was shocking only because he had been so good at hiding it. They weren't friends, but she had considered their relationship to be at least professionally cordial. That she was so off base was disconcerting. What else had she been wrong about? Who else?

The more she read, the more Michaela realized concealment seemed to be Hiro's speciality. She jumped to her feet, so fascinated she couldn't stay still. She paced around the pagoda, only distantly aware of Cormac's eyes tracking her, comforting rather than invasive.

When done, she checked the sheaf to see if she'd missed a page. "Is that it?" The last message ended midsentence.

"Unfortunately." Cormac joined her on the grass.

"Damn." The messages definitely described an alliance between Hiro and Frieda's army. More concerning was that Hiro and his mysterious associate seemed to have been in touch with some of the very cells Michaela had been working hard to eradicate.

She held up the papers. "Hiro supplied at least some of those dead humans Eric's teams found."

Cormac nodded. "With vampire collusion. Did you get the sense that they were going willingly or the vamp was using their compulsion?"

"My bet is on willingly. Hiro promised them something." She slapped the papers down. "What? What could a group of masquerada traitors give humans?"

Her question was rhetorical. They both knew the answer. Humans had yearned for arcane powers for millennia.

"Could Oksana be involved?" she said.

Cormac laughed out loud. "Would you include that woman in a highly dangerous and secret plot?"

True. Oksana loved drama, and Madden had kept a close watch on her to make sure she stayed in line. She'd taken it as special interest in her opinions and had preened unbearably under his attention.

"None of this points to why he would be killed."

"Besides looking like you at your desk in your office?"

"I know. They wanted me. I thought so even before I was poisoned." She raised her eyebrows. "At least you know it wasn't for your forest."

"A relief." His light words were betrayed by the dark expression on his face.

"This still doesn't answer why Hiro was in my office," Michaela said. "Or why he was killed there. There's no proof he was spying, although it seems likely."

"I'd almost believe we could chalk it up to an unhealthy obsession with you, but it's too coincidental." He held up his fingers to count off. "One, we have a human in touch with your personal enemies. Two, he's involved with your enemies to overthrow your Hierarch and our entire way of living with the humans, the whole Law. Three, for some reason he's supplying humans to the masquerada to kill."

Michaela thought about this. "Your last point."

"Was as cogent and as well-articulated as the rest."

She resisted an eye-roll. "Is a fallacy. He's supplying the humans and the humans are dying. It's not certain the goal is their death, though."

Cormac tucked his hair behind his ear, and she stared at the thin gold band again. Why did it attract her so much? She had earrings herself. "Then what?"

"The punctures on the remains," she said. "They could be experimenting."

"They could also be very tidy killers."

"Which is the opposite of whoever killed Hiro." All that blood. "We need to talk to Eric. Is there a signal out here?" No comms towers, but who knew what the fey had set up. Maybe hummingbirds took messages.

"Back in the tree." He placed his hand on her back to guide her through and her entire body trembled. His hand was almost large enough to span her waist. For a moment she wanted to retreat into Yuri's huge masque but she restrained herself. There was nothing to be frightened of.

It wasn't fear she was feeling. Her tattoo pulsed and Cormac's hand stiffened on her waist.

Hold on. She cleared her mind and took a few more steps before suddenly thinking of when they had been together in her bed, and Cormac telling her how she would eventually beg for him.

Behind her, she heard a groan and Cormac stumble.

She spun around. He was looking at her with a hot desire that made her thighs shake. Instead of speaking, he simply pressed a hand down on his cock—which she could see through his jeans was already big and thick—and watched her body. He walked towards her, his eyes now on hers.

It only took two steps for her to be backed up against the trunk of a big, smooth birch tree. Her mouth was too dry to speak as she looked up at him.

Slowly, so slowly she had to stifle a moan from the anticipation, he leaned forward until his body almost touched hers. Then he stopped.

What was she supposed to do? Michaela was never uncertain, but this had her thrown for a loop. It was all the more exciting for being unknown. In any other situation, she would have taken the lead and pulled him in.

She didn't know what Cormac wanted her to do.

She shivered as she realized she wasn't sure. For the first time in a long time, she didn't know what she wanted.

* * * *

Alana Delacroix

In the dim recesses of his mind, Cormac knew it was extremely important to get back home and tell Eric Kelton what they'd learned. They could save lives. They might stop a war.

It didn't matter. Michaela Chui stood in front of him, her breath coming in quick gasps from excitement and so aroused that he could feel the desire flow off her in waves. It was physically impossible for him to stop.

She was also nervous and he knew why. He'd prayed for this to happen, but in all of his years, he'd never been lucky enough to encounter it. This was his ultimate fantasy, his eternal wish. A ball-bustingly strong woman who wanted him to take the lead, at least in bed.

Or in the forest. He took a step back. Then another.

"If I do anything you don't want, you say 'flower.' Do you understand?"

She nodded silently, her eyes wide. The thin linen tunic trembled with the rapid beating of her heart.

"Take your shirt off. Slowly."

Michaela hesitated, looking around the clearing as though wondering what the chances were of being observed. Cormac watched her struggle. She wanted to do as he said—he'd seen the pulse leap in her throat—but at the same time, she didn't. Obeying him went against everything she thought about herself and the independence she'd honed over the years.

She took a deep breath, caught the hem of her tunic in both hands, and lifted it off. Cormac's brain nearly shut down. Michaela's hair had caught in one of the buttons and she wrestled briefly with it, all the while exposing her gorgeous body to his gaze. Then she tossed the shirt down on the grass with a defiant gesture and stood proudly in front of him.

Cormac's mouth was dry. She was perfect, standing there in the dappled shade of the tree. Her breasts were high and small, and his hand ached to cup them. She was slender but smoothly muscled, with a dancer's trained physique. Her waist dipped in only slightly.

He reached out and lightly brushed one finger on her left nipple. Instantly her entire body goosebumped.

"Take off the rest of your clothes."

The leggings were tied with a bow at the hips and she pulled it slowly, teasing him, before letting them drop to the ground. She wore nothing underneath.

If Cormac died right now, at this very moment, he would die a happy man. Michaela's thighs were gorgeously full and where they met he saw the thick thatch of hair that called out for his fingers.

Control. He swallowed. She was still nervous, and was forcing her hands to her sides to prevent herself from covering herself from his gaze.

He moved close enough to make sure her nipples rubbed against his rough shirt. To be naked while he was fully clothed would throw her more off-balance and highlight his power over her. He nearly groaned out loud at the thought of it. This was the most excited he had ever been.

Don't fuck this up.

"Keep still." He undid her braid and let her hair unravel, keeping it behind her back. It was so heavy the weight pulled her head back slightly. Michaela. He wanted her. Not only this body, perfect though it was. He wanted everything she was and everything she could be. Wanted to call her his.

Wanted to be hers.

He leaned down to kiss her throat. Under his tongue, he could feel the beat of her pulse, a butterfly's wings under her flesh. Michaela panted under his mouth. Her tongue darted out to lick his ear and he barely stopped himself from pulling out his cock right there.

He dipped a leg between her thighs and she opened them wide, then clenched shut on him, grinding against him.

No. He would dictate her pleasure. Cormac stood back and looked at her, treating himself to a single moment to appreciate the utter eroticism of how she looked. It was time to make her beg. He hardly knew where to start.

Yes, he did. He dropped to his knees and flickered his tongue across her thighs. The soft inner flesh was already slick and he closed his eyes. She was as aroused as him. A soft bite caused her to cry out loud and push her hips out, a wordless ask he was happy to answer. He reached out and drew a single finger across her belly and slowly dropped it between her legs. She moaned and he leaned forward, his tongue flickering across the wet flesh as she ran her hands through his hair.

Now Michaela screamed out loud and pushed frantically against him. "Cormac," she breathed, the first thing she'd said since they began.

"Yes?"

"Please."

He didn't answer. She might be looking for a quick release, but he had other plans. He licked and sucked until she was almost sobbing underneath him, her body flushed and writhing under his touch. He pinched her nipples and bit at her flesh.

"God. Stop. Stop." The words were no more than a moan as Michaela's body started to clench around his fingers. He couldn't take it. Cormac rose swiftly to his feet, releasing himself at the same time. He pushed her thighs apart and cupped her face in his hands and kissed her, his mind a glitter of light.

Then he found himself on his back, halfway across the clearing. In front of him was a huge man, naked and scowling.

It was Yuri. And man, did he look pissed.

Chapter 23

Michaela took another sip of tea, still wishing the floor would open up and swallow her. They were back in the tree after a very fast and horribly uncomfortable walk back through the woods. "I don't know what happened," she finally said. She traced a drop of water into a thin line across the table.

Cormac winced as he took the ice pack off his shoulder and moved it gingerly. "You turned into Yuri and threw me."

"I know. I'm sorry." She had never apologized so much in her life.

To her astonishment, Cormac burst out laughing. "There's nothing to be sorry for. At all."

"I hurt you."

He shook his head. "I pushed you too far, too fast."

No. Please don't let him want to talk about it. She had been the one to bring it up, but now she wanted nothing more than to pretend the entire last hour had never happened. Michaela went bright red as Cormac sat down in front of her. "Were you aroused?" He sounded serious, as if this was important to him.

"Uh, yes." What was wrong with her? She'd never been ashamed of her sexuality. "We should call Eric."

"Soon. We need to talk about this. Did you not want me?"

"I did," she mumbled. God, did she.

"But…" He leaned forward, his dark brows arched in inquiry.

"Nothing." She didn't know. Why so much talking? There didn't need to be so much talking. She must be purple now.

"Like hell," he said amiably. "I kissed you. You don't like being kissed. You told me and I forgot." His gaze held hers. "I apologize. It wasn't my intention."

"It's fine." These were feelings. She did not like to talk about feelings.

Cormac ripped off some bread, slathered it with honey, and handed it to her. "When was the last time?"

Michaela concentrated on keeping her fingers clean as she ate. "For what?"

"You kissed someone. Let them kiss you."

She couldn't take her eyes off his mouth. It would be sweet with honey. "About four hundred years."

"I beg your pardon?" He sounded genuinely shocked.

She sighed. "I don't like it. The idea of it."

"Too intimate?"

"It's not something I enjoy."

"When was the last time you had sex?"

"Do we need to speak about this? Now?"

He considered this as he dipped his finger in the honey and licked it off. She had to look away before she started squirming on the chair. "I think we do. This is important to you and I need to understand it so I don't offend you."

"It wasn't offensive," she protested.

"Right. That's why a Russian giant threw me into a black ash."

He had a point so she grit her teeth. Might as well get this over with. "About two months ago, if you must know." She made sure to find partners semi-regularly, knowing how easy it would be for her to stop trying completely in that area of her life.

"How was it?" He sounded merely curious but Michaela noticed his eyes darken. Was he angry at the thought of her finding release? Or did it arouse him?

She struggled to find a word. "Therapeutic."

He winced. "Aye. Poor bastard."

"I think not. He got what he wanted and so did I. It was mutually satisfactory."

Now he groaned out loud. "I think you rang the death knell of sex. Didn't you want more than mutual satisfaction?"

Michaela struggled to find an answer. Of course she wanted more, wanted the kind of fireworks that came when partners were emotionally involved. But, since she avoided involvement, satisfaction was as good as it got. It was still pretty good.

While she contemplated this, Cormac came over to her side of the table and straddled the bench. She couldn't help but look down.

Even through his jeans she could tell he was hard.

"No," she said stubbornly. "Can you deny that sex is physical? Your *physical* reaction to *physical* stimuli?"

There was a long pause as he thought this through, looking for a trap. Finally he nodded. "I do not deny this."

"Then there we go." She smiled at him and he groaned and dropped his head in his hands.

"Michaela."

"You didn't deny it."

"Do people eat?"

"Of course they do."

"Would you prefer to nibble on a stale crust of bread or sit down to an exquisite meal?"

"It would depend how hungry I was," she said loftily. "Where are you going with this?"

"Be patient. Is there a difference?"

"Fine. Yes."

He stepped closer. "As it is with sex. You can enjoy it because your body wants to release some tension. That's your mutual satisfaction. Or, you can revel in it bite after delicious bite."

"It's still a release, and when it's done, it's done."

"Michaela."

"What?" Her heart beat so hard that she could barely form the words. Was this his reaction or her own? Where did the mating connection stop and start?

He frowned. "That's it. Michaela."

"Why do you keep saying my name?"

"Michaela is as much a masque as Yuri. She's tough as nails. Emotionally closed."

He was making it sound like it was a bad thing. She opened her mouth to protest, but he put a finger on her lips. "Listen. Think about it. Maybe Miaoling will be able to enjoy what Michaela can't let herself experience. Openness. Vulnerability."

Experiencing those things was the exact reason she had hidden Miaoling. Before she could answer, her cell phone buzzed. Michaela grabbed at it guiltily, grateful to have a valid excuse to stop this conversation.

It was Eric, checking in. She put it on speakerphone and filled him in on what they'd learned from Hiro's phone. Mentioning that Hiro was probably killed as a case of mistaken identity wasn't useful, so she kept that back. That was her problem, not Eric's. He had enough to deal with.

"This is not great news," he finally said. He sounded tinny, as though he was speaking through a tunnel and underwater. Where was this tree, exactly in terms of space-time? Most arcana eventually gave up trying to understand each other's magic and simply accepted it without thinking too critically about the mechanics, like Wi-Fi or the judicial system.

"There's more." Michaela went over her experimentation theory.

"It sounds crazy, but I can't discount it," Eric said. "Are you ready to come back? I need you here."

"Tomorrow," interrupted Cormac. "She needs one more night."

"Fine. Come straight to the house and Stephan will meet you. I want you two working together on this."

"We three," Michaela said without thinking. "Cormac too."

"Naturally," Eric said, sounding surprised. "I never doubted your mate would be part of this."

She caught Cormac's eye across the table, but his expression was unreadable. Was he angry she'd included him without asking? Her mate. Not for long, though. Just until this mess was all sorted.

"Eric," Cormac said. "The favor I asked."

"All good," he said immediately. "I've got two teams on her. Well hidden."

"Thank you."

They ended the call and Michaela raised an eyebrow. "Favor?"

"I asked him to watch Ivy while we were here."

"You did?" Tears sprung into her eyes. "I…thank you."

"You're welcome. Thank you for telling Eric I would be part of the team." He gave a small, formal nod.

"You're welcome." She smiled. There was a moment of silence, then she coughed. Time to change the subject. "You know, you promised me you'd show me your practice. My muscles are stiff."

He rose up and held a hand out to her. "I know the perfect place."

Chapter 24

Cormac gathered some mats as Michaela filled a bottle with water. Exercise would be a good idea. A great idea. His mind felt almost fragmented and the structured, flowing poses of the *dolmatan* would help refresh him.

He led the way to a small clearing that he'd found by chance a decade ago. Trees sheltered it from the wind and provided welcome shade. Michaela gave a delighted gasp and he felt as pleased as if he'd created it just for her. In the clearing were few sounds beyond the whisper of the wind through the elm leaves and the soft rustle of grass under their feet. He'd taken care to keep the clearing tidy and the practice area was clear of twigs and stones and had been closely scythed.

"Will you start?" she asked. She stripped off her long-sleeved top and stood in a black tank and the loose pants he'd found for her.

Not surprisingly, Michaela was a quick study, following his movements as if she was born to the knowledge. As he led her through the final sequence—a series of deep twisting bends designed to recall a windstorm, he was astounded to find that her breath remained smooth and steady. She didn't even break a sweat.

"I usually do it several times," Cormac said when they finished.

She nodded and moved through the sequence again. Cormac simply watched and tried to keep his jaw from hitting the ground. It had taken him years to learn all fifty-three poses properly. He'd heard the masquerada were physically gifted, as expected from a race of adept mimics, but he'd never seen it in action quite like this. Michaela was as strong as a warrior and as graceful as a dancer.

He joined her for the last sequence, finding a quiet peace in their joint exercise. He'd missed this, he admitted, being with another as they worked in tandem. When they finished, both simply stopped to absorb the world around them. For Cormac, this was the most dangerous moment, when the lure of the *dolma* came as a physical tug.

A quick shake of the head and the temptation was broken. "Your turn," he said.

Michaela blinked away from the trees she had been contemplating with a puzzled expression. "I think they're speaking."

"Trees like to talk. You can sense them now because you are mated to a fey." And a *caintir*.

She nodded as if this made sense and moved into the first tai chi pose, with her knee bent and arm outstretched. This time Cormac followed. He'd heard of tai chi in his travels, of course, seen the lines of men and women at dawn in parks and along waterfronts, but he'd never tried it himself. There was little challenge to his body, but Michaela's soft voice as she named the poses soothed his mind. His sigil radiated warmth as though he'd dipped it in sunlight.

He could see a matching reaction in Michaela. Even as she bent and stretched, an unconscious tension seemed to go out of her. Like him, she was eased by their connection.

By mutual agreement, they lay down on their mats when finished, searching for a few more moments of tranquil contemplation. A surge of contentment ran bone deep and his sigil fluttered against his very heart.

Michaela gasped and put her hand to her chest. "The tattoo," she said wonderingly. "It moved."

"It's more than a tattoo," Cormac said. Their voices were small under the canopy of branching elms that stood over them.

"You called it a sigil. Why do we have it?"

"We don't know. It's one of the mysteries of the mating. Most think it's the physical representation of the bond."

"It's more than a representation," Michaela accused. "It connects us for real. How could it do that?"

Cormac shook his head and sat up to wrap his arms around his bent legs. "Magic? I've never been mated, or know many who have."

"Impossible. Fey don't mate?"

"Not often." He patted the spot where his sigil lay. "It's permanent, you know. Forever."

"So you keep telling me. What exactly do you mean?" She sat up as well. "What kind of forever are we talking about?"

"You won't like it."

She laughed wryly. "Will me not liking it change it?"

"Not at all."

Cormac rubbed his eyes. How much should he tell her? They were mated, which meant there should be no secrets. Yet they were only mated because of a mistake, almost a bureaucratic error, so he shouldn't be bound by the same expectations as a real mate, one with whom he had jointly discussed the gravity of the situation and the depth of commitment before coming to a mutual decision. He could get away with telling her most but not all, he decided. He should probably limit the information to the mating bond and not get sidetracked with things like being a *caintir*.

"You're trying to decide how much to tell me," she accused.

"I am," he admitted. That would at least prepare her for the bad news. "What do you want to know?"

"You said the bond was serious," she said promptly. "What does that mean, exactly?"

Figures she'd start with the big one. He took a breath, then ripped off the bandage. "Until we die."

A small frown twitched her mouth. "That is a very long time. What if only one of us dies? What happens to the other?"

"Death. Usually within a week. Sometimes at the same moment." For the lucky ones.

"You don't think we can fix this?"

"Isindle is a very good scholar, but I don't think she will find us a solution."

"Even though I'm not fey?"

"I don't think so. The bond took."

"Okay." She thought about it. "Can anything break this bond?"

He raised his face to the sky to feel the warmth of the sun. "No."

She covered her face in her hands. "Seeing a pattern here." Her voice was muffled.

"I'm sorry."

"We're always apologizing." She laughed wearily. "Another thing to blame on the poisoner. Do we have to be together? I mean, what if we're bonded but live separate lives?"

"Do you want to?" The question came out before he could check himself and he found himself holding his breath for her answer. This was the first time he'd had a true partner in centuries. He wasn't sure how he felt about it himself.

"I want to know the parameters of what we're dealing with." She skirted the question.

"I don't know. I've heard that it weakens each partner. The bond is meant to keep us together. The forest wants our combined strength."

"Did you tell me the truth when I asked if I took you from someone?" she asked in a voice so low he could barely hear her. "Another man or woman?"

"I did." He watched her carefully and was surprised to see her look relieved. Well, he didn't blame her. It was hard enough to be mated to someone you didn't plan to be, let alone a person who resented you for taking them from their true love. Doubt crept in. He was fairly sure Michaela had been alone, but they didn't know each other that well. "What of you? Did you tell the truth about whether the bond stole you from another?"

She shook her head and he exhaled, relief filling him. "What else do you want to know?"

Michaela walked to the edge of the forest. "This is utterly ludicrous," she said finally.

He twisted to look at her. "Which part? The surprise mating, the magical tattoos, or the simultaneous death?"

"All of it, but mostly what you said about the forest's approval. Why does the forest even care?"

He saw the gap in her understanding. It wasn't unusual. Many arcana simply thought the fey had a generic connection to their trees, like pets. Nothing could be further from the truth. "Some background might be useful here. You've heard the fey are soulless?"

"Yes."

"It's not true. We place our souls to care for our forests. My soul resides in my red oak."

"Since when?" she asked. "Are you born with one? A soul?"

"There is a ceremony when we're quite young when we become bonded to our forests. They take it then."

"When fey mate"—she paused, thinking it through—"it's not only individuals, is it? I'm connected to your forest?"

"Exactly. Your actions can rebound on it, as mine would on yours if you had one."

"I don't get why your forest would have approved this since I don't." She frowned. "It's bizarre to talk about trees this way."

"The forest is more than trees. It has a spirit, part of the *dolma*."

"Nature."

"The natural world, yes. As for your question, I can't tell you why it did either. I can't speak with it in exile."

"Is it hard?"

"Yes." He left it at that and decided to change the topic before he ended up telling her about being a *caintir*. He would trust his mate with his life, but that...that was different. "Your masques."

"What about them?" She sounded defensive.

"Today I was surprised by Yuri's appearance. Will that happen often?"

Michaela turned suddenly serious. "It's the same risk as a werewoman shifting, or a vampire sinking her fangs in unexpectedly. Today was a mistake and should never have happened."

"I won't put you to the test again." He leaned over her and pushed her back into the grass. "I promise."

She curled into him, trusting, her face buried into his chest. He bent down and kissed the top of her head softly, loving how his lips almost slid across the smoothness of her hair. It was sleek as mink and as dark as a night forest.

Michaela lifted her head but he was careful to avoid her lips. She relaxed under his touch, melting into him, warm from the sun and exercise and he pulled her even closer, so they touched down the full length of their bodies.

He wouldn't fuck this up this time. He couldn't, because if he had to go another day without her, he would die. A soft moan escaped her lips and he flipped them so that she was on top. He would give her the knowledge she could end this any moment but kept a firm grip on her hips. She would feel desired. She would know how much he wanted her.

She pulled back to nibble on his ear, causing him to see stars. Her bites were sharp enough to hurt perfectly. Michaela's hands came up and stroked his chest. When her fingertips slid over his sigil, they both trembled in unison. Her eyes widened and she bent her head to lick at the green brand on his flesh.

Cormac groaned out loud. It was as though the soft feel of her tongue had been amplified to fill his entire self. Michaela gasped and rolled over, urging him with her and on top of her.

He couldn't stop. With a single tug, he ripped off the loose pants and pressed her thighs open. She tilted her hips up as he buried himself in deep.

Then he stayed there for a moment, letting her get used to him and forcing himself into an inner calm. He'd make this perfect for her.

"Now," she said.

Cormac raised himself up on his hands as he pulled almost completely out then thrust in hard. Michaela lay below him, fully revealed. He could hardly bear it. Her nipples had turned a gorgeous raspberry and he leaned down to lick each one, feeling each grow in his mouth. Her eyes were wide and fixed on his cock as it slowly slid in and out of her. He glanced down but the sight of himself entering her was too much. He wouldn't be able to hold back.

She moved her hips against him, wordlessly urging him to go faster, deeper. Cormac was happy to oblige. She was perfect. Her body shook against him.

He buried his face in her shoulder as he burned into her one last time.

She screamed, a sound of utter release that he echoed a second later as he felt her come deep inside his mind. Their bodies came together and he could feel the flutters as she came. His vision was almost black.

Never had he experienced anything like that. The mating bond had intensified every sensation until he could barely think.

Cormac rolled them over so he could wrap his arms around her. Michaela was still trembling against his chest, and he covered her hair with kisses.

"I..." She didn't even finish the sentence.

"Yeah." He wasn't doing much better.

"That was."

"It was."

That seemed to be enough for her. She stretched, smiling in a way he'd never seen, her heart in her eyes. Miaoling instead of Michaela. He opened his mouth and then shut it again, knowing that whatever he said would be the wrong thing. Instead he held her close and for a brief and shining moment, it seemed like a promise.

Chapter 25

Later that afternoon, Michaela sat at the table and nibbled on some of the flowers they'd gathered. Cormac had insisted she take it easy—medic's orders—and for the first time in a long time, she'd simply enjoyed time passing without worrying. There were no lists. No deadlines, self-imposed or other. She'd gone for another bath in that strangely effervescent stream. Cormac had taken her for a walk and brought her almost to silence by his encyclopedic knowledge of every plant, animal, and even cloud type they'd encountered.

She even gradually became more used to the sigil on her chest. She'd demanded they do some experimentation—she hadn't changed *that* much—and forced Cormac to try different emotions so she could feel them. To his credit, he had tried. She let him stop after the fifth attempt.

"I can't do it," he said, exasperated. "You need to actually scare me."

Unfortunately, it had proved almost impossible to do that too. The sigil had given them such an intimate awareness of the other that it acted as an early-warning system. It wasn't as intrusive as Michaela feared it would be, but it was definitely there.

They had spent most of the day in roving conversation, talking about nothing in particular. Michaela had told him stories of when she was a merchant and the strange things she'd witnessed. The ghost at her uncle's house had intrigued him.

"You saw it?" he asked skeptically.

"She was in the same robes as when she'd died. She'd hanged herself with a belt." It had been an old concubine of her uncle's, and she'd changed the topic before he'd asked more about her life there. It was too pleasant a day.

Cormac poured her another glass of the sweet watery birch sap. "Are you tired?"

"I had two naps."

"Like a cat in the sun," Cormac said with satisfaction. "You enjoyed it."

She had, too, leisurely waking to a plate of berries and cool water by her side. Cormac had been out in the woods somewhere but the sigil told her that he was fine.

After tidying up after their evening meal, they went outside again. Cormac pulled out two blankets from a chest before he followed her out. "Where would you like to go?" he asked.

She pointed to a fallen log a short walk from the door. "Here. I want to watch the stars come out."

He arranged the blankets and they settled down, staring at the sky. The soft hoot of an owl sounded deeper in the woods.

"There was a place like this near my parent's house," she said. "Different plants, of course, but the feeling I had was the same."

"What's that?" Cormac rolled over on his side and propped his head on his hand.

"Peaceful. The house wasn't very happy for me, so I ran out of the back gardens to the bamboo grove whenever I could."

"Weren't you watched?"

Oh, was she. "The *amahs* weren't very attentive. My father's second concubine was kindest to me, but she died." Suicide by poison after Michaela's mother beat her.

"What about when you went to your uncle's house?"

"Was sent," she corrected. "In Melaka. It was Dutch then and much different than home. More alive. I liked the city, liked watching everything going on around me."

"And you became a merchant? How?"

"My uncle tried to marry me off." To another old man, another set of soft, wrinkled hands.

Cormac's eyes were narrow. "Did you go?"

"No." Not this time. "I waited and made my uncle believe I would obey. That was the day I decided to make my own way. I snuck out, took on a boy's masque and wore some servant's clothes. Captain Lu took me on."

Cormac pulled her close. "It was exciting to be at sea?"

Exciting? "Thrilling. I loved it. Captain Lu taught me everything and when he died he left me his ship because he had no sons of his own. The crew were human, so I had to keep bringing on new men so they wouldn't notice I didn't age as they did. No one could tell me what to do. I was in charge."

The stars were sparks against the deep indigo sky. "I had a Captain Lu. Her name was Kiana."

"Tell me." Michaela lay down on the blankets and let Cormac's voice surround her.

"She was Tismelda's sister. Smart, driven, moral. Kind. Generous." He moved so their heads touched. "She trained me as if I was her own."

"What happened?"

"She and Tismelda were never friends. Kiana was to be queen and Tismelda wanted the throne. She's a political animal, Tismelda, and Kiana was not. She wanted what was best for the Queendom. Tismelda bought alliances with promises of land and honor. There were enough greedy families to support her."

He was holding something back, but Michaela didn't want to press him.

Then he sighed. "When Tismelda captured and killed Kiana, the war was over. I was one of the last commanders. I was banished before I healed from my wounds."

"Not killed?"

He laughed bitterly. "If I was dead, how could the queen lord it over me? Banishment is worse. I can't see my tree. My forest is without stewardship. Each year"—he paused—"it's difficult."

He reached for her hand and grasped it hard. For a long time, they lay staring at the stars and taking comfort in each other.

* * * *

The next morning, Michaela stayed curled up in the bed. Cormac had left to take a bath but she'd been too lazy to join him. She'd been so stunned by her honest admission that she was too lazy that she'd simply laid there thinking about it. That was a Miaoling thing to say. Miaoling had always been clear-eyed enough to acknowledge her feelings, even when they brought beatings. She considered that. It was lovely to allow herself to be Miaoling again, to lower her barriers enough to trust that she could be herself without fear that another being would see her vulnerability as weakness. Here in Cormac's enchanted place, it felt right to be herself and to peel back the armor that protected her from the sometimes crushing emotions that came with being a masquerada.

She needed to scale that back. The sex had been amazing. Incredible. Mind-altering. It was still only sex. Physical. She would remember to keep it that way.

She swung her legs out of the bed, feeling good. The poison was probably gone, but it would be wise to have one of Eric's medics check her over.

Someone had poisoned her. She frowned and sat on the floor to stretch her hamstrings. There was no way to get around this. It was a poison deliberately designed for a masquerada.

Hiro had been killed by accident by a knife meant for her. The further mutilation could either be explained as the killer acting out in anger, horrific as that was, or a desperate attempt to cover or mislead.

She dressed quickly and had poured a decadent-smelling cup of flower nectar when her phone rang.

"Stephan!" As always, hearing from him cheered her up.

"How are you feeling?" he demanded.

"Good. Very good."

"That feyman treating you well?"

"He is." She averted her eyes from the tumbled covers of the bed.

"I've been looking into the mating thing." Stephan sounded troubled. "It's not looking good for you."

She drew out a chair and sat down. "I know. He told me about it."

"I've got hope, though. Caro and Evie are on it."

Caro was one of the most tenacious journalists on the planet and Evie was an unsurpassed data shark. They were basically a research dream team. "Thank you." Sex was great and all, but Michaela still hated the idea of a forced bonding.

"Eric said you were coming back today so I wanted to check in. You only come back if you feel ready, understand? We can survive without you another few days."

"No, you can't." She smiled at the phone.

"Yeah, I know. Seriously, though, your recovery comes first. You won't be much use to us if you keep passing out in the war room."

"I'm good, Stephan." She lowered her voice. "I want to come back."

There was a short pause. "We're here for you, Mike. Always."

"Thanks."

"By the way, Estelle is going to join us," he said. It was a good try at being casual.

"Estelle?" She refrained from saying, *Your vampire ex-girlfriend?* He didn't need to hear it and she definitely didn't need to hear another explanation of how it had gone wrong and how they'd decided to be friends and that he was completely fine with that.

"She's a bit more than a vampire and she can help us. I'll let her tell you."

More than a vampire? Interesting. Estelle was one of Caro's best friends. Michaela had liked her more every time they'd met but she'd always been under the impression that Estelle was more concerned with Estelle than with the politics swirling around her.

They chatted for a few more minutes and she ended the call when Cormac came back into the tree. He glanced at the phone in her hand. "All good?"

"Stephan. I told him I was coming back today, after I meet Ivy and her parents for lunch." She'd almost forgotten until Stephan had mentioned that it was Sunday. Time seemed to run on a different clock in the tree. Michaela observed Cormac, who stood shirtless and with wet hair. He was always clean-shaven and she wondered if fey even grew beards. There was a lot to learn about her mate.

Wait. What was that? Mate in name, only.

"We sorted that out with Eric already." Cormac pulled on a black T-shirt that did nothing to hide the perfection of his chest. He also looked pissed and that was what eventually drew Michaela's attention.

"Yes, he was confirming."

"I don't like it."

"You what?" She would give him the benefit of the doubt and not automatically assume he was about to go caveman on her.

"You are my mate. He has no right to you."

And...he blew it. She didn't even know what to say at first; there were so many things wrong with his head.

He kept digging the hole as she stared openmouthed. "Protecting you is my responsibility," he said, throwing his towel into the corner of the room. "Not another man's."

That was enough. She held up her hand. "Let me stop you right there. I'm going to talk and you're going to listen."

"Michaela, I—"

"I *said* you were going to listen. Stephan is my colleague and friend. You think you can dictate who I will and will not speak to?"

His lips thinned and eyes darkened but he simply crossed his arms over his chest. She continued, surprising herself with her calm. "I protect myself. As we've discussed before. In fact, so many times I'm tired of discussing it at all. Last, no one, especially you, who have known me the least amount of time, has any fucking right over me. Mates means nothing to me, Cormac. It was a mistake, okay? All this is a mistake."

"Yesterday?" he said stiffly.

"Was great, but I fail to see how sex suddenly transformed me into a possession." The pent-up anger suddenly filled her. Her whole life she'd fought to be treated on her own terms, not owned by someone stronger than her. Her mouth filled with bitterness as she remembered her parents and her uncle and she shoved the thoughts out of her mind. They were gone. Cormac was here and he was going to treat her as Michaela. Not his toy.

"I can't help it," he said. "You're mine."

She shook her head, almost unable to speak over her anger. "No, that's exactly what I'm saying. I'm not. Not ever. So deal with it."

They stood in the tree, glaring at each other, before Cormac gave an exaggerated and extremely irritating shrug. "Fine," he said. "Then let's get you to your *friends.*"

Chapter 26

Saying that he needed to go for a walk in the woods before they left may have sounded like a weak excuse, but it was true. A few more moments in this in-between place, the exile's woods, would help to calm him before he made a complete fool of himself about Stephan. He lifted his face to the sky and let the shade of the leaves cool his skin.

"You might as well come out." He could feel the intruder lurking.

"The queen is not pleased with you." Rendell stepped out from behind a tree.

"Nothing new there." As if he needed this, right now.

"I've been sent to inform you that the queen is considering taking Yetting Hill as her property." Rendell's voice was a purr of satisfaction.

Impossible. "By law the forest has to be offered by free will. I don't recall making an offer."

"You mated."

"As you so promptly told Tismelda, yes."

"Michaela Chui is a masquerada." Rendell's voice implied that mating a masquerada was a mere step up from joining with, say, a marmoset. "But she is still intelligent. I thought she would have known better."

Cormac wouldn't let the little weasel get to him. "The forest?"

"You broke your exile agreement, Redoak." Rendell shook his head. "Too bad."

When Rendell disappeared, the birds rose in a chorus, as if they'd been silenced during their conversation. Cormac stood in the clearing, staring at the place where Rendell had stood. Broken his exile? How? He needed to find his exile decree, now.

As he made his way to the tree, he heard Michaela mumbling to herself. She looked up, pale with two bright spots high on her cheekbones. "Are you ready?"

"Soon." Even distracted by his concern about breaking his exile, Cormac couldn't help but notice that Michaela's voice was toneless. He didn't like that it had to do with him but right now…He brushed past her to throw open a trunk that lay on the floor. The decree was wrapped in linen tucked in the very bottom.

She followed him over and watched as he unwrapped and unrolled the parchment. "What's that?"

He stayed silent, so she came around and read over his shoulder. "Oh."

Should Cormac Redoak, Lord of Yetting Forest, come to break his exile, he shall forfeit his ancestral lands to the Crown.

Yes, yes, he remembered that. He skimmed over the rest looking for the list of what counted as breaking exile. He dimly recalled reading it when he'd been forced out, but that had been long ago and nothing had jumped out. Entering the Queendom without permission, threatening the queen and her family, fine, okay, all expected.

His eyes stopped. *Mating without the express permission of the queen.* It wasn't against the law, and so he'd forgotten it was part of his exile. Not like he'd had a choice but it didn't matter. The queen wouldn't care.

He was going to have to go back and try to reason with her. That meant leaving Michaela alone with her enemies—and Stephan.

"Tell me what's going on," Michaela demanded.

Not a chance in hell. Her sense of fair play would crush her with guilt if she knew that her action could lose him his forest, not to mention all of their lives. He tucked the decree into his pocket. "Ready to go?" He wouldn't even hint at a problem.

She narrowed her eyes and muttered something about men, which he accepted silently. If she thought that he was sulking, all the better. "Ready when you are."

They emerged from the side of the tree in the middle of High Park and shivered. Although it had been warm and cloudless where they'd been, Toronto was windswept and rainy with gloomy fog that clung to the trees like shrouds.

"Let's go." Cormac pointed to the east. "Car park is that way."

Michaela followed him silently, still stewing. He glanced behind after they'd walked a few feet to see that the door in the tree they'd left was no longer visible. Had it not been for a newly broken twig by the roots, no one walking by would have even known it was different than the others.

They walked quickly, each caught up in their own thoughts. Cormac's concern had shifted from his forest to Michaela. He didn't like leaving her alone. Someone had tried to kill her, and all he wanted to do was make sure it didn't happen again. Why was that a bad thing? Also, he didn't trust Stephan more than he could throw him, but that was natural.

She needed him. Needed his help, his protection. Why was it so hard for her to admit it?

They got to the top of the hill and Michaela stopped abruptly beside him. Raindrops clung to her skin and hair, making it even darker under the clouds. Her thin jacket stuck to her, outlining the thin lines of her shoulders and arms.

Michaela turned to him. "This is only what you want to see, Cormac."

"What do you mean?"

She pointed at herself. "This is my natural self, but not my only masque. You've seen me shift but you still don't seem to get it. I don't need a man to protect me because I can be a man. I can also protect myself as a woman. This is what it means to be a masquerada."

"How did you know what I was thinking?" he demanded. Were the masquerada mind readers as well?

She put a hand on her hip. "Not hard. You're stomping around and muttering to yourself."

Cormac sighed and ran his hand over his eyes. He was being a dick. "I know you're right. Isindle told me almost the exact same thing when I tried to look out for her." Multiple times, and even after it was clear that her mage's power far outstripped anything he could offer while in exile.

"Please don't tell me you can't help it. That's such a cliché."

Now he laughed. "A true one. I can't."

"You have to."

He sighed. "I'll try," he lied. Anything to at least get them off this topic.

"Good." She paused for a moment. "I was a possession before, you see. When I was younger."

A light rain started to fall, and he pulled them under the shelter covering some small picnic tables. "In China?"

"When I was born, girl-children were not welcomed." She sat on the top of a picnic table with her feet on the bench. "It was different in my family. They saw me as a way to make money."

She shivered and Cormac wrapped his arm around her to keep her warm. He forgot how small Michaela was at times. "What happened?"

"None of our neighbors knew we were arcana. We blended and humans at the time…the men had multiple wives. They all wanted sons. My parents found an old, desperate man and sold me to him."

Cormac held her closer and said nothing.

"I was to make children. I didn't, of course. My parents wanted me to because they could have gotten more money out of an heir, but I took the tea my *amah* had given me."

"Then what happened?"

She laughed grimly. "He died. Luckily not in the room with me. My parents took me back and forced my first shift on me. It…hurt." She paused. "They couldn't wait until I was ready to do it on my own. They wanted me to look different, younger, so they could sell me again."

Cormac's throat was tight. "How many times?"

"Six." She rubbed a dead leaf between her fingers. "When I finally said no more, they sent me to my uncle's in Melaka."

"He did the same thing?"

"He tried. I was named after my mother, Miao Hua." Cormac blinked at this abrupt change of topic but let her speak. "Exquisite Flower."

"What does your name mean?"

"Exquisite Bell. The chime of the bell. My father called me Braying Donkey."

"Tell me more."

Michaela squinted at the drizzle falling outside their shelter. "He thought I owed him for my room and board. That I owed it to the family to increase our wealth. We were an old lineage but our family's masquing abilities varied. I was the strongest and it was my duty to help them all. I thought there was another way I could contribute. He disagreed, said I was too young to know the world and that humans didn't deserve what they had, those riches and prestige."

He sounded like an asshole. Cormac stayed silent, keeping his rage inside.

"He sent me to my uncle in Malaysia. Put me on one of Uncle's merchant ships and sent me off like a package. He was smiling when the junk left."

A couple walked by holding an empty leash in one hand. Behind them bounded a lean husky, rain beading on its fur. It looked into the shelter and paused before being distracted by a fat black squirrel. All around him, life went on.

Michaela sighed, a small sound like that of the young girl who'd been expected to be less than what she was. She gave herself a shake and him a thin smile. "I learned that I was my own protector, there. It's held me in good stead."

She moved his arm off and hopped off the table with her usual grace. "We should get going."

Cormac caught up to her with a few steps. It was hard to tell if the water on her cheeks was rain or tears, but he touched her arm then pulled her into a hard embrace. Words were inadequate, so he gave her a kiss on her wet hair. "You're incredible," he said softly.

Michaela gave a little shake. "We should go," she repeated.

* * * *

The drizzle had turned to rain by the time they reached the car. She started the engine, then rubbed her hands together against the chill damp. "Tell me where to drop you off before I go for lunch."

"I want to come with you."

She didn't even look at him. "Did you not hear a word I said?"

"I'm still your Watcher," he reminded her.

"So you are. As you also tell me, we are connected through our mating bond. That will do for the two hours I'm at dim sum."

Michaela turned out into the light traffic on Bloor Street. At the first red she glanced at her phone and put it back down. Cormac couldn't resist reading *Kings noodle on Spadina. See u soon. xo*

She glared at him. "Done spying?"

There was no defense so he gestured at a little parkette he saw. "I can walk to Eric's from here."

She didn't even look over as he got out of the car but the way she floored the accelerator told him what he needed to know.

That he knew he was in the wrong was not helping him. Rationally, yes. The story of her past had been wrenching and he could see that the woman he knew had been formed out of a crucible. There was nothing he could do to make up for the way her family had degraded her in the distant past.

He steered himself towards the wood and automatically headed southwest. He hadn't wanted to worry her, but her attempted killers would know by now that the second try had failed. Maybe they would try again. Today. He pulled out his phone and shook his head. There was no way Michaela would listen to him now. Better to keep an eye out.

Off to Chinatown.

Chapter 27

Michaela and Ivy left the restaurant together burdened with bags of heavy Styrofoam takeout containers for Eric and the others. They barely managed to get around the corner onto Dundas Street before they burst out laughing. Ivy wiped her eyes.

"Ma really lost it this time," she said admiringly. "What about when she started to cry and said I would never find a doctor to marry if I failed med school?"

Michaela groaned. Ivy's mother had a deeply admirable belief in the benefits of higher education. Ivy wanted to be a doctor and her mother supported that. However, she couldn't hide the fact she also desperately wanted her only daughter to marry a doctor. Ivy's father didn't care who or if his daughter married, but thought any second away from studying was time stolen from a future career.

Ivy's sweet heart-shaped face had taken on Yao's mulish expression as her mother went on—and on—about how Ivy was in school to learn and not work as a barmaid. Michaela had done her best to keep plates and teacups full.

"Anatomy test on Monday," Ivy said regretfully. "Time to hit the books. I'm going to walk back. It's not far."

As she spoke, a plump raindrop splattered on the ground. "I'll drive you," said Michaela.

She and Ivy walked slowly to the car park, laughing about other parts of the lunch. Ivy chatted about what she was learning in school. Michaela listened with real pleasure, wondering what it would have been like to have her learning encouraged like Ivy, who would have every opportunity to learn and grow. Her own past must have been on her mind, to have told

Cormac so much in the park. That was a mistake. She needed to guard herself against such disclosures.

The garage was emptier than she expected for a Saturday. She juggled the three bags of food to get at her keys, deciding to pick up some wine as well after dropping Ivy off. It would be her apology to the others for missing most of today's planning session.

Ivy made a choking noise.

Michaela spun to see four huge men surrounding them. Not human, she knew that instantly. Masquerada, though she didn't know them. Three faced her and the last, who was already reaching his hand out, stared at Ivy with the avid stare of a hunter who had sighted prey.

She didn't hesitate. In a second, she had taken on her toughest, meanest masque. Yuri had none of Michaela's usual intellectual approach. Where Michaela might have hesitated, looking for a more strategic method, Yuri assessed his opponents and attacked in a single moment.

The attacker focused on Ivy had a gun and the girl's wide eyes looked from the weapon to the giant who had burst through her auntie's clothes before she collapsed. Michaela approved. The dead weight would make her harder to move and less likely to get accidentally killed if she tried to run.

She flung out her arm, grateful that Eric loved congee. The hot rice porridge flew out of the bag to explode in the face of her nearest enemy, giving her enough time to drive her foot into his knee and hear a rewarding scream of pain. In the same motion, she turned and brought her elbow into the unprotected throat of the second. He went down.

The gun fired but the bullet went wide. Michaela pulled out her knife, but before she could throw it, a shining blur of man leapt into the fight. Cormac didn't even bother with a weapon but took the masquerada down with a kick to the knees and slammed his head into the ground.

That left the final attacker, who stared at the carnage with wide eyes before pivoting on his heel. He managed to get about four strides before Michaela tackled him, brutally slamming his face into the concrete until it was a gruesome red mess.

When she turned, Cormac had Ivy gathered in his arms. His eyes were green fire and his voice rough. "Into the car."

He tossed her the dropped keys and Michaela didn't hesitate. Cormac lifted Ivy's small body into the backseat. Then he paused and motioned for her to pop the trunk. With one hand he hauled up the closest body and threw it in.

Michaela shifted out of her Yuri masque and was ready to go when Cormac got into the backseat beside Ivy.

"Eric's?" he said.

"Yes. How is she?" It was difficult to keep her attention on the car.

There was a long silence before Cormac responded. "Good. Looks like she knocked her head when she passed out, but no other injuries. What the hell happened there?"

She glanced back in the rearview and her eyes widened. Cormac had the face of a solider—hard, stern, and focused. "You tell me," she said.

"Another attempt to kill you." His voice was tight.

"Why are you here?"

"I was worried about you." He said it simply and honestly.

Their gazes met in the rearview mirror. "Thank you," she said. She had almost expected him to be there, she thought with surprise. She'd known he would be there for her, that she could depend on him.

She turned the corner. Later. She could think about all this later, after Ivy was safe.

* * * *

Cormac looked up when the medic stepped out of Ivy's room. They'd been waiting for over an hour and he thought Michaela's pacing was going to wear a hole in the corridor floor. His sigil throbbed with each step she took, like an alternate heartbeat.

The medic pulled down her mask. "She's asleep."

Michaela sighed with relief and finally stopped pacing. "Her memories?"

"Michaela," said Tom in a warning tone.

She held up a hand, clearly still furious. "I wasn't talking to you."

Cormac bit his lips so as to not interfere. The vampire Estelle appeared behind the medic, pale and with dark circles under her eyes. Her voice rasped when she spoke. "She'll remember feeling dizzy. You can tell her that it was probably stress-related." Estelle fixed her hair with trembling fingers. "I want her to stay here for a day or two at least. Tell her she's at the house of a doctor friend of yours."

"Thank you." Michaela had fought Tom about using Estelle's compulsion abilities to erase Ivy's memories and had only agreed reluctantly when Caro pointed out that she would be doing Ivy a favor.

Cormac had agreed. "Letting her know that she shares the world with what she considers monsters is a huge psychological hit for her. It could be devastating. Let her live her life in peace."

Estelle had offered to work with Ivy, promising to be gentle. "She's good," said Stephan in a stiff voice before excusing himself to check on the attacker they'd pulled out of Michaela's trunk. Estelle had watched him go, her expression tight, before following the medic into the room.

There had been enough there to put Cormac's nerves at rest about Stephan's potential interest in Michaela.

"You know it was for the best," Tom said.

Michaela glared at him. "Stop rubbing it in." Then she sighed. "I know. It's…"

"Taking her memory of a confusing and terrifying attack won't reduce her as a person," he said softly.

Michaela sat down heavily in a chair and Cormac rose to stand beside her. She said nothing, but a small pulse in his sigil told him she was comforted. He put a hand on her shoulder and rubbed it softly.

"Why the attacks on me? It's too coincidental that it's all happening now. There was only one other real attempt in the last six months." She said it so casually. Cormac tried not to react.

Tom shook his head. "Frieda Hanver. The Dawning. It's coming to a head. She must know taking you out would cripple us."

"That would go for any of us," Michaela argued.

"Not quite. After Eric, you are the most likely target, as head of the Advisory Council." He tapped a pen against the table. "Not to feed your ego, but you're the best we have. Losing you would be devastating."

Cormac fought down a rush of pride to focus on the issue at hand. "What about Ivy's security?" asked Cormac. "Today shouldn't have happened."

Tom shook his head. "My fault. I told them to take a break when Ivy was with Michaela. I apologize."

Michaela nodded. "It was reasonable. I want more on her now, and until this is resolved. They're targeting her to get at me."

"I'm going to set a patrol on her when she returns," Tom said. "I've had her apartment checked as well and someone watching it."

"Thank you." Michaela ran a hand over her face.

"We managed to get one of ours heading the police investigation, so we're fine there," Tom said.

One less worry. The masquerada were quick.

"The one you brought back was dead by the way," Tom said. "As in already dead when you pulled him into the car."

"Sorry." Cormac shrugged. "Best I could do."

"We can still get information out of him, although it would have been easier to ask. Still no identification."

They went down to the basement and pulled on gloves and masks before going in to the makeshift autopsy room. Stephan was already suited up, and Cormac was pleased to note that he experienced no overt feelings of dislike.

"This is weird," Stephan announced, looking at the slim, dark body that lay on the table.

Cormac saw the dead attacker was a young man no more than seventeen or eighteen. He looked as though he'd led a rough life, with a missing tooth and an earlobe that looked like it had been chewed off. An old wound. "He looks different."

"He masqued back to his natural self," Michaela said. "That shouldn't happen. We keep our masques when injured or killed."

Then she pointed at the man's arms. "Punctures in the same location as Hiro's wounds and the dead humans in the rebel cells."

"Not a coincidence," said Tom.

"No, and look at this one's skin. At him."

The men stared at the body. Cormac did too, wondering what was so important about the skin.

"Jesus," said Stephan. "Stretch marks."

"What's that mean?" Cormac asked.

Michaela pulled off the shroud and examined the man's skin closely. She gestured to thin shiny lines that crossed over his skin at the arms, legs, and chest. They were definitely stretch marks.

"Masquerada never get stretch marks, no matter how drastic our changes," she told him.

"This is a new way of turning humans." Stephan looked grim. "Not like how we were."

"The punctures are the result of the procedure," Michaela said. "Hiro hated us. Why would he want to be one of us?"

Cormac tapped a gloved finger on the steel table. "Tell me how masquerada are usually turned."

Michaela gestured for Stephan to answer. "It's difficult," he said. "We're totally drained of blood and only given a small dose of masquerada blood to metabolize."

"What's the survival rate?"

"Poor. There are very few of us."

"Recovery time?"

"Weeks if you're lucky. Months for some."

Tom's phone beeped and he pulled off his gloves to check it. "Finally. Ahmed Kalar, aged eighteen," he announced. "Missing for three weeks."

"Family?" Stephan asked.

"They're human."

"As a rule, turned masquerada are extraordinarily powerful," said Michaela. "Ahmed was too young and weak to have been fully recovered in the three weeks he'd been missing."

Cormac looked at the body. "You said that when you were turned, they drained you? Infected you with another masquerada's blood?"

Stephan grimaced. "We prefer not to think of it as infection, but yes."

"What if they used, say, Eric's blood instead of an average masquerada. Would there be a difference in the one being turned?"

"Of course." Stephan shrugged. "The more powerful the donor, the faster and more..." His eyes widened. "Yangzei."

Cormac felt Michaela's body tighten in horror. "Taking the blood of an Ancient would definitely hurry the process."

"Jesus." Stephan shook his head. "We found some unusual traits in the DNA sample. It could be. Frieda has Yangzei."

"She's building herself an army." Michaela walked around the table with her eyes on the body. "Frieda doesn't care how many die, or how powerful they are at shifting. She's going to overwhelm us by numbers."

"Shock troops," said Cormac with sudden understanding. "She's preparing for battle."

Chapter 28

The discovery put Michaela in a somber mood. There was little else to learn from the body, so they returned to find Estelle, Caro, and Eric speaking quietly in the war room. Maps covered two of the walls and laptops projected satellite data on the others.

Michaela reported their findings and Eric shut his eyes. "Do we have any sense on how many she might have turned?"

Tom shook his head. "No idea, but I have to assume it's still not many in the city itself. We'd notice that many more masquerada, even weak ones."

"Frieda is smart. She'll have spread out her operations to make it more difficult to track the missing and dead," said Michaela.

Estelle took a seat near the table and pursed her perfectly painted crimson lips. "It would be easier if we actually knew where that bitch is."

Stephan looked up from his laptop. "Ask and ye shall receive. This came came through a few seconds ago." The display on the wall flashed a new map, this one with shaded zones and a big red dot in the central Atlantic.

Caro squinted. "Please don't tell me she's got the mers on her side."

"Nope. She tried, though, and they told us. She's on her way."

Michaela leaned forward and examined the shading with a sinking feeling. "She has far more sympathizers than I thought."

Estelle nodded. "I can explain that. She's made an alliance with some vampire clans."

That made sense. Although the human population had grown, the Law's strict rule made it more difficult for vampires to feed and forbade them to feed to the death. Although most had accepted that surviving this modern life meant compromise, traditionalists had always protested what they called an attack on their culture. Despite the establishment of blood banks, drinking "dead" blood had not gained a lot of traction.

For some, not even seven hundred years had been enough time to adapt.

Estelle pulled up a complicated flowchart that mapped out the relationships between the different vampire clans and a detailed analysis of the power dynamics within each one. It was impressive.

"How do you know all this?" asked Michaela. This astute assessment did not fit into the idea she had of Estelle as apolitical.

"I have good contacts," Estelle said vaguely.

"No secrets," Stephan said. "Tell them."

She sighed. "I'm what we call the seneschal minor."

Michaela blinked. This was unexpected. Caro, meanwhile, glared at Estelle. "Something you forgot to mention? What is it?"

"Vampires have two parallel lines of authority," said Estelle, her expression wary. "There's the actual clan chief. The chief has moral authority, I guess you'd say, but has no military power. That's the realm of the seneschal."

"Like samurai and with extraordinary psychic abilities," said Eric, looking at Estelle.

Caro went purple. "You didn't tell me?"

"It's a long story and I'm only the deputy," Estelle said, her face a deep red. "My mentor, the seneschal major, is in charge."

"Which means that Estelle has a very good grasp of the politics of the situation," Stephan said in an oddly cagy tone. "She'll eventually take over the job for this hemisphere."

Michaela wondered briefly about both Stephan's tone and why a woman so influential was working as the receptionist in an arcane public relations firm. Then she put it out of mind. Now was not the time for questions, and Estelle looked pained enough. "Good," she said, turning from Estelle to look at the shading on the map. "Because we're going to need it."

Tom made a pot of black tea and a special blend for Michaela from the supplies on the far table. It was as sweet and fragrant as a sunny meadow and as she sipped, small pinpricks came through her sigil. Cormac was watching Stephan closely. Jealousy? Although the idea of being attracted to Stephan was laughable—he was so, well, if not in love, in *something* with Estelle—to have someone feel possessive about her was unusual. She wasn't entirely sure how she felt about it until she thought of Cormac in another woman's arms.

That was unpleasant. Was she jealous as well? The feeling was new and unwelcome. That sort of possessiveness meant emotional connection.

Mind you, she had a stamp on her chest that alerted her to another being's emotional state at all times. *That* was attachment.

Her phone rang and she moved to the other side of the spacious room to take it. "Hello, Madden."

"Where are you?" Her heart sank when she heard the tone of his voice. He was furious.

She answered the question with one of her own. "Is something the matter?"

"I have council members banging down my door wanting to know who is hunting them down and my security chief went missing. That is the matter."

"I was ill." She hadn't liked that Cormac had texted Madden from her phone but accepted the necessity. Now she was glad Cormac had been so evasive. No need for him to know she was poisoned, not after what he'd been like lately.

"So your message said." A slight pause. "Ill. A masquerada with a cold? Unlikely."

She ignored the blatant accusation of a lie. "My team is still onsite and working on the investigations."

"They have reported nothing."

"Because there is nothing to report." Anjali had kept her apprised.

"Days go by and not a single suspect?" Madden sounded almost amused. "How do I explain that to the council?"

"Tell them we're working on it. The councilors are hardly being hunted down. They have nothing to fear."

"I hope you aren't going to tell me that this revolves around you."

Michaela took a deep breath. "Madden. Hiro was in my office, dressed like me. You don't think this is even a possibility?"

"Perhaps a very slight one, but it remains that you are not dead. Michaela, your illness must have weakened you."

She had a sense of foreboding.

"I'm removing you as security chief. Anjali will act in your place."

"This is unnecessary," she said coldly. "Madden, what are you doing?"

"As your mentor, I should have known your limits," he said almost sadly. "I failed you. Rest now. I'll tell the council of your failure."

He hung up before she could reply.

Which was probably good, because all she had to say was not very flattering.

Cormac came over and put a hand on her shoulder. "Madden always was a piece of shit," he said in a conversational tone. His face told a different story. He looked enraged.

Michaela looked around. "You heard?"

They all nodded. "His voice carries," Stephan said.

"That council is a nest of vipers if Madden is in charge," Estelle observed dispassionately. "He claimed clan neutrality in the late eighteenth century, but Madden is the equivalent of a mercenary. He had no loyalty to anyone but himself."

Michaela said nothing. Madden was—had been—her mentor, and she had benefitted greatly from his wisdom. She couldn't fault the logic of his decision to remove her, though she still wanted to tear a strip off him for acting so unreasonably. Part of her felt guilty at having failed him. Most of her, to be honest.

That asshole.

* * * *

Dinner that night was subdued. Michaela had insisted on sitting with Ivy, who was now awake , and Cormac promised to check in after dinner. He wanted to get to know the girl better, and if she fell asleep, well, it would give him time to figure out how to convince the queen to leave his forest alone despite his mating. The meal itself was delicious—the entire arcane world was jealous of Eric's legendary chef, Cynthia—but it might as well have been minced cardboard for all of the enjoyment Cormac got out of it.

He was too focused on the ways he was going to make Madden pay for what he'd said to Michaela.

"*Mei mei*'s strong," said Baptiste, leaning over to speak to Cormac. He sat to Cormac's right and peeled a small but intensely fragrant orange. The old masquerada had come earlier, first to inform Eric that he had been part of the Pharos Council, which had caused Eric to sigh and ask rhetorically which of his trusted advisors weren't, and then to tell Michaela that Madden had prorogued Pharos until Hiro's killer was found. She had simply nodded and gone up to be with Ivy, but Cormac's sigil had sent a pang through him. Baptiste raised his bushy eyebrows. He must have heard the same thing Cormac had—the almost audible *snap* of Michaela cutting what was left of her relationship with Madden.

"How did you know what I was thinking about?" Cormac took an orange for himself. It smelled like bright sunshine.

"What do you know of the masquerada?"

Cormac suddenly realized he and Estelle were the only two outsiders here. "Not much," he admitted. "Probably no more than what the average arcana knows."

Baptiste touched his fingers to the sides of his head as if he was a human fortune-teller. "Let me guess. Michaela has already torn a strip off you for assuming she's weak."

"Not quite." *Time to change the subject.* "You were consecrated to a tree."

"In the bayou, a big, beautiful bald cypress." He gave Cormac a broad, knowing smile. "Good try. To be with a masquerada means you need to be able to embrace change. We can't go without shifting. We have to."

"It's difficult to deal with." Since it was going to be impossible to move the masquerada from this topic, Cormac decided to be honest. "Not knowing who she is."

Estelle leaned over before Baptiste could answer. "She's always Michaela. Always."

Michaela or Miaoling? What was the true masque? The dinner table was no time to discuss it, so he finished his orange and wiped his fingers. "Tell me about being a seneschal."

Baptiste's eyebrows hit the middle of his wrinkled forehead but he stayed silent. His masque today was an elderly grandfather with long, greying locks that reached to his waist and dark eyes weepy with age.

"The training is intense," Estelle said vaguely.

"The psychic training?" He'd always wondered about the range of the vampires' compulsion power. If there was an extreme to the impact a vampire could have on the minds of others, the seneschals would be the ones to possess it.

"Part of it," she said. "You know vampires have compulsion skills and we build on those. You've both felt Madden's, I'm sure."

Baptiste tapped the gnarled walking stick by his side with one bent finger. "He's strong."

"Very. Don't underestimate him."

"How well do you know Madden?" Cormac asked. He made sure to let his gaze rove casually around the table, as if the three of them were talking about nothing more interesting than the weather. Stephan stared at them, his fist clenched around his knife. Cormac gave him a serene smile.

"We had a few of the same teachers, although he's much older than me. He wasn't able to—" She glanced over and grimaced. "Never mind."

Cormac wanted to know more about Madden. "He's not seneschal level."

She laughed. "Did that ever piss him off. Tell me why you want to know about Madden."

This was easy enough to answer truthfully. "I don't trust him, and the way he speaks to Michaela makes me want to slam his head through a wall."

"He's an asshole who accused Michaela of murder," Baptiste said at the same time.

"Legitimate reasons." Estelle turned to reply to one of Eric's remarks and bestow a megawatt smile on Stephan. The deputy clenched his jaw and turned away.

"The problem is, there's not much to tell. We trained together, as I said, but I was much younger than he was. It wasn't until later that I found out the training was in part to weed out the weaker students and direct them into other important clan roles. If you failed a single test, you were automatically out of the running for seneschal."

"Madden failed, obviously," Cormac said.

"The very last test." She looked pensive. "Quite sad, actually. I was sorry for him. He took it well. The trainers were impressed enough by his poise that they recommended him to Wavena. I don't know what for."

Baptiste poured out more water with a shaky hand. "What did he fail?"

She raised her eyebrows. "That, I'm afraid I can't tell you."

That was fair enough. Cormac sipped his tea as he looked around the table. "Can you tell us about your training?"

"Nope." She said it cheerfully. "Treason."

Michaela came into the dining room and was greeted with questions about Ivy. Cormac examined her. She looked tired, with huge dark circles around her eyes. Her long hair was in a loose braid down her back, as if she didn't even have enough energy to tie it up. His sigil pulsed in sympathy with her exhaustion.

Stephan was about to blast her with more questions when Cormac stood up. "Michaela. I want you to rest. I'll bring you food."

Her back stiffened so quickly that he thought he heard it crack. "I'm fine."

He was about to order her to bed when Baptiste and Caro shook their heads almost imperceptibly. He could almost hear their voices chant in unison in his ear. *Don't be a dick.*

Instead, he softened his voice. "Please. Let one of us watch Ivy. Go rest and let me bring you something to eat."

Baptiste put both hands on his stick to haul himself up. "I feel like taking a break and telling some stories. I will sit with her."

"I've given you the room you like, the green one," said Eric. He didn't urge her to rest, though. In fact, he, like the others, seemed fascinated by the exchange between Michaela and Cormac.

Michaela hesitated and Cormac walked over to her. "Rest, Michaela. Let us help."

Chapter 29

It was how he said her name that caused Michaela to give in. Well, simply melt, to be honest.

"I'm a *bit* tired."

Cormac nudged her out of the dining room, and the moment the door closed behind them swept her up into his arms.

Michaela struggled until he bent and kissed her ear. "I'm carrying you to bed," he said firmly. "You look like you're going to pass out."

She couldn't deny that it felt good. Unable to contain the heavy sigh that escaped her, she closed her eyes and let her face rest against his chest. His question seemed to come in from a long distance.

"How's Ivy?"

She roused herself enough to answer, though she kept her eyes closed. "Dozing on and off, and the medic says that's to be expected. All her vitals are strong. She doesn't remember anything and believed the stress story."

He kissed her ear again and Michaela smiled at how comforting it was. Even her sigil radiated a sense of cozy warmth, an encompassing feeling of comfort and safety.

Strange. She hadn't experienced anything like this in a long time. Even with Yao, the pain of their everyday life have been enough to dim the edges of the pleasure she took in his company. Before that, well. As a child she'd been fearful of her father's anger and mother's temper. There had been very few moments of quiet contentment and most of those had been with objects, her books and pens and paper and art, instead of people.

Cormac kicked open the door for the green room and took her right to the bathroom. "Strip down," he said as he turned on the shower and tested the heat. "I'm not even going to watch, as hard as that is. I want you refreshed and between those sheets. You need to rest."

Michaela was about to protest that she was fine and would nap on top of the bed when the warm steam from the shower enveloped her. A shower *would* be lovely. Cormac left and she stripped down and stepped in. Water poured down on her and she simply stood, enjoying the hot needles on her skin.

"I lied."

The shower door opened and Cormac came in, already naked. Michaela felt her eyes widen as she took him in. Cormac was gorgeous. The sigil on his chest, partially hidden by the pendant he never removed, was a bright green. She hardly spared it a glance. She was too busy admiring the rest of him.

"Turn around." His voice was husky. She moved instantly and closed her eyes against the shower spray that beat against her chest. A sweet fragrance filled the shower as Cormac washed her hair.

Michaela sighed as his strong fingers rubbed against her head. Each stroke drew more of the tension and stress out of her. He pushed his thumbs into her shoulders and she bent forward to let him massage her painfully tight muscles. His hands glided across her wet, soapy skin as he worked his way down her arms, back up to her neck, and then over her back. By the time he was done, she was almost sagging.

The shower was filled with heavy steam. Cormac drew her hair over her shoulder, then slid a lathered cloth over her. Her skin tingled from his closeness and the intimacy of his washing. Slowly, he drew the cloth around to her chest. In a single motion, he pulled Michaela back against him as he stroked her breasts and stomach with the cloth. Her legs widened and he dipped the cloth between her thighs, making her jerk against him.

That was all it took. Cormac twisted her around and silently picked her up. With a single motion, he leaned her up against the cool wall of the shower and thrust into her. Michaela moaned into his shoulder.

"Let me do the work," Cormac said into her ear before he bit her earlobe gently. "Let me take care of you."

Even if she had wanted to, she couldn't. Cormac's arms were under her ass and then he hooked one arm under her thigh to open her wider. She buried her face into his chest to muffle her scream of pleasure at how deep he was. Cormac moved slowly, and in the hot swirls of steam, Michaela felt as though she was in a dream.

Michaela could feel her climax coming, slow waves of ecstasy that began to bring her to the edge.

Cormac drove into her again and again. He slammed into her one final time and she cried out loud with the overwhelming sensation. Green fire filled her vision as she shook in his arms. Cormac held her close, whispering something in her ear. He seemed as shaken as she and when he kissed her temple, Michaela could feel a faint flutter as her sigil responded to his.

Cormac released Michaela slowly but kept her tight, as though he was afraid of letting her go. It was a good thing he did, because her legs were like jelly. Silently, he rinsed her off and wrapped her in a luxuriously fluffy towel.

Then he swept her up and carried her to the bed.

Michaela had curled into his arms when the thought came to her that she might not mind being mated to Cormac as much as she thought she would.

* * * *

Cormac made sure Michaela was tucked under the covers and warm before getting up and ordering a tray from the kitchen. She'd be hungry when she woke. He pulled on a pair of jeans and sat on a chair to watch her sleep. He'd prefer to be beside her, pressed against her, but that would be distracting and he wanted to think about Hiro's death.

Occam's razor. The simplest explanation is the likeliest. Right now, the simplest explanation was that a killer went into Michaela's office while Hiro was at her computer, assumed it was her, and struck with that lethal blade. When they'd realized their error, they erupted in that frenzy that had resulted in half of Hiro's blood supply on the ceiling. The gashes on his forearms were to remove proof of Hiro's connection to the Dawning's masquerada.

His gut told him it was Madden. His brain told him there was no reason it should be Madden. He and Michaela might have issues but grisly death was not necessary to dissolve a mentoring relationship.

Shite. He leaned back in the chair and stared up at the ceiling. He needed to find out what happened in that office.

He would need to ask the only witness.

The wood.

He'd avoided contact with the *dolma* since before the war. Kiana herself had sworn him to secrecy, telling him that to let other fey know his power would be a death sentence. "I've managed to cover us until now but Tismelda sees the *caintir* as a threat," she'd said. "Forget you can do this. Forget your training. Live."

When Kiana had revealed her power, her sister had reacted with predictable fear and rage. Kiana had been too moral to use the *dolma* to her advantage where it would risk harming innocents, and this had led to her capture and brutal death. Cormac had learned his lesson. To be a *caintir* was to live in danger. He had done as Kiana had ordered him for centuries. After a while, even the dull ache left him. A little longer, and he no longer remembered what it had been like to have such a deep connection with the world.

Kiana had told him not to do it.

He didn't want to do it.

He had to, even though he knew that her prophecy was correct. The moment he opened himself fully to his *caintir* powers again, he would be a target for Tismelda. The fey queen was paranoid enough already and wouldn't stop until she had him under control and probably dead. His dying forest would be at more risk. All fey feared the extreme power of the *caintir*, their ability to bend all of nature to their will, and Tismelda wouldn't hesitate to play on that fear to justify any actions against him. At least Michaela would be safe—Tismelda would think seriously before going up against a woman under Eric Kelton's protection.

"What are you doing over there?" Michaela's drowsy voice interrupted his thoughts.

He walked over to her. "You only slept for an hour. Are you hungry?"

She yawned. "Yes. And curious about what you're up to."

"Food first." Cormac went to the door and collected the tray that had been left outside. Propping it up on the bed beside her, he uncovered a gorgeous platter of fresh fruit, cheese, and bread.

"Oh, wow," Michaela breathed. She sat up and Cormac's gaze went immediately to her bare breasts. She was perfect. Also, she would be cold. He rose to fetch a robe, which he draped around her shoulders as she attacked a mound of strawberries. Then he stepped back, bemused. Caring for his mate had given him a satisfaction so deep that he would have felt it in his soul, had he possessed one.

"Here." She passed him a berry. "They're perfect. Try one."

He did and realized that he was hungry as well. He joined her on the bed and took another. They ate in companionable silence for a minute, offering each other tidbits from the tray that were particularly delicious.

"Are you ready to tell me what's bothering you?" Michaela asked as she passed him over an almost translucent lychee.

"I want you to hear me out." Despite what had happened between Michaela and her old mentor, her logical, rational mind was underpinned by an extraordinary core of loyalty. Her instinct would be to question any accusations against Madden.

She put down the wedge of cheddar in her hand. "This doesn't sound good."

"I think we need to consider the idea that Madden killed Hiro."

Her eyes narrowed and she pulled the robe tighter around her shoulders. "You're kidding."

"Estelle told me he failed the final test to become a seneschal. He's powerful."

"We knew that, and it has no bearing on why he would kill Hiro."

"Not Hiro, remember. You. We know it was supposed to be you."

"Give me a reason."

"I just know." He pursed his lips as he regarded the bright berry in his fingers like a jeweler assessing a diamond. "I feel it."

"Do you have any proof?"

"No."

"Nothing?"

He should have known that she would demand physical evidence. He had none.

He was going to have to find it.

* * * *

He knew? That was *it*?

There it was, that impulsive part of Cormac she had always shied away from.

"A gut feeling is not proof," she said.

"He tried to get you off the idea you could be the target."

"Yes, because I wasn't the one who was dead."

"He accused you of murder in front of the council."

"I seem to recall you did the same thing, *Watcher*." Michaela pushed the tray away and climbed off the bed, needing to move around.

Madden had acted like a total ass the last few days, but that was the pressure of what was happening. He'd been her mentor for decades, a steady rock she could turn to. A voice for other ways of thinking. She'd respected him.

Madden's own voice appeared in her head, advice from a conversation they'd had years ago. *You have a logical mind*, he'd said. *Except you think too much in terms of the rational. That others will do what is reasonable for success or even survival. All beings are inherently irrational, to some degree.*

Fine, she argued with herself. Even if he was acting irrationally, what good would her death have?

Cormac stood as well. She glared at him and masqued into a version of herself that was a foot taller. The robe now came up to her thighs and Cormac's gaze flickered down her legs before meeting her eyes.

"I wanted to stand up," he said mildly.

"Right. You weren't trying to intimidate me."

He laughed. "To do what? Believe me? Only the facts and your heart will do that." He looked her up and down. "In fact, I don't mind this at all."

As if to underscore his point, he crossed the room and sat in one of the low lounge chairs. Michaela clomped over to him. "Is that all you have? What's his motive?"

"That's been bothering me as well," Cormac said slowly. "Have you considered that Madden might be aligned with Frieda Hanver?"

"You're kidding." She masqued back to her natural self and sat in the chair across from him to see his face. "Why on earth would you even think such a thing? Madden is the chair of the Pharos Council. He's the one person we can absolutely depend on to uphold the Law."

Cormac leaned forward and caught her hand in his. "You're thinking too black and white," he said softly. "Think of the other attempts on your life. Someone wants to kill you. I think it's Madden and he's working with your enemies."

"Why?"

He shrugged. "Power is the best answer. He failed at becoming seneschal. Perhaps Madden is tired of being behind the curtain. He wants everyone to know who he is. Hiro's messages spoke of an ally. Remember, Dev saw them together."

"I don't believe it."

"Don't, or don't want to?"

"I need to think about this," she said. "Alone."

He froze. She thought of tempering the rejection, but the words didn't leave her mouth. The truth was, she'd seen what was behind his accusation.

This was more of Cormac's idiotic jealousy. He hated all of her old friends. Stephan. Madden. Would Eric be next? Yao's poor ghost, already forced to spend eternity away from his ancestral land? Part of being arcana meant that any individual came with an entire around-the-world set of relationship baggage including centuries of love lost, gained, and unrequited. No doubt Cormac had his own.

There was no point in even bringing it up because it would move this argument nowhere. He'd deny it, or admit it and then what? The accusation had been made. He'd accomplished his goal of trying to drive a wedge between her and another man she admired and respected, despite their current rough patch.

"I'm going to get some sleep," she said to his stiff back. "I'll call you when I'm awake." That would at least prevent him from disturbing her.

"You're angry." He touched his hand to his chest.

Thanks to that sigil, she couldn't have any privacy. She didn't even want to think about that. "I'm tired."

Cormac paused at the door. "Rest well," was all he said.

Michaela waited until his footsteps disappeared to jump out of bed and lock the door. Then she turned off the ringer on her phone. No. She contemplated it and turned the phone off completely. Eric could fetch her in person if Ivy woke.

This was a good reminder of why she swore off relationships. Men were too possessive. Look at how her family and then her husbands had tried to control her life. It wasn't enough for Cormac that they were mated. He had to deliberately sow discord between her and the men she cared about.

She went back to bed and pulled the covers over her head. Accusing Madden of killing Hiro was so patently ridiculous that she didn't even know what to say about it. He had no way of getting into her office without Hiro seeing him.

What if they went together? asked a little voice in her mind that sounded too much like Cormac for Michaela's comfort. *What if they were both working for Frieda and they had an argument in your office?*

That was only slightly cheering, because although it still centered on Madden as a traitorous killer, at least he had gone after Hiro deliberately. She wasn't his target.

Cold comfort.

It was stuffy under the thick down blanket and Michaela threw it back and sighed. She might as well admit that Cormac had destroyed any chance she had at getting back to sleep. She turned her phone on and pulled up the photos from the crime scene. It was as repugnant as the first time she'd seen it. This time, though, she used the small screen of the phone to her advantage, zooming into sections of her blood-sprayed office to isolate different areas.

As expected, there was nothing unusual about the splatter patterns. Her team would have caught it if there was. What was she expecting to find? Nothing.

Catching sight of a pad of paper, she found a pen to make a list. The simple action of noting what she knew in tidy lines and columns soothed her mind. Logic always won the day. She'd been thinking with her heart about Cormac's accusations. She paused, pen poised above the pad. With Cormac, she gave in too much to sentiment, allowing her gut to rule her mind. This was not the woman she was.

Reason. Strategy. Rational planning. These were the traits she valued. Not Cormac's wild accusations and leaps of fancy.

Her list made no connections. Nothing new. She expected to find nothing. Was that the problem? What if instead of expecting nothing, she expected...something? She grabbed the phone again. No marks on her office door. With a sigh, she slid her finger on the screen to re-examine all of the areas that she'd given only a cursory check, assuming they were less likely to yield evidence. The upper reaches of the walls were clear. There were no strange trapdoors on the floor—she'd checked years ago after finding one in the kitchen. The bookcase behind her desk. Hiro had been killed from behind, so she examined this carefully and focused on a single book she hadn't noticed before. What was that? A blood smear?

Whatever it was, it was all she had. Michaela made a final note on her pad, then grabbed her clothes.

Time to go into the office.

Chapter 30

Cormac stood outside Michaela's Pharos office. He didn't blame her for being upset, but it was infuriating that she'd decided to blame the messenger, particularly since the messenger happened to be him. He glanced up at the CCTV. His glamour was strong enough that he'd be invisible to any observer, but that advantage would disappear if he entered Michaela's office. Not only was it spelled to prevent arcane advantages such as glamours, but even a security guard as obtuse as Nadia would notice a door opening by itself.

For a long moment, he stared at the heavy oak door. He raised his hand. Lowered it. Did it again. Listened to his heart hammer against his chest. It wasn't fear. More foreboding. The moment he deliberately touched that oaken door, the connection with the wood would open him up to the *dolma*. Tismelda would know who he was and what he could do. Despite the fear, eagerness filled his chest. For Kiana, he'd made a vow on his tree to not use his power, but it had been the equivalent of cutting off a limb. He'd nearly gone mad in those first years of silence. *Caintir* lived in a world of song, speaking with the natural world as easily as they did to other fey.

In some ways, exile had saved him. Had he been forced to stay in the Queendom and never speak with the *dolma*, he would have died from the agony of it.

He hesitated again. Perhaps he could find what he needed a different way. Then he shook his head. There had been three attempts on Michaela's life. Cormac wouldn't let there be another. He touched his sigil. *I'm sorry, Isindle. Forgive me, Kiana.* With a quick, deep breath, and before he could think his way out of it, Cormac reached out for the door.

The moment he made contact, he jerked back.

He couldn't do it. Not even for Michaela. He'd find another way to prove his point.

* * * *

Michaela bent over with a sudden quick burning pain through her chest. Her sigil throbbed for a moment, then subsided, making her wonder if she was imagining things. No doubt. For all she knew, she'd get such a feeling every time Cormac stubbed a toe.

She had no trouble getting into the office, although for a moment she thought Madden might have cancelled her access despite her remaining councilor status. Luckily, it worked, and Nadia merely waved her in with a dour expression. Michaela nodded as she passed. The minute she was back in charge, that one was out.

Although it was only late afternoon, she saw no one and wondered if Madden would be in. Her throat caught when she thought of him. Cormac's accusation was obviously ridiculous, but was there another issue that she hadn't seen? She wasn't one given to much self-doubt, but this had shaken her. They'd been coming to the end of their relationship, but that was natural, nothing to make him turn on her like this. Was she not working as hard as she could? Had she failed him in some way?

Michaela kept her back straight and expression neutral as she walked through the halls, hiding any trepidation from the cameras. She reached her room almost with relief, although she could smell the noxious cleansers used to clean it even in the hallway.

She unlocked the door, turned on the lights, and stepped in.

It was her office, no more and no less. Cleaner than usual, and with her chairs moved out of their usual spots, but other than that, there was no evidence of the brutal murder that had taken place mere days ago. Michaela didn't dwell on that. She had seen plenty of death in her many years and for people far more worthy of her grief.

Instead she pulled out her phone and brought up the image that had caught her interest. Behind her desk was a set of built-in bookcases she had packed tight with volumes that spanned the gamut from true crime to the philosopher Mengzi. Her gaze went between the image and her books. There. It was easy to see why it had been missed. The book spines were a riot of color and the smear blended in.

She went up to examine it closer and held her breath. It was the exact shape and size of a fingerprint, minus any identifying whorls and spirals.

A flat, blank fingerprint.

Like a vampire's.

Michaela's breath whooshed out. *Don't jump to conclusions. That could be any vampire's finger.*

Fine. Assume it wasn't Madden. What was this unidentified vamp doing in her office? Maybe killing Hiro. Maybe coming in after his death.

Why the bookcase? She frowned and looked up at the smear. Up. That's what had bothered her. Whoever it was had reached high. For one of her books?

She stared down at the floor and dropped to her knees. What she had assumed was residue from the cleaning was a faded line across the bottom of the shelves, as though they had been moved back a millimeter.

Michaela jumped back to her feet and eyed the cases as she gnawed on her lip. What was behind her office? She closed her eyes to help recall the convoluted Pharos floor plan.

Madden. Madden's office was on the other side of the wall.

* * * *

Michaela hesitated outside of Madden's office. She knew by the thin band of light under his door that he was inside but she needed a moment to marshal her thoughts. What she had to say was difficult.

Impossible, rather.

The killer had come from Madden's office. Reason told her Cormac was correct and the most likely suspect was Madden, but it was possible that his office had only been used. The first thing she needed to confirm was whether it was possible to move between their offices.

She steeled herself and knocked.

"Enter." As always, his voice was low and calm.

Michaela pushed the door open and stood inside. Madden pushed himself away the table. "Michaela. A pleasant surprise." He gave her a friendly smile. "Sit down. Your health has improved?"

This was so like the old Madden that she paused, suddenly uncertain.

"Yes, thank you. Ready to discuss the transfer back from Anjali."

"There's no hurry, since I've prorogued the council indefinitely. I can't have them here if I can't guarantee their safety."

She stayed close to the door and took in the room. There, to the right and in the corner, a tasseled gold rope hung down. It had been so part of his office that Michaela had hardly registered it before. Now she stared at it. There were no servants' quarters in the Pharos building, no one to summon.

"You killed Hiro." She said it without emphasis, knowing in her gut it was true.

"Don't be ridiculous."

"You did. You came through a door in the bookcase. You killed Hiro. You thought it was me. You saw Hiro's back when he was at my computer and thought it was me. You skinned his arms. I bet you were the one who put Hiro in touch with those rogue masquerada."

Madden's face shifted and she knew that she'd struck home.

"This is no longer your case, councilor." He glanced indifferently at his computer screen. "You should bring your concerns, however outrageous, to Anjali."

"I'm bringing them to you." Anger unfurled in her chest. "I trusted you. You were my mentor. My guide."

Madden's shrug was so supremely uncaring that it hit her like a blow. "You were convenient, Michaela. You masquerada. All the same."

"What?"

"As if I would take one of you into my confidence. I was almost a seneschal. Then you came strolling in, acting as if it was an honor for *me* to work with *you*."

Despite herself, Michaela's eyes blurred with tears. She was struck silent.

Madden stood and she suddenly knew she was in danger. Even as he lifted the gun towards her, she masqued into Yuri and leapt to the side, slamming into the wall hard enough to crack the wood paneling. The sharp crack echoed in her head.

There was no time to think about how to react. Shoving herself away from the wall, Michaela attacked, hoping to knock the gun away.

He fired again, this time skinning her arm. She grunted in pain even as she kicked out. Madden dodged and she landed heavily on the ground.

The heavy oak door burst open. Michaela had twisted behind the desk to protect herself when Madden's gun landed next to her with a thump. She whipped out her hand to grab it, then jumped to her feet.

Madden was fighting with…what? Who? There was definitely someone there, but she couldn't see a thing. Then she caught a faint scent of pine. Cormac. It was Cormac. She swore. There was no way she could shoot with Cormac fighting in close quarters.

Madden's head snapped back with the force of a blow and he tumbled away from Cormac's grasp. As he fell, he reached out, frantically looking for a way to break his fall, and yanked on the pull. The wall slid away noiselessly, revealing Michaela's office in the room beyond. Anjali stood there, hands on her hips and with her mouth open.

"Help us," called Michaela. "Madden killed Hiro."

The witch didn't hesitate. She raised her arms and muttered a quick spell. Wind swept through the rooms, blowing books and papers towards Madden and pinning him in place. When Cormac shimmered and became visible, Madden roared and thrust out both of his arms with a huge effort, catching Cormac on the chin. As the fey stumbled back, Madden ran straight through, ramming into Anjali and shoving her into the wall. The wind stopped.

Then Madden threw open the door and was gone.

Chapter 31

Cormac sprinted past Anjali and into the hall to find Madden had already disappeared. Shite. He turned back. Anjali was on her phone giving a flurry of instructions to the security team and Michaela, still in her Yuri masque, was at Madden's computer.

He slammed the door shut and returned through the now-joined offices. "How hurt are you?" he asked Michaela.

She rumbled a negative and slammed her meaty hands down on the desk. "Nothing here. He must have wiped it or used his phone."

Anjali came back in. "He's gone," she said angrily. "Went out the window."

Michaela's stare was stone-cold. "Nadia let him go. Bring her in for questioning."

The deputy rubbed her eyes. "Too late. Dev said she left in a big hurry."

"Michaela. Are you hurt?" Cormac took a step forward as she returned to her usual self, her stretched-out clothes bagging around her slim frame.

She checked herself over and shrugged. "Grazed my arm." She showed them the thin line of blood and Cormac closed his eyes in relief that the wound was so minor. A bandage and she would be fine.

Of course, he still wanted to make Madden pay for harming her. That was a given.

Anjali's eyes were narrow. "What was that about, sir?"

Michaela bowed to her. "First, thank you. Madden killed Hiro. He thought it was me."

"What?"

"He's not who we thought."

Anjali sagged against the desk. "This is big, isn't it? I've seen the signs myself."

She was a witch, Cormac remembered. "What signs?"

"Ripples in the threads of nature we use for our spells, but I can't tell you more. It's too nebulous." She sighed. "I need to report to my coven."

She left the room. Cormac went to Michaela and took her in his arms. She stood stiffly against him. "How did you know I was here?" she asked.

"I didn't. I came here to get proof for you."

"You were right." She bent her head to his shoulder. "Madden. My old mentor. He hated me." Her voice was wondering, as if she couldn't believe it.

"He's a hate-filled man. It has nothing to do with you. He wants to hurt." Cormac's desire to kill Madden upgraded to a need to kill the treacherous bastard with maximum pain.

Michaela heaved a shaky sigh and pulled away from him. "I should have believed you."

He shrugged. "Well, of course. I'm usually right."

"I…Madden."

Cormac tucked her under his arm, wordlessly urging her to lean on him. She did. "It will hurt for a long time. I know. Then it will pass."

"I can't believe how he tricked me. What else was he lying about?" She pulled away. "What else could he be hiding? Why did he want to kill me?"

Kill Michaela. Tom's comment about how devastating her loss would be. "The Dawning."

She sagged in his arms. "The Dawning. He's how they received their information, not Hiro. We need to get back to Eric's. Right now."

* * * *

The next morning, Cormac opened the door to Eric's busy war room. He'd taken a shift with Ivy so Michaela could finally get the rest she needed.

Michaela looked up from her laptop the moment Cormac approached her. "How's Ivy?"

She looked revitalized and her hair was held up in a high ponytail that made her look so young his heart ached. In the bright early sun, her long, dark eyes caught the light, and he saw flecks of amber deep inside.

"Sleeping well and the medic's pleased. She can probably go home today. He said not to come up. He'll call you when she wakes."

Michaela made a face. "I'd prefer to go up, but fine."

"What are you doing?"

She pointed at the screen. "Yangzei."

Eric came up beside Cormac. "Morning, fey. What about Yangzei?" The Hierarch peered down into his gigantic coffee cup as though willing it to be full again.

"I think he's it." Michaela rubbed her sigil, an unconscious movement that made Cormac catch his breath. That was what he'd been feeling all night. Occasionally, a small quiver had run through his chest, exactly the same feeling that he had now.

It was Michaela's touch.

Michaela cradled her forehead in her hands and stared at the wooden table. Cormac was momentarily distracted by the nape of her neck, as pale as birch bark. "Iverson brought back Yangzei," she said slowly. "The Ancient helped him gain power and is now helping Frieda build her army."

"How could Iverson do that?" asked Eric. "None of us knew where Yangzei was."

Michaela sat up straight. "Only because we didn't look," she said. "How many resources had we put towards finding the Ancient? We were happy enough that he wasn't around."

"We fooled ourselves he was gone." Eric's lips were a thin line. "I fooled myself."

"We had other concerns," said Michaela. "Iverson was motivated. No wallowing, sire."

Eric shot her a wry grin. "No wallowing. As you say, he was motivated."

"It makes sense," said Stephan. "We thought Iverson was able to build his power base a little quickly."

"Then what does Yangzei get out of it?" asked Cormac. "What would an Ancient want?"

The rest stared at him, but it was Eric who finally answered. "I don't know. What I do know is that I can't let it happen. First we stop Frieda. Then the Eye Thief. Stephan, do we have reports of other Ancients appearing?"

Stephan and Tom shared a glance and both shook their heads. "They could be out there, though."

"Not on the vampire side," said Estelle. "Our Ancients are kept in a crypt, and I would know if they were tampered with."

Stephan addressed her without looking in her direction. "How many do you have?"

She gave him a level stare. "Our Ancients are kept in a crypt, and I would know if they were tampered with."

"Fine." He crossed his arms.

Cormac hid a grin and noticed Michaela and Caro very carefully avoiding each other's gaze. Eric cleared his throat. "Right. Good to know. Redoak, is there a threat from Queen Tismelda?"

"Always. Tismelda is greedy."

"What would the queen want?" Tom stood by the window in his usual stiff posture. "The Queendom has always been on the outskirts of the arcane world."

"Land," said Cormac simply. "The humans are taking over forests at an astounding rate. Though people are trying to dial back some of the damage, for some places it's too late."

"The fey depend on the forests here, although their realm is—" Stephan stopped. "Where is it exactly?"

Cormac gave him a tight smile. No need for the masquerada to know. "Existing elsewhere."

Stephan rolled his eyes. "Excellent. Fucking amazing. I'm so glad we can come together for this generous sharing of information and ideas. This meeting has been so instructive."

Eric shot Stephan a warning look. "That makes sense. The Dawning wants to subjugate the humans. There's no guarantee that any arcane race will be more ecologically minded, though."

"In many ways, it won't matter. Queen Tismelda is constrained by the Law, as are we all. If Frieda overthrows that, the fey will be able to act aggressively and openly to protect what we need."

"We?" It wasn't surprising that Caro, the former journalist, was the one who caught the word. "Do you agree with Tismelda?"

Here he was on safer ground. "Not me, but this is not an unpopular philosophy. Not many fey like humans."

"It makes me wonder why we even have the Law anymore." Michaela looked up from her laptop. "Does anyone want it?"

Eric nodded. "We do. I know you're frustrated but the Law is what keeps peace. Don't let Hanver and some disillusioned arcana stop what we know is good."

"I know." Michaela sighed. "I worry."

Cormac ran a finger along her neck. A thrill vibrated his spine when she leaned towards him and lightly touched her hand to his.

"We need a plan," she said. "Eric has laid out our orders. Hanver and the Dawning is our primary concern. Then Yangzei."

"Could be one and the same," warned Tom.

Michaela pushed a button to reveal a concealed whiteboard and flashed a marker. "Time to work it out."

Chapter 32

"I've got it." Stephan tapped frantically at his laptop as the images from the smartboard uploaded to his computer. Michaela clicked the button on the board to get a fresh screen.

"That's our complete asset list. Any additions?" she asked.

The others shook their heads and she went back to her work, sketching a map of the eastern seaboard, the Dawning's current location, and possible landing targets from memory. Stephan flashed up a map—the geography was a match.

Low whistles erupted from around the room, but Michaela was too focused to acknowledge them. She stared at the map, seeing only potentials. Frieda might go south. They had limited intel on her assets, though the mers were feeding constant updates to Evie, Eric's data hound. Evie was too busy running analyses to come join them but she was watching Michaela develop the strategy on her desk screen and suggesting modifications as more information arrived.

You are Frieda. What are your goals?

Abruptly, she took on Frieda's preferred masque, a blond bombshell of a woman. Behind her, Caro hissed. Not surprising, given that this was the face of one of her kidnappers. Knowing Eric would soothe her, Michaela closed her eyes and let Frieda's persona permeate her. The woman was smart, cunning.

She wanted revenge. Michaela opened her eyes and stared thoughtfully at the map. Frieda wanted to strike back at Eric. It was personal.

Madden, though. He wanted power through the end of the Law.

"Frieda will win that struggle," she murmured. Yangzei would be more likely to side with a fellow masquerada, or be under her control.

She shifted back to her own self with a sigh of relief and spoke into the wireless mic. "Evie."

"Here."

"I need you to run simulations based on the landing coordinates I'm sending you. Vary the troop strength."

"Will do."

Michaela paused. "Tom."

"Yeah?"

"You need to map out all of the satellites in the area"—here she gestured at the map—"and match our embedded assets to them. We need to make sure every single one is covered. Madden will want humans to know what's going on when they strike."

Tom nodded. "I'll get my team on it."

"Good." Michaela turned back to the screen, no longer seeing the room with the others. Now it was only her and the plan. She was immersed in possibility and it was her job to bring order to the chaos.

She began to write.

* * * *

Cormac had not realized how much intelligence turned him on. He shifted uncomfortably in his seat, trying to adjust himself without calling attention to how hot he was getting watching Michaela kick some serious strategic ass. Even Eric sat and listened as she created a complete campaign on the fly. Occasionally he or one of the others would ask a question or seek clarification, but for the most part they took notes and nodded. Michaela was the expert here, her generations of experience informing her every decision, and they knew it.

How different from his own methods. His success as a commander had been based on intuition formed by what he'd learned from the *dolma*. It wasn't that he didn't respect commanders who were able to formulate and then act on a plan; it simply wasn't his way.

Perhaps if he'd thought like Michaela during the war, he wouldn't be in this situation now. If he'd had Michaela during the war, Tismelda wouldn't be queen.

Michaela put down the marker and stared at the fortieth or fiftieth board she'd filled. Stephan shook out his hands, wincing. He'd been in charge of making sure every one of Michaela's points, maps, charts, notations, and plots had been captured from the smartboard and Cormac had seen his hands flying over the keyboard as he tried to keep up with Michaela.

His mate's cheeks were flushed and her ponytail had slipped, letting her hair soften around her face. This was a serious moment. Michaela had laid out a plan so comprehensive it made his mind spin. Military commanders would sell their souls to have that level of insight and creativity.

Since Cormac was a crass bastard, all he could think about was getting her into bed.

"There's only one thread we need to knot off," Eric said. "Pharos. Can the councilors be depended on to uphold the Law?"

"No." Cormac knew his answer was brutal but it was honest.

Eric turned to Michaela. "Do you agree?"

"Unfortunately. There were already divisions prior to Hiro's death." She looked at Cormac. "In some ways, I'd say his death was a release on some pressures that were previously hidden."

A huge booming noise echoed through the house and Cormac leapt to his feet as devices on Eric and his team burst out in a flurry of crackling and vibrating.

"Intruder," Tom barked. "Eric, I want you in the security room."

"No," said Eric calmly. "We'll discuss this later but we have an Ancient in play now and the rules have changed. Caro, get to the security room."

Caro was already on her feet and holding a nasty-looking knife. "No."

"Intruder is heading for the medical bay." Tom spoke smoothly into his phone. "Get all nonessential staff out."

"Ivy!" Michaela was up and out the door before Cormac could even react.

"I want all security at the medical bay." Tom ordered his team. "We have a human there. Repeat. After the Hierarch and his consort, the human is the priority."

"Belay that," Eric interrupted. "If they want Ivy, we need her safe."

Cormac only heard the end of this as he sprinted out of the room with Stephan and Estelle at his heels. The sound of gunfire erupted from up ahead. Cormac burned around the corner and nearly fell back as a wave of heat burst out. "Michaela!" He and Stephan huddled against the wall, Estelle tucked behind them.

"He's here," Estelle whispered. The heat died down and her eyes had turned all black. "The Eye Thief. He wants them, the two of them."

Cormac didn't hesitate. In the room, a gigantic shadowy figure wrapped itself around two struggling women. Cormac's heart dropped. Michaela had been caught mid-shift and her features were mixed with those of another. Ivy's face was blank with terror and her mouth open in a silent scream.

Eric's security poured in behind him and paused, uncertain. Cormac knew why: wave upon wave of ancient malevolence emanated from the constantly changing figure in front of them. Even Stephan and Estelle seemed frozen.

Fey magic was from a different realm. Cormac stepped forward. "Release them!"

The primeval masquerada twisted one of its heads to regard him, then returned its attention to Michaela and Ivy. Michaela was still fighting. She needed help. Distraction.

The fey battle cry rose to his lips unbidden and Cormac dove towards the struggling trio. At first, his hands felt nothing, not even Michaela, but he focused and drove his hands deep into the darkest part of his enemy. Yangzei's form slid over and around him, as ephemeral as smoke. Inside was nothing but swirling chaos, thousands upon thousands of Yangzei's masques. Cormac's entire body chilled as though cold fingers dragged along his flesh. The sensation was obscene.

Yangzei must have been diverted because Michaela managed to complete her shift, roaring as she rose to her full height. If Cormac had thought Yuri had been an intimidating masque, he was nothing compared to what Michaela accomplished here. Yangzei's shadow grew as she did, but thinned when Michaela slapped a hand on her sigil.

Cormac groaned as the connection between them lit up. She was pulling something from him, dragging out the fey essence and using it against Yangzei.

Then Michaela quickly bent down and exploded her arms and legs outward, shattering the shadow that enveloped her. The force of Yangzei's disappearance blew Cormac to the ground and for a moment, everything was black.

Chapter 33

"Ivy, come back. Ivy. Come back to me, Ivy." Michaela sat on the floor next to the young woman, who lay on her back, breathing and with her eyes open.

Ivy, her smart, wonderful Ivy, was gone. The medic pushed her away for a series of tests that Michaela knew would be useless. Yangzei had come and taken what he wanted—Ivy's soul, to join the multitude of others that he'd stolen over the eons, all clamoring for escape. The old myths about him were true.

Strong arms wrapped around her. In the aftermath of the attack, it had taken her and Cormac several minutes to come to their senses. Eric, luckily, had been further away and had started issuing orders instantly.

Get the medics.

Secure the house.

Find Yangzei.

The medic leaned back and pulled her stethoscope off her ears. "Physically, she's fine. Breathing and heart rate are good. I'll need to take her to the lab to do neurological testing. She's catatonic."

"I'm coming too."

The medic frowned. "We need some time with her."

"A full security unit will be with her at all times," Eric said. He put his hand on Michaela's shoulder and squeezed hard. "You're hurting, but we need your help here to get her back."

"I'm going with Ivy," Stephan told the medic in a tone that brooked no dissent. "She doesn't leave my sight."

Michaela's throat tightened with tears. "Thank you."

Stephan looked fierce. "We're going to get that bastard," he promised. "Ivy will be well again."

He followed the stretcher out, leaving Michaela staring at the empty place on the floor. All she'd wanted was to keep Ivy safe. Instead, she'd led her enemies straight to her. What defenses would a young human have against any masquerada, let alone Yangzei? Her heart fluttered in her chest as guilt weighed her down. She was the guardian of Yao's line and she'd been the one to lead tragedy to it.

"Stop," Cormac said softly.

She looked up to see him look stern. "What?"

"You think you're to blame."

Michaela's entire body felt heavy and her very skin hurt. How could it not be her fault? "If it hadn't been for me, they wouldn't have found her."

Cormac pulled her close. "I told you about the fey war."

"I know. It led to your exile."

"I had more than a thousand fey under my command. A civil war is hard, Miaoling. It kills the heart of you."

When he called her by her real name, a soft relaxation ran through her body. She listened carefully, knowing that they didn't have much time but craving a forgiveness she knew was impossible for him to give.

"There was a battle. I'd say it was a hard one, but by that point, they were all hard. Queen Tismelda's forces were stronger and she'd supported them with a tougher magic than we could. I ordered my troops into a battle. I knew there was a very good chance they couldn't win."

"What?" She twisted to look at Cormac but he was staring at the wall. A muscle jumped in his jaw and one hand pressed hard against his leg.

"There was one last opportunity. The outcome on the war hinged on control of a single fortress. Tismelda had it and if we could gain it, her supply trains would be disrupted. We were outnumbered but there was a chance, a very small chance, that we could win. I ordered the attack."

He looked down at her. "You know all fey have a special bond with nature."

"Yes."

"Did I mention that some fey are slightly more connected to the *dolma*?"

Michaela raised her eyebrows. "You may have forgotten that."

"Good, because it would have been mostly a lie. They are very much more connected. They're what we call *caintir*. Forest talkers."

"All fey speak to trees, don't they?"

"Not like this. I'm the last one I know of. My trainer Kiana was a *caintir*. It was her downfall. We're feared because of our power."

"What kind of power?"

"Other fey can sense aspects of the dolma, but only *caintir* can bend it to our will. I can speak with animals and trees, and get them to act for me."

"The pigeons," she said.

"That was a mistake. I can't use it without Tismelda knowing and she would do to me as she did with Kiana. A slow, torturous death."

"What happened in the war?"

"I might have been able to use my power to help the troops. It was possible. I don't know. If I had, I would have doomed my sister and our forest. Had she known I was a *caintir*, and that I was willing to use it so openly against her, Tismelda would have stopped at nothing to end me. She would have killed Isindle as a precaution."

"You needed to keep your sister safe." She had been right to discount Rendell's story.

"In the heat of battle, there's often no good decision. I told myself I could bluff my way through but Rendell saw the weakness in my troop formation. I chose my family over my soldiers. You know how this ends. We lost. Most of my people were slaughtered. I heard their death cries in my ears for decades. In my sleep I listened to their accusations. I could have reached out to the *dolma*, caused the trees to form a barrier, the wind to rise. I didn't." He took a deep breath. "It was my fault they were dead. My fault that their children wept. My fault Tismelda was queen."

He stood and pulled her to her feet. "I'm telling you this because it was my fault. I made that decision. You made the decision to guard Ivy for Yao and perhaps—not certainly but perhaps—led Yangzei to her."

His every word beat into her like a drum. Her fault.

"However." Now he placed his hand under her chin and tilted her head up so she looked him right in the eyes. "That doesn't matter. Right now, stewing in fault and guilt are a self-indulgence you can't afford. The question you need to ask isn't whose fault it is."

Michaela nodded, understanding pushing away her doubt. Cormac was right. "What can I do to fix it?"

Cormac kissed her hand. "What can you do to fix it."

Chapter 34

A day later she was no closer to a solution. Cormac and the others had forced her to sleep but her dreams had been so tormented with nightmares she woke more exhausted than when she had gone to her rest. Cormac had been lying in bed beside her and had reached out to pull her close. They had lain silently and his touch had soothed her enough to at least calm her thundering heart.

Michaela stared wide-eyed at the dim shadows on the ceiling. The last twenty-four hours had been maddening. A masquerada had been sent to take Ivy's place in her classes and reply to her mother's texts within the expected two minutes. This was in clear violation of the masquerada tenet of not taking on the masques of others without permission, but Michaela didn't care. She would not complicate Ivy's life more by creating an absence the young woman would need to explain if she became well again.

When. She cursed herself. Not if, when. Because she was going to find Yangzei and pull him apart until she found Ivy's stolen soul.

They'd taken turns staying with the catatonic girl, each doing what they could to whisper assurances and tell stories to help bring Ivy back to them. Michaela had told secrets about Ivy's parents, while Caro had brought in a dog-eared copy of *To Kill a Mockingbird* and settled down to read aloud in a soft Southern-accented voice. Tom had discussed military tactics of the Romans before Estelle displaced him to chat about how to create the perfect red lip. Cormac had told the still girl about Yetting Hill. He'd stopped when he'd caught sight of Michaela listening at the door.

"You make it sound alive," she had said to him. Despite Cormac's impressive storytelling ability, Ivy hadn't moved.

"It is alive."

Now he spoke into the darkness of their bedroom. "I didn't get a chance to ask earlier. Any updates?" Michaela had been working with Eric's team to try to understand what had happened.

Michaela sighed. "Not much. Eric has Evie working with historians to understand more about Yangzei but there's not much hope."

"Why not?"

"We don't know enough," she admitted. "Our archives were largely destroyed during the arcane war. Estelle is checking to see if the vampire historians can shed light on Yangzei and what happened to him."

"I don't know much about the masquerada, but Yangzei's capabilities seem far beyond what any current masquerada is capable of doing."

"They are, but I couldn't tell you if those are what he could do initially, or if his powers have grown over time. We don't even know where he's been hiding, how he found us, or why he attacked Ivy. I can only assume it was on Frieda's orders."

He had said nothing but held her closer until she finally dozed off.

When she dragged herself into the room where Stephan sat with Ivy, he was drawing pictures on her palm with his fingers and murmuring in a soft voice.

"How is she?"

He glanced up and didn't answer. She didn't expect one. The question was a formality. Had there been a change she would have been notified.

"I've been thinking," Stephan said instead. "Perhaps we've been looking at this wrong."

Michaela pulled over a chair to sit on Ivy's other side and gripped the girl's cool, limp hand. Her throat tightened to the point where she could hardly swallow but she ignored it. Breaking down was not going to help Ivy. "I'm listening."

"Sitting here, I've been thinking of the past." He had a distant look on his face as he stared over Michaela's shoulder at the wall. "Thinking about my life before I was taken."

Stephan had been transformed into a masquerada in Africa before he was kidnapped and sold to a sugar plantation. He rarely spoke of his early life. Now he turned his gaze over to her.

"What was your first shift like?"

He'd probably assumed that it had been a gentle and caring experience, as it should have been. Michaela shuddered, still traumatized centuries later. "Not good. I was too young and ill-prepared for what happened."

This was an understatement. It had been brutal and cruel. Masquerada children underwent their first shift in a long ritual after months of training.

She had a week of preparation and then her parents forced her first shift on her by keeping her awake for four days. Michaela had been sold to her second husband a month after.

"Tell me what you saw when it happened," he said.

"What I saw?" she echoed.

"I saw the multitude." He held up his hand to prevent her from speaking. "I don't know what it is, but I felt thousands of masques. So did Eric."

"The multitude." Astonishment caused Michaela to drop Ivy's hand.

"I've spoken to others—Tom for instance—and they all said their focus was inward. I assumed it was different for true-borns." He stared at her with his dark eyes. "You saw it, didn't you?"

"I thought I'd hallucinated it," she said. She'd called it the horde in her head, but it sounded like the same thing—a feeling of endless masques surrounding her and calling her name. They were desperate, wanting her to acknowledge them. She'd completed the shift into a new masque babbling about what she'd seen and had been told she was ridiculously hysterical.

"I have a theory," Stephan said softly. "We know Yangzei as the Eye Thief. We've talked about what this means."

"Souls." She repressed a shudder.

"What if the multitude we sensed are the souls Yangzei has stolen? What if traumatic transformations, like ours, open our eyes to it?"

"It's possible. When I touched Yangzei, I had a similar sensation, like many souls calling to me."

"There's another thing. We're all very strong, you, Eric and I."

She nodded. "But my lineage has pockets of strength, and you need to be strong to survive the transformation, don't you?"

"That's what we thought. What if there's another reason? What if when we shifted, we all connected with that multitude and Yangzei?"

"Well, what if?" She tightened her grip on Ivy's hand, excited by where he was going.

"This might be crazy."

Like any of this could get any crazier. "Go on."

"I think that if I'm right, then we can help Ivy by reconnecting with Yangzei."

Michaela wondered if it was a measure of how tired she was that this sounded like a perfectly reasonable idea. Her mind went straight to the logistics. "We'd need to find him."

"I've thought about that too. Tried meditating, but no go. Cormac?"

Now it was getting a little nuts. Stephan must be tired as well. "Cormac is fey," she reminded him.

"He also has access to an older magic than we do. Your mate was the only one who was able to withstand Yangzei."

She *had* used his energy. She mulled it over. It made sense. "How does that work for actually finding an Ancient?"

Stephan rubbed his dark eyes. "For that, you'll need to ask him."

"Ask who what?" Cormac's voice came from the doorway.

* * * *

Cormac tightened his lips. He wasn't pleased to see Michaela and Stephan together, but they were at least on opposite sides of Ivy's bed. Deep down, he knew he was overreacting. He'd watched Estelle carefully. Vampires were possessive, and if she'd had the slightest suspicion Michaela was competition for Stephan, Estelle would have had her throat. Or tried to. His woman was tough.

Then there was Michaela herself. He could trust his mate. This might not be the relationship she wanted, but she would be true to it until it was annulled.

He didn't know how he felt about that. He had no desire to be mated, but mated to Michaela was not what he expected. Her presence was a comfort more than an interference.

Rendell's comment came back to him, Tismelda's threat to seize his forest. Not much point in being mated if they both ended up dead. Hiro's Japanese forest was in a legal limbo as the executor sorted out his will and refused to communicate with Cormac until he was ready. Damn the man.

Michaela looked up with a tired smile and he moved closer. "We were talking about Yangzei." She filled him in on Stephan's theory.

Cormac stood beside her and looked down at Ivy's face. Although she would still not respond to stimuli, he occasionally thought he saw a small spasm run through her muscles. It was as quick as a blink but left the impression of a powerful internal fight. His gut clenched at the terrors Ivy's soul was experiencing, and that settled what he'd been considering.

"I had a similar feeling during the attack, but I wouldn't know how to use that to our advantage," he said. "I need to see Isindle. Fey magic helped bring Yangzei down. It could be our hope to get back Ivy."

"Your sister is back home."

"I need to return to the Queendom." He'd been mulling it over anyway, considering finding some old allies to help him protect his forest before Tismelda could act on her threat to take it.

Michaela stood abruptly. "Then you break your exile."

Stephan glanced at the two of them and murmured an excuse as he sidled out.

"I think I can help," Cormac said.

Michaela pulled her hand back from where she had laid it on his arm. "When you're executed?"

"Tismelda won't even know I'm there." Michaela didn't need to know about his plans to save Yetting Forest. "I'll meet my sister in a place we both know and be back before you know it."

"How long, exactly?"

"I don't think long."

"That is not an answer." She took a step back and planted both hands on her hips.

"I know." He tugged her close and and rested his chin on her hair. Her sweet tuberose embraced him and he breathed deep. She struggled briefly, then sighed and leaned into him.

"Yangzei is a monster," she mumbled into his chest. Her breath puffed onto his skin. "He could come back while you're gone."

He'd thought of this as well. "He's taken what he wants from Ivy. I need to go. Isindle is the scholar in the family. I'm the muscle."

Her laughter tickled him. "Only that?"

Estelle poked her head into the room and Michaela pulled away from him. "Out you go," Estelle chirped. There were two bright red spots high on her cheeks and her eyes were sparking. "My turn with Ivy. Today I'm going to tell her how to do the perfect smoky eye."

"Ivy doesn't wear make-up," Michaela said absently.

"She will when she hears how easy it is. Now, get some rest." Estelle made a shooing motion with the one hand that was not carrying a briefcase of cosmetics.

Michaela dropped a kiss on Ivy's forehead and left with Cormac. Once out in the hall, she sighed. "I'm lucky," she said simply.

Cormac nodded. While fey families would rally around a member in need, it was rare that friends would interfere or offer intensive support the way Michaela's had.

He led her to the dining room and sat her at the table before going to the buffet that Cynthia had left out. Michaela needed to refuel. He picked out the juiciest fruit and filled a plate with toast and eggs that he placed before her. "Eat."

She picked up a fork without answering. "Isindle," she said. "Tell me more about her."

Cormac poured them some tea. How to describe his sister and do her justice? "She reminds me of a white flower at home we call the star rose. Its vine is so strong you need an axe to cut it. The flowers are delicate enough that a summer breeze can blow off the petals."

Michaela offered him a strawberry. "An iron core, then."

"One that needs to be protected. A star rose that loses its blossoms too many times will wither and die." His parents had been the ones to provide him this analogy when Isindle was a child and absorbed in her books.

"Yet she's a scholar." Michaela sniffed the tea and nodded with unconscious approval.

"The best in the Queendom." It was impossible for Cormac to keep the pride out of his tone. Isindle spent most of her life in either the library or roaming the land hunting for rare books. It was the one area of her life where she was fearless and would take any risk to obtain knowledge. Before his exile, he'd made a private visit to the magehood to insist they send an escort with her at all times and supplied the funds to pay for it. There was no need to tell Isindle, but it was for her own safety. He'd heard she'd once swam a flooding stream to get to a castle that held a text she wanted.

Michaela shoved her plate away. "You're sure she can help Ivy? It's worth the risk?"

Cormac stared out the window. Light streamed through the wide windows and the clouds in the sky were like the wispy breath of a tired goddess. "I think that you have no choice." He paused. "If Yangzei comes back, he will do the same with others as he has done with Ivy, and perhaps on a broader scale."

She planted her elbows on the table and laid her head in her hands. "Eric said as much."

"Since it's also reasonable to assume that every soul that he takes makes him stronger, I think we have to act. We need Isindle's knowledge."

She nodded slowly. "Fey magic is different than that of other arcana."

"Older. We aren't like you. That's why you were able to use mine to fight Yangzei." He touched his sigil.

"You're right."

"Good."

"I still don't like you breaking your exile. Can you not summon her here instead?"

"I tried." It had been his first thought and he'd rushed back to High Park last night while Michaela sat with Ivy. He'd failed. Isindle might be too weak to appear so soon after her last astral visit. Or she might be in danger. More reason to go home.

"Okay." She pushed her chair back. "When do we leave?"

Chapter 35

Cormac ducked into a small, manicured park behind a row of houses. There were no portals into the Queendom he was permitted to use, so he was going to have to do it the hard way. He walked nonchalantly by a group of mothers doing stretches and jumping jacks with their babies in strollers next to them. Hopefully they would be too engrossed with their quads to call the police when they saw a man ducking into the copse of trees by the path.

He glanced back to see if Eric's house was still within sight. At least Michaela had finally seen reason. Caro had come in the middle of their argument—apparently she'd heard them from two floors away—and had whisked his mate away for what had apparently been an effective talk. When Michaela returned, she still looked furious but had been realistic. It was for her own safety. Queen Tismelda was not to be trifled with, and he was already in her bad books. To bring his illegal masquerada mate as he tried to sneak into the Queendom without the queen's knowledge would be in the world of high comedy, it was so absurd.

A couple strolled by, holding hands. They saw Cormac and whispered to each other as he tried to look casual, a regular guy hanging out alone in a bunch of trees. He waited until they were out of sight and sank deeper into the Douglas firs. Better move fast before they came back to check on him.

Cormac reached into his pocket for the knife he'd grabbed before he'd left Eric's house. A quick slice removed the bark from the largest fir and revealed the cold inner wood.

He paused. This was it. Once he carved those three runes into the tree, he was irrevocably committed and completely within the queen's power.

It had to be done. He carved the runes. Whispering a short invocation, he slashed his palm and pressed the cut to the characters. Blood filled the sharp channels and the needles at his feet moved as the wind picked up. Tingles ran from his hand into his body and he shut his eyes. Opening a rogue portal was the roughest way to enter. He groaned as a hundred fists pummeled him and a thousand feet kicked. The air was sucked out of his lungs. He was going to die.

There was someone holding his foot.

* * * *

Before Cormac left for the Queendom, Michaela had watched him pack the few things he would need. They were all weapons.

She'd assessed Eric's knife collection. "Take the throwing blades."

"Good choice." He'd wrapped the holsters around his wrists and thighs as she'd taken a moment to admire him.

"We're mated," she'd said.

He had smiled in a way that had made her flush. "A fact of which I am most intimately aware."

"If you die there, then I die here?"

He'd paused only for a moment. "I'm not planning to die."

"Hypothetically. Until it gets fixed, we're in this together. It's not like someone can suddenly take over your place as my mate."

His eyes darkened as he'd laid a hand on her arm. "No one else will take my place as your mate, Miaoling."

The use of her real name had caused Michaela to catch her breath. It had been so intimate, how he said it. "No," she whispered. "No one else."

"Stay safe here. This is bigger than Hiro and Madden now. You're a target."

"I was before. Also, I've got Stephan and the others." That was a comfort, though Cormac's jaw had twitched as she said it.

Cormac had leaned down and grasped her arms hard as his mouth almost came down on hers. Then he pulled back and instead kissed her ear.

It was Michaela who sought his lips. She cupped his face in her hands and kissed him, lightly at first and then with a passion that took her by surprise. Cormac. Her head spun. She wanted everything she could take from him. Wanted to call him hers.

Wanted to be his.

This was the first kiss she'd shared and the intimacy she so feared instead increased her desire. Their mating bond connected them at a deeper level than she could have imagined.

He pulled her closer and Michaela panted under his mouth. Her tongue darted out to lick his lip. Their bond made every sensation more intense. This kiss was magnified by her feeling him feeling her.

His kiss was such a clear claim that it left her breathless.

"We may have been mated by accident but we are now mated. You're mine."

"Then you're mine." The words came out before she thought but it was true. They belonged to each other now, however it had happened.

"Yes." He kissed the side of her mouth. "I thought that was clear."

Then he had left.

Michaela. Michaela.

She forced her eyes open, the memory of Cormac's earlier kiss still on her lips. It was the only pleasant thing about her current situation. It hurt to blink. "Are we here?"

"Jesus God in my forest." Cormac was almost incandescent with rage, his eyes a bright glowing green. "What the hell happened? You were supposed to stay at Eric's."

"I lied. Why can't I move?" She didn't want to sound anxious but knew her voice had ended on a bit of a squeak.

He shut his eyes. "I know you lied. Why?"

"How about first you tell me why I can't fucking move?" She managed to twist her head slightly and saw that Cormac was in no better shape. Unsure of whether it made her feel better this seemed to be a common side effect of entering the fey realm or worse that neither of them could defend the other, Michaela decided to opt for the former. From what she could see, they were in an isolated meadow, pretty and serene.

"You can't move because I was trying to sneak in here by taking an alternative and rougher route," he said with exaggerated calm. "This is the unfortunate side effect."

"Look, Cormac." This was terrible. She couldn't even argue from a position of power since her body had the strength of jelly. "I know you're upset."

"Aye. Upset is one way to look at it."

"You said if one of us dies, we both die."

Now he groaned. "I don't believe this."

She plowed on. "I talked it over with Caro and she agreed with me. Better we face this together with our combined strength." This was a slight gloss on what Caro had actually said, which had included the phrases *Don't be an idiot, I don't like this,* and *Fine, I'll help but I'm not happy about it.*

"The couple in the forest." He looked unbelieving and shook his head as he looked at her clothes. "Those men were you two. I am such a blind idiot."

"Caro wanted to make sure I was able to follow you here."

Cormac put his hands on his eyes in a series of jerky motions. "You could have died."

"I didn't, though. What's our plan?" She tested out wiggling her toes and fingers and was relieved to find the life coming back into them. Beside her, Cormac did the heavy breathing of a man who was very obviously trying to cope with the woman in his life without going insane. She waited.

"Fine. You win."

"It's not a matter of—"

"No. Enough. The Queendom is dangerous and I am an exile. I can be executed on sight. We are going to get back alive and to do that, you are going to listen to me. Am I understood?"

He spoke to her like a commander and she nodded. This was professional now, and his tone had changed to reflect that.

"I can't send you back alone."

"Then what do we do?"

"We stay here until we recover. It should take an hour for me and then if you are longer, I can at least hide you."

"Are we safe?"

"We're on the edges of the Queendom and in a relatively out-of-the-way area that has an alliance with Yetting. There are no guarantees, but this is as good as it gets for us."

"We need to get to Isindle."

"She lives in the magehood's fortress and I would keep her safe there. We only need her astral body to come. When I'm stronger I can send her a message."

Michaela's mind cleared and she sighed with relief. "Is there a way to speed up this process?"

He snorted. "None. That's why we only use this route in emergencies. It's a bit like working out pins and needles. Keep trying to move. Speed is our friend here. We need to get what we need from Isindle and get out before we're spotted."

A voice from behind them made Michaela's heart drop.

"Oh, I think you're much too late for that."

* * * *

Shite. Naturally the queen would send her most annoying lackey. She must have been monitoring the borders with an eagle eye. This was exactly why Michaela should have stayed at home. Now he had to worry about her. She should be safe and he couldn't keep her safe here.

Why. Did. She. Not. Listen.

"Hello, Rendell." Michaela greeted Queen Tismelda's torturer with an insouciance that Cormac appreciated despite his anger. "How have you been?"

"Councilor. I am astonished to see you. It takes great courage to illegally enter the Queendom, especially as the unlawful mate of an exile." Cormac sensed a grudging admiration in his tone.

"After Cormac told me so much of the beauty of your land, I couldn't rest until I'd seen it."

"Then I can only apologize you will not see more of it." Pleasantries complete, Rendell walked around until he stood in Cormac's line of sight.

"Rendell." Although he had recovered some of the use of his limbs, Cormac didn't move. Better to make Rendell think he was as weak as possible. It might give him an advantage.

Rendell rolled his eyes. "Pathetic." He snapped his fingers at the servants who were out of Cormac's sight. "Treat Councilor Michaela with respect and make sure she is comfortable."

The stress on *Michaela's* comfort was not lost on Cormac. Rough hands stripped his weapons off before rolling him onto a litter they wrapped with linen and attached to a pair of black mules. Michaela gave a gasp of wonder as she was placed in an open-roofed palanquin. Rendell rode a white stag with a rack of antlers so wide Cormac knew only magic was keeping the poor thing's head up. "The queen wishes to see you both immediately."

"Cool." Cormac didn't have to see Rendell's face to know he was pursing his thin lips in distaste. He hated all slang and particularly modern English vernacular. Cormac wasn't a fan himself, but he was willing to embrace anything Rendell disliked.

"I must say that I was surprised you brought your mate here."

Like it was his decision. "You've worked with her."

"Ah. I see. She didn't ask your permission. The queen may like that. Or she may not."

To say anything to this would be fatuous, so Cormac lay back on the litter and relaxed despite the constant bouncing. The best way to recover from a rogue portal was mental and physical stillness to allow his mind and body to reconnect.

But he'd never had to deal with Rendell before. The other fey kept talking, his voice a snake in Cormac's brain. Rendell would edge right up to a topic that he knew would interest Cormac—usually for reasons of self-preservation—then veer off into a totally different subject. Thus, on the long ride to court, Cormac *almost* heard about Yetting Forest, his sister, and Rendell's thoughts on Pharos and Hiro. It was like following a goddamn hummingbird.

Then there was his fear for Michaela and how she would react to Queen Tismelda. Did she realize that the queen ruled the Queendom with an iron fist?

Cormac? Is it true?

Isindle. He went straight into his request. *You need to find out how to defeat the Ancients, especially the masquerada known as Yangzei, the Eye Thief. He attacked a human, and she is alive but catatonic. Michaela was able to defeat him in combat, we think in part with fey magic. Bring your findings to the Hierarch, Eric. Every minute counts.*

What? She sounded stunned.

The balance of the world hinges on this, sister. Please.

Cormac, I need to talk to you.

Suddenly her voice disappeared and Rendell's smirking face appeared over his. "Having a private conversation?"

That asshole. Rendell had somehow managed to interfere with his connection to his sister before he had a chance to ask her about finding allies to help him alleviate the queen's anger.

"Of course, the rumors about Madden are getting out of hand," said Rendell casually as Cormac grit his teeth and stared at the canopy of golden leaves that shook in the wind overhead. "I even heard…ah, and here we are."

The litter dropped to the ground with a thump and Cormac rolled out and stumbled to his feet. Rendell and the others watched him without offering help, which he wouldn't have accepted. Once the dizziness wore off, Cormac stood straight and went to assist Michaela. She was able to walk but leaned heavily on his arm.

"Scenic," she said.

Cormac held on to her and gazed at a scene he'd thought was lost forever.

The fey court was exquisite. Staircases formed from living vines led up to the upper branches of the great trees that formed the pillars of the main throne room. Fey drifted through, each dressed more beautifully than the others. He looked around, seeing familiar faces from years ago.

Silana looked Michaela over curiously and gave him a small wink before tossing her lavender hair and strolling off. She was friends with Isindle and kind at heart but not even she would have the courage to greet an exile with a masquerada mate openly at court.

Whispers passed through the court and more fey arrived, some coming out from rooms formed within the trees, others from the gardens that lay for acres around the throne room.

"Lord Yetting." The pure voice rang out and the court stilled.

Cormac bowed gracefully. "Your Majesty stripped me of that name years ago." The polite words rolled off his tongue. Beside him Michaela fielded the stares with aplomb and a faint superior smile worthy of a fey princess.

Queen Tismelda stepped out to the tinkle of bells. Her flame-colored hair was caught up in intricate coils dressed with green leaves and her gown was a vibrant sapphire. She was lovely, but Cormac knew her beauty was no more than a glamour designed to awe. He bowed lower. He might not like the queen, but he still respected the throne she represented.

Also, it was possible that he'd gotten wilier as he'd aged. The young hothead who chafed at the idea of bowing had been replaced by a man who understood the rules of the game. If bending his head ten degrees lower would help get him what he wanted, then so be it. He would give what he didn't prize in exchange for what he did.

Not that even the queen was silly enough to swap his exile for a bow, but it might dispose her to be more generous than she planned.

Before he could introduce Michaela, Tismelda turned and disappeared through a gated filled with a gossamer haze.

"Let's go," Rendell said. "The queen doesn't want an audience for what she wants to say to you."

That was somewhat cheering. Usually she loved a crowd to admire her authority. Cormac turned to Michaela and leaned down. His sigil had been unusually silent, and he was concerned about how she was coping with the tension. The Lilac Court was notoriously cruel, so ruthless there was a garden of tall trees in the very back with strong low-hanging branches. The courtiers called it the Grove of Tears, where those who could not bear the shame of the sharp, subtle ridicule of court left this life. "How are you?"

The smile didn't move. "I've had better days."

"This one's probably about to get worse."

"Oh, good. I was worried. The queen seems charming."

"You're kidding."

"Yes."

"Please don't take on a masque," he muttered. Scaring the hell of out the Lilac Court by turning into some monstrous giant was definitely a second-visit action.

"Have they never seen a masquerada before?" she asked. "They're gawking like I'm some rare animal."

"For them, that is probably a close analogy. Some have never been out of the Queendom."

"They should. Travel is mind-opening."

"No one accused the fey of being open."

Still with that smile she took his arm and they strode across the glossy stone floor. All eyes were on him, and he made a deliberate effort to look as many courtiers in the face as possible.

Assailed by memories, it affected him more than it should. Leith, by the pillar, had fought beside him during the war and had saved his life more than once. Otero had been his first commander and had lifted a tree off him with her extraordinary strength.

To his shock, he saw many of those he thought to shame and intimidate by his direct gaze were watching him openly and returned his look with a tiny, almost imperceptible gesture of recognition and...pity?

Pity for what? A lead feeling settled in his gut as they moved through to the gardens. The Snow Field was Cormac's least favorite of all the gardens at the fey court and Tismelda knew it. During the war it was here he'd been found unconscious, the white snow around him pitted with bright blood. It was here that she'd proclaimed his exile. This glittering, barren scene had been the last sight he'd had of his homeland.

He pulled Michaela closer, both grateful to have her with him and wishing she was safe in Eric's house. This was not going to be good.

Chapter 36

Michaela had seen many wonders during her journeys around the world. She had seen a bay of ships on fire, lighting the water for days with their hellish glow. She had seen miracles in medicine. Geniuses creating art that spoke directly to the soul. Priceless jewels and porcelain and sculpture had passed through her hands.

None of it prepared her for the spectacle of the Queendom. Even though she hadn't been able to see much from the litter she'd been carried on, the delicate scent of the breeze that flowed through the silken curtains had been intoxicating. Fuchsia birds sang songs of stunning complexity and golden fruit hung heavily on the trees.

Then there was the court. The fey were physically magnificent, decorating a palace that looked like a filigree dream. She'd done her best to look as though all of these beauties were boringly mundane but she'd almost become dizzy as she tried to take it all in.

At least Cormac was beside her, and her sigil had warmed and reassured her. She stepped cautiously through a causeway to what Cormac murmured was the Snow Field. He didn't like it; she could tell from the way her sigil almost cringed back into her flesh. Without thinking, she pressed her palm on it.

Cormac relaxed beside her and for a moment, Michaela accepted the power they had over each other. It was a responsibility she hadn't wanted but now felt natural. Perhaps it wouldn't be so bad to continue being mated: being mated as a woman was nothing like being married as a child. They could discuss it if they survived the next hour.

Queen Tismelda strolled over the ice path to stand near a crystalline frozen waterfall. Shards of sunlight lit the scene and Michaela had to stop from rubbing her eyes against the harsh white—it would be seen as a weakness and she couldn't afford that here. Cormac remained silent and she followed his lead, conscious of Rendell standing near the gate with his bow in his hand. The threat was unmistakable—one false move and Rendell would shoot them full of arrows. It was clear Cormac respected Rendell's aim: he walked slowly with his hands in sight and Michaela did the same.

"You have brought your mate, Lord Yetting. Introduce her."

"Michaela Chui, High Councilor of the North American masquerada and personal friend to the Hierarch and his consort." Michaela approved of his clear point: mess with her and Tismelda would have to deal with Eric.

"Madame Chui." The queen stared at her, unabashed. "You are inside the Queendom."

Michaela wasn't sure if that was a welcome, but decided to pretend as if it was. "Thank you."

"Lord Yetting." The queen paused and ran her hand down a long, gleaming icicle, then turned and pulled the hood of her white velvet cape over her head, draping it with supreme elegance over her crimson hair. "I do not know where to start. You broke your exile by mating without permission, and not even to a fey. I still cannot decide if that is better or worse. At least I have only one traitor to punish instead of two."

Mating broke his exile? That's why he'd been looking at his decree. It wasn't coming here that was the problem. It was her.

Cormac said nothing. Michaela cleared her throat. Perhaps the queen was reasonable and she could fix this mess. "The mating was because of me."

The queen's heavy red brows shot up. "Did you speak?"

Bitch. "I was the one who insisted on the mating. Not Cormac. He is innocent."

Cormac squeezed her arm and was speaking before she even finished. "My mate exaggerates. I could not live without her."

What the hell was that about? Was his stupid male pride getting in the way of the out she'd given him? Now was not the time to hash it out. God only knew how many others were listening.

The queen turned to Cormac, and Michaela had the distinct sense she was now dismissed from the conversation. When she spoke to Cormac it was in the silvery fey tongue.

"My mate does not speak our language," Cormac said smoothly. "Let me translate. The queen said that I have been much in the human world."

"Of course the masquerada would not know our speech." The queen sounded pitying. "I will speak hers so she does not linger in ignorance."

Yes, a class-A bitch, decided Michaela.

The queen continued speaking. "Tell me what you know of the outside world, Lord Yetting."

"I know much," Cormac said airily.

"As proud as always." Tismelda sounded merely as though she was stating an observation and despite the situation, Michaela nearly laughed. The queen knew her man. Her sigil pulsed and Tismelda's gaze went to her chest as though she could see through to the dark green design that was their claim on each other.

"Only the truth. Tell me what you wish to know."

"Describe for me what you've seen since you've been there."

They were there so Cormac could give the woman a history lesson?

Cormac didn't react. "The world has transformed in the last centuries, but the beings who live in this altered world remain selfish and selfless, base and noble. They haven't changed."

"I heard an Ancient has returned."

"Ah?" He said no more. Michaela listened carefully. How did Tismelda know?

"Lord Yetting, you should be executed where you stand, but I will give you a gift. A choice where there should be none."

Cormac stiffened and Michaela prepared herself to fight.

* * * *

Then, shockingly, Tismelda threw back her head and laughed. "But you disobeyed in such a fashion. Very impressive and not what I expected of you, Cormac Redoak. It made me wonder if I had underestimated you."

Cormac kept his face very still and prayed she hadn't found out that he was a *caintir*. No, if she had he would already be in chains. *Please let Michaela stay quiet.* Better that Tismelda think it was a true love bond— she would feel that she had leverage on him, which might work to his advantage. "I merely live in exile, your majesty."

"Which is why I brought you here. Rendell, leave us. The mate as well."

Beside him, Michaela sniffed. "You may refer to me as Councilor Chui."

Cormac and Rendell shared a glancing look of disbelief. This was not how one spoke to the Blossom Queen.

"I could," said the queen indifferently. "Rendell, leave. Take the masquerada with you."

"I think not," said Michaela.

Cormac glanced over. The queen didn't like challenges or strong women. Michaela's mere presence might be enough to set Tismelda off. "Please," he murmured.

His mate tightened her lips but nodded. She ignored Rendell's politely proffered arm and followed him out a side door. Cormac was grateful she would at least be spared the stares and whispers of the court.

He'd have a lot of explaining to do when they got out of here, though.

The queen looked pointedly at Rendell's retreating back. "The perfect courtier, is he not?"

He couldn't help it. "Ideal. For a dog."

Again, she laughed. "I've missed your sharpness here, Cormac. I want you back."

Time to tread carefully. "Majesty?"

"The world outside is changing and this time, the fey will not be able to stay detached. We are arcana, though of course not diluted by the root human stock. I mean to be on the winning side."

He did his best to look encouragingly interested. "Majesty?" Christ, he sounded like a parrot. Never mind. There was nothing Tismelda loved more than hearing her title.

"We've had an ambassador come with an offer of alliance. You will be my intermediary."

"What about Rendell?" Rendell was the perfect diplomat, handsome and evasive.

"Rendell is too wed to the old ways. He wants to stay out of what is happening in the world. If he had his way, we would destroy most of the portals and stay here, isolated and safe. Stagnant. You are different and always have been."

"I'm honored, but…"

She went on as if she hadn't heard. "This is a time of much opportunity for us, and much risk. For instance, you lost Yetting Forest because of your mating. I had played with other ways of punishing you, but Isindle was kind enough to gift me your land only this morning. I would naturally need to reward you if you stayed."

Cormac felt the blood empty from his face to fill his arms as he clenched his fists behind his back. He'd hoped Rendell's threat had been exaggerated. "Isindle would never do that." Surely he would have known, sensed his forest's anguish. Then he remembered what Isindle had said. This is what she'd wanted to talk about. *Shite. Shite, shiteshiteshiteshite.*

"Not even to save a beloved brother and his new mate? I admit I was quite angry when I found you mated a masquerada, and so very sneakily.

The *ihune* had already left when Isindle managed to placate me with her generous gift. I was able to call them back in time."

Tismelda had sent assassins? The *ihune* were a fey secret. They never missed a kill. Michaela could never survive against them, not even with her masquerada strength.

Tismelda smiled with all her teeth. "The choice, Cormac. Stay and regain your forest for your family. The mate returns to her own world. Or go with her and your forest remains mine."

Cormac reminded himself that Rendell was waiting close by, so to strangle Tismelda bare-handed in the snow, though a pleasant fantasy, would likely end badly for both him and Michaela.

Michaela or his forest.

His forest or Michaela.

The sigil on his chest burned like lightning, but he kept his hands loose at his sides and his face unreadable. Curses bubbled inside of him, catching in his throat until he thought he would choke. Tismelda waited in perfect silence as though she had all the time in the world. She played with a glistening icicle and he noted distractedly it didn't melt in her hands.

In some ways, there was no choice. If the queen already had Yetting Forest, severing the Redoak connection to the land had begun. Once complete—and it could take days or weeks—his tree would die to let the new owner name another steward. Cormac would die and when he died, Michaela would die. Linear connections.

To leave Michaela and remain in the Queendom meant that all of them would survive. He would keep his forest and his sister safe. Perhaps he could even feed information to Michaela to help the fight against Yangzei and the Dawning.

He would never see Michaela again, but she would be alive.

"How long do I have to decide?" he asked.

The queen tossed the icicle aside. "Why, there should be no decision to make," she said softly. "You choose now."

Chapter 37

"I'm staying."

"What?" Michaela turned from the garden she'd been staring at—a strange grove filled with tall dark trees—to see Cormac standing on the step. Rendell watched them both without expression, his hands still ready on his bow.

"Queen Tismelda has offered to commute my exile," he said.

She kept her face still, conscious of Rendell's avid stare. "Why?"

"Michaela, neither of us wanted to be mated," he said slowly. "It was an accident."

"You are not answering my question."

"I'm not sure how long," he said, moving down a step towards her.

"What's going on?"

"I need my forest," he said simply. "A small service for the queen and I can live in Yetting again. It's important to me."

"Important to you," she echoed. "For how long?"

"I don't know. Tismelda wants me to be at court for a while." Behind Cormac, Rendell made a face.

Michaela stared at her mate. Cormac was evading the question because this was his excuse to get away from her. At first, Michaela didn't believe Cormac was picking a forest over her.

Choosing trees over her. Bloody *trees.*

He'd claimed her as his and then at the first opportunity had turned his back.

Tears of rage built up behind her eyes and she bit her tongue so hard her mouth filled with the metallic taste of blood. She still had her pride, and no one in this land would see her cry, not even if they held her down and cut off her limbs one by one. That would hurt less than what Cormac had done to her heart.

What a gullible idiot you are. Even after all the hints he'd given her about his disloyalty and his love of his forest, she'd been stupid enough to think they'd found something in each other.

Self-recrimination could wait. Her goal now was to return home, alone, with as much self-possession as she could manage.

"A good choice," she said to Cormac in her old, cold voice. He didn't change expression, another knife in her chest. "However, I am concerned about the lingering connection of the mating. This will limit me."

"Do you have another lover back home?" called Rendell with idle interest. "I didn't think you did."

Michaela had to restrain herself from masquing and throwing the fey into the air like a rag doll. Then she'd do Cormac for good measure. Not that a masque was necessary. Even as her core self she was angry enough to take them on.

"Miaoling," Cormac said in a low voice, pitched so only she could hear.

"No." Her freezing refusal was so harsh that he stopped dead.

The faint sound of silver bells heralded the queen's arrival. Tismelda surveyed the scene. "Good, you have told her."

The queen snapped her fingers and Rendell snapped to attention. "Bring the councilor to the main portal and escort her home." She smiled. "Lord Yetting and I have much to discuss."

Michaela could not even risk looking at Cormac as she left, nor did he try to stop her. His pine fragrance seemed to linger on her skin and she promised to take a long, hot shower to scrub it off the moment she was out of this nightmare. Then she would carve the sigil, that *thing*, off her flesh.

Now it was time for the ultimate walk of shame. She didn't relish returning through that throne room, but of course that's where Rendell led her, and she would not stoop to request a more private exit. Word of their arrival and meeting with the queen had spread throughout the Lilac Court and the fey were now gathered to watch them leave. Rendell led the way as though she was a prisoner being taken to the gallows.

The courtiers didn't bother to lower their voices and Michaela heard their malicious, gleeful or bored tones discussing Cormac's choice as she kept her focus on holding her head high.

A masquerada. What a taint on the Redoak bloodline. How kind the queen was.

Kind? Tismelda?

As handsome as ever. Silana will be happy.

Of course he'd jump at the chance to leave her. An outsider?
She's unusual looking. Rather like a cat.
Small and hideous. How could he?

Rendell paused at the last comment and twisted to face the silver-haired feywoman who'd said it. "Ah, Mesinda. I didn't see you there. Have you recovered from your...incident? Tell me. Did the scars heal?"

Mesinda's face went impossibly yellow and she ran from the room as vicious laughter rose in waves around her. Rendell nudged Michaela and ushered her quickly to the empty courtyard.

"That one was always a bitch," he said conversationally. "I should thank you for providing me with the opportunity to put her in her place."

"You're welcome." Michaela didn't have the energy to make a wittier rejoinder. If Rendell showed her the smallest sign of pity she would burst into tears. Her chest tightened until she could barely draw breath. The last time she had cried had been with Cormac and beyond that, at Yao's death. Cormac had wrested more tears from her than he was worth.

"Redoak never did know what was best for him," Rendell said casually.

"As I told him, I approve. This mating was not by my choice and it will be a pleasure to be rid of it. How do we get back home?" Michaela looked up at him with a wide smile designed to hide any feelings. "Please tell me it's more comfortable than the route I took here."

Rendell gave her a steady look that she met without blinking. "The portal is close by and we can walk there."

"Good. Let's go."

The walk was interminable and although Rendell tried to make conversation about the flowers ("very unique flora") blooming along the side of the path, all Michaela could manage was to put one foot ahead of the other with as much attitude as possible.

She had no right to think Cormac should have chosen her over his forest. After all, their mating had been a mistake. It had been forced upon him, on both of them.

Fine. She would admit it here. The mating had been a mistake, yes, but it had grown into something special to her, something she hadn't ever thought she would feel. She trusted him. The mating might not have been planned but it had changed, grown. They fit together. However, she couldn't win against his forest.

She should have known better.

They were two flowers into Rendell's botanical dissertation when they arrived at a shimmering circle on the ground. Surrounding the light were carvings of animals so lifelike that they looked as though they would simply walk away. Rendell pointed at the light and stepped back.

"All you need to do is walk into the center."

Michaela regarded the circle with some suspicion. "Will I be able to move when I arrive back home? Or will I be a jellyfish again?"

"It will be as easy as a moonlight stroll," he assured her.

Well, it's not like she had a choice if she wanted to get out of here. She took one last look around at the gorgeously Technicolor Queendom. So much beauty disguising so much rot.

"Farewell, councilor." Rendell gave her a low bow.

She stepped into the light.

* * * *

Tismelda didn't even bother to watch Michaela go. Cormac refused to give her the gratification of knowing that she'd ripped out his heart. Even his sigil felt cold, thin shafts of ice digging into his skin.

"Rendell made me a wager that you would choose your mate," she said. "Of course I knew better." He allowed himself the brief and delicious fantasy of slicing off the queen's head. In the distance, thunder rumbled. That wasn't good. He'd have to watch his *caintir* power even more closely here to make sure he didn't unconsciously slip.

Self-absorbed as always, Tismelda had noticed nothing. "You will leave soon."

"Who will I meet with?"

She smiled. "Her name is Frieda. Frieda Hanver, and she's expecting you."

If Cormac thought he hated the queen before, it was nothing compared to what filled his heart now. The assignment had multiple layers of sting that he would have admired had he not been so filled with rage. Tismelda was well-informed and would have known about Michaela's role in the fight against Frieda and her allies. Did Tismelda have any idea what she was involving the Queendom in? If Eric and the others were correct, this went far deeper than a claim for power. An Ancient could mean destruction on a level they couldn't even comprehend.

Michaela would never understand why he decided to act as a liaison for the queen. Despite being able to shift into multiple personas, at heart she was not duplicitous. In fact, her masquerada traits made her more honest as she took on the personalities of each masque she inhabited. She wasn't pretending to be Yuri. She *was* Yuri. The depths of empathy that transformation required made him shiver. If Michaela was a sea, he was a puddle drying in the middle of a hot concrete street.

This way was better, Cormac assured himself. He would be privy to information that would help Michaela and the others. Perhaps it wasn't loyalty as she would define it, but it was loyalty all the same and driven by the decision to do what was best.

"When do I leave?" he asked.

Chapter 38

Michaela trudged into Eric's house. The world looked decidedly dull after the fey homeland, but she couldn't tell if it was her eyes adjusting or heartache.

Stephan said nothing when he saw she was alone and gave her a quick hug as she came in the door. This time she accepted the comforting embrace. Last year, her relationship with Stephan and the others had been more formal. She'd respected them but true friendship had been missing. One good thing had come out of the entire Iverson mess.

Caro flew down the stairs. "How was it? Where's Cormac?" She sounded almost breathless. "Ivy is the same and Eric is with her now."

The Hierarch came down behind her. "Got kicked out by the medics, so I have twenty minutes." He grabbed Caro by the waist and gave her a kiss that caused Stephan to sigh and cover his eyes.

"Cormac is staying in the Queendom." Better to get it out now. "The queen has ended his exile."

"What did you say?" demanded Caro. A small line had appeared between her eyes.

"I followed Cormac to the Queendom, and we were taken to Queen Tismelda."

Eric raised his eyebrows. "Is she as bad as we've heard?"

"Yes." No more needed to be said. "She was very interested in Cormac's experience with the outside world. I think she means to use him as an ambassador of sorts. Since it is clearly not with us, I believe it's with the Dawning."

Eric frowned. "That's a leap."

"It's logical," she said. "I was right there. I am the head of your High Council. If she wanted to parley with us, she had a grand opportunity right there."

"You don't know that she wants him as an ambassador," Eric said gently. "It's possible, but with the fey so are many things."

"I know it," she said stubbornly. "She wants him for a reason."

"Even if she does, why does he need to stay there?" asked Caro. "Can't he commute?"

Michaela took a deep breath. "You all know our mating was a mistake."

"It didn't look like he was treating it as a mistake from my perspective," said Caro heatedly. "He chose to stay and not come back?"

"Yes. He chose his forest."

Caro coughed. "Sorry. Did you say he left you over some plants?"

"The fey have a complex relationship to their forests," said Eric pedantically. Then he added, "The fucking bastard son of a bitch."

Michaela had to snap her teeth down on her tongue again. It would be shameful to burst into tears here.

As if Eric read her mind, he said, "I think we need some time to consider this, and Michaela will want to see Ivy. We'll reconvene with the others in an hour."

Michaela walked out with her head high. Ivy. She almost ran down the hall to her room where the girl lay unchanged, pale in the bed, tubes connecting her to softly beeping machines. "How long can she exist like this?" Michaela asked the attending medic.

"Indefinitely. She's not getting worse. Physically, she's fine. Her heart and the rest of her organs are working as they should."

"Her mind?"

The medic's eyes were on Ivy. "There's much we don't know about how the human brain works. Add into that an attack by an Ancient? We're in a world of unknowns."

With that, the medic left. Michaela took her place by Ivy's side, smoothing the girl's black hair back from her forehead. She spoke in Chinese. *"Wo ai ni." I love you.*

She told Ivy about her trip to the Queendom, finding the hidden beauties even as she described them. As she spoke, she drew small pictures on Ivy's palm with her finger. A lovely flower. The queen's icicle. Cormac's smile.

Erase that.

She was drawing an intricate design on Ivy's still hand when Eric came in. "Ivy wants to be a doctor. Did I tell you that?" Michaela's gaze stayed on the girl's slack face, the lashes a dark smear on her cheek.

"You did." Eric pulled out a chair and sat across from her, dark hair tumbling over his forehead. He pushed it away and leaned forward to take Ivy's other hand.

"Did you learn anything that will help Ivy while you were there?" he asked.

Michaela shook her head. "Cormac was able to get a message to his sister. Or at least he said he did."

"There might be more to this than we know," said Eric. "The relationship between the fey and the natural world is something they've never explained to outsiders."

Michaela glared at him. "Do you know how long it took for him to decide to stay? No time at all. He was the one telling me the mating bond meant something and didn't even hesitate."

"How do you feel?"

"Angry." The word burst out of her mouth. "He played me for a fool and I'm so angry I could kill."

Eric gave a wry laugh. "Good to hear, since that's what's probably going to happen soon."

She stared at him. "What do you mean?"

A rustle came from the door and Estelle cleared her throat. "Couldn't help but overhear. First, Cormac is a total jerk and Caro and I are going to take you out for wine tonight." She glared at Eric, who had sighed heavily and put his hand over his face. "Problems?"

"Last time you did that, you nearly burned down the kitchen making Kraft Dinner. Cynthia was furious."

"Shut up, Eric. We left you some."

"You made it with orange juice."

Despite herself, Michaela smiled. "The fighting?"

Estelle became serious. "I told the others already. I know more about the vampires allied with the Dawning."

"Tell me." Facts would help bring her back to herself.

"First, Madden has gone underground. No one has heard from him."

Michaela leaned forward, pushing back the many layers of worry that gnawed at her mind. Madden. Ex-mentor. Murderer. Poor Hiro.

"I think I told you a bit about Madden before. He is very strong. He's also not very well-liked. We have some"—here she paused as though deciding what to say—"*issues* among a few of the vampire clans."

Michaela remembered. "When Iverson was around he tried to make alliances with some of them."

"Yes." This was no longer Estelle speaking, or at least not the Estelle Michaela was used to dealing with. In front of them stood one of the ruling class of the vampire clans. Whatever was involved in seneschal training must've been intense. "Madden picked up where he left off. He's looking for trouble and he's finding it. The same as you, we have our disenfranchised, our power-hungry, and our chauvinists. Iverson spurred your people to action, or at least some of them. Madden is doing the same to us."

"How many vampires are we talking about?" asked Michaela.

"Many. At least a third of the vampires in North America, and I assume more would join a winning side." Estelle ran her hand down her hair, smoothing out the stray strands. "Those on other continents will stay quiet until there is a need. They view this as our issue only."

A morose silence filled the room. The masquerada were the most populous of all of the arcane races, but vampires were not far behind.

Michaela closed her eyes. She'd wanted something to distract her from Cormac.

World war hadn't been what she'd had in mind.

* * * *

Cormac was escorted to a small suite in the least salubrious part of the palace, near enough to the servants' quarters that it was almost, but not quite, an insult. He didn't care. The moment he was alone, he went into the bath. He assumed Tismelda had set a watch on him and he needed to check his sigil. Not until steam filled the room did he strip off his clothes and force himself to look. It was still there, but as dim and faded as a dry autumn leaf. He dipped under the water to run his fingers across it, praying for a connection to his mate.

Nothing, but whether that was because of his location in the feyland or Michaela's refusal to open to him was not clear.

The door banged open, sucking the fragrant steam out into the main room. Cormac spread out his arms against the back of the tub and eyed the intruder.

"Rendell. I hope you didn't wish to join me. You're not my type."

"You go more for the small, sad ones. Like your poor mate, fighting tears to walk through the Throne Room and all the fey mockery." Rendell shrugged. "I can't even give her the dignity of calling her your ex-mate, as she's stuck with you."

Despite the hot bath, Cormac froze. "You took her through the Throne Room?"

"Don't play ignorant. Do you think the queen would have it any other way?" Rendell paused. "She did well." A peculiar respect filled his voice.

Cormac wasn't sure who he wanted to pummel more—Rendell or himself. "Did you come here simply to taunt me or do you have a real purpose?" Their conversation had been in the nuanced fey tongue and the word he used for the last indicated that Rendell's purpose was one disgusting to all living things.

Rendell swept a deep bow. "Nicely done. I had worried that your time among the barbarians had dulled your already dismal wit."

"When in fact it was good training." Another insult: that outsiders were better at wordplay than the fey, namely Rendell. Cormac rose from the bath and wrapped himself in a towel, then walked back to his room. New, fey-approved clothes were already arranged on the bed.

Rendell followed him and made a sad noise. "Unfortunate. All those dull tones. So unfashionable."

Unfashionable, but he preferred that to looking like a butterfly. Cormac dressed quickly, giving his sigil a last secret touch. Still nothing.

"I came to inform you that you are not to enter your forest, which is now the queen's property. Guards are posted by your tree, and your sister's." The threat was clear—step out of line and he would be responsible for his own death, Isindle's death, and indirectly, Michaela's. He was a puppet on a string. It would be so easy to kill Rendell right now, he mused. He'd wanted to for years. Tismelda had already taken his family forest. What further punishment could she give?

"You are to leave immediately for your meeting," Rendell said. "Here." In his hand was a paper with an address that he let drop to the floor before he left.

Cormac's pendant tapped against the table as he bent to pick the paper up. The leaf was brown and withered.

His heart plummeted.

His forest was almost gone.

It looked like working for the queen was now his only hope at getting it back.

And to save his mate's life.

Chapter 39

When Michaela finally woke, the first thing she did was drink a glass of water, thirst luckily being the only side effect of the promised marathon drinking session with Caro and Estelle. They'd talked of everything but men and then gone dancing in a dark, seedy bar until the early morning.

The second thing she did was flip her pillow to the dry side. Cormac's pillow was on the floor where she'd pitched it in a rage after smelling his scent. Then she'd ripped the bed apart and remade it with fresh sheets.

That had helped, but not enough to prevent her from finally shedding the tears she'd managed to hold back since Cormac left her without a moment's thought.

She curled up on her side and sniffed, wishing it was only her pride that had been hurt. In a way, it was. *Michaela*'s rage was based on Cormac's infidelity, the breaking of a promise.

Miaoling, on the other hand, had seen her heart ripped out.

In part, her fury was self-directed. She'd known how stupid it was to get emotionally attached to any person. Look where it had got her, not to mention those she'd opened to. Yao—dead placing dynamite in her place. Ivy—soulless and half-dead. Cormac—happy and single, his exile reversed.

Perhaps the last wasn't the best example.

The tears came again, and this time she didn't even bother to check them. Here at least, in the privacy of this room, she let herself feel the grief she'd done her best to deny. She'd fallen for Cormac, fallen for all his talk about their bond. For the way he touched her. The mating had gone from a burden to a comfort. A need.

Cormac hadn't texted or called. She didn't expect him to, although like a desperate idiot she checked her phone repeatedly. She glanced down at her chest to see the sigil was a dead gray.

There was no point in touching this physical reminder of his rejection.

She sighed and rubbed her eyes roughly. She'd had her breakdown and that was it. *Time to pull yourself together*, she scolded. *You didn't cry when Baba and Mama sent you to old Zhang's house. You didn't cry when you made your first shift unprepared. You didn't cry when you ran from your uncle's house as a boy on one of his competitor's junks, leaving everything you knew.*

You were strong then. Be strong now. Put one foot on the ground.

Nothing happened.

Michaela. You will not let a man, of all things, beat you down. Ivy needs you. There is a war. Now. Get. Out. Of. This. Fucking. Bed.

Nothing. She lay there.

Chui Miaoling. Now. Do it for Ivy.

The image of her niece, almost as white as the bed she lay on, was what finally got Michaela out of bed. Isindle may have responded to Cormac's message. There might be hope. A hot shower followed with an ice-cold rinse left her gasping and alert. She rummaged through the drawers and covered up her sigil with every bandage she could find. That would do until she could get it surgically removed.

When she left the green bedroom she'd shared with Cormac, there was nothing left of the desolate, lonely Miaoling who had cried quietly into her pillow.

She was Michaela again, and she was ready to get shit done.

* * * *

Michaela left the house without seeing anyone and made her way to High Park. A few morning joggers panted their way up and down the hills when she arrived and parked in the same spot as before. She would need to navigate by landmarks and it would be easiest to retrace her steps from a familiar point.

Michaela left the main path. Apart from her boots crackling dead leaves and fallen branches, the forest was pleasantly quiet with only the occasional crow caw or owl. A familiar large rock at the base of a fallen tree told her she was on the right path, and Michaela moved more confidently through the forest.

Then she stopped. There was someone close by.

Not human. Fey.

She shifted instantly into one of her older masques. Taili had trained as a temple warrior and was cunning, fast, subtle and deadly. If Yuri was a sledgehammer, Taili was a rapier. She bent down and picked up a strong stick, cursing herself for coming so unprepared. Had Cormac been taken unaware by an enemy?

"No need for weapons, councilor. Violence is overrated, at least when directed at me."

Michaela didn't relax. "Rendell. What are you doing here?"

Now he came out from behind a tree. His dark hair melted into the forest shadows but his eyes had the luminous fey glow, though reflecting the sky rather than Cormac's earthy forest tones. Draped over his shoulders was a long cape, which should have looked ludicrous but instead filled Michaela with an odd sense of dread.

"Waiting for you, of course." Rendell took a step forward, but instantly retreated when she raised the stick. "As I said, no need for violence. We're both Pharos."

"That seems to mean less and less these days."

"True, but nothing lasts forever. That era is over."

He spoke with a certainty that made Michaela shudder but she refused to show him how his words affected her. "What do you want?"

He looked her up and down. "An interesting look. Rather monkish and self-flagellating. He isn't worth it, of course."

"Answer the question."

"To say hello."

"Not in the mood, Rendell."

"Perhaps not. By the way, did Cormac ever tell you the rest of the story about his losing battle?"

She lost all patience. "Fuck off, Rendell."

"Soon. I like this story because I won. Imagine the final battle of a long and bloody war. He had a lovely formation and my heart sank when I looked at it. It was formidable, strength matched to my weakness. I was puzzled because I knew he didn't have the forces."

"Point?"

"His arrangement was designed to hide the weakness on his left flank. Naturally I saw it. He never forgave me for that one." Rendell's smile was exultant.

"Take the rest of your pointless stories and leave." She moved her stick from one hand to the other to underpin the point.

"On my way." Rendell backed off. "A word of advice, though. You're better off to forget him. Cormac belongs to the queen now."

She was welcome to him. Returning to her natural self, Michaela moved around the forest looking for Cormac's tree. She could almost feel it, but it was such a tiny flicker that it was probably her own mind playing tricks. His tree had looked like the rest, but she remembered looking back at it after they'd left. The branches of two nearby trees had bent towards it like sentries offering protection.

She put her hand against the crevassed bark of an oak and took a deep breath, trying to calm herself before searching further. She had to find it. Ivy's cure might be right here, only meters away. Her palm itched where she'd laid it on the tree but before she could move it, a soft song rose in her mind. No, not a song. It felt like a song, but there was no music or melody.

The tree spoke to her and she blinked, suddenly seeing hidden connections between the many living beings that lived there. Insects that lived for days and trees that lived for centuries. They were all interconnected, and pulling her in. Below her feet was an entire network passing information to each other.

She yanked her hand away with a gasp. This was as bad as convergence, when a masquerada risked losing their natural self among the many masques they had created. As part of the forest, she would stop being Michaela.

She took a deep, shuddering breath and moved away from the siren tree in the shape of an oak that had lured her in. From now on she would be cautious about what she touched. A fey might be able to withstand that call, might already be so deeply embedded in the natural world that they would have no fear of losing themselves in it, but she was not fey.

One good thing came out of that experience, though. With unerring feet, she walked straight over to Cormac's tree.

* * * *

An hour later Cormac stood on the corner of the deserted parking lot on the far eastern edge of the city. His message to Frieda had been answered with disturbing promptness and precise instructions. Now he waited alone, surrounded by concrete.

About to betray Michaela for his forest and his sister.

Several black cars pulled into the lot with their lights off. He stood his ground—after all, wasn't this what he was waiting for?—and managed to watch the procession with a bored expression. In some ways, the situation was almost humorous. The black cars, the creepy lot. It might have been taken out of any of a thousand human movies.

When the man in a long leather jacket and sunglasses got out from the car to motion him in, Cormac nearly laughed out loud. This bunch was too much.

They'd also threatened his mate and her ward. That sobered him up, fast.

A woman sat in the back seat of the car, waiting for him. Knowing he was with masquerada, the woman could be anyone, but chances were good that it was Frieda Hanver. The car started.

"Cormac Redoak. So pleased to meet you." The woman didn't offer her hand. Her face was so perfect it was hard to know where to look—a mix of Barbie and Aphrodite, the same as the masque Michaela had taken on in Eric's war room. He very cautiously kept his eyes away from how her curves filled out the plain black tank and jeans she wore.

"Queen Tismelda sent me."

She giggled, a disconcerting sound from a being he knew was at least two hundred years old. "Of course she did. I asked for you."

Cormac decided not to play her game. "Do you have a message for the queen?" Not his queen. Never his queen.

"Tell me about Eric. I know you've seen him." Conflicting emotions flickered across her face. Hate. Desire. Jealousy. Rage.

He could tell her that Eric and his consort were wrapped in a passionate love that would span a thousand lifetimes, but instead said, "He's fine."

That terrible giggle came again. "No, he's not." She leaned forward. "We're about to blow his world open. It's time for arcana to take our place in the open again."

This situation was bad enough without having to listen to a bigot run through her grievances. He tried again. "The message for the queen?"

"In a hurry, feyman?"

"My haste is for the queen."

"Fine." Frieda sat up facing him. Her fragrance, a thick amber, filled the back of the car and he wanted nothing more than to get out and into a clean forest. "Tell the queen her offer is accepted and the terms are agreeable."

Cormac paused. "Is that it?"

"Yes."

"You couldn't send her a message?"

"I will. Or rather you will." She cocked her head to the side. "Didn't she tell you?"

A sense of dread overtook him. "Tell me what?"

The car stopped and the driver opened up Frieda's door. She thrust her leg out. "You can send the message from here. She's offered you as a military consultant. You're with us now."

Chapter 40

They'd taken his phone for "security reasons" Frieda explained smoothly to him over dinner. He'd made a point of eating heartily, not wanting to give her any indication of his inner turmoil. There was now one way of being able to possibly beg Michaela's forgiveness, and it involved returning with the most information possible.

That was presuming that she even let him live long enough to tell her.

They'd been served with the main course when Frieda smiled sweetly. "I'm sure Michaela will not be in the best mood when I return you."

Cormac laughed out loud. "You assume I'm going back."

"No?" She took a sip of wine and looked over the edge of the glass, blue eyes wide.

"The queen was generous enough to make me a deal. My help here for a reversal of my exile." Cormac shook his head. "I'd be a fool to give that up."

Frieda frowned slightly and he prayed his lie would hold up. He'd never get information if Frieda thought he valued his life with Michaela. Every word he uttered was like sand in his mouth.

"I was told you were mated," she said.

"A mistake that will be remedied once I'm back in the Queendom." He made sure to make eye contact and hold it. "I'm not one for monogamy."

"Mmmm," she purred. "Good to hear."

She even licked her lips. *Better tone it back.*

"More wine?" she asked. Cormac refused. They were dining alone in a small room that gave the impression of being underground, though it was brightly lit. When their plates were cleared and they'd been served a delicate dessert of candied flowers, she gave him a smile that said they were about to get to the real business.

"I couldn't help but notice that you seemed surprised at Tismelda's offer," she said, putting a violet into her mouth. Her lips were red and wet. A maw.

"I was," he said. There was no point in lying when it could be so easily confirmed with a conversation with the queen. "I thought she would offer Rendell. He's served her well and was on the winning side of the war."

A faint frown showed on her perfect features. "I was told Rendell doesn't have your power."

"He's much better trained than I am."

She laughed at the ambiguous wording. "No doubt, but I don't want you here for a pet. A week, maybe less, and you'll be back in the feyland."

"I'm in no rush. What do you have planned?"

She said nothing but instead tapped her fingers on the table. The side door opened immediately.

Cormac nearly leapt up from the table as power surged through the room, a blast that seemed almost insane. In the doorway stood—what? It must be Yangzei. Cormac blinked and saw a red-haired woman become an old man, eyes white with cataracts, then a plump and laughing youth with ebony skin. An Arabic woman. An albino child. Yangzei flickered through the masques so quickly that Cormac barely had time to register one before the next had taken its place. He averted his eyes, trying to keep from getting dizzy.

"Speak," Frieda ordered.

"Help me, Auntie! Help me. It's so cold and I don't know where I am." Ivy's anguished wail came from Yangzei's mouth, echoed with the sounds of thousands of other voices, and Cormac knew horribly that it was the real woman he was hearing.

"How?" Cormac's voice came out raspy.

"Yangzei obeys my orders," said Frieda. Cormac raised his eyes high enough to see that a small collar had been bound around the Ancient's throat. Some sort of controlling device, but based on the aura of malignant power that surrounded the Ancient, he was grateful that he was under control.

"He attacked Ivy."

Her full lips pursed. "A misunderstanding. He was to get Michaela, but the little girl is as good as a hostage. Almost better."

Cormac managed to maintain his neutral expression. "It's always wise to have a hold on your enemy's heart."

"We understand each other, then." Frieda appraised him. "I didn't believe Tismelda at first, but she assured me you would be an asset."

"I want my exile finished."

"Good." She nodded. "Then we'll begin."

* * * *

Michaela stopped dead and stared at the stranger.

"Who are *you*?" Both women spoke at the same time.

A minute ago, Michaela had been in Cormac's tree slapping at the smooth indent on the wall that he'd pointed out as a portal. Now she stood in the middle of a spring meadow with bluebirds singing overhead. She would have thought it was a hallucination except for her sigil, which almost seemed happy and gave little warm pulses every few moments. Then the woman had appeared, her pale pink dress tattered around the hem and holding a gigantic knapsack that nearly bent her double.

A shout came from a distant hill and the woman—clearly fey—frowned. "Introductions can wait. Do you like dungeons?"

"No."

"Torture?"

"I can live without it."

"Then you'd better come with me." Adjusting the backpack with a heave, the feywoman brushed by Michaela and gave a tree a gentle kick. "Open," she said peremptorily.

The tree shimmered and projected a small gate. "In," ordered the woman.

Dogs bayed from the same direction as the shouting and Michaela didn't hesitate. The fey came right behind her, muttering something under her breath. Michaela paused and turned in time to see her toss out a handful of powder that burned so brightly it left white spots in her vision. Then there was nothing but emptiness.

"Are you the opposite of claustrophobic?" asked the woman. "You're afraid of open spaces?"

"Agoraphobic and no." Now that the woman had mentioned it, Michaela noticed that they were simply standing in space. There was no floor or ceiling, but they also weren't floating. "My God. Where are we?"

The woman said a long fey word and, "It is better for you to think of it as the in-between. We need to stay for a moment so I can ensure the hunters don't come after us."

"That gives us enough time for you to tell me who you are." Michaela wasn't exactly afraid of where she was, but at the same time decided that concentrating on something solid would help calm any potential fear immensely.

"Isindle of Yetting Hill." Isindle spoke her name with a kind of aplomb.

"You're Cormac's sister?"

"I am. How do you…" Isindle's voice trailed off. "You're his mate. My brother's mate."

"Michaela." She had a name and enough of being a man's property when she was young, thank you.

Loud voices and fierce dog barks erupted from all around them and Isindle held up an imperious hand. Michaela got the hint and stayed silent. For some reason, she'd gotten the impression from Cormac that his sister was a powerless young girl who needed protection. That was definitely not this woman. Isindle exuded authority and wisdom.

Plus, she was breathtaking. She and Cormac shared the same coloring, with pale hair, golden skin and mutable green eyes. Isindle's hair flowed in smooth waves to her shoulders, held back by a simple band of golden leaves. "Come closer to me," Isindle whispered. "It's easier for me to keep us covered."

Michaela knew when a woman was an adept and she moved closer. Cormac's scent, that intoxicating pine, rose from Isindle's skin, but mixed with peony. A voice came from what sounded like right beside her. "Can't find her, sir."

"Queen Tismelda will have our heads if we come back without her." This was a woman, with a high voice. "You're sure that was her? It's more likely Isindle would stay in Yetting Forest."

"The queen has the Redoak lands now," said the first hunter. "Another family she's destroyed."

Isindle and Michaela both winced at the heavy sound of a blow. "Never say that out loud," hissed the woman. "You don't know who is around."

"If Princess Kiana—" Another grunt of pain.

"Enough." Now the woman's voice was cold. Another blow. "You never learn."

"You refuse to see the truth," said the man sullenly.

"The queen wants to question Isindle. Do you want to be the one to say we failed?"

A slight pause. "No, but Lady Isindle is not here. The dogs must be confused."

"What about the woman we saw? The one in pink?"

"There is no woman here," the man said. "Are you sure your eyes weren't playing tricks? There are stories about the Redoak woods."

There was a short pause. "You could be right. We should check the mage's fortress again. I heard a rumor she was still there."

"A good idea."

Isindle held up her hand for continued silence, but it was unnecessary. Michaela knew enough to stay quiet well past the point when an enemy could still be around. After what seemed like an hour, the fey turned to her.

"Well," she said cheerfully. "Shall we go?"

Michaela glanced around the empty space. "Why don't you lead?"

In a moment, she stepped right from the gray emptiness back into Cormac's High Park tree. Isindle dropped her pack with a heavy thud and rolled her shoulders back before turning to Michaela.

"I am told you are a warrior, so I will keep my distance." A faint smile played on her lips. "One day I hope to embrace you as my sister."

"Not likely."

Isindle sat down in a smooth swirl of dirty skirts. "I have come to help with Ivy. I have some information."

Michaela stared at her, torn. Isindle smiled thinly. "You don't trust me, but rest assured that Cormac's actions are not what you think."

"No?"

Isindle ignored the brittle tone. "No. The queen forced me to give her our forest in return for his life. He is getting it back for us, so we can live. Without our connection to Yetting, we die."

Michaela could barely speak. "What did you say?"

"He did this for us. He is the steward of Yetting Forest. The exile was bad enough, but he was at least still connected to the land." She sighed. "The queen wanted to punish him for mating without her permission. She was going to send the *ihune*, the assassins, but I begged her to take our forest."

It all began to fall into place. "You need the forest because your souls are in the trees. They help keep you alive."

Isindle nodded. "As you say."

Another betrayal. Another truth he hadn't trusted her with. He should have told her what the mating meant for him, that he was going to lose his forest and his life.

If this was even true.

"Cormac *is* a master strategist," Isindle said clinically. "Do you know what task Queen Tismelda entrusted him with?"

"No."

"We can find out."

Isindle stood and went to the wall, laying both hands and her forehead against it. A slight hum built and Michaela knew it was the sound of life around her. Isindle's voice rose in a song without words, her pure voice bringing purpose to the forest's purr. She lifted a hand up and reached it behind her. Knowing what she wanted, Michaela took the outstretched hand and placed her other on the wall as well.

It was as though she was on a highway through space. In that instant she was on the verge of knowing everything. Her sigil vibrated against her skin.

Cormac. She thought his name and he rose up in front of her. It was dark, and he was at a table with laptops and maps spread around him. Leaning over him, her chest pressed against his shoulder, was Frieda Hanver. It was a cozy scene.

A third person was in the room. He looked up and the empty light of his eyes hit Michaela like a physical punch. With pained cries, both women released their hold on each other and the tree and fell back. It was a moment before Michaela caught her breath and when she did, she saw that their handprints had been etched in black on the wall.

"Who was that with Cormac?" Isindle gasped the words out as she clambered to her feet. Her hair was in a huge frizz around her head. "I've never met such strength."

"Yangzei," said Michaela grimly. "Our enemy." She remembered again Cormac's words about the fey war—that he had chosen his forest over loyalty to his troops.

"That traitor." Yuri came out of nowhere with a roar of anger and Isindle stared up in shock. "You're coming with me." In a moment, she had Isindle's bag over her shoulder, the feywoman's arm in her hand, and was heading back to her car.

Now that she knew where Cormac stood, it was time to get this finished.

Chapter 41

Two days later, when Cormac was out of excuses to avoid Frieda's bed, it was almost a relief to see Madden come through the door. Almost. He was overtaken with an intense desire to feed the man his own teeth. Never mind. Michaela would not be pleased if he killed her former mentor before she had a chance to do it herself.

Yangzei had not been out again after that first night, and he'd learned that the ancient masquerada was held in a secure cell. He was a tool for the Dawning, to be maintained and used when required, but Frieda was obviously wary of his capabilities and uncertain of their extent.

Madden laid a hand on Frieda's shoulder and flashed an urbane smile at Cormac, who watched with detached interest. Was this the affectionate show of a lover or the dominance play of a competitor? The uprising was obviously Frieda's show. She had been the one to collect the Dawning. She had been the one to work with Iverson. Cormac suspected that as a masquerada, she was the one with the primary relationship to Yangzei.

He also knew Madden was a political animal with no morals. He would use Frieda and whomever else he needed to get what he wanted. Cormac looked closely. What *did* Madden want? Should the Dawning succeed in instigating another war it would be as devastating for vampires as the other arcane groups. Did Madden think he could create a new society out of the ashes, one where he was in charge? It was possible. He certainly had the ego to think he could. He would be one to watch. While Frieda was driven by revenge, it was Madden who wanted much more.

Frieda put her hand on top of Madden's and faced Cormac with her golden smile. "Present your plan."

"Yes, sir." Cormac had found it easier to treat this as if he was still a soldier. "Eric Kelton has made certain preparations that indicate he's about to move his headquarters. To maintain the Law, it's logical to assume it will be to a more isolated location. His goal will be to minimize human exposure to the arcana."

It took over an hour to walk through the battle plan. Judging from what Eric and the others had said when they were together, Cormac now knew they had drastically underestimated the number of troops the Dawning was able to muster. The most stunning revelation had been the sheer numbers of troops they had prepared to sacrifice, those newly made masquerada Hiro had been helping to supply. Then there was Yangzei, who Frieda insisted be kept as a final weapon. The nuclear option, so to speak, and Madden had not disagreed.

Madden sat and listened, making only a few comments. When Cormac finished, he moved his laptop to the side. In his defense, he had provided only information that should have been clear to them through their knowledge of the enemy and mere common sense, nothing sensitive or secret.

At least, that's what he told himself to placate his conscience.

"I'm impressed what you can do when you put your mind to it," said Madden. The tone was so condescending that Cormac choked back a laugh. "It's missing a major element though."

"What's that?" Frieda tilted her head to her side. "We've been over everything."

"Yet you've forgotten the Law. They want to keep us hidden from the humans, living in the shadows like sub-creatures. We need chaos. We'll break the Law by opening their eyes before we subjugate them."

"Chaos," said Cormac thoughtfully. He didn't point out that Eric and the others had trusted masquerada in positions to monitor and manipulate what humanity knew—government, media. Instead he said, "Tell me how you'd do it."

Madden pontificated for an inordinate amount of time and Cormac duly added his thoughts into his tactical plan. Madden had no concern about the damage he was about to inflict, which, with the revised plan, was tremendous.

Cormac stared at his notes. "I recommend neutralizing the Hierarch first to make this easier to do. He's weak and isolated up north, unable to get more troops. We can overwhelm him, then move on to the important core of your plan." We, not you. He had to make them think he was part of the team, and his suggestion would at least delay the Dawning from attacking major urban centers and feed into the strategy Michaela had developed.

Alana Delacroix

Madden looked like he wanted to disagree, but Frieda nodded. "Agreed. Let's get the troops ready," she said. "We begin tomorrow."

They put him back in his room and locked the door. A collaborator he might be, but they didn't trust him, a fact made clearer when he had first realized there was no wood in the room, or anything natural. His room had been cunningly designed out of plywood, wood so mangled that he wouldn't be able to sense it at all. The floor was laminate. Even the sheets were polyester.

It was like living in a sensory deprivation tank.

Cormac slid his hands under his shirt to rest on his sigil. It stirred, a soft flutter against his skin, but he couldn't reach Michaela. *Michaela. Miaoling.* It was an internal call into the void. He needed to reach her, now more than ever.

He had to warn his mate that she was about to die.

Michaela.

Nothing.

* * * *

Michaela stared at the map in front of her. It was no use. Three days had passed since Cormac's betrayal and she still couldn't concentrate. Eric and the others had not wanted to believe what she'd seen but had no choice once Isindle had waved her hand and made a cloud appear with the same scene they had witnessed in the tree.

Isindle was another problem. Michaela winced. This was a lie. The feywoman was a godsend who had rarely left Ivy's side since she arrived. They had to remind her to eat, and when she did it was in front of the huge texts she had brought with her from the Queendom, all the while muttering to herself in the lovely fey language and making esoteric notes on the pad beside her.

Eric had taken the new addition to his household with his usual self-possession. "If she can help Ivy, she can stay for as long as she wants," Eric had said when Michaela told him the full story.

"She's being hunted by the queen," Michaela reminded him. "Plus she's the sister of the man who betrayed us to the Dawning." She had to force the words out. What Michaela felt was so far beyond hurt that she couldn't even bear to think about it. Even looking at Isindle was difficult because she looked so much like Cormac. The sigil over her heart was almost gone now, and she felt nothing from it.

"Yeah, well, I'm not too happy with the queen myself these days," said Eric. "So if taking in a refugee from the Queendom is going to piss her off, then that sounds good to me."

Michaela didn't blame him. Eric had sent a message to Queen Tismelda, the usual *Hey, what's going on, heard you were thinking of joining forces with my enemy, is it true?* note between rulers, and she hadn't even bothered to reply. Eric had taken this deliberate rudeness as acknowledgement that they were no longer friends, which Isindle had confirmed when Eric had summoned her for her opinion.

"The queen has not been satisfied with ruling her own lands for many years now," Isindle had said. She had changed the tattered pink dress for a pair of jeans and a casual T-shirt. She preferred to go barefoot and her blond hair was tied in a messy ponytail at the back of her neck. Although she had been dressed as though shopping at the farmers' market on Sunday morning, Isindle still wore her authority like a gown. "Since she has nowhere to expand the Queendom in our own realm, she's been looking elsewhere."

Estelle walked into the room and broke in on Michaela's train of thought. "This place is pretty," she said. Eric had moved his headquarters to an isolated island in northern Ontario, which was currently aflame with autumn colors, hoping to draw away some of the Dawning's attention.

"It is." She had listened to the loons on the lake last night, and thought that the birds' lonely cry was exactly what she was hearing in her heart. It had not been a cheerful thought.

"Trying to work?" Estelle asked.

"Trying and failing." Michaela shoved the papers away and took a big drink from the cold coffee that sat at her elbow.

Estelle frowned. "You don't drink coffee," she accused. "You never drink coffee. You only like tea."

"Maybe I've changed."

Estelle sighed and sat down beside Michaela on the couch, tucking her feet underneath her body and leaning back against her hand. "Maybe, but I doubt it. Coffee's not your style. Do you want to talk about it?"

"About coffee?"

"About Cormac."

"No." An easy answer. She was doing her best to avoid thinking about him.

Estelle flashed her a smile full of fang. "Too bad, because you're going to. You can't keep this bottled up inside of you, not if you want to heal or at least be functional. You've been moping around and that is totally legitimate. Girl, you got fucked over."

Michaela ran her hand over her eyes. "Thanks for pointing that out."

The vampire wasn't done. She raised her fingers to tick off Michaela's recent catastrophes. "Your mentor tried to kill you. We're facing a war. Ivy's hurt. Cormac's gone."

"Hold on." Better clarify that right now. "Cormac is not 'gone'." She used finger quotes to emphasize the word. "That makes it sound like he simply disappeared. He deliberately turned his back on us to join forces with Frieda and the demon who took Ivy's soul. For his forest. That isn't *gone*."

"You're right."

That was it. The gate that been locked in front of Michaela's mouth burst open. "I trusted him. We were mated, for God's sake. Even though I was the one who said it was a mistake and that we should try to get it annulled right away, he persuaded me to try. What sort of man does that? He wanted me to fall in love with him so it would hurt more when he left. That's the sort of mind games the fey play, and I was dumb enough to believe it."

Estelle said nothing, but cocked her head to one side and made a *keep going* gesture with her hand.

Michaela didn't need any encouragement. "For how long was he planning this? He wanted to keep his damn forest safe and even said so. He must have been trying to engineer this for ages. First, he would get in with Eric through me and find out information that would be useful for Frieda. Then he'd dance on over there and help them win the war. Oh, and lead Yangzei to Ivy for the hell of it."

"Michaela—"

Michaela spoke right over her. "We all thought it was the fey magic that helped beat Yangzei. It wasn't. I bet they had an agreement beforehand."

"Do you believe this?"

"I do." Michaela stared at her, dry-eyed and furious. "You know why? Because he's not here and Ivy is half-dead. Of course Cormac would pick the forest over me."

"Or because he would die otherwise? As would you?"

Michaela snorted. "Would I? That's what his sister said. I don't believe it."

"It's true." Isindle came into the room with a tray of nuts and berries. "The chef was very disappointed that this was all I wanted to bring to you, but these are my comfort foods and I wished to share them with you."

Estelle jumped up but Michaela waved her back down. "Stay. I know you love strawberries."

"I do," the vampire admitted. "As a child I used to wear them on my fangs and pretend I was a circus walrus."

The other two women stared at her, but Estelle had her head down to pluck through the nuts to find her favorites.

Michaela sighed. "Any news about Ivy?"

"Yes. This is what I came down to tell you, but then I heard your conversation."

"Were you eavesdropping?" Michaela demanded.

Isindle chose an almond and popped it in her mouth. "I'm not sure. The door was open and I was listening. We all do this at home. It's how we learn. It's expected."

"Well, we don't do that here."

"Understood. However, since I did hear, I feel I must address your concerns. What I told you is the truth. We are deeply linked to our forests. They are our lives."

"Then why didn't he tell me?" asked Michaela. "Why didn't he say what the mating could cost him?"

Isindle tilted her head to the side. "Why? What would it change?"

Nothing, but...they were mated. He should have trusted her.

Even though you said it was a mistake? That you wanted it over? To not think about it?

Isindle, not part of Michaela's internal debate, spoke again. "Shall I tell you about what I learned about Ivy?"

Priorities. Michaela clasped her hands together, trying to keep her impatience under control. Isindle only had information—it might not be good, and she needed to prepare herself for that.

Isindle ate some more almonds and settled back in the chair. Michaela noticed that she had some of her large books with her, including the notebook in which she'd written all of her ideas. She opened the largest tome, which looked as though it was bound in a piece of the sky, and flipped through until she found the page she wanted. Smoothing it down with her hands, she read something in the lovely fey language.

"This is the diary of one of my ancestors, who was both a mage and a *caintir*, a forest talker like Cormac. They are very rare and are usually hunted and killed by weaker rulers. Stronger queens have used their abilities wisely."

"How did you know Cormac was a *caintir*?" asked Michaela. She'd thought it was a secret he'd only shared with her.

"I knew." Isindle shrugged. "His closeness with Kiana was suspicious."

She twisted the book around so Estelle and Michaela could see the image etched onto the page. It looked like a fey but with twelve faces instead of one. "Is that a masquerada?" asked Michaela.

"I believe so. It's an artist's rendition of an experience my ancestor had when he was here in your realm. He met a masquerada, the first one he had ever seen. This was many years ago, and judging from what you've told me I think it may have been Yangzei."

"Why?" asked Michaela. "It could be anyone of us."

"It could be, but you told me Yangzei was known for stealing souls. This story"—and here Isindle tapped the page in front of her—"tells of an evil being with many faces who took part of my ancestor with it."

Michaela and Estelle exchanged glances. "What else?" asked Michaela.

"Many arcana believe the fey don't have souls, but this is inaccurate," said Isindle. "Our souls are in the keeping of our forests. Because of this, my ancestor didn't realize that Yangzei had stolen part of his until many years later."

"This is all very interesting, but what does it have to do with Ivy?" Michaela glanced out of the window.

"What is interesting is what my ancestor did next. He returned to your realm and hunted down Yangzei to take his stolen soul back."

"Now this is more like it," approved Estelle. "How did he do it?"

Michaela's heart was racing. "When Yangzei was here, I used part of Cormac's energy and weakened Yangzei. It didn't stop him from taking part of Ivy's soul, but there is something about the magic." Michaela realized that she had cut half-moons into her palms from her nails. Finally they were getting closer to something that could help Ivy.

"It's the relationship to our forest," said Isindle. "My ancestor had the sense that Yangzei needed to feed itself by stealing souls. This was where it took its power from. This was why it was so powerful."

Michaela nodded. "Stephan came up with the idea of a horde all stuffed inside Yangzei's shell."

"I need to do more research but I think my ancestor was able to use the power of the *dolma* against Yangzei. I don't know how but I'm going to find it for you."

"Thank you." Even this little bit of information helped to raise Michaela's spirits. Knowing there could be a solution was much better than hopelessly staring at Ivy's still face every day.

"There's one problem with this," said Isindle. "Cormac is the head of our forest, the same way that my ancestor was head of the forest in his time. If my hunch is correct, we will need Cormac in order to target the spell against Yangzei."

"Cormac, who is working with our enemy?" asked Michaela.

Isindle looked at her steadily. "Yes."

Great.

Chapter 42

Michaela touched her pen to the battle plan. "We need reinforcements here."

Tom and Stephan scowled in unison. "Think again," Stephan said. "We don't have the numbers."

They all stared glumly at the map. Estelle and her mentor had guaranteed the vampires, at least those who Madden hadn't swayed. Wavena, Estelle's queen, hadn't been pleased at the degree to which the Dawning had penetrated her ranks and was involved in a purge even as they prepared for the attack. The weres were allies but limited in where and how they could fight. The mers would help but were most formidable in the water. The other masquerada Hierarchs stood united and ready, having already sent their best troops to serve under Eric.

Eric pounded the table in frustration. "I need to know about the fey," he said. "They can make or break it."

"Judging from what Isindle says, the fey can't be counted on to stay neutral," said Caro. Like the rest of them, she had dark purple shadows around her eyes. "They gave Cormac as an advisor and she says this guy Rendell is almost as good. He's the queen's right-hand man."

"Then we're screwed." Tom said what they were all thinking. "They don't care about harming the humans, so we're already working at a disadvantage."

"We don't go without a fight," said Eric grimly. "We have good people. Strong people who are fighting for what's right."

Michaela agreed. "The transformed masquerada aren't very resilient. They'll be fueled on adrenaline." Tom had developed what he called a "newbie" trap to get most of them.

"I'll say it," said Caro. "What about the Ancient?"

Alana Delacroix

Yangzei was still the greatest unknown. They knew nothing about his motivation, which meant it was almost impossible to plan for what he could do. Ivy's condition remained unchanged, and Michaela feared doing any harm to the Ancient that could rebound on the girl. That was, if they could hurt him. He might be able to come in and disable every one of their soldiers in the blink of an eye.

"We can't prepare for him," said Eric finally. "We'll have to deal with it when it comes." When, not if.

The Hierarch stood up, Caro by his side. "There's no going back," he warned. "The Dawning will attack, so be ready. It could come any time."

The meeting broke up and Michaela went to sit on the enclosed porch at the front of the house. Eric's northern base was an island compound used for training his elite troops, but it was empty apart from his defensive force. He'd ordered the teams out to protect logical landing spots along the eastern seaboard.

Michaela drew a deep breath of the fresh evening air and felt the cool breeze coming off of the lake. She wanted to wander in the forest, but Eric had asked everyone to please not act like fools when they were expecting an attack. Nonetheless, she wasn't surprised to see a lone woman walking up from the shore. Isindle had told Eric very simply that she needed to be in nature and that was it.

Cormac's sister was restful to be with and Michaela wasn't upset when she sat down on the Muskoka chair next to hers. "I tried to reach Cormac," Isindle said.

Michaela strove to be polite and managed to come up with a noncommittal "Oh?"

The fey shook her head. "I could not. Then an idea came to me."

"I don't know why you bother," said Michaela. "He's not on our side. He's trying to destroy everything that we value."

"If the forest dies, then he dies. If he dies, you die," said Isindle stubbornly. "He is doing this for us."

Michaela laughed but it was a bitter sound. "Tell me again how sending an army after me and my friends is helpful. I forgot how that works."

"Please." With surprise, Michaela saw Isindle had tears in her eyes. "Please. I must talk to him. I almost did it. I need only a bit of help."

"No." The refusal came fast and hard and surprised even Michaela. She stood up, almost shaking in anger. "No. He can rot, for all I care. He has nothing to say that I want to hear."

Leaving Isindle on the porch, she went back inside and managed to hold the tears until she was alone in her room.

* * * *

They summoned him in the middle of the night.

"Change of plans," said Frieda. "Tismelda has formally pledged to join us."

She pointed to the wall where a large map showed the different sides and where their forces were. Cormac stared at it. The Dawning was by far the strongest of the two combatants, and that wasn't even including what they expected from the Queendom. Part of him had believed that the queen wouldn't commit troops for this fight, but it was possible that she understood the threat from Yangzei as much as he had. The queen may be greedy, nasty, and vengeful, but she was not stupid.

"I need you to rework our attack plan," Frieda said. "Incorporate the fey troops."

"That will take time."

"You have two hours."

He took a laptop and moved as far away from Frieda as possible.

When she was absorbed in her maps again, he maneuvered his hands under the table. He had to tell Michaela. Even if it caused his death and Tismelda sent the *ihune* after him again. He had to reach her, to tell her about the fey.

It was time to touch the *dolma* again.

He took a deep breath and laid his palm on the wood. At first, nothing changed. A sick shiver ran through him. After all these years of rejecting his ability, could it be possible that it had left him? Withered and died from disuse?

He squeezed his eyes shut and slowly placed his other hand on the wood. A tingle tickled the outermost edge of his consciousness and grew into a whisper, then a call. There it was. He could feel the wood under his hands speaking to him, energizing him even as it told him stories from its existence.

No. He ripped his hands back, almost panting. He couldn't. Yetting Hill was already at too much risk. He couldn't make it worse by declaring himself as a *caintir*. Tismelda would raze his forest before killing him as she did Kiana. Michaela would know to plan for the fey. She was smart.

Madden strolled in and Cormac bent to his revised attack, cursing his weakness.

"I must say, Cormac, you're being much more accommodating than I had expected," he said. "It's almost as if you have something up your sleeve.

I hope not. I don't think I mentioned it, but I was speaking to Yangzei the other day about what happens to the souls he collects. Like Ivy's."

"I assume it's nothing good." Cormac refused to give him the pleasure of knowing every word was a sword thrust.

"No, not at all. Yangzei can determine the experience each of those little ghosts has. Ivy can be in agony, or in heaven. It's up to you."

Cormac's jaw hardened. "Me? Sounds like this is a decision Yangzei makes for himself."

"Not while he wears his pretty little necklace." Madden smiled and again Cormac thought about how nice it would be to shatter those goddamn fangs onto a piece of granite. "Here's where it's up to you, Cormac. You're going to be with us and you're going to help us win. If you do a good job, Ivy won't hurt. If you do a bad job, Yangzei will crush her mind so completely there will be no point in helping her anyway."

If they hurt Ivy, they would break Michaela's heart. Cormac didn't even pause. *Stay in character.* He rose to his full height and stared back at Madden. "I'm here for my forest and for my exile. Nothing else. You can take your pathetic threats and shove them up your ass."

Crude, but worth it to see Madden's face harden.

"Boys." Frieda stood up. "Enough. Let's think with our upper heads only. Cormac knows his job."

"Good." Madden stood up and pointed to the door. "Then let's go. The battle awaits."

Chapter 43

"Move Mai and her team over to the western border." Michaela studied the satellite images coming in. "Tom."

"Here." His voice crackled in her ear.

"I need you to hold there. You've got sniper cover to the east."

"Roger that, base."

"Stephan, are you connected with the mers?"

"Affirmative. Glad I splurged for the quality wet suit."

Michaela sat hunched over the table in the war room. Around her buzzed tense conversations but she ignored it all. She pushed away the pile of lists, made in her personal shorthand, then sighed and picked one up.

Better sort them neatly. A cluttered space meant a cluttered mind. She needed to concentrate.

It was so hard. Although now greatly faded, she could feel the sigil's cold weight pulling on her skin on her chest. She hated it. Hated that she'd allowed herself to be so fucking vulnerable. So many warning signs—he'd even confirmed Rendell's story for God's sake—and she'd still walked right in.

She stood, shaking her head to rid herself of the pain of Cormac. Eric ruffled through another set of maps while Caro pounded away on a laptop. Estelle was on the phone with her mentor, ready to direct the vampire contingents. On Michaela's screen a small green dot held steady—she'd insisted she have a real-time update as to Ivy's status since the girl was hidden safely away from the battle zones. Isindle sat in a corner surrounded by her magical books. Right now the fey had both eyes closed and her hands working in a complicated contraption she'd made of oak leaves, bark, and wood. She'd called it an amplifier. Eric wanted her close to keep an eye on, but none of them suspected that she was a spy for the fey. Isindle's hate for Tismelda was simply too strong.

They'd been in the underground bunker since the first Dawning sightings about fourteen hours previous. As they'd expected, Frieda had targeted her first real attack to take out Eric. Their own forces had moved silently to neutralize Eric's internal enemies the day before, which Frieda had clearly not expected them to do with such thoroughness. Without direction from the mutinous masquerada, the shock troops were confused and easy to round up.

"It won't all be this easy," Stephan had warned them before he left to take position near the water. "She's testing. Remember those numbers. We need to fight smart and hard."

"Here it comes." Caro tapped a button and the wall lit up with video of the island's borders. Several helicopters appeared from the south and troops poured in from ships that landed.

"Evie, confirm the humans aren't seeing this," said Eric.

Evie was stationed at the hidden southern command post. "Affirmative. We have them blocked."

Eric had placed trusted masquerada in positions of power in human institutions years ago in preparation for any crises. At least that was one thing they didn't need to worry about. Michaela stared at the video streaming through. Their strategy was sound. They had done the best they could.

The updates came quick and fast as all teams reported in. The mers had engaged with Frieda's forces. The vampires were still holding, waiting for Wavena to give the order when required.

"Incoming," called Caro. More of the recently turned masquerada, the shock troops, converged on Eric's island. Michaela moved between the video and the display of trackers around the island, commanding Eric's forces. She was in a state of icy calm. This was what they had dreaded and prepared for, a fight they hadn't wanted but they would end.

"I'm going out there," said Eric.

"No." Caro didn't even look up from the display. "You are not."

"I belong with my fighters," he insisted.

Michaela looked up to see Caro and Eric staring at each other. "You are the one they're protecting," Caro said coolly. "Go out there and you'll distract them. Let them do their job and you do yours."

"They're dying."

Caro stood up. "That's right. They are. The same way we would, and you would. They know they need to protect the Law, Eric. Trust them."

Eric breathed out. "I should be with them."

"They need you here." Caro's tone was final, and there was a tense silence. Finally, Eric nodded. "You're right. Always right."

"Damn straight," said Caro. "Now get to work."

* * * *

"Status check on the fey." Cormac spoke into the mic. They had placed him in a room with multiple feeds and a human tech to show him what he needed. All he knew was that he was on a ship—he could feel the slight dip of the waves. He had no idea where Frieda and the others were, but he assumed they were monitoring him. Even before he'd started, a woman's desperate, agonized cry had come through the speakers in the room, causing the tech to cringe and cover his ears.

Ivy's pain, and the message was clear. He'd better stay in line.

He shuddered. The fey. Tismelda kept her soldiers well-trained. Michaela was looking at a catastrophic loss and he was partly the cause of it.

"Report, Minh." Madden's voice blasted through the room.

The huge Vietnamese tech coughed and spoke into his mic. "Still nothing."

"How are they doing it?" Madden sounded infuriated and had already raged that Michaela had kept Eric's defensive secrets from him. Cormac hid his smile. Anything that bothered that asshole was a brief joy. Right now, Madden was expecting the humans to be going insane with the battle right on their turf between monsters out of myth. There had been none. The most exciting news story had been some celebrity divorce.

"I assume they have some human contacts, sir."

Cormac almost heard Madden grinding his teeth. "Break it down. I don't care how."

The human rolled his eyes at the mic and Cormac filed that for future use. Minh wasn't a believer.

"The fey?" he asked Madden with exaggerated patience.

"Talk to them yourself." Madden was gone.

Cormac caught Minh's eye across the room and made a very slight and careful *What are you going to do* expression. Minh's lips quirked before he mastered his face and bent down to his monitor. Good. He'd made a connection. He glanced down to see Minh's arms had two healed punctures. Perhaps he was one of Frieda's turned masquerada and not human after all?

"Lord Yetting." The familiar voice came over the comms speaker.

Cormac closed his eyes. "Rendell. What do you want?"

"Orders, apparently."

"What?"

"I know. I can't believe it either. The queen has said that we are to obey your commands. She ordered us into battle on this realm." Rendell sounded halfway between appalled and furious.

Rendell. Here was his chance. His opportunity. He kept his voice mockingly calm. "Good. At least she recognizes talent."

"Fuck you, Cormac."

"Another time." His mind worked furiously, trying to work out what he needed. Then he had it. "Listen up."

Rendell listened as Cormac laid out his plan. "I know this battle formation."

This was the moment. Was Rendell's loyalty to the queen, or to the Queendom? "I thought you might."

Another pause. "Perhaps, Cormac. I rather like the idea of you owing me a favor."

Then the connection was broken.

Chapter 44

"Stephan, pull back. Pull back!" Michaela shouted into the mic, but it was too late. Stephan's voice disappeared in a steady stream of static. "Stephan! Reply. I repeat."

Estelle came over and hauled her away from the screen. "Michaela."

The grief in the vampire's voice broke her. "Get him back. Pull them back."

"We can't."

Michaela slumped in the seat. The last three hours had seen their forces overwhelmed by Frieda's soldiers. Madden had rallied the vampires, and they were wreaking havoc. Tom had disappeared hours ago. The shock troops had been more numerous than anyone had expected. Estelle spent most of the time in a frantic conference call between Wavena and her mentor, the seneschal major. Sightings of Yangzei had terrorized their troops, the more frightening for its apparent randomness.

The only thing that had gone in their favor was that they had managed to keep the massacre away from the humans. The Law stood. At least for the moment.

Now Stephan was gone.

"No." Caro only breathed the word, but it was enough to stop every conversation in the war room.

Eric stood immediately. "Caro?"

"The fey." It's all she had to say. Michaela looked at the screen to see gorgeous warriors stepping out of trees all over the island.

This was it. The end. They watched silently as the fey moved with an almost balletic precision. *There are so many*, thought Michaela. So many.

It was over.

Isindle tumbled her books aside and joined them at the screens. "Fey," she said, as though commenting on the weather. She looked more closely and hissed. "Rendell."

"With many others," said Michaela, unable to tear her eyes away.

Isindle was silent as she studied the screen. "This is a message from my brother."

Every head in the room turned to her. Michaela was the one to finally say, "What?"

"I know this formation. Cormac used it in the last war." She pointed at the display.

The last war. Michaela stared at it, remembering the story Rendell and Cormac had both told her. The inherent weaknesses in Cormac's battle formation.

Isindle was right. It was a message.

Did she trust him? Was it a trick? He'd lied to her so many times. The fey thrived on deception. He'd gone to her enemy. He'd worked against her.

"Why would Rendell agree to do this? He's on the queen's side."

Isindle continued to look out, a slight flush on her cheeks. "Rendell does not want to be in this realm, or associate with you."

That seemed reasonable enough for Rendell. Still not enough. She couldn't do it. The wrong choice would be the end of them.

Then her heart spoke. "Eric. I want what's left of Tom's team to strike here and here." She pointed at the screen.

Eric regarded her steadily. "You're committing all we have," he said. "This is it. Are you sure?"

She took a deep breath and for the first time touched her sigil. It fluttered under her touch. "Do it."

Eric nodded and gave the orders.

* * * *

The door slammed open and Cormac looked up.

"You son of a bitch." An unfamiliar man in a wetsuit, bleeding copiously from his face, lurched in and yanked him up with a single hand. He was built like a tank, with long arms and a chest like a barrel. "You fucking betraying son of a bitch." He threw Cormac against Minh, who collapsed under him with a groan of pain.

Cormac had only managed to get one foot under him when his head was knocked back by the force of the stranger's blow.

"Fucker," he gasped through the blood. Was this one of Madden's minions? Had they realized what he'd done with the fey?

The man leapt on him and the beating began in earnest. Minh was still, either playing dead or knocked unconscious.

"Stephan, come in. Please. Tell me you're okay."

Cormac froze. That was his mate's voice. "Stephan?" He managed to roll away to give himself a moment's reprieve.

Stephan didn't hesitate. "I'd kill you now, but then I'd deprive Michaela of the pleasure of doing that herself."

"I didn't—"

"Fuck you, fey, and fuck your pathetic excuses. Michaela trusted you and you fucked her over good. You don't deserve her."

At least Stephan had that straight. He didn't deserve her.

"My, this is quite the reunion." The sweet tone barely covered Frieda's obvious fury.

Both men shot to attention, their mutual animosity put aside in light of this larger threat. Without saying a word, Cormac and Stephan moved slowly away from each other. Frieda didn't look visibly armed, but that meant nothing. In a moment she had blasted up to become physically as large as Stephan. Cormac did his best not to gape at her. She was at least twice as broad and a good foot taller than him. These damn masquerada. A quick check around the cabin confirmed what he already knew. There was nothing to use as a weapon, except for a few monitors and the microphone. On the floor to the right he saw Minh inching his way towards the wall and trying to make himself look as small as possible. He didn't blame the poor guy. Things were about to get messy.

"Frieda, this is all over." Stephan stood to his full height and for the first time in his life Cormac felt short.

"It's only beginning," she said. Behind her appeared several of the new masquerada that Eric had been busy disposing of on the mainland. They looked intent on murder but Cormac saw they seemed unsteady in their new bodies. This was his only advantage, and he would use it.

Frieda and her underlings rushed the room. He ducked down behind the desk and when he rose again his glamour ensured he was invisible to his enemies. On the other side of the room Stephan had engaged two of the newbies and brought them down with almost insulting ease. One had raced to Cormac but came to an abrupt stop when he realized the fey was no longer to be seen. Cormac moved slowly from the table, careful to avoid touching anything that would give his location away. On the floor,

Minh stuck a foot out and tripped one of the attackers, who fell face first into a monitor bank.

Frieda stayed at the door and watched as her guards were decimated in seconds before calling out for reinforcements. Cormac didn't wait. He brought down the last guard with a blow to the back of his neck before leaping towards Frieda. Stephan, alerted by the collapsing man's grunt of pain and the mass of equipment that fell in Cormac's wake, did the same.

The two men struck at the same time, but Frieda was ready and armed. Cormac fell back and shimmered back as his glamour retreated. Going against Frieda was like pounding a brick wall.

Out of the corner of his eye, he saw a shadow at the door, but Frieda aimed at him with a small smile and fired as Stephan managed to slam into her. The bullet went wide, through the door, but Frieda was faster than Cormac had anticipated. She slashed down with the knife held in her other hand and Stephan fell as blood gushed.

There was no time to help him. Cormac lurched to his feet. In his hand was a cable he'd scrounged off the floor. There was no wood, nothing of the *dolma* that he could call on in this technological tomb, but he was still a soldier. A cord was as good as a vine.

Frieda said nothing but raised the gun again. Cormac whipped his arm out, snapping the cord down to smash against the brute's forearm.

Then the giant was gone and in her place was a thin whippet of a woman who flashed down and under the table to roll against Cormac's legs before he could blink. He fell to the ground and slid in the blood that pooled under Stephan's still body. Frieda was on him before he could move, her long body snakelike and flexible. She bit down hard on his unprotected neck and he wrenched back with a roar of pain as her sharp teeth sank into his flesh. Instinctively, he hit back with his arm and flung her away. In an instant, he was on her, taking advantage of her momentary surprise.

It was enough to get his arm around her throat. It was slippery with the blood streaming from his neck so he wrapped his legs around her, wrestling with her as she fought for breath.

A figure came through the door but Cormac didn't stop.

"Yangzei," Frieda croaked. Cormac tightened his arm around her throat so her next words were more thoughts than said out loud. "Help me."

Yangzei stared at her and tossed his broken neck piece, split where Frieda's wide shot had shattered it, down at her feet. "No," he said in that horrific echo.

Then the Ancient left.

Cormac gave one final wrench and Frieda went limp in his arms.

* * * *

"Now." Michaela stared at the screen, praying that she was right. If she wasn't, they were looking at total defeat. If she had been right to trust Cormac, well…At the moment, it was still defeat, but not on a grand scale. She was willing to take any advantage.

Eric's forces charged the fey, focused entirely on the left flank. That was the hidden weakness. It only looked strong because of the troop formation, strong enough that she would never have dared to hit there first.

"You trusted my brother," said Isindle. The feywoman stood at Michaela's elbow, watching with her. Michaela glanced up to see that Isindle's attention was mostly on a man dressed in dark green, camouflaged to blend in perfectly with the trees. A white light blew up from one of the trees and Isindle nodded as if she was expecting it.

"They've got mages," called Caro from the other side of the room. "I count one, five. Maybe eight."

"That is not many," observed Isindle.

Michaela stared at her. "It's more than we thought," she pointed out. "Especially as we have no magic to counter them with."

"That will be my role." Isindle leaned down and kissed Michaela softly on the cheek. "Good-bye, sister."

Before Michaela could respond, Isindle shimmered and disappeared. She and Caro gaped at the spot where she stood while Eric paused in his orders to the field. "What the fuck is going on?" he demanded.

Michaela looked back at her screens. In the middle of the battle— fey moving like shades against the subtle vampires and the shifting masquerada—a woman in jeans and a white shirt picked her way with bare feet through the trees. A frosty light illuminated her and she held up both her hands to the sky. Lights and fire flared across the island.

"This is it," Michaela said into the mic. "Now. Now."

The generals in the field acted as one. As Isindle's eerie glow intensified, the allied troops moved hard against the fey, who slowly fell back.

Then a green light exploded noiselessly through the forest.

Michaela stood up from her seat staring at the monitor, her cry frozen in her throat. Isindle lay still on the ground, her pale hair spread around her. The allied fighters stood in shock, staring at where, only seconds ago, they had been fighting. Not a single fey could be seen.

Then a young Chinese man strolled up, waved, and opened his mouth.

"Oh, Auntie," he wailed in Ivy's voice, but with a demon's horde echoing behind it. "Make him stop. Make him stop."

* * * *

"Come on, you son of a bitch." Cormac heaved over the dead weight that Stephan had become so he could get a better look at the wound that crossed high on his chest. "Minh. Get over here. Give me a hand."

The human scrambled up, eyes wide as he stared at Frieda's still body. "What the fuck happened?"

"Your leaders are working with a masquerada Ancient who now seems to have gone totally off the rails," mumbled Cormac as he ripped Stephan's shirt off. The wound was long and deep, but he breathed a sigh of relief. Frieda hadn't managed to go deep enough to hit any organs. Blood loss was the main problem. Luckily masquerada healed quickly. "Hold this against him."

"Okay." Still looking stunned, Minh reached out his hand for the shirt and Cormac passed it over.

"Stay here." He glamoured himself and did a brief check of the yacht. No Madden or Yangzei. What guards there were seemed to have either gone overboard—he saw a motorboat speeding off in the distance—or had come to answer Frieda's summons and were now dead.

He went back into the cabin, where Stephan's breath was shallow but steady. "Where are we?"

"Where do you want to go?"

Michaela. He needed to get to her before the demon could. "The Hierarch's base."

"We're almost there." Minh looked at him narrowly. "What are you going to do with me?"

Cormac laughed. "Get us to Eric and I'll throw you a fucking party. Unless you want to stay with your side."

"I don't want to be here at all. I made a mistake." Minh shuddered. "I'll get us there."

"Good man." Cormac took over holding the pressure steady. "Can we communicate with them?"

Minh cast his long dark eyes around the room. "You did a pretty good job trashing our stuff here."

"Sorry."

Minh shrugged, already on his way out. "Best bet is to try this guy's communicator. It was working before."

Cormac rummaged through Stephan's clothes with one hand. It took less than a minute before he fished out a cracked and battered case. He shook it, but it remained dark.

Under his knees, the floor hummed.

He was on his way back to Michaela.

Chapter 45

Michaela rose from her seat blind to everything except that slender laughing figure standing in the forest. Yangzei took a careful step to the right and nudged Isindle with his toe.

"A fey," he said in Chinese. He bent down and lifted her up with a single hand. Isindle's head lolled to the side. "She is related to the other one," he said, staring at her curiously. The voice, with its terrifying echo, boomed through the forest.

Then he started to laugh.

Michaela didn't realize she was already at the door until Eric grabbed her arm to hold her back.

"I forbid you to go out there," he said.

"Sire. I must." She grabbed a gun that was set near the door and left as he bellowed her name and shouted for the others to cover her. Yangzei regarded her as she stepped into the forest surrounding the compound. By now Eric and the others would be targeting Yangzei, but they wouldn't be able to fire without fear of hurting Isindle. She kept her gun behind her back.

"Put her down." She didn't take on a masque but boosted her voice so that it rolled through the forest in Yuri's rough baritone.

Yangzei rattled the unconscious Isindle like a rag doll. "They all want to keep me. This one's relative was different. She will be different." To Michaela's intense relief he spoke in his own voice and not Ivy's.

Keep him talking. Find out what he wants. Find out about Ivy. Michaela smiled as best as she could. "Keep you? Who kept you?"

Yangzei looked at her with pity. "Do you hope to keep me talking in some misguided attempt to understand me? To stop me? I was summoned here by one of my own, promised all I desired and then tricked. They tricked me." The voice rose to a wail.

"What did you want?" She took a cautious step forward. If Stephan's theory that she had witnessed the multitude was correct, perhaps she could connect with Yangzei with a touch, even without Cormac's magic.

"I wanted nothing but sleep for a long time. Then I was pulled out." Yangzei gave Isindle another shake. "The world has changed and it appeals to me. Now I want to live again, as I did before."

Not good.

His eyes narrowed. "They lied to me. Put the collar on. I couldn't keep a masque. It hurt. They bled me. Weakened me."

For the new troops. "Madden? Frieda?"

"Of course." Madden stepped out from the dense forest. "Yangzei was going to help us put the arcana in our rightful place, until he began disobeying." Michaela didn't hesitate, but brought her gun up and pulled the trigger. As she did, an accompanying barrage of bullets rang out from hidden spots around her. The vampire hit the ground and rolled to safety in the trees.

Jackass. As if she would be here without cover. Trusting the others to keep Madden occupied, she turned her attention back to Yangzei. "Give me Ivy."

"No."

"Please." The word stuck in her throat.

"No. Ivy is mine. Soon all will be mine." Yangzei flickered in the same way he had during his original attack, with multiple faces appearing as he grew in size.

Isindle's feet lifted off the ground.

* * * *

Cormac checked the knots carefully. "Sorry about this," he said. They were at the island, but he couldn't leave Minh without making sure he couldn't make trouble.

"I get it." Minh wriggled slightly and winced. "Don't scuttle the damn boat with me in it."

"No promises."

"What about him?" Minh thrust his chin in Stephan's direction. The big masquerada hadn't regained consciousness but he seemed to be breathing. It would have to do. Cormac couldn't go dragging dead weight all over the island.

Also, Stephan's chances of survival were better here than where Cormac was going.

"He's staying with you." Cormac turned to leave.

"Do you know what that thing is?"

Cormac nodded. "I do."

"You're still going out there." Minh regarded him skeptically, as though wondering if Cormac would take the opportunity to run.

"My mate's there."

His expression altered. "Shit, man. Go."

As if Cormac needed his captive's urging. The moment he stepped onto the beach the land sang to him. He could feel the traces of the fey, blown back to the Queendom by Yangzei's incomprehensible power. Only two remained.

His sister, diminished in his mind.

And...Rendell? Why was he here?

Then there was Yangzei, hanging over them like a malevolent god. It was ridiculous to think that he would be unnoticed by the Ancient, but there might be other threats lingering on the island. He took each step agonizingly slow.

Michaela.

Still no answer.

* * * *

Michaela hesitated, unsure if she should shift and not willing to antagonize Yangzei before she got Ivy. *Cormac.* She could almost hear him calling for her. She beat down the pain.

Yangzei's voice was now the same multi-toned horror she remembered. "All but the fey. I will rid the world of them. They hurt me."

"No." Behind Yangzei appeared another fey, dark where Isindle was light. "Drop her."

It was Rendell, fully armed and pointing what looked like a silver firearm at the demon masquerada's back.

He fired and Yangzei flickered swiftly to the side.

At first Michaela was conscious of nothing but the strange booming chime the fey weapon made as it discharged. Then she noticed a strange trickling sensation in her leg.

The pain hit a moment later.

Michaela collapsed as Yangzei laughed. Through eyes blinded with tears, she saw him toss Isindle's limp body to the side as he turned on Rendell, who fired again and again. Each hit caused Yangzei to diminish slightly, as though the fey magic was feeding on him.

Ivy. What was it doing to Ivy? Michaela clawed at her gun, but her legs were too weak to stand or kneel. Rendell had to stop before he did something to harm the girl.

Cormac.

Her last hope. At least he might come for his unconscious sister, if not for her.

She slid her blood-slick hand to what was left of the sigil and threw her voice into the darkness around her heart. *Cormac. I need you. Isindle is here. Help us.*

Nothing.

She pressed down hard on the wound in her thigh and forced herself to shift to Taili. She no longer had the strength for Yuri, but at least as Tai she was slightly stronger.

She tried again. *Cormac.*

Still nothing.

A final inspiration hit. She slid one hand deep into the soil and kept the other on her sigil. This time the power stirred through her and she threw herself into her call, wavering as she did. The light was going dim.

Cormac. Please. We need you.

This time the response came like a caress.

Miaoling. I'm coming. For you.

* * * *

No answer came except a flash of pain from his sigil. She was hurt.

Enough with this. Cormac broke into a sprint, desperate to reach her. A fey blunderbuss fired, a deadly chime that triggered memories of agony and destruction.

At the edge of a clearing, he paused. A concrete compound loomed to the south, Eric's headquarters. As if in a vision, he saw Yangzei, huge and daunting, with Isindle's motionless body at his feet. Rendell stood behind a tree, his blunderbuss now trained on a sneering Madden.

He cast the thought into the air. *Miaoling. Answer me.*

There was only the faintest whisper, hazed with pain, but it was enough for him. She was hiding, huddled behind a rock that protected her from Rendell and the others.

He didn't even pause. Yanking a glamour over him, he sprinted across the clearing and leapfrogged over the rock to get to his mate.

When he saw her, he couldn't even speak. Blood covered her, smearing her pale face and white lips and caking her long black hair. She was so still. The wound, where was the fucking wound? She moaned as he moved closer beside her. There. Her hands were pressed hard against her leg. He stripped off his shirt and pried her hands off long enough to slide the cloth underneath.

"I'm here, Miaoling."

"We know you are." Yangzei's voice was mocking, but in the smallest of mercies, it was not Ivy's agonized tones. "No one cares. You can do nothing."

This was not the weakened being Frieda had kept. He would worry about that later. First Michaela.

Always first.

Her eyes flew open and she shifted back to her natural self. "I'm fine."

"You've been shot."

"Not badly. Cormac. Ivy. We need to help Ivy."

"I love you." Before anything else, he had to tell her.

She gaped at him. "Now? *Now* is the time for this?"

"Since there is a very good possibility one or both of us will be dead soon, yes."

The blunderbuss fired again and Cormac slid around the rock. "Rendell and Madden," he reported. "What is Rendell doing here?"

"He tried to kill Yangzei when he attacked your sister."

"Did he shoot you?"

"It was an accident."

His lips tightened. "I'll deal with him later."

"Eric and the others are in the compound. Armed but probably hesitant to strike against Yangzei because of Ivy and Isindle."

Yangzei screamed in Ivy's voice, a keen of total agony that made Michaela jerk and raise horrified eyes to his.

"Stop, stop. You're hurting me." Ivy's screams were tortured. The blunderbuss fired again.

"We need to get her before Rendell gets her killed," Michaela said urgently.

"Do you have a plan?"

She shook her head.

Incredible. "I do." He peered over the boulder. "Try distracting him. Get his attention on you."

"What are you going to do?

Cormac touched her beautiful face. "I'm going to get Ivy."

* * * *

That was it? All he was going to tell her? Michaela couldn't even call after him, because he had already disappeared. She squinted at the place he had been and saw a wavy impression of the glamoured Cormac bent low and moving around the periphery of the clearing.

Distraction. Michaela wracked her brain for something good. She could throw a rock.

There were no rocks. She had no rocks, no weapons, and a bum leg.

Fine. She hauled herself to her feet and waved.

That was enough to get Yangzei's attention. She refused to look where she thought Cormac might be—broadcasting his location would not be in the spirit of distraction—and instead forced herself to look straight in Yangzei's face. It shifted and shimmered, dancing through masques. Yet even as she stared at him, she could see a small fragment of his natural self, his true core. It was chilling.

She needed to keep his attention. She dragged herself around the rock, praying that Rendell wouldn't shoot her again.

"Yangzei, let her go."

"Who, this one?" With a snap of his fingers, the demon summoned a ghostly-looking version of Ivy on the ground in front of him, small and terrified. "You're welcome to her. All she does is cry."

"Such a bore," she said tightly. Her Ivy.

"Ah, you are a woman after my own heart. You know, perhaps I will keep her." His eyes moved over her face. "You're tethered by that fey. Interesting. You trust him with your lives."

She remained silent.

Yangzei regarded her curiously. "You know, of course, that he was lying to you. How ridiculous that he was on loan and simply happened to reappear when you needed him. This is their plan. They want to use us."

"Who does?"

"The vampires. Frieda was in their pay, as were my resurrectors. They wanted to practice calling an Ancient to this earth before they summoned their own."

"Liar." An uncomfortable feeling scratched at her: Estelle's admission that the vamps had their Ancients under lock and key.

"What can you know of any other race but yours? Madden. Cormac. Which of the men in your life have been true to you, *mei mei*?"

Involuntarily, she glanced down at her sigil.

"Which men tried to control you?"

She shook her head. "No."

"Tricked you? Lied to your face?"

Cormac had. Madden. Stephan, Eric, Tom? Never.

"So join with me and get your Ivy back. Nothing will hurt us again."

The ghost-Ivy reached out her hand pleadingly, then flickered and disappeared as Yangzei reeled to the side.

When he turned back, there were two Cormacs. Michaela's heart skipped a beat as her injured leg gave out beneath her. She grabbed the boulder for balance.

"Shit." Estelle appeared beside her and flipped her a gun. "Who do I shoot?"

Michaela shook her head as the two grappled. Unlike the other masquerada, Yangzei was able to take on Cormac's clothes as part of his masque. They were completely identical. She watched the two carefully. No. In Cormac's masque, Yangzei seemed to be absorbing the fey magic much better than he had before. The two were moving lightning fast, Cormac's fey grace and speed more than matched by Yangzei.

Cormac was losing, badly.

Chapter 46

He was losing, badly.

Yangzei had shifted into a masque that looked like him—Cormac had not realized how difficult it was to put full strength in a punch when the fist was aiming at your own face—but fighting the masquerada was like fighting a swarm. It wasn't one of Yangzei's punches that landed, but twenty, thirty.

It took only two more endless minutes to know he was going to lose, and in losing, fail his mate.

Again.

Yangzei threw him to the ground with a single hand and Cormac heard his ribs snap. He thrust his right hand into the ground. This time there were no slow tingles, no gradual reconnection. He threw his mind open to the grasping claws of the *dolma*.

For Michaela.

It had been waiting for him, a wild power heaving at the edges of his sanity. A slicing pain ripped through his chest and a trickle of blood ran down his flesh. A mournful sigh filled his mind as his tree acknowledged the broken covenant.

There was no time to grieve for his tree's pain or pause to think of the waves he was sending through the dolma. No fey alive would miss that a *caintir* had survived and was now, abruptly, unexpectedly, in full possession of his power and at one with the *dolma*.

Tismelda would never give back Yetting Hill.

He didn't care. He'd sacrifice a thousand forests to save Michaela right now.

The *dolma* reached out and he threw himself into its embrace. It hurt, and he wondered if the pain was related to loss of his forest. It felt different as well. The song was more distant, and he needed to reach out to hear properly. Each note rang with a sadness and desolation he had not felt before but was achingly familiar. For a moment, he gave himself to the song, letting it swirl around him and push aside the bleakness that had been part of him for so long that he'd assumed it would be there forever.

That is, the song took up residence in the areas that hadn't yet been filled by Michaela. She was part of him.

He opened his eyes. The forest shivered overhead, the leaves trembling in the quiet air, but their song continued. Kiana had told him of this once, and warned him of the danger of becoming too connected to the world. *It wants you*, she'd said that day they'd sat out in the meadow. Her hands had played with a long vine and it had wrapped itself, almost lovingly, around her wrist. *The* caintir *are part of nature, and the goal of nature is to take over what lies in its path.* She tugged at the vine, which tightened around her arm. *You need to remain strong within yourself and not let it too far, no matter how tempting.*

The warning echoed again in his ears as he stopped to assess the scene in front of him.

Yangzei, ready to kill him. Michaela, already injured. His sister, unconscious.

Fuck it. He opened himself up completely. If the *dolma* wanted him, it could take him. He would be the sacrifice it wanted.

It started with his feet, which sank into the ground. Cormac didn't fight it. *Take me. Do what you want with me.*

The *dolma* responded with violence. The wind picked up and swirled around him like a tornado. Branches and stones cut his flesh and his blood streamed out but Cormac stood, eyes open and hands outstretched. He would give it up, give up everything, if the *dolma* helped him.

Suddenly, there was silence. Cormac looked around with eyes that were no longer his, seeing jagged fragments of light surround all the living things. Every animal in the forest acted as his ears. The trees were his eyes.

He could see all, including Yangzei.

"That is what the other fey did," the Ancient said, that echoing voice furious. "He made me hurt."

Cormac ignored him. The power of the *dolma* was his now and he had no qualms about using it.

The trees first.

* * * *

"What the hell is happening?" asked Estelle in awe.

Michaela couldn't answer, partly because she wasn't sure, and partly because she felt very...odd. Dreamlike. Cormac had opened himself to the *dolma*, and she could feel the edges of it, a huge presence that slowly prodded at her, as though wondering who she was.

"That fey with the gun is moving Isindle away from the fight," murmured Estelle. "She's still out. Caro has him in her sights, just in case."

Michaela nodded but couldn't take her eyes away from the fight in front of her. The two men had gone past any recognizable fighting style and were now holding on to each other and wrestling for dominance. Trees dipped down around them, but the two fighters were so close that she couldn't tell who they were trying to reach. Around them swirled wind, lifting up rocks and raining them down on the fighters.

Then the two broke apart for a moment and she saw one of the Cormacs lift his hand to his heart as if for strength.

Not his heart. His sigil.

That was him. She rose up behind the boulder, her eyes on the other Cormac, Yangzei.

Ivy was trapped in that Yangzei hell, so Michaela was scared to shoot to kill. She pulled the trigger, aiming for his hip. Yangzei's Cormac masque flickered and disappeared as the bullet hit.

She scrambled around the rock, dragged her leg, desperate to get to the fighters.

Instead, Madden appeared from the trees and raised the gun.

Then everything happened at once. Madden fired but in front of her rose a pale flash.

Cormac.

Cormac lying on the ground, bleeding.

Madden's laughter, suddenly stilled as Estelle shot him.

Cormac.

Michaela's leg gave out as she tried to reach her mate, screaming something that might have been his name.

He was already in a pool of blood and her sigil was colder than cold against her flesh. "Cormac," she gasped.

His eyes, a pale green as though they'd been drained of life, found hers. "Told you I was right."

"God, right about what?" She pulled his shirt open and sagged at the sight of the wound, a gaping hole through his shoulder, his lung.

"To tell you I love you, Miaoling." He chuckled, but groaned as the blood gushed out. "Go get Ivy."

Then he stopped breathing.

* * * *

Michaela knelt beside him, stunned. Dead. Cormac was dead.

Impossible. He couldn't die. She loved him. They were mated.

"Another to have failed you." Yangzei's whisper came from behind her.

She twisted silently. The Ancient's face was appropriately solemn but his eyes were gleeful.

"Give me Ivy," she said.

"No."

She could hear the whisper of the horde inside him, captured souls held prisoner but they were too weak for her to join with. She needed Cormac. Without knowing why, Michaela put one hand on Cormac's sigil and raised the other to the sky. Cormac was a *caintir* and they were mated.

The *dolma* would not let him die. He wouldn't let Ivy die.

Which meant it was up to her.

Michaela took a deep breath and sliced through the wall that had built up around her heart for centuries, protecting Miaoling and all of her love, her trust. *Protecting? Don't lie.* Avoiding. Shunning. Fearing the pain that came when she let herself care. Tears blinded her as she relived every little wound, the injuries big and small that had forced her to become Michaela. The rejections. The hate. The pain. As each peeled off, it flayed her soul, but she forced herself to go on.

She had to, even if it killed her in the process. She needed to become part of the *dolma*.

Help me, she thought. *I can't do it alone.*

It was the *dolma* that replied in a voice that seemed to echo through the world. *You must.*

A vision of Cormac came to her, his hand on her back. Soothing her. Supporting her.

She remembered Ivy's laugh. Yao's gapped smile as he presented some delicacy he'd stolen for them to share. Stephan's stories. Caro. Baptiste. Captain Lu.

There had been much love and kindness in her life. Enough to overwhelm the selfishness? The anger?

If Cormac died, the pain she would feel would be more than she could handle. She would break, shatter into a thousand shards of glass.

He was not going to die. Nor was Ivy.

I am the mate of a caintir *and I will join him.*

Then do so.

Shaking with fear and agony, she opened herself completely to the *dolma*. For a moment, she was in that same in-between place Isindle had shown her.

Then she was on her hands and knees, screaming with all of the memories that came tumbling down around her. Strong arms embraced her as she wept, feeling herself knit back together.

Cormac.

"I never thought you'd be here," he said. "The in-between is only for fey."

"You need to come back with me. I need you."

He turned to face her, his eyes now a green so bright that she could barely meet his gaze. "You don't need anyone, Michaela, let alone me."

"I love you."

Cormac stilled. "What?"

"I love you."

"It's too late." His smile now was sad and gentle as he laid a hand on her cheek and leaned to kiss her. Desperately, she clung to him, trying to press her lips against his as he murmured broken words of love. Her arms clashed together and to her horror, she drew back to find he was a mere ghost. The light behind him turned incandescent.

"Cormac!"

"Good-bye, Michaela."

"No. I love you. I do need you. You've become part of me." Frantic, she struck her hand against the sigil that had started to fade from her chest. She wouldn't let him die.

She reached down deep and searched for their connection. It lit her up from the inside and this time when she reached for him, he was already taking her into his arms.

Their kiss was like nothing she'd experienced. It filled the small cracks left behind in the torture of breaking herself down to become her real, true self once more, a Miaoling stronger and more open than she could have ever achieved alone. Cormac's love was a light in her darkness and as he breathed into her, her sigil warmed against his.

Now, finally, they were true mates.

Then he was gone.

* * * *

As if from a distance, Cormac saw Michaela's face twist in agony as she tried to hold him back. He wanted to comfort her, to tell her that he would wait forever on the other side.

Except he didn't want to wait. Michaela needed him. She loved him. Fuck death. *She loved him.*

Cormac lifted his head to fight, knowing that it was a lost cause.

Michaela.

I'm here.

Help me.

She opened her mind to him in a gesture of trust that clutched at his heart. Within her he could feel all the pain and isolation she'd experienced.

He also felt the love. She had a capacity for love he'd only dreamed of. For Yao. For Ivy.

For him.

He wouldn't fail her, not his Miaoling.

With tremendous effort, he forced himself from the edge of the precipice. Michaela stretched out with both hands and a line of light flung out to twist around him. His mate heaved back, trying to wrestle him close, swearing like the merchant-sailor she had been, her face almost gray with fatigue and effort. He could do nothing to help but resist the gaping emptiness behind him. It called him in, luring him with sweet promises of rest.

There could be no rest without Michaela. She was his and he was hers. Simple and true.

"Help me!" She screamed at him as her grip wavered.

"Tell me what to do."

"I don't know! I don't have a plan!"

Despite everything, her frenzied declaration made him laugh. That was all it took. He stumbled forward, death's grip on him lessened enough to move away from the danger.

Then into Michaela's arms. She bent into him, her fingers clawing against his back as though afraid he would return to the void.

"Don't leave me," she said.

"Never."

They stood for a moment in the timelessness of the in-between and all Cormac knew was a rushing coldness and the feeling of air bursting into his lungs.

He was alive. Healed. A *caintir*. Mated.
Michaela had brought him back.

* * * *

Michaela had no time to marvel over the miracle she'd experienced. Cormac was alive, but Ivy was still a prisoner.

They were back on the island, in the fight that had killed Cormac only a moment ago, still laying in a cooling pool of his blood. The in-between was gone. She was the first to get to her feet, pulling her mate away from Yangzei and stepping in front to shield him. In her peripheral vision, Eric and the others were all waiting, guns trained, for her to make a move. They wouldn't shoot for fear of hitting Ivy, whose ghostly form still wept on the ground near Yangzei's feet.

She had no idea what to do and she didn't care. The *dolma* had opened her eyes to a perception beyond what she'd limited herself to before.

Cormac rose behind her, covered in blood with a severe expression. "You are not going in that fight without a plan," he said grimly. "I have one."

"Never thought I'd see the day."

"I even have some lists somewhere. You need to trust me, Miaoling."

She looked up. "With my life."

"Then we strike together. Both of us." He placed his hand on his sigil and Michaela's responded. Their minds linked and Michaela knew what he was doing even as he did it.

Together, they ran at Yangzei, who flinched back with their combined force.

"Now." Cormac's command was quiet.

Simultaneously, they reached out to the *dolma*, channeling the energy that swirled around them and thrusting it into the Ancient. The vindictive coldness she'd experienced in Eric's house fell over her like a blanket.

She attacked.

* * * *

Before his eyes, Michaela shifted into a masque he'd never seen before, a tall being who moved with the strength and stealth of an assassin. Yangzei laughed and shifted himself to become an older man with a wiry frame.

"You are not the only one to have studied with the mountain monks," he said.

Michaela didn't reply, but moved slowly towards him, her hands held loosely at her sides. Yangzei's eyes tracked only her, so Cormac took a small step towards the small, translucent Ivy who sat huddled to the side. Then another.

When the fight began, Cormac halted, his eyes dazzled. Michaela fought like a snake, darting in and out with rapid attacks. Yangzei was more of a mountain, an immovable force that simply deflected her blows. He was trying to wear her down.

She had told him she was strong and that she didn't need his protection. He would always be there for her, but she had this.

Instead, he focused on Ivy. It took three more steps before he reached her. "Ivy."

She looked with red, pleading eyes. "Get me home."

"We will." He laid a hand on her head. "As soon as your auntie finishes this bastard off."

He focused on the fight again. Yangzei was still a mountain, but Michaela was now more of a tiger, fierce and remaining on the attack.

Yangzei shifted, his new masque now a cheerful looking Chinese man with a shaved head, missing teeth and one eye. He knew instantly this was Yao.

Michaela's mind was a welter of devastated thoughts and emotions and she fought to force them down. How had he ever thought she was cold? Michaela was a volcano, a solar flare.

Ready to explode.

He could be her tinder.

Let me help, he thought. *I have an idea.*

There was a long pause. *Yes.*

Cormac gathered Ivy to his chest and ran to Michaela. As Yangzei slashed out with a clawed hand, he pulled his mate close, feeling the hammering of her heart through their connection.

"Let go," he said. "Use me and let go."

She understood instantly. Grasping both of his hands in hers, she combined the *dolma* with her rage, sending it towards Yangzei. Cormac's heart stuttered as she drained him of everything he had, and he focused hard, reaching deep to replenish her again.

The resulting blast knocked them both off their feet. Yangzei let out a shriek of mixed agony and fury and backed away. In a moment, he'd grabbed Madden's limp body and simply disappeared.

It was over.

Chapter 47

Miaoling—Michaela no longer—stood on the richly woven rug in the middle of Eric's war room and assessed its new configuration. There was enough space for the newly named High Command. They were no longer facing a threat limited to masquerada, and the layout reflected this. There were spaces for all of the arcane groups who wished to ally with Eric. Their recent rout of Frieda's forces had both swayed groups that initially hedged their bets—and these were not part of Eric's inner sanctum—as well as confirmed the loyalty of others.

As long as Madden and Yangzei were out there, the war room would remain operational.

"Councilor." Eric came in and handed her a cup of tea.

She accepted it with a smile of thanks. "How is Stephan?"

Eric shook his head. "Not good."

Despite Cormac's efforts, infection had set in, affecting his arm. Although they hadn't had to amputate, he'd been greatly weakened. Stephan was having trouble adjusting, lashing out in rage. Estelle had done her best, but Miaoling didn't blame the vampire for her absences from Stephan's side.

After all, the woman was now also the seneschal major, her mentor killed fighting against Frieda's rogue vampires. She had responsibilities.

"Is he still threatening to go after Tom?" The dark cloud hovered over her again. Tom had not been seen since the battle, and no one on his team could provide information about his last moments. Since they had no body, they'd been loath to declare him dead. Stephan had taken it particularly hard.

Eric's silence was answer enough. Tom's loss had been difficult for all of them.

Ivy poked her head in. "Time for class, Auntie. I'll be back for dinner." She waved and left.

Miaoling watched after her with a small smile. Estelle had said the memories were too deep and intense to allow her to take them away, and they'd been forced to tell Ivy that she lived among beings out of fairy tales. To the girl's credit, she'd only fainted once and then blamed it on lack of food. For now she lived in Eric's house and spent most of her time with the medics, who adored her. With Yangzei and Madden around, they were taking no chances.

"Tell me some good news," Eric said as he leaned against the chairs.

"I need to resign as head of your council."

"Your idea of good and mine are very different things." He sighed. "I thought this was coming. Pharos?"

"I've been chosen as the new leader. I'm going to be busy making some changes."

"No more secrecy?"

She nodded. "I want it to be as transparent as possible. Except with the humans, obviously."

She rose to leave and Eric stood and kissed her on the cheek. "Good luck, Miaoling."

She bowed low. "Thank you, sire."

* * * *

Cormac glanced around his tree. It was all ready for his mate. Life had been a flurry for the last few days but Michaela—Miaoling—was coming by.

To talk.

That part, he was not looking forward to, but he was desperate to see his mate. Despite their constant connection through their mating bond, he craved her physical presence like a drug.

"It's still a hovel."

"Shut up, Rendell." Cormac made the branches outside rustle menacingly. A silly use of his *caintir* power, but Rendell brought out the worst in him.

Rendell laughed and uncoiled himself from the chair. "Is the Lady Isindle near?" he asked with studied indifference.

"Isindle is busy."

Another laugh. "I only wish to pass on a message from the magehood."

Although they had publicly repudiated Isindle to please Tismelda, the Fern House mages had set up a secret line of communication to Isindle in her exile, keeping her abreast of all the news and sending messages of support. Rendell had become the unlikely go-between and Cormac tried hard not to think of their relationship, if a relationship there was. They weren't together, but in the aftermath of the battle he was sure he'd seen Rendell watching Isindle in a way that struck him as much too interested. He didn't like it but when he'd idly commented that he should tell Rendell to keep his dirty paws to himself, Miaoling had told him in no uncertain terms that it was none of his damn business.

Maybe not, but if he didn't butt his nose in where it wasn't welcome, life would be very dull.

Rendell paused at the portal back to the Queendom. "Another day, Cormac."

He disappeared through the portal and Cormac dropped the silken curtain over it. Rendell's silver tongue had transformed the loss on Eric's island into an inspiring story about the victorious battle for the survival of the fey—stressing the Dawning as the ones to have failed in their understanding of Yangzei. He'd been persuasive enough that the queen had decided to promote him to chamberlain, then agreed to close off the borders to the Queendom.

Two hidden portals survived. The first was the one Rendell used to secretly communicate with Cormac. Rendell had seen Yangzei's power, and Cormac didn't blame him for wanting to keep an eye on things on this realm, even if it meant working with an official enemy of the state, something Cormac twitted him about on a regular basis.

Cormac also had a direct path to Yetting Forest, safely back in his control. The moment the battle was done, with Michaela still in his arms, he'd had wolves chase out Tismelda's guards and he'd placed a glamour over his entire forest.

Not even Kiana had been able to do such a feat.

The queen had still tried to kill them. Isindle lived in a High Park tree close enough to render aid if needed, and Cormac had set the entire forest up with traps and a complex early warning system of trees, squirrels, and bats. The ubiquitous Toronto raccoons did their part as well, gossips that they were. He and Isindle had already dispatched five *ihune* Tismelda had sent after them. The sixth he'd sent back with a message and a warning.

Leave me alone or I take your throne.

Cormac had accompanied the *ihune* with a personal thundercloud that had followed the poor woman all the way home, then had lingered over the Lilac Court to pelt it with hail for a week. Tismelda had stopped after that, but Cormac was under no illusion that it would remain that way.

That was when he decided to triple the protection on Yetting Forest as well.

His sigil throbbed and he stood as Miaoling tapped politely at the door. He gave the tree a silent command to open it.

When his mate came in, it took him a moment to catch his breath. She was so gorgeous, inside and out. She gave him a quick kiss and unrolled a scroll of paper she held under her arm. "Look."

"I am looking." Her hair was loose down her back.

She waved the scroll. "At my plans."

"Later."

* * * *

When Cormac looked at her like that, all of Miaoling's willpower disappeared. He took the plans gently from her hand and laid them on the table. "I've got something to show you."

Outside, the air was warm, a sweet kiss on the skin. Cormac led her to a ribbon of a path that wound through the forest before stopping at a tree surrounded by a sea of intensely fragrant white flowers.

"Tuberoses," she said, bending down. The breeze wafted up her favorite scent.

Cormac pulled her close. "Look up."

She peered up, then gasped. A small staircase made of branches led to a high platform covered with a canopy of deep green leaves. A small bed and comfortable chairs sat in the center, surrounded by low bookcases and a desk.

"I thought you might want a place to come now that you're in charge of the Pharos," he said. "A workplace might as well be beautiful."

The stairs were perfectly placed, and she scrambled up to the platform. The desk overlooked the distant valleys and the leaves puddled light onto the smooth floor.

"I love it." She hadn't realized how much she had craved such a space. Her fingers itched to write at the desk. Solitude and inspiration.

"Look in the desk drawer."

Curious, she pulled it open to find a small wooden box. Inside was a long golden rope studded with gems, rubies, emeralds, and sapphires all glowing in the light. She pulled it out, stunned. "It's beautiful."

"Good." He drew her close and she lifted her lips to his. All those centuries she had dreaded the intimacy of a kiss, but with Cormac she was learning an entire new language of love, desire, and hope. His kiss deepened and her sigil began to glow, warming her flesh.

Convenient that he'd placed a bed here, but that's not what she wanted. She stood back and closed her eyes, calling for the *dolma*.

"What are you doing?" Cormac gaped as a thick branch lowered down until it hovered over the bed.

"I thought of something." Cormac wasn't the only one who could act on an impulse.

"Looks interesting." He eyed the branch. "Tell me."

Instead, she stepped over and pulled up the hem of his T-shirt. If she lived a thousand years, she would never tire of seeing his body and running her lips over his cool skin. Cormac stood obediently in front of her, letting her undress him. His eyes turned a bright leaf-green as she ran admiring hands over him, letting her fingers linger along the long muscles of his shoulders.

Cormac leaned down to capture her mouth with his. After it swished down her back, he ran his hands through it, tightening his grip to pull her head slightly back. Small kisses rained down on her throat and she gasped.

In seconds, her clothes had dropped to the floor and the soft breeze ran along her skin. Cormac groaned and stepped away, his gaze lingering on her before he took the jeweled chain and wrapped it around her waist, the cool metal causing her to shiver. "Perfect," he said.

Michaela guided him to the wide branch, now covered with soft moss, and then smiled as he lay down.

Then she climbed on top.

Cormac's entire body jerked as she rubbed against him, then lifted herself up to tease them both.

In a single motion, she buried him deep. The branch was low enough that she could ride him standing up, hands planted on his abdomen, which rippled as he moved his hips under her. She'd never been filled so deep or had so much control over her partner.

Cormac's hands reached out to stroke and pinch her nipples as she moved up and down, going high up on her toes until he almost slipped out before slamming back down. The slippery friction made her even hotter and she bent forward, desperate to get even more of him in. Cormac moved in her rhythm, building her excitement even higher. She was so close. Time slowed.

From her sigil came a soft explosion that reverberated through her at the same time Cormac roared out, his hands gripping her shoulders as he jerked beneath her. It was enough to send her over the edge, her orgasm spreading out from her core to shake every part of her body.

Then she collapsed on Cormac's chest, both of them slick with sweat.

* * * *

Cormac lay on the bed panting and exhausted, Miaoling nestled under his arm. They'd tried her branch idea out one more time, but forked and with him standing between her spread thighs, before attempting a vine swing that had broken and tumbled them onto the bed.

Still, the last one had potential. Beside him, his mate smiled. "I like this place."

Like was an understatement. He was going to get hard every time he saw her damn tree. "I like you," he said and kissed her hair.

She stretched, that slender body arching like a cat. "Good, because someone told me that mating's a pretty serious thing."

"Thank God." Miaoling. How had he ever lived without her? He leaned down and captured her lips under his.

His mate. Forever.

Fascinated by the masquerada?

Keep an eye out for more in the
Masked Arcana series

Coming soon

And don't miss the first in the series
MASKED POSSESSION

Available now
From Lyrical Press
Wherever ebooks are sold

Masked Possession

A MAN WHO CAN WEAR ANY FACE

Caro Yeats doesn't run from much. As a former investigative reporter now working PR for Toronto's supernaturals, what she hasn't seen mostly isn't worth seeing. But the assignment to "rebrand" Eric Kelton's out-of-control alter egos has her on edge from the start. Kelton is the Heirarch of the masquerada, beings able to change their face—their entire persona—on a whim. Eric's charisma muddles her instincts. How can she trust a man who can become anybody?

A WOMAN WITHOUT A PAST

Eric has never met anyone like Caro, with her lightning wit and uncanny insight. But desirable as she is, he'd be a fool to let her near. Struggling to hide the sudden loss of his powers, Eric can't risk becoming entangled with a woman who scorns her supernatural side and claims not to play politics. The enemies on her trail are strong, clever, and vicious. And when they force Eric and Caro together, the fallout could shatter far more than two hearts . . .

Chapter 1

Caro Yeats entered the lobby cursing her new stilettos. Sure, they were sexy as hell and made her legs look a mile long but they were terrible for, say, *walking*. It had been a mistake to wear them, but they'd sat at the back of her closet for weeks and she'd grabbed them in a moment of uncharacteristic boldness brought on by the perfect spring day.

Estelle, receptionist at Julien D'Aurant Public Relations, gave a low whistle as Caro strutted past her desk. The strutting wasn't deliberate; it was impossible to walk any other way in the damn shoes. "What's the occasion? Hot date tonight? It's sure not for any of us here."

"Not true," Caro said. "I wore my mouthwatering baggy jeans and stained sweatshirt ensemble to impress you last week."

Estelle winced. "Forgot about that. Anyway, you clean up nice. The boss will be impressed."

Caro rolled her eyes. Julien D'Aurant was so stereotypically French that she suspected it had to be an act. "Why do you not dress *plus comme une femme*?" was a question she'd had to dodge on multiple occasions. Her usual wardrobe of jeans and ballet flats seemed to cause him real anguish.

"Speak of the devil," Estelle muttered.

Julien strolled into the lobby, his crisp, pressed, blue button-down tucked into his perfectly creased gray dress pants. The caramel-brown belt was the exact shade of his casual summer loafers, which he naturally wore without socks. In his hand—Estelle had told Caro that he went for weekly manicures and she'd never been able to look at his buffed and shiny nails again—he held his phone, regarding it as warily as he would a snake coiled to strike.

He glanced up, then back at the phone. After a moment, his head flew up in such a comical double take that Estelle burst out laughing and Caro felt a bit insulted.

"*Mon ange*. This is what I mean by dressing like a woman." He strode over and grasped Caro by the shoulders, giving her a lingering kiss on both cheeks before stepping back and looking her over in admiration. "*Quelle différence*. Dress like this every day. You must." His expensive Hermès cologne wafted over her.

Although it was nice to have her efforts appreciated, Caro suddenly had the impression that her black pencil skirt was a little too tight and definitely too short. Time to deflect his attention. "Good morning, Julien. What were you frowning about?"

"Ah. Yes, that." He waved the phone at her. "Emergency meeting in the boardroom in an hour. New client."

"Who?" She didn't particularly care, but knew enough to feign enthusiasm once in a while. Or at least interest.

The phone rang out with the opening bars of Nina Simone's "I Put a Spell on You." Instead of answering, Julien pointed a single, pampered finger at her before murmuring "*Allô?*" and breaking into rapid French.

Caro raised an eyebrow and looked over at Estelle, who shrugged and shook her short, black, Louise Brooks bob into place. Caro caught a quick glimpse of Estelle's wickedly pointed fangs. How the vampire avoided slicing up her own lip was something Caro always wondered but was afraid to ask. Friendly as she was, Estelle could bring on the predator when she wanted. She called it her resting-death bitch face and Caro had seen it reduce grown men to inarticulate lumps.

When Caro first started working at JDPR, she'd been surprised that a vampire could be out during the day—Estelle was the first one she'd ever met. Estelle had laughed and said silly rumors made for amazing camouflage. "You can see us in mirrors and I put garlic in everything," she had said. "We're like humans. Except for being almost immortal and drinking blood. Minor differences."

Now Estelle said, "It's a masquerada. That's all I know."

"Masquerada?" A fine tension weighed down Caro's shoulders—her usual reaction to masquerada, the powerful shapeshifters who took on human forms.

"We don't usually get many but why are you complaining? You were the one who pulled the ghoul client last month. This should be a cakewalk."

Caro could not deny the sewer-dwelling ghoul had been a nasty piece of work. The office had to be professionally cleaned after his visit to dispose of the residue he'd left behind, and the meeting room had both looked and smelled like a post-plague charnel house.

She shuddered and slowly teetered her way to her office, where she kicked off the shoes with a sigh of relief. Taking one poor foot in her hand, she gently rubbed the feeling back into her toes as she waited for her computer to boot up.

A light-brown ring showed where her coffee cup should be—and wasn't. One of the misfortunes of working for a feyman was that items constantly went missing. Apparently minor theft was a fey thing. Last week Julien had pilfered her lipstick. When she first started, Caro had thought he did it as some sort of hazing prank, a test for how much the newbie could take. Now, many discussions with Estelle later, she realized that Julien often didn't even notice his thieving.

Not for the first time, she wondered if she'd made the right decision by taking this job. The supernatural arcane world was one that she had avoided for years. Now she had deliberately placed herself in the direct heart of it.

Inside the drawer of her minimalist white acrylic desk lay evidence of her past life—a battered envelope containing a single *Washington Post* newspaper clipping, the pages still crisp. Lynn Butler's first A1, over-the-fold story was an exclusive scoop tracing criminal kingpin Franz Iverson to a string of illegal activities that reached right to the Mayor's Office and even to the Senate.

Every time she looked at it, she felt a thrill that was immediately followed by deep aches in the year-old scars that traced pale, jagged paths along her abdomen, chest and back. The doctor had said the pain might never completely subside. It was a miracle she wasn't dead from the attack, he'd added. "I don't understand how you didn't bleed out from those wounds. You're one lucky woman."

She rubbed her stomach with a shaking hand. The police had never caught the men who left her for dead and she didn't expect them to. There was no need. She knew exactly who had ordered the hit.

Not even incarceration had limited Franz Iverson's reach, or his need for revenge.

Those knife thrusts had ended her career in journalism and her life as Lynn Butler. When she finally got enough courage to walk back into the *Post*'s newsroom after her recovery, she barely managed to smile through her colleagues' standing ovation before limping to the bathroom and collapsing in a shaking heap. The thought of writing another story made her hands shake uncontrollably and she had known, suddenly and without a doubt, that the life she loved as a reporter was done. Over. That had been a year ago.

The sea of multi-colored project folders that sat in neat layers on her desk made a knot twist in her stomach. Caro twirled her chair away to cast her eyes over the gray accent wall in her office. A single print hung there, a huge close-up of Banksy's iconic protestor throwing his bouquet. Trendy and ironic, exactly the image that Julien worked hard to maintain in an industry where perception was everything. Caro rubbed her eyes. The job at JDPR was as far away from investigative reporting as she could get while still staying, however peripherally, in media. She'd left Washington in a panic to create a new life for herself in Toronto at JDPR. She was lucky the city was big enough to hide under a new name and new job, but with neighborhoods that gave her the homey feel she craved. It had turned out as best it could, but sometimes she regretted the move from hack to flack so much she felt numb.

Quit this, she told herself sternly. *Enough. You're alive, you're working. Just because you're not a reporter, it doesn't mean it's a bad life. It's different. You chose different, remember? It's what you wanted. It's what you* needed.

JDPR was definitely not a typical PR agency. It represented only arcane clients. Humans who stumbled across it were given such an outlandish rate list and cold welcome from Estelle that they didn't return. For the most part, the company dealt in the delicate art of keeping humans unaware of the fantastic beings who shared the world with them. Most arcana could either pass as human, pass as odd humans, or lived as isolated as possible from populated areas. Regardless, there were enough incidents to make for some interesting days. She was grateful for that busyness at least.

Caro tapped her fingers on the table. Julien had made it clear that she had gotten the job at JDPR because she was part masquerada, although a latent and an extraordinarily and determinedly ignorant one at that. Before her death, her mother had tried to train Caro in the basics of taking on a masque, but Caro had stubbornly opposed any arcane education. Nor was there anybody else to learn from, even if she changed her mind. Besides her mother, she'd never knowingly met another masquerada and she often wondered if this avoidance was as deliberate on their side as it was on hers. Her mother had made it crystal clear that being a half-blood was nothing to be proud about, so she wasn't surprised if none of them wanted to make themselves known to a pariah. One of the things Caro did know about masquerada culture was that it was unusually hierarchical and status-driven, like some time-traveling medieval court.

Not that any of this mattered to Caro, who had always despised the fundamental trickiness of masquerada and had done her best to ignore that entire part of her heritage. Her mother had changed masques the same way other women changed clothes. As a child Caro would often kiss one woman good night and wake to an unfamiliar one in the morning. It was years before Caro even knew what her mother truly looked like and that was only because she had found an old photo in a shoebox.

"Oh, her?" Her mother had shrugged dismissively when Caro showed her the photo of the dark-haired, dark-eyed woman who looked like Caro herself. "That's my natural self. A bit of a wet blanket. I much prefer this one." At the time she was a curvy platinum blonde with Asian eyes and features, and so stunning that people stopped on the street to watch her walk by.

"Can't you at least look like this when you're with me?" Caro had asked, shaking the photo. She'd been nine or ten. Her mother had glanced at Caro's reflection in the mirror with an unreadable expression, mascara wand steady in her hand.

"Sorry, darling."

That was the day Caro decided she would never take on a masque. She would never give in to that pathological need to be someone else—she was going to be good enough as she was.

However, Caro's boo-hoo, sad-face childhood issues turned out to be an advantage in her new job. Although she'd rejected her arcane heritage, it meant JDPR's clients would trust her, Julien had explained when he'd hired her. "You have an insider's knowledge of the human world, without the taint of humanity," he had said. "Our clients don't trust humans. *Et bien sûr*, protecting our clients' confidentiality and interests requires more layered complexity than it does for humans working with some vulgar reality star from Atlantic City."

She had nodded, but wondered how on earth it was possible to keep decrepit ghouls and pale creatures with fangs hidden from the public eye. Julien had stressed that upholding the Law—the ancient agreement made by all arcana to stay secret from humanity—was their primary task, but surely at least one damning image would go viral. Then one did and Caro watched as it was ripped apart, ridiculed as fake, and sent to join the ranks of fringe theories about the Bermuda Triangle and the Illuminati. It wasn't that hard to keep the arcane world a secret after all, Caro reflected. What normal person would admit to believing it?

Meet the Author

Rebecca Springett

Alana Delacroix lives in a little house filled with books in Toronto, Canada. She loves exploring the city, on the hunt for both the perfect coffeeshop as well as ideal locations to set her paranormal romances. A member of RWA, Alana worked as an archaeologist before forging a slightly more stable career in corporate communications. You can follow her at @AlanaDelacroix or learn more at alanadelacroix.com.